BY THE
BLOOD OF
HEROES

ALSO BY JOSEPH NASSISE

THE GREAT UNDEAD WAR

By the Blood of Heroes

THE JEREMIAH HUNT CHRONICLE

Eyes to See

THE TEMPLAR CHRONICLES

The Heretic
A Scream of Angels
A Tear in the Sky
Infernal Games

BY THE BLOOD OF HEROES

★ ★ ★

THE GREAT UNDEAD WAR: BOOK I

JOSEPH NASSISE

HARPER Voyager
An Imprint of HarperCollins Publishers

For Dad.
A love of history and a love of speculative fiction were two
of the many things you instilled in me in my youth.
This book is a direct result of both.

BY THE BLOOD OF HEROES. Copyright © 2012 by Joseph Nassise.
All rights reserved. Printed in the United States of America. No
part of this book may be used or reproduced in any manner what-
soever without written permission except in the case of brief quo-
tations embodied in critical articles and reviews. For information
address HarperCollins Publishers, 10 East 53rd Street, New York,
NY 10022.

HarperCollins books may be purchased for educational, business,
or sales promotional use. For information please write: Special
Markets Department, HarperCollins Publishers, 10 East 53rd
Street, New York, NY 10022.

FIRST EDITION

Designed by Paula Szafranski

Library of Congress Cataloging-in-Publication Data has been ap-
plied for.

ISBN 978-0-06-204875-2

12 13 14 15 16 OV/RRD 10 9 8 7 6 5 4 3 2 1

ACKNOWLEDGMENTS

LIKE MOST BOOKS, *By the Blood of Heroes* wouldn't have happened without the assistance and input from a group of incredibly awesome folks, including: my terrific editor, Will Hinton, whose timely suggestions made this a better book; my marvelous agent, Joe Monti, who heard my pitch for an "alternate history series set in World War One but with steampunk and zombies!" with complete enthusiasm and who went on to make it a reality by selling it; and to my loving and ever-patient wife, Dawn, who supports my literary endeavors no matter how crazy the storyline.

And, last but certainly not least, every reader who has ever picked up one of my books with the expectation of being entertained. I hope I have lived up to my end of the bargain.

CHAPTER ONE

★

This godforsaken place!

Captain Michael "Madman" Burke set aside the trench knife he'd been using to clean the mud out of the clockwork mechanism that powered his left hand and closed the access panel with a firm push. He'd been at it for almost a half hour but didn't think he'd done more than move the dirt from one set of gears to another; he knew he'd need a trip to the rear in order to get it properly cleaned. Unfortunately, he wasn't due for another of those for at least two more weeks and was stuck with his own meager efforts for the time being.

Such was life in the American Expeditionary Force.

His fingers clicked and clanked as he worked them back and forth, testing to see if his field repair would do any good. There was still some resistance in movement, but not as much as before; for that he guessed he should be thankful.

He rolled down the sleeve of his wool uniform shirt and got up from the camp stool he'd been sitting on. A glance at his pocket watch told him it was time to start getting the men up and ready for the morning "Stand To," as dawn was less than an hour away and the shamblers wouldn't be far behind.

It might be March, but the morning air was far more winter than spring, and Burke knew it would have a nasty bite. He pulled his greatcoat out from beneath the blankets he'd slept under and slipped it on, grateful for the warmth his body heat had imparted to the material during the night. The extra heat wouldn't last long in the cold morning air, but it would at least ward off the initial chill for a few minutes and Burke had been a soldier long enough to know that you indulged in the little things while you could.

Helmet and rifle in hand, he stepped out of the makeshift tent to find Staff Sergeant Moore waiting for him, just as he had been waiting every morning for the three years that they'd been stuck here at the front together.

"Morning, Charlie," Burke said.

The sergeant gave a noncommittal grunt and handed Burke a tin cup with steam rising off it. The coffee was weak—they'd been using the same grounds for over ten days now—but Moore had put a generous taste of rum into it and Burke sighed in satisfaction despite the taste.

"What have we got?" he asked.

The sergeant shrugged. "Nothing unusual, sir. McGraw's men reported hearing movement beyond the wire around 0300, but the scouts we sent out came back without having encountered anyone. Probably just more of what we've been getting all week, if you ask me."

Burke nodded. The enemy had been probing their defenses for six days straight. Never anything too serious, just quick little engagements that forced his men to react, revealing their locations and letting the enemy get a sense of what they would be facing if they did come in force.

Not if, when, he corrected himself. If there was one constant in this war, it was the enemy's implacable desire for the living.

So let them come.

His men were more than a match for any German unit, with or without shambler accompaniment. Lord knows they'd had enough practice.

The Great War was in its seventh year, but it seemed to Burke that it had been going on forever. He could barely remember what life before it had been like, though he was honest enough with himself to admit that his forgetfulness might have more to do with his own desire to put the past behind him than the length of the conflict. Truth was, after Mae's death, he just hadn't given a damn anymore. The days flowed past in an endless haze of gray, one after the other, until he wasn't able to tell where one ended and the next began. In the end he'd enlisted, not out of some misguided sense of duty or vain quest for glory, but simply to try and feel something again. If he couldn't feel alive while staring into the face of death, well, then, perhaps he didn't deserve to live anymore. Of course that had been during the early years, back when a bullet was a bullet and the man you killed with it stayed dead afterward.

Once the Germans invented that damned corpse gas, everything changed.

The last three years had been particularly brutal. While the Allied powers had managed to hang on to the small stretch of ground won at the end of the Somme Offensive, it had been by only the thinnest of margins. Even now the Americans continued to increase their support of the beleaguered French and British armies, sending fresh troops to fill the gaps being carved in the Western Front. As the death toll mounted and the ranks of the opposition swelled, reinforcements continued to arrive; doing anything else could mean certain doom for everything from the English Channel to Moscow.

The line had held, but only just.

"All right then, Charlie, let's get the men up."

The two of them began moving in unison down the length of the trench, waking up each man in turn and ordering him to fall in at the fire step, ready to defend his position if need be. And most mornings, that was exactly what was needed.

A mere two hundred yards separated the two sides, but that two hundred yards of no-man's-land was composed mostly of bomb craters, minefields, abandoned trenches, and row upon row of barbed wire, making it some of the most treacherous ground on the face of the planet.

Recently, the enemy commander opposite them had made it a habit to order dawn assaults on the section of the Allied line that was under Burke's command. Which meant Burke had to rouse his troops out of their bedrolls every morning, get them assembled on the raised earthen "step" that allowed them to see over the top of the trench, and wait in the chill morning air for an attack that might not come.

There was a peculiar feeling in the air this morning, a tension that hadn't been there during the past week. Burke had the feeling that the Germans were done testing their lines; an attack was sure to follow, and he sensed that today was the day.

As the men scrambled to take their places along the line, Burke had a quiet word with each of them. They were good men, though many of them were relatively untrained, having only recently been sent to the front to replace the losses suffered over the last month. He gave them a few words of encouragement, reminded them that the men on either side of them in the trench depended on their actions, and then left it alone, confident that Sergeant Moore would handle any other needs the men might have.

All that was left at that point was to wait to see what the enemy would do.

Fifteen minutes later, the man beside him, a corporal named Ridley, suddenly stiffened.

"There's something out there, sir," he whispered.

Burke followed the man's frightened gaze, out across the muddy battlefield to where the first of the barbed-wire emplacements was buried beneath the weight of a thick curtain of fog, but didn't see anything.

After a moment, he heard it.

The sound of movement.

Out beyond the wire.

It was a sound he'd become intimately familiar with over the last few years and one he knew he'd hear in his sleep long after the war was over.

"Steady," he told the men nearest him, and the command was repeated down the line. Any moment now . . .

The first of the shamblers emerged from the fog on the far side of the barbed wire, lumbering toward them with the peculiar gait for which they'd been named. Behind it came at least a dozen more, though Burke was sure that was just the first wave.

They'd once been men; that was easy to see. Some were still dressed in the tattered remnants of the German uniforms that they'd worn while alive, scraps of gray cloth hanging on their desiccated frames; others were naked, their rotting flesh exposing bone in more than a few places. The control devices they wore stuck out as the only intact thing about them; dark collars that encircled their necks and rose up on the left side of their faces to cover that side of the head in a mixture of leather and electrical components.

But thinking of them as men was a grave mistake, however, for they had ceased being anything remotely human the moment their corpses responded to the call of the corpse gas and rose anew, hungry for the flesh of the living and driven nearly mad from their desire to consume it. The control devices rendered them manageable, but only just. This was fine with the German commanders in charge of the shambler brigades, for soldiers like these were best used as shock troops anyway, fodder to weaken the Allied lines and pave the way for the human divisions that usually followed in their wake.

A rifle went off to his right, then several more, but Burke held his own fire, wanting to be certain of his shot, wanting to make it count.

Back in the days before the war, most soldiers were taught to shoot for the center mass but that didn't do much good anymore. Shamblers were long past the point of feeling injury or pain. You could knock one down with a shot to the middle of its chest and it would simply get back up again. Even blowing off a limb didn't do much good; as long as it could move forward the shambler would do so, dragging itself forward with its bare hands or wriggling its body along the ground. The only way to stop one was to put a bullet in its brain.

Even that wasn't final, Burke thought. Being exposed to the corpse gas would cause the creature to rise once more, which was why his side had taken to burning the bodies of friends and foe alike in giant bonfires after every conflict. The air had become so saturated with the smell of burning flesh that he barely noticed it anymore.

Burke had learned through long experience that if you waited until the shamblers got hung up in the barbed wire, you'd have a better chance of making that head shot as they struggled to pull themselves free. He propped the barrel of his weapon on the lip of the trench and used his mechanical hand to hold it steady, sighting in on one of the enemy soldiers that was currently squirming its way through a hole in the wire. A moment to steady his breathing, a few extra ounces of pressure on the trigger of the rifle in his hands, and he put a bullet smack in the center of the creature's skull. Without hesitation he swung the barrel of his rifle to one side, sighted it on another target, and began the process all over again.

His men were firing regularly now, the sharp cracks of their rifles and their shouts of hatred for the undead blending together into a mad cacophony of sound. From somewhere farther down the line came the rattling burr of a Hotchkiss machine gun and he glanced that way, watching with satisfaction as an entire squad of shamblers were cut down in midstride. Once on the ground, it was an easy matter for the sharpshooters to finish them off.

Just as he'd expected, however, this first group turned out to be just the tip of the enemy's attack. Wave after wave of the ravenous creatures followed, attempting to make their way through the hail of gunfire and reach Burke and his men. Behind them came the German regulars, firing from the safety of the back of the pack and not caring if they accidentally hit some of the shock troops that were trying to clear the way before them. Burke kept up a steady rate of fire, alternating with the man next to him when one or the other of them needed to reload and snatching quick moments of rest in between waves of the assault.

Some two hours after the attack began, it was finally over. The stretch of no-man's-land directly in front of them was littered with the still bodies of the enemy dead. Thankfully none of the shamblers had reached the trench itself. If they had, the outcome would have been very different, Burke knew.

He reloaded his rifle for what felt like the hundredth time that morning and then, seeing Sergeant Moore making his way back along the floor of the trench toward him, stepped out to greet him.

They were still standing there, chatting quietly and comparing notes on how the new men in the platoon had reacted to the attack, when the ground beneath their feet trembled.

"Did you feel that?" Burke asked.

Moore nodded. "Felt like an earthquake. We get ones like that back in San Francisco all the time."

An earthquake? Burke thought. *In godforsaken France?*

Before he could express his doubts, the ground trembled again, this time with more force. It shook them about for thirty or forty seconds and knocked several of his men off their feet. Rats burst out of their holes all along the sides of the trench, swarming around the soldiers' feet before charging en masse down its length. Burke had a moment to stare after them in surprise before the ground began shaking for a third time.

The makeshift tent he'd been using as a command post collapsed, as did the stockpile of crates containing ammunition and food stores just beyond. The sides of the trench itself even began to shake apart, great clods of dirt breaking free and falling around them so frequently that Burke began to fear that they all might be buried alive before the trembling stopped.

He wasn't the only one with the thought, apparently, for he saw several of his men praying aloud or gripping good luck charms as the shaking continued. A young private named Hendricks scrambled up out of the trench, silhouetting himself against the sky, only to take a sniper's bullet through the throat a moment later, his body dead before he hit the ground.

Just when Burke thought they wouldn't be able to take any more, the trembling stopped as the trench wall ten feet in front of him burst open from the inside. Dirt flew in every direction as a strange machine rose into the morning sunlight, the three massive drills attached to its snout still spinning wildly as its tracks drove it up out of the earth.

As Burke looked on, stunned into immobility by the machine's sudden appearance, hatches clanked open along its length and a horde of shamblers spilled out of its dark interior, falling upon the men of 4th Platoon with a vengeance. In seconds it was every man for himself as hand-to-hand combat stretched from one end of the trench to the other.

CHAPTER TWO

TWELVE MILES AWAY from where Captain Burke was fighting against a horde of ravenous undead, Major Julius "Jack" Freeman stepped out of his tent into the brisk morning, pulling on his thin leather flying gloves as he went. The sun was just breaking through the cloud cover, its feeble light barely visible through the smoke and dust that seemed to be the only constants in this never-ending war.

Despite the early hour, the home of the 94th Aero Squadron was anything but quiet. The mechanics had taken the aircraft out of the hangars and had them facing forward down the airfield where they were being prepped for the dawn patrol. The enlisted men were already up, manning the machine-gun pits that were scattered throughout the airfield, ready to protect the Allied aircraft on the ground in case of a German attack. If the enlisted men were up, so too then were the men of the hospital company, ready to drag the wounded to the hospital tents and the dead to the fire pits. The din of men at work filled the air around Freeman.

He snorted at himself in disgust at his characterization of the enemy. *Germans? Could they even be called that anymore? Each new assault swelled the ranks of the undead, and they had long surpassed the number of living troops left under the German High Command.*

An army of the ravenous dead didn't care about nationalism; all they wanted was their next meal.

Freeman had been involved in the war from the very beginning of America's support, when the 94th had been activated at Villeneuve in March of 1918. It seemed like a long time ago now.

He jammed a cigarette into his mouth and then removed a battered silver lighter from his pocket. It'd been a present from Rickenbacker, back before the invention of the gas, when this war had only been a war and not a struggle for the survival of the human race. He turned the lighter over in his hands and held it up so that he could read the inscription in the thin morning light. "A Gentleman and a Flier" it read.

Instead of cheering him, the sight of it made the airman shake his head in near despair. *Rickenbacker was gone now and Marr with him. At least they had perished in fires on the ground instead of rising to fight against their own men like so many of the others. Facing off in the air against his longtime friend would have been unthinkable.*

A glance at the weathometer on his wrist told him that it was just after seven, with the air pressure holding steady in the green zone. Another hour and the wind would disperse the clouds enough to fly. Then the real day's work would begin.

Might as well use the time to get some breakfast, he thought.

The mess hall was set up in the old farmhouse. His squadron mates—Samuels, James, and Walton—were already there, waiting for the day's briefing.

Not that today's mission would be any different from the hundreds of others they'd already flown.

The aerodrome at Toul was only twelve miles from the front. Nancy lay fifteen miles to the east, Lunéville ten miles beyond that. The highway from Toul to Nancy to Lunéville ran parallel to enemy lines and was within easy shelling distance of their guns, making it difficult for the Allies to move troops and supplies up to the front in support of the men holding the line there. The 94th's job was to patrol that long stretch of highway and do what they could to keep it clear so that the infantry wouldn't be cut off.

Freeman joined his men as they were sitting down to a breakfast of syntheggs and ham. They both tasted like paste, making it hard to tell them apart once they were in your mouth, but he was glad to have them; all the men were. Real food was growing scarcer than a pig in Berlin.

As happened most every morning, the men in the squadron were discussing the enemy, and the argument went round and round without really getting anywhere. There were far more questions than answers. Why did the shamblers crave human flesh? What caused their ravenous hunger? Why did a small percentage of the dead come back as revenants, their physical dexterity, their mental acuity, and perhaps even more important, their memories, all perfectly intact? Understanding the answers to these and other questions was an issue of the highest priority. Solving them could bring an end to the war, but there was no way this group of farm boys was going to manage that. Freeman kept quiet throughout the discourse, just nodding noncommittally over his coffee, for he had nothing new to share on the topic.

After breakfast, while the men were still enjoying their coffee, a runner arrived with news that a wireless call had just come in from Nancy. Several enemy aircraft had been spotted heading in the direction of the aerodrome.

"Time to earn our pay, boys," Freeman said as he led the way out of the mess hall and to the field.

The entire squadron now flew Spad XIIIs, and while Freeman missed his old Nieuport 28, he had to admit that the Spad was a nice substitute. Introduced in the fall of 1917, it had a maximum range of two hours' flying time and a ceiling of just under twenty-two thousand feet. Armed with two synchronized Vickers machine guns mounted in front of the pilot, it had quickly become a favorite among the fliers attached to the American Expeditionary Force (AEF). Rickenbacker had flown one until his death, and Freeman had decided to switch to the Spad in tribute to his old friend.

Mitchell, Freeman's mechanic, had the major's bird in the lead position and wasted no time getting the propeller spinning when Freeman climbed aboard. Being the careful type, Freeman took a few extra moments to be certain everything was in proper condition.

He checked the tachometer first, watching it as he opened the throttle and then closed it back down again to an idle, making sure the engine was running normally. His gaze swept over the fuel pump and quantity gauges. Next he moved to the physical controls. Waggling the control column, he tested the aileron and elevator movements, taking them through their full range of movement. The rudder was a bit stiff, but he attributed that to the cold morning air and didn't give it another thought. A quick tap of a finger on the altimeter, a brush of his hands over the petrol cocks and magneto switches, and he was ready to go.

Freeman lowered his goggles, made sure that the lenses were adjusted to the same polarization by nudging the selector on either side of the goggles with the tip of his finger, and then gave Mitchell the thumbs-up.

When the same signal was received from the rest of the pilots manning the aircraft strung out in a line behind Freeman, the mechanic turned to him and swept his arm forward in a wide arc.

Freeman advanced the throttle, watching as the propeller's flickering dissolved into a darkened haze. The Spad came to life, awkward at first as it tentatively moved onto the grassy field. As the engine surged into a throaty roar the machine picked up speed and its forward motion smoothed out, though the creaking and groaning of the undercarriage didn't cease until the Spad eased itself off the ground and into the chilly air above. Just a few short minutes later the entire flight of four aircraft was up and headed east, following the roadway.

Freeman flew low over the Allied lines, knowing the Jack of Spades painted across the underside of his wings would be visible from his current height to the men on the ground. As America's top ace, he felt it was his duty to encourage the men every chance he could, and the sight of his distinctive plane was sure to give a lift to those in the trenches below. A dark cloud of smoke was already spiraling upward from an area a hundred yards behind the Allied positions, the stench of burning flesh wafting through the air along with it, and he steered slightly to the east to get away from the stink of the corpse fires.

He couldn't imagine the horror this infantry had to face on a daily basis. How the Germans had gone so horribly wrong in creating that hideous gas was anyone's guess. It was bad enough up in the air, fighting aircraft flown by pilots who were long dead. How much worse it must be to sit there, mere yards from the newly risen opposition forces, knowing that the other side saw you as nothing more than that evening's meal. Once when he was laid up in the hospital at Reims, he listened to the survivors of the Battle of Soissons recount their experiences. The opposition made assault after assault, charging out of that venomous green gas and through no-man's-land as fast as their rotting forms could carry them. The long miles of barbed wire became heavy with bodies and still they came, stepping over the still-moving carcasses of their comrades to rush the trenches, dragging off those Allied soldiers unlucky enough to be near the break in the lines. The Allied troops fell back to the secondary and then the tertiary trenches before the attack had been repelled.

While that was bad enough, the descriptions of the Allied dead waking up later the same night in the abandoned trenches and crawling under the wire to assault their former comrades was far worse. Freeman remembered vividly the look on one private's face as he talked about the horror he felt bayoneting the man who he'd just spent the last forty-five days huddled with in a foxhole and of his shame at then having to burn the body in the bonfires to keep his friend from rising a second time.

Remembering it now made Freeman shudder in his seat.

Thank God the gas only worked on inert tissue. If it had the same impact on the living as it had on the dead, this war would have been over years ago.

As they neared the outskirts of town, Freeman began to climb higher, the possibility of being jumped at so low an altitude by the opposition's pilots outweighing his desire to boost the morale of the soldiers on the ground. The haze was thick, the cloud cover fairly low, and Freeman wanted some clear sky beneath their wings before they were forced to engage the enemy.

Fifteen minutes later they crossed into enemy territory and ended up getting lucky right away. The observation balloon first appeared as a small dark smudge against the blue-green earth below. Reaching up with one hand, Freeman pushed the magnification lenses into place over the left eye of his goggles and took a good, long look at the aircraft ahead of them.

The balloon was one of the Caquot styles, a long teardrop-shaped cylinder with three stabilizing fins. There was a symbol painted on the rear fin, but it was too far away to see clearly with the goggles' current settings. Reaching up with his left hand, he flicked through the magnification selections until the black German cross painted on the dirigible's rudder swam into view.

They had the enemy in sight; all they needed now was an attack plan.

Freeman had the flight in formation at six thousand feet with his plane in the lead, followed by Samuels and James flying parallel. Walton brought up the rear, forming an aerial diamond. He didn't give the signal to attack, at least not yet.

Instead, he craned his head around from side to side, huddled against the rushing wind, searching the sky below for the fighter cover that he knew had to be present. The opposition never sent the balloons aloft without the fighters.

They had to be here.

And they were.

Both aircraft, Pfalz D.XIIs by the look of them, were approximately a few hundred feet below and to the south of the balloon, drifting lazily along as though they didn't have a care in the world.

Freeman waggled his wings, getting the attention of his fellow pilots. He pointed downward at the balloon and then tapped the side of his head with two fingers. He then pointed at the escort aircraft circling below and then at his men.

They understood. It would be their job to take on the opposition's aircraft while Freeman went after the balloon.

They all circled back around, staying in the cloud cover until they could bring their planes into position with the sun at their backs. Then as a group they fell into a rushing power-glide designed to bring them up on the enemy as swiftly as possible.

Freeman watched the balloon grow larger and larger in his field of vision, his comrades forgotten as he focused on his attack. He covered more than half the distance to the other craft before its crew noticed his presence. He could see them floating beneath the wide bulk of the balloon in their wicker basket, frantically calling the ground crew on the field phone. Those on the ground were equally desperate, rushing to the mechanical winch in the hopes of getting the balloon and its crew pulled out of the sky before Freeman could reach it.

With his Vickers guns thundering in his ears, Freeman closed in. Even in the weak sunlight he could see the incendiary tracers arcing away from his aircraft and slashing into the fabric of the balloon. Before he got too close he pushed hard on the stick and banked his Spad, sending it around the edge of the balloon just as a bright arc of color danced along its surface. Seconds later the sky around him was filled with the glare and heat of an explosion as the gas inside the balloon ignited.

He looked back to see the observers jump out of the now falling basket, taking their chances of surviving the fall rather than burning up with their craft. He roared in exultation as he watched the flaming balloon crash to the ground atop the moving forms of the ground crew, trapping them in the blaze.

That's four more of the bastards that won't rise again, by God!

For the first time since he began his dive, Freeman noted the whine and crack of the machine-gun bullets coming from the troops below. He pulled back on the stick, taking his Spad up and out of reach of the weapons that were trying to claim his body for their masters.

When he was safely at altitude, he surveyed his chariot, finding a good number of holes in the fabric of his wings and several splinters gouged out of the leather-wrapped wood surrounding his cockpit area, but nothing that would suggest he needed to return to the airfield.

Satisfied, Freeman looked down once more. Now only one German biplane occupied the sky, and even he wouldn't be up for long. A thick stream of black smoke was pouring out of the engine and Samuels was hanging doggedly on the Pfalz's tail, firing as he chased it around the sky. As Freeman watched, the enemy aircraft suddenly collapsed on itself, falling away in pieces to the ground in a graceless ballet of destruction.

The flight regrouped, smiles on the faces of the younger pilots. Even the veteran, Freeman, couldn't help but feel that this was going to be a good day. Both the balloon and the two Pfalzs had been downed in full view of the other pilots in the squadron, so there should be no quibbling with headquarters about credit for the kills. That made for an auspicious beginning.

They spent the next forty-five minutes edging their way farther into opposition territory without sign of another aircraft. The cloud cover had retreated a few thousand feet but was still pretty thick so the squadron took advantage of it, hiding their aircraft up among its lowest reaches.

It was from this lofty position that they first spotted the damaged aircraft making its unsteady way across the sky below them.

It was a lone Fokker Dr.1 triplane, painted a bright red, the black Iron Crosses easy to see. A thin stream of black smoke was pouring out of the engine and the pilot seemed to be engrossed in maintaining control of his aircraft as he fought to keep it moving along a straight path.

Freeman knew that only one man in the entire German air force flew a red Fokker triplane; it could be none other than Baron Manfred von Richthofen himself.

Flush from their earlier victories and excited at the chance to down the legendary ace, the less-experienced pilots reacted without thinking things over. As if of one mind, they banked over and swept downward at the opposition aircraft.

Freeman stared after them in shock. *What did they think they were doing?!*

Holding the stick steady with his knees, he snatched up the radio mike with his left hand and cranked hard on the handle with his right, but he saw right away that it would be no use. The radios were not designed for emergency use. It took time to build up a sufficient charge and the squadron would come in contact with the enemy aircraft before he'd be able to get a message out.

He had no choice but to follow them down.

Freeman watched as the Allied aircraft closed in on the Fokker, their Vickers guns winking in the sunlight. They opened up as soon as they came within range. The opposition pilot continued to ignore them, a large mistake, and it wasn't long before Freeman's squadron mates blasted the plane right out of the sky.

It was at that point that the other side launched its carefully planned surprise.

From the west, out of the sunlight, came seven Albatros D.III fighters, their guns primed and firing before the others knew they were even there. Samuels was taken down in that first pass. One moment his Spad was there and the next it was not, replaced by a cloud of inky black smoke and small pieces of fluttering debris. James followed suit only moments later, though he did manage to take one of the enemy with him.

From there it became a tenacious duel in the sky, the opposition forces swarming around the two remaining Allied planes in a choreographed dance of death and destruction. Freeman and Walton managed to give a good accounting of themselves, taking three more of the enemy aircraft out of the fight in a dazzling display of marksmanship.

Freeman had just begun to think that they might survive this encounter when both of his Vickers guns jammed. One minute they were roaring steadily, the next, nothing. Suddenly furious and more than a little bit frightened, Freeman clawed at the charging handles, trying to clear the mechanisms.

Once.

Twice.

Three times.

Nothing.

Knowing he would be no good in the middle of a dogfight without operational guns, Freeman broke away from the fight, climbing in an attempt to find time to fix the problem.

The opposition let him go, choosing to gang up on Walton instead.

From his higher altitude Freeman watched the enemy aircraft make short work of his lone surviving subordinate.

Walton's Spad suddenly dipped and headed for the ground in an uncontrolled spin, a clear sign that a well-placed bullet had ended the life of its pilot. Freeman could watch no more.

When he turned his gaze away from the destruction below, Freeman recoiled in surprise to find a previously unnoticed aircraft sitting directly off his right wing tip!

It was one of the new Fokker D.VIIIs, the "Flying Razor Blades" as the British pilots were wont to call them. The single-wing aircraft was the current pride of the opposition's air corps and one of the most deadly aircraft in the skies. It could outmaneuver, outshoot, and outfly anything the Allied powers could put in the air. This aircraft was painted a bright red, like the triplane that had baited the trap, but the Iron Crosses on its wings and fuselage had been replaced with the double-headed eagle and skulls of the Richthofen family seal, the insignia looking stark and menacing against the brightly colored background. The D.VIII was so close that Freeman could see the other pilot clearly, right down to the missing flesh across the lower half of the right side of his face.

Instantly, Freeman recognized the true nature of the trap to which his squadron had just fallen victim. The triplane his fellow pilots had exuberantly chased had been a decoy, designed to pull the younger pilots into the fray just as it had so brilliantly done. The flight of Albatroses that had dropped out of the clouds to the rear of the Allied planes had been there to whittle down the Allied fliers, leaving Freeman isolated and alone.

Ripe for picking by the commander of the enemy flight.

Freeman did not wait around to see how the trap turned out. He stood his aircraft on its beam and whipped around in a turn that came close to pulling the wings off.

Too good a pilot to be taken in so easily, the other chased Freeman into the tight turn so that the two aircraft were spinning around each other in a vertical helix. Looking directly "up" from his cockpit, Freeman could see straight into the former German's cockpit, where the other man was looking "down" at him in return. They flew that way for several moments, getting closer to the ground with each revolution as they arced around each other in opposite directions, Freeman sitting hunched against the chill wind while Richthofen ignored both the cold and the centrifugal forces created by their movement.

A sudden change in the sound of his engine let Freeman know he suddenly had a bigger problem than the presence of the opposition's most deadly ace. It was barely discernible at first, just the slightest change in tone and pitch, but he was too experienced a flier to not know that it represented a major problem. His eyes swept over the gauges where he immediately noted the change in fuel pressure. One of the attacks by the Albatroses must have damaged his fuel line, something he hadn't noticed before now. He was about to pay the price for his negligence.

There was no way he could continue this ballet of motion in an aircraft with jammed guns and a faltering engine and he knew it. He waited another moment, watching, until his opponent looked away for a split second to check on his own aircraft's controls, then broke out of the spin, headed east in a straight line, praying that the German pilot would take the bait.

Like a cat with a mouse, the enemy pilot had been waiting for just such a move, and he pounced just as Freeman had hoped he would. As the enemy's Spandau machine guns began hammering Freeman's aircraft to pieces, the American launched his own surprise.

With a sudden turn, Freeman arced his Spad over into what

first appeared to be an Immelman turn. As the other pilot altered course to intercept his arc, Freeman abruptly turned, steering directly into the German's path.

The enemy reacted quickly, shoving his stick over in an attempt to get out of the way, but his reflexes were not quick enough. The edge of the Spad's upper wing struck the Fokker's solitary one. Cloth, leather, and wood flew in all directions as the two aircraft collided and then tumbled away from each other.

Freeman fought the stick as it jumped in his hands, trying to get his aircraft under control, but with most of the Spad's upper wing now shredded, his options were limited. He managed to get the plane into a flat spin, using the entirety of the aircraft's surface in an attempt to slow his plunging descent, but it wasn't enough to prevent the crash altogether.

He could see a dark space off to his left and he did what he could to angle the aircraft in that direction, hauling on the stick and hoping that the shadow was a farmer's pond or a copse of trees, or hell, even a wide hedgerow, anything that might give him a bit of a cushion.

As the ground rose up to greet him, he prayed the resulting fire would be hot enough to prevent him from rising again.

There was a thunderous crash, a moment of agony, and then nothing.

CHAPTER THREE

As THE WAVE of shamblers poured out of the strange machine in front of him, Burke calmly drew his pistol and began to fire into their ranks. His first shot struck the closest shambler in the face, knocking it backward into the one directly behind it, sending them both to the ground. He'd hoped it might slow the others down, even if only for a moment, but the rest of the horde didn't even notice as they pushed forward, trampling their comrades into the mud beneath their bare feet as their chilling cries of hunger split the morning air.

Charlie's rifle sounded from close by and the two veterans had time to get off several more shots, sending half a dozen of the enemy to the ground, at least temporarily, before the shamblers were too tangled up with their own troops for them to continue.

At that point there was little choice but to wade into the melee. They had to hold the line; if the shamblers managed to get past his unit and into the rest of the trench complex, there was no telling the damage they might do.

With his pistol in his right hand and his trench knife in the metal fingers of his left, Burke charged forward. He'd been here before, too many times to count, and his body knew what to do without conscious thought. Shamblers were not only slow, but they also fought without any sense of self-preservation, their only thought the food they saw in front of them. As long as you weren't overwhelmed, a well-armed man could hold his own against several of the creatures at once.

He scythed about him with his trench knife, aiming for an unprotected neck or maybe the soft spot behind a knee, the well-sharpened blade cutting through the creature's rotting flesh with ease. Once he had one of them down, he'd thrust his pistol out and put a bullet through its skull, ensuring that it didn't get back up again. Within moments he was covered with blood, gore, and the stench of rotting flesh.

After what felt like hours but was probably only a few minutes, there was a lull in the fighting directly in front of him and he had a moment to survey the scene. The world seemed to shift, everything slowing down, letting him get a good look at the action going on around him, as if he'd suddenly stepped out of time and was looking back in, the details popping out with stark clarity . . . one of his men, openmouthed, screaming his fury as he bashed in a shambler's skull with the broken shaft of his Enfield rifle; another standing, firing his pistol at the shambler that was latched onto his leg, gray teeth tearing meat from his calf; a hysterical young man cradling the body of another in his arms while blood streamed down his own face as the enemy closed in.

The arena was pure, unadulterated chaos, the stuff of battle, and to his secret shame Burke felt his heart cheer at the sight of it all.

This was what he had been born for; this was what made him come alive, what had kept him at the front even after losing his hand in the midst of a battle very much like this one.

Motion near the strange burrowing machine caught his eye. As he watched, a hatch opened down low in front between the treads and a gray-faced shambler peered out. It was the creature's very caution that drew Burke's attention; it should have been charging out into the melee like someone had just rung the dinner bell, not checking to be sure the coast was clear.

Burke dealt with the shambler directly in front of him by jabbing his knife into its eye socket and twisting sharply, then turned his full attention on the newcomer. He was in the perfect position to watch as it apparently made up its mind and burst out of the hatch at a run. It dogged friend and foe alike as it headed for the opening of the communications trench in a lumbering gait.

Shamblers can't run, Burke thought to himself.

Shamblers CAN'T run.

But this one could. It was doing a damned good job of it, too, like a tight end who'd just caught the football and was giving it everything he had to get into the end zone ahead of the other team.

The end zone in this case was the communications trench that ran perpendicular to the one in which Burke and everyone else now stood.

One of only two such trenches that led into the unprotected area behind the lines.

That's when Burke noticed the belt of potato masher grenades the shambler wore around its waist. Wires ran from one device to the next and, seeing them, Burke had little doubt that setting one of them off would detonate all the rest. In the close quarters of a communications shack or a command bunker, the explosion would cause one helluva lot of damage.

Urgency spurred him forward.

"The block!" he shouted at the men manning the communications trench, trying to be heard above the din. "Release the trench block!"

Every trench at the front had one, a wood or an iron frame that was covered with barbed wire and ready to be wedged across the path of the trench to keep it from being overrun if the enemy broke through. At least one man was supposed to be near it at all times, prepared to cut the rope and allow it to fall into place if circumstances required it.

Except that no one seemed to be paying attention.

Burke's cry went unheeded.

The men in the communications trench were no doubt hunkered down, waiting for their comrades to either defeat the horde in front of them or fall back to the next position behind. This would ensure that a fresh force was ready to take the fight to the enemy if they managed to break through the lines. No one was watching for a runaway shambler and, even if they were, the thing's speed and dexterity would make them think it was one of the living, rather than one of the undead.

"Block the trench!" Burke screamed again as he raced after the creature in front of him.

There was no way he was going to catch it. The blasted thing ran like hell itself was snapping at its heels. Burke skidded to a stop, raised his pistol, and fired off three quick shots. The first two missed, but the third struck the shambler in the back, knocking it forward off its feet.

Burke lined up his next shot with the back of the creature's skull, took a breath to steady himself, and pulled the trigger.

Click.

The hammer fell on an empty chamber.

The rotting thing in front of him climbed to its feet, snarling.

"Damn you!" Burke yelled. "Seal the trench!"

The shambler was almost to the entrance, was less than twenty feet away in fact, when someone finally heard him. There was a loud grinding sound and then a massive iron plate covered with a roll of barbed wire dropped in front of the entrance to the trench, blocking the way forward.

Burke wanted to scream and dance and shout for joy.

Until, that is, the shambler slowed down and came to a stop. It paused there for a moment, staring at the trench block, then turned to face Burke, clearly making a decision to try this another way.

They're not supposed to do that, either!

Burke transferred the gun to his left hand while he dug in the pocket of his coat with his right, fingers fumbling for the extra cartridges he kept there.

The creature angled its head one way and then the other, like a dog might when considering something it hadn't encountered before.

Burke knocked the breech of the pistol open and began shoving cartridges into the chamber, never taking his gaze off the thing in front of him.

He'd only managed to get three of them in place when the shambler's head lifted and it looked directly at him.

A kind of crafty intelligence glinted in its eyes.

"Fuck me," Burke said softly.

The shambler sprang forward, pushing off with its hind leg like a sprinter and tearing down the length of the trench toward him.

Burke managed to get off one shot, then a second, both of which struck the shambler in the fleshy part of its chest, but neither did anything to slow it down. He was trying to line up the third and final shot with the creature's skull when it barreled into him like a runaway freight train.

He hit the ground hard, the full weight of the thing atop his chest, and the back of his head struck something unyielding behind it, momentarily stunning him.

He shook his head to clear it, opening his eyes to find a shambler staring down at him with undisguised hunger. Once upon a time it had been a blond-haired, big-boned German lad who had stood a few inches taller than six feet and weighed more than 250 pounds. Now its skin was gray and laced with black veins that stood out against the slowly decaying flesh, its eyes a filmy white rimmed with yellow pus.

Burke didn't hesitate; he swung the pistol around and pointed it up into the creature's face.

Only to have it knocked out of his grasp by a backhanded blow.

Trapped as he was beneath the shambler without a weapon to use in his defense, Burke could only watch in horror as the thing's mouth opened wide, revealing broken teeth that dripped thick, greenish-gray mucus. A shambler's bite was poisonous, and rescuers had to act fast to save a man if he was unlucky enough to get bitten. The toxins contained in a shambler's bite spread through the body at an incredible rate, causing a raging infection, crippling pain, and ultimately, death. The really unlucky would turn into shamblers themselves, rising a few hours later once the transformation was complete, though this didn't happen very often, thank God.

The creature reared up, drawing its head back like a snake preparing to strike, and then thrust its face downward toward Burke's unprotected neck.

Focused entirely on keeping those slavering jaws away from his unprotected flesh, Burke did the only thing he could think of at the time.

He shoved the prosthesis on his left arm into the creature's mouth, jamming it between its jaws.

Burke knew from prior experience just how strong a shambler's bite could be; his lower left arm and hand had been crushed by one three years before, ultimately requiring his forearm and hand to be amputated. But losing a hand was better than losing his life. This time the creature's jaws slammed shut on the metal skin of his forearm with a sharp clank, crushing it like a tin can.

The once-human creature yanked its head to the side, expecting to pull itself away from the offending limb and try again to reach the soft tissue at the base of Burke's throat, only to discover, to its increasing frustration and Burke's growing horror, that its teeth had become trapped in the twisted metal of Burke's mechanical arm.

For a moment, the two of them froze, staring at each other, and then the shambler went berserk, slashing at Burke's face with overgrown nails and digging at him with its feet, as it fought to free itself from its precarious position.

The shambler's thrashing only served to jam its teeth farther into the tangled mess that had once been Burke's forearm.

Meanwhile Burke beat at it with his free hand, driving blow after blow into its hideous face, but it was like swatting an elephant with a blade of grass; shamblers didn't feel pain.

Unable to free itself by twisting from side to side, the shambler changed tactics. It beat its fists against the other side of Burke's arm in furious rhythm, its animal intelligence able to identify the threat but not able to puzzle out a means of release. Each blow further dented Burke's already damaged prosthesis. If the shambler kept it up for much longer, he knew he'd have nothing left but a piece of flattened steel for an arm and no hand at all. Panic bloomed. Desperate, Burke abandoned his attempts to hit the thing and began looking around for some help.

Where the hell was everybody else?

As if in answer to his summons, he suddenly spotted Sergeant Moore rushing in his general direction, a thick black case the size of a sea chest held in his arms like a load of firewood. The case's weight was evident by the way the sergeant staggered to a stop and dumped the thing on the ground with a resounding thud.

It had only been delivered to them the week before, and they hadn't yet used it in action. When he'd first seen it, Burke had laughed aloud. *What the hell were they going to do with something like that in the midst of a battle?* he'd wanted to know.

Looked like he was about to get his chance.

The shambler wasn't sitting still for it all, however. Unable to free itself from Burke's prosthesis, the creature apparently decided it was going to gnaw all the way through the mechanical apparatus instead. It was working its jaw in every direction it could while shoving its face forward, its teeth grinding against the inner workings. Oil suddenly spurted free in a long wet arc, splashing across Burke's face. Half a second later he lost the use of his fingers.

Another glance in Charlie's direction showed that he now had the case open and was in the process of setting up the device inside it. What had started out life as a Vickers machine gun had undergone substantial modifications in Tesla's laboratory. Belts and glass tubing ran over the barrel and stock like creepers in the Deep South, and a big ball of glass sat where the sights should have been. A short-legged tripod supported the front of the barrel and allowed the "gunner" to point it in the right direction. Perhaps most incongruous of all was the hand crank that stuck out the side of the contraption, reminding Burke of the mechanism used to start the Model T Ford he'd owned before the war.

Before he knew it, Burke found himself staring down the business end of the device as Charlie pointed it in his direction.

The barrel of a gun had never looked so big.

A synapse or two must have finally fired somewhere in the depths of the shambler's brain, for it stopped trying to masticate Burke's arm and instead simply seized it between its two hands, using the extra leverage to attempt to pull itself free. Burke was surprised it hadn't done that from the start given the intelligence it had displayed earlier, but he was thankful just the same.

Burke used the respite to raise his head out of the dirt and look past the creature in the direction Charlie was pointing Tesla's experimental weapon.

One glance was all it took for him to understand what it was that had his sergeant so spooked.

Another wave of shamblers had crossed no-man's-land and was a dozen feet or so from reaching the edge of the trench. Most of Burke's men were engaged, fighting off the horde that had burst out of the digging machine, and this new wave of enemy shock troops would provide the reinforcements needed to finally overwhelm the defenses.

Once they were eliminated, there was practically nothing standing between the enemy and the rest of the division camped out in the rear.

It would be a complete slaughter.

"Do it, Charlie! Do it!" Burke screamed.

His sergeant didn't need to be told twice. Burke watched Charlie turn the crank as quickly as he could. A high-pitched whining filled the air as the dynamo inside the gun rapidly spun up to full speed.

Charlie's fingers reached for the trigger.

The glass ball atop the weapon filled with a harsh light, and then twisting, churning arms of bluish energy lashed out of the front of the barrel. One arced across the dozen or so feet that separated them to strike the shambler sitting astride Burke dead in the chest, while others snaked past them to strike those in the front of the onrushing horde.

The scientist from Tesla's staff who'd delivered the "suitcase" to Burke's platoon had gone into a long-winded explanation about magnetic fields, opposing charges, and a bunch of other technical mumbo jumbo that hadn't meant squat to him, nor to any of the men listening to the briefing. But the one thing Burke did understand was the fact that the discharge from the device was supposed to zero in only on nonliving tissue, protecting the troops that might accidentally be caught in the cross fire.

Burke prayed they'd gotten it right.

And, in those first few seconds, it looked like they had. A web of twisting electrical balefire spread across the shambler's entire form, outlining him in a blue light that sparked and popped with a life of its own.

A grin began to slide across Burke's face as he watched the thing shake and twist under the power of the beam.

The grin swiftly vanished when one of those twisting bands of energy jumped from the creature's face to the arm that was still trapped inside its mouth.

Burke's metal arm.

A bolt of power shot down the length of his prosthesis and exploded across the cluster of dead nerve endings in the stump of his elbow, making his arm twist and jerk from the pain.

As they both danced to the energy coursing between them, Burke thought he saw a dead man's smile on the shambler before he was shocked into unconsciousness.

CHAPTER FOUR

WITH A PLUME of black smoke spilling from beneath his engine cowling and his left wing vibrating hard enough to beat the devil, Baron Manfred von Richthofen carefully nursed his dying Fokker D.VIII toward the airfield that was just coming into view in the distance.

Failing at this point would be more a blow to his pride than anything else. He had little doubt that he'd live through a crash; after all, his altered form had allowed him to do so twice already and from heights far greater than this. But the thought of crashing within sight of his own airfield, and the resulting humiliation he would feel when facing the rest of the Jasta's pilots later that evening, sent a red-hot fury burning through his veins.

No one bested him in the air, especially not that ridiculous American playboy, Freeman!

For months now the American and British press had been comparing the two fliers to each other, and Richthofen had grown tired of the nonsense. Not only was he an officer and a gentleman, but he was also a *freiherr*, a titled noble in the Prussian Empire! There really was no comparison. Freeman's "daring exploits," as the press liked to call them, were examples of poor planning and careless decision making in the Baron's eyes. If the idiot paid more attention to what he was doing, perhaps he wouldn't end up in so many difficult situations.

Like the trap he'd fallen for today, for instance. Richthofen was confident even his rookie pilots would have been able to recognize it for what it was and would have had the intelligence to avoid engaging the "injured" aircraft. Freeman had gotten what he'd deserved, in Richthofen's view.

Unfortunately, the damned Yank had also managed to cripple the Baron's aircraft in the process, which was why Richthofen was doing everything he could to get the dying Fokker back to the ground in one piece.

He nursed the plane through the last quarter mile and was making his final approach toward the grassy field that served as the takeoff and landing area when a loud *WHUMP* came from the engine. Tongues of fire joined the billowing column of smoke. The air rushing over the cowling fanned them into flames three feet high, which quickly began to make their way back along the fuselage toward him!

Richthofen was close enough that he could see the crews on the ground pushing some of the other aircraft out of the way, clearing as much of the landing area as possible in case he should lose control as he brought his damaged plane in for a landing. A flash of anger at their lack of faith bloomed deep inside, but he squashed it before it could spread. The situation must look much worse from their point of view, he realized, with the way the aircraft was wobbling all over the sky due to the wing damage it had sustained, never mind the visible flames now completely engulfing the engine.

By the time he felt the wheels strike the ground beneath him, those same flames were enveloping the Spandau guns mounted a foot in front of the cockpit in their heated embrace. Richthofen taxied away from the other aircraft as far as he dared and then, as the fire began to cook off the 7.92 mm ammunition in the twin-mounted machine guns before him, he scrambled over the side of the cockpit and retreated to a safe distance.

From there, he watched in fascination as the flames swept over the aircraft, consuming it like a hungry beast. The sight of the fire caused a wave of fear to well up inside his chest, for fire was one of the few things that could permanently damage his resurrected body and end the strange new unlife he'd been granted, but it took several minutes of effort before he could look away, so drawn was he to the spectacle. The effort left him trembling slightly.

Disgusted by the loss of another aircraft, Richthofen stalked across the airfield toward the tent that served as both his living quarters and work area, leaving the ground crew to deal with the flaming wreckage. As he approached his quarters, his adjutant, Leutnant Adler, stepped out and snapped off a parade-ground salute.

"A good patrol, Herr Richthofen?" he asked.

Richthofen's eyes narrowed as he scrutinized the expression on Adler's face, but he couldn't find any hint of insolence and so he did what he could to quell his irritation at the question.

Adler had once been a prime example of excellent Prussian breeding—tall, strong, fair skinned and fair haired—but little of his natural good looks remained after undergoing Dr. Eisenberg's special procedure. His skin had gone sallow, and his veins stood out in thick black lines. Most of his hair had fallen out; the rest hung limp and lifeless, despite his efforts to comb it over with what little vanity that remained. His lips had thinned, his teeth had elongated, and his nails had thickened into what might almost pass as weapons, if necessity demanded it.

The procedure was not an easy one. It took a strong man, both physically and mentally, to withstand the crippling agony and mental confusion that came along with it. Those who were too weak or those who lost their sense of who and what they were came through the procedure broken in more ways than one.

Adler was a "graduate" of the supersoldier program Eisenberg ran out of the secret facility in Verdun. It had been Richthofen's brainchild, but even he would admit that the program would have failed long ago if it hadn't been for Eisenberg's ruthless determination to succeed. It had taken months and literally thousands of test subjects before they had seen even the slightest success, but those days were far behind them now. In the next few weeks, they would reveal what they had been creating in the depths of the Verdun forests and the world would never be the same.

The war had been mismanaged right from the start, in Richthofen's view. Not wanting to fight on two fronts, the High Command had decided to strike west with overwhelming force in the hope of taking Paris from the French before their Russian allies to the east could mobilize. Seven field armies under the commands of von Kluck and von Bülow had marched into Belgium in August of 1914, completely confident that Paris would be theirs within six weeks. No one expected the Belgian army to put up such a fierce resistance, nor the series of poor decisions made by General Moltke in early September that had resulted in the German retreat following the Battle of the Marne and the loss of much of the ground they'd occupied. By October, both the British and the Russians had mobilized to help their French allies, and Germany had been faced with exactly what the plan had been designed to avoid in the first place—a war on multiple fronts.

Still, it hadn't been completely hopeless. Kaiser Wilhelm might have regained momentum at that point if he'd listened to those who called for a renewed push toward Paris with the help of a beefed-up Army Air Service, Richthofen's mentor, Oswald Boelcke, among them. It had been Boelcke who had brought Richthofen into the kaiser's inner circle, and from that point forward the German ace had seen for himself the indecision and fear that were a hallmark of all Wilhelm's decisions.

The stalemate might have continued indefinitely if it hadn't been for the invention of the corpse gas in the spring of 1918. The massive influx of additional manpower had allowed them to push the Allied lines back almost all the way to Paris, and they might have even taken the city itself if the Americans hadn't entered the war.

A fresh influx of American troops, combined with tactical errors on behalf of several German commanders, had allowed the Allies to regain some of the ground they had recently lost. German forces retreated to a line bisecting France that ran from Ypres in the north to Nogent in the south, and there they had stayed for the last two years. Now, at last, they had a way of breaking the back of the American forces. All that was needed was a man with enough determination to see it through; Richthofen knew he was that man.

The sight of Adler, and what he signified, mollified the Baron's anger a bit and allowed him to appreciate what he had achieved that morning, ruined airplane or not.

"Ya, a good patrol indeed. That stupid American, Freeman, has flown his last flight."

Richthofen stepped inside the tent, and Adler followed at a suitable distance. The interior was spartan, as befitted the warrior asceticism that Richthofen sought to cultivate amid the rest of the squadron's pilots. The furniture consisted of a simple table, desk, and bed. The walls were covered with maps of the Western Front, many of them containing notes in Richthofen's spidery hand. He took meticulous notes of every patrol, placing the most important of them directly onto the maps for future reference. This was the secret of his success, the very thing that had allowed him to rise from a lowly cavalry officer to the head of the most feared aerial fighter unit in all of Germany, the Flying Circus. Information was power, and power was something Richthofen had become very good at acquiring over the years.

His days of freezing in the trenches and charging the front line atop a Prussian stallion were long over. The cavalry had effectively become extinct in the face of tank warfare and the development of the machine gun. Richthofen couldn't have been more grateful, either. A chance meeting with Boelcke in October 1915 had spurred his joining the German Army Air Service and his meteoric rise through the ranks to his present command.

The meeting had changed his life, for it led directly to the circumstances that left him lying dead in the ruins of his Fokker D.III biplane in April 1918. The wreckage, and the corpse it contained, *his* corpse, had been enveloped by thick clouds of green gas later that afternoon as the German High Command initiated battlefield tests of a new weapon, a special gas that was intended to replace the mustard and chlorine compounds that had been used in the war up until that point.

The gas had performed far better than anyone expected. Corpse gas had been born and with it the zombielike death troops, the *Tottensoldat*, who soon swelled the ranks of the kaiser's army in seemingly endless numbers. Once the German High Command learned how to control them, they became the perfect frontline shock troops.

But that was not all that had risen anew that chilly April afternoon. In an unusual confluence of events, that same gas had worked its own twisted brand of magick on Richthofen himself, resurrected him as a better, stronger, more intelligent version of the man who had died at Allied hands.

He had no need for air, for he didn't really breathe. His body felt no pain and was equally impervious to the weather, be it heat or cold. Even sleep was no longer a necessity. His reflexes were faster, as were his thought processes. Where before he was a methodical thinker, now he found himself making leaps of logic and seeing plans unfold twenty steps ahead, like a chess master, and he'd used that newfound ability to fuel a ruthlessly ambitious rise to the top of the military juggernaut. His unique nature, combined with his hereditary title, had allowed him to move in the highest circles of German society, eventually coming to the attention of the kaiser himself. Sensing a kindred spirit, the kaiser had promoted Richthofen to his inner circle of trusted advisers, never once realizing that he'd just let a wolf in sheep's clothing loose among the herd.

Richthofen stripped off his smoke-infused flight suit and undergarments, handing them to Adler, who stood nearby.

"You are certain it was Freeman?" Adler asked, as he took the Baron's clothing over to a rack near the entrance to the tent to let the wind air them out.

The question made Richthofen pause for a moment in the

midst of pulling on a new set of clothes. *Was he? Had it truly been Freeman?*

He thought so. The plane had been decorated with Freeman's trademark Jack of Spades, but that alone was not enough to confirm the pilot's identity. His own little stunt with the Fokker triplane that had lured the Yanks to their death proved that. Still, the skill with which the pilot had flown, the tenacity he'd brought to the task, even the last-ditch effort to ram the Baron's own plane rather than succumb to the enemy—all that required a rare combination of finesse, skill, and bravery, something the average flier just didn't have.

It had been Freeman; he was certain of it.

But it would be prudent to confirm the kill just the same. Thankfully the dogfight had occurred on the German side of the lines so that shouldn't be difficult.

Richthofen got up and walked over to one of the maps tacked to the tent wall. He studied it earnestly for a few minutes, then beckoned Adler closer.

"We came upon the American patrol about here," he said, pointing to a spot on the map a fair distance inside German lines. "Which means Freeman's craft went down in this general area." He circled another spot a few inches away. "I want you to take a patrol out there and find the wreckage. If you can recover the body, do so; otherwise, just take photographs and bring me something we can send to the Yanks to confirm the kill."

Adler snapped to attention. "For the empire!"

Richthofen nodded absently, his attention still on the map, then called out to the younger man before he slipped out of the tent. When Adler turned at the door to face him, Richthofen said, "If you can't recover Freeman's entire body, I'll be content with just his head."

CHAPTER FIVE

★

FIELD HOSPITAL

BURKE AWOKE TO the scent of blood, vomit, and unwashed bodies. Underneath it all was the smell of lye soap, which, rather than hiding the stench, only seemed to somehow magnify it. That was all he needed to know that he was in the casualty clearing station.

The casualty clearing station, or CCS, was set up in a series of large tents about five miles behind the front lines. If a man's injuries couldn't be treated at the front with bandages and simple first aid, he was brought here for more in-depth care and assessment. Those needing immediate surgery received it in a sectioned-off portion of the main hospital tent and were then shipped farther back behind the lines to one of the area hospitals near the larger coastal towns like Boulogne and Calais. Needless to say it was always a busy place, the tents filled to overflowing with the wounded.

Burke had been to the CCS before, not this one but one just like it, and so he knew what to expect. He'd get a few days' rest, a hot meal or two, and then be sent back to his unit at the front. Which was fine by him; the sooner he was out of here the better. He hated hospitals even more than he hated the enemy, or the Boche, as they were commonly known among the troops.

He opened his eyes to find himself in what passed for a private bedroom at the CCS: a corner bed set off from the others by two walls and a couple of tacked-up blankets. A chair stood in the corner, near a shuttered window. The half-drunk glass of water sitting on the windowsill told him someone had been sitting there recently, waiting for him to wake up.

The blankets gave him some visual privacy but did little to filter out the sounds surrounding him. He could hear men moaning and calling for their mothers, doctors arguing, the endless creak of cot springs under a heavy load, even the far-off whine of a bone saw being prepped for its next victim. All that, combined with the smell of the place, was too much for Burke.

Screw the hot meals. I'll be better off at the front.

He reached out with his left hand, intending to pull off the thin blanket that covered him, and found himself staring at the newly bandaged stump of his left forearm instead. For a moment he was back in the mud and muck of Ypres earlier in the war, watching in horror as Sergeant Moore brought the machete whistling down toward the unprotected flesh of his forearm, a few inches past the mangled remains of his shambler-bitten hand. Moore's action had saved his life, had kept infection from spreading through his tissues, but that didn't lessen the power of the memory. He could hear the mortars going off overhead, could smell the cordite in the air and the mud beneath his feet, could see the grim determination on Charlie's face . . .

"It's not what you think."

Burke jumped. The memory held him in its grip for a moment longer, just enough so he could feel the bite of that shining blade, and then it dissolved like rain and he found himself staring across the room at his sergeant's smiling face poking through the curtains.

"It's not?" Burke croaked, not realizing until he tried to speak how parched he was. He waved at the glass on the windowsill and Charlie dutifully retrieved it and helped him take a drink.

"Nah. Graves took it, that's all."

Burke cringed. Losing his hand to a shambler for a second time would have been bad, but hearing that the ghoulish Graves had taken it might just be worse.

"Did he say when he was bringing it back?"

Charlie must have sensed what he was thinking for the big man grinned sympathetically. "He's not. It was too crushed to repair so he's giving you a new model. I'm supposed to take you down there tomorrow for a fitting."

Great, Burke thought. *Can't wait.*

Something about the man's utter fascination with the undead unnerved Burke, so much so that he only dealt with him when it was absolutely necessary. He much preferred having Graves's boss, the great inventor Nikola Tesla, handle any maintenance work that might be needed on his mechanical forearm and hand, but this time it seemed he didn't have a choice.

Graves it was.

Not that he wasn't thankful for what Tesla and his assistants, Graves included, had done for him. He knew it had been pure luck that Tesla had been there in the field ambulance when he'd been rushed in from the battlefield at Ypres. If they'd brought him in for surgery even ten minutes later, he'd be wearing a brass cap over the end of his stump like so many other wounded soldiers rather than the clockwork arm that had been his constant companion for the last few years. He'd been the next patient scheduled for amputation that day when the inventor had come looking for a human guinea pig. A mechanical arm had sounded better than no arm at all to Burke when the deal was offered and he'd willingly volunteered.

Hopefully this "new model" would stand up better to shambler teeth.

"How bad was it?" Burke asked.

Charlie knew from long experience just what he was asking.

"Eight dead, eleven wounded, including yourself. Other sections of the front were hit at the same time. We threw them back, but just barely."

Burke nodded. Eight dead wasn't bad at all, considering what they'd faced, but he still felt responsible. Each of the casualties was another man who wouldn't be returning home to his wife or family. Each represented a letter he had to write to whoever was waiting at home.

"What about that digging machine or whatever it was? Do we know anything about it?" he asked, to get his mind off the difficult duty that lay ahead.

His staff sergeant shook his head. "Word is that it was a complete surprise; headquarters hadn't even heard a rumor about its existence. It didn't stick around to let us check it out either, but bugged out of there shortly after disgorging its cargo. Several men from the Engineer Corps tried to follow it back through the tunnels, but the Boche were smart and collapsed the passage behind them as they retreated."

"Damn!" It wasn't what Burke wanted to hear, not by a long shot.

The digging machine worried Burke, and he wondered just how many of them were out there. The enemy could destabilize the entire front with just a couple dozen of them, burrowing underneath the lines and coming up anywhere they wanted, including in the Allies' rear. That would effectively pin them between a rock and a hard place, and it wasn't hard to imagine what would happen at that point, with both sets of enemy lines closing in on them like a vise.

And if that wasn't enough to worry about, there was also that new type of shambler to deal with.

As if reading his mind, Charlie handed him a clipboard. On it was the after-action report form, the same one he was supposed to complete after every engagement with the enemy. Burke had long ago become convinced that if the enemy didn't kill him, the paperwork would.

"Christ, Charlie," Burke said. "Can't it wait?"

"Sorry, sir, but it's best that you get the details down now, before too much time has passed and you forget 'em." The big sergeant hesitated for a moment, and then asked, "You going to tell them about the shambler?"

Burke scowled in frustration as he considered the question and the issue it addressed. At last he said, "I've never seen a shambler act that way before. Have you?"

Charlie shook his head.

"I don't see that I have any choice then," Burke replied.

And he didn't, not really. Any development that might end the current stalemate and give the enemy a tactical advantage had to be taken seriously. A shambler that acted with foresight and initiative was definitely something that could upset the balance of power. It was bad enough when they behaved like unthinking automatons. But give them intelligence, even at a rudimentary level, and things would get a whole lot more uncomfortable for the troops at the front.

Charlie clapped him on the shoulder. "Leave it with the nurse when you're done and I'll swing by later and see to it that it gets filed properly. You need anything else?"

"No, thanks. I'll see you in the morning."

As Charlie took his leave, Burke turned his attention to the report before him and began jotting down his preliminary thoughts. There were a lot of details and if he was going to stick his neck out like this, he at least wanted to be certain that he got them right . . .

CHAPTER SIX

THE FIRST THING Freeman noticed was the pain.

A white-hot spike of pain poked and prodded at him, like a metaphysical branding iron, jarring him back to consciousness. He knew right away that the pain was coming from his right leg, and the fact that it blocked out any of his other injuries told him that this one was probably more serious than the rest.

The pain wasn't necessarily a bad thing, as it let him know that he was still alive, but it certainly wasn't good either. If he'd been injured too badly to walk, his chances of getting out of occupied territory alive were pretty slim.

Make that zero chance.

He'd deal with that when the time came.

Focus, Freeman. Get out of the wreck, then worry about getting out of occupied France.

Right.

He opened his eyes and looked around, discovering that what was left of his Spad was a dozen feet or so above the ground, crammed between the trunks of several trees. He was still in the cockpit, hanging upside down, held in place only by the thick leather belt bolted to the underside of his wooden chair on the right-hand side and extending up and across his chest to the hook above his left shoulder.

The morning's events came back to him in a rush. The ambush. The loss of his squadron mates. The long dogfight with Richthofen that had ended with his fateful decision to ram the Baron's plane. He remembered aiming his mortally wounded aircraft at a nearby copse of trees, hoping the vegetation-laden branches might slow him down enough to keep from being splattered all over the landscape.

Apparently, by some miracle, it had worked.

His arms, hanging limply over his head and down toward the ground, were full of pins and needles. That told him he hadn't been hanging there very long. Fifteen, maybe twenty minutes tops. Any longer and he wouldn't have felt them at all, so coming to when he did had probably saved his life. He simply hadn't had time to bleed to death.

For now, an inner voice said.

You've still got to get down from these trees.

His hands didn't particularly want to listen to what his brain was telling them, but eventually he managed to reach up high enough to snatch hold of the edge of his cockpit and hold on.

The effort caused fresh spasms of pain to shoot up from his leg, stealing his breath away. He took a minute to steady himself and then got ready for the tricky part.

In order to get out of the plane, he was going to have to release the seat belt and let himself drop to the ground below. He didn't want to do that until he knew exactly what shape his leg was in.

He was going to have to reach down there and see.

Freeman took a couple of slow, deep breaths, mentally preparing himself. The pain coming up from his leg told him the news wouldn't be good. All that was left to find out was just how bad it actually was.

When he was ready, he quickly bent forward as far as the strap would allow and ran his right hand down the outside of his leg to a point just past his knee.

He found the problem right away.

The Spad was nothing more than a wooden frame supported by wires and covered with a hardened cloth to help it resist the wind loads that it was subjected to while flying. When it had come down through the trees, the impact had crushed the outer frame and splintered the spars that lined the fuselage. The remains of one of those spars was currently jammed through the meat of his calf, holding him in place.

Just touching it sent a wave of pain and dizziness washing over him. Darkness loomed at the edge of his vision, and he had to lean back and stay still for several long moments while he waited for it to recede.

Breathe, Jack, breathe.

Now that he knew what the problem was he imagined he could feel the blood dripping down his leg, could feel the pressure of the wood against the muscles of his leg, but really, all he could feel was the pain.

There was no doubt about that.

Getting himself free was going to be a bitch.

He couldn't stay here, that was for sure. He'd gone down in sight of the enemy, which meant they'd send someone out to check on the wreckage, if only to go through it for spare parts or evidence of technological improvements the Central Powers hadn't come up with yet on their own. His people did it, so he knew theirs would as well. If he could get away from the wreck, he might stand a chance. They wouldn't expect him to survive the crash and the lack of a body in the wreckage wouldn't set off any alarms; many pilots didn't bother with seat belts . . .

So what are you waiting for?

Gingerly touching the inside of his calf let him know that the spar hadn't gone all the way through his leg. That was good news, but getting himself free was going to be compounded by the downward pull of his body weight. He was going to have to ease the pressure while at the same time sliding his leg free.

Any way you looked at it, it was going to hurt like hell.

Keeping one hand firmly on the edge of the cockpit, he used the other to unwind the scarf he wore around his neck. It had been given to him as a gift from a Frenchwoman he'd met on his last liberty. He couldn't even remember her name now, but he said a silent thank you to her just the same because her little gift was going to keep him from bleeding to death.

Scarf in hand, he mentally rehearsed the steps he was going to have to take.

Shift his body to the left, using his hands to pull his leg off the jutting piece of wood. Wrap the scarf around the wound to stop the bleeding. Pull up on the cockpit to take his weight off the seat belt. Unhook the belt and drop to the ground below.

Nothing to it.

Now or never, Jack.

He moved his other leg to the left as far as it would go, creating a bit of space between them, then laid the scarf across his thigh where he could get to it quickly.

He took a couple of deep breaths, clenched his teeth tightly shut, then grabbed his leg at the knee with both hands and wrenched it to the left.

He'd thought he'd been in pain before, but that was nothing compared to what he experienced as that jagged piece of wood made its way back through his leg a second time. He could hear it sliding wetly out of his flesh and he couldn't help himself; he screamed.

"Aaaiiiieeeeee!"

Over the sound of his cry he could hear a faint sucking sound and then he was free.

Sweat poured from him in buckets, and all he wanted to do was let go of it all and sleep, his body desperately wanting to escape somewhere that the pain couldn't follow, but he knew if he did, he'd never wake up again.

Trembling, Freeman grabbed the scarf, wrapped it once around the wound, twisted the ends together into a knot, and yanked it as tight as he was able.

That did it.

As another wave of pain coursed through him with all the grace of a tsunami, he passed out.

WHEN FREEMAN CAME to, he found himself still hanging upside down, held in place by the strap of his seat belt. The belt was stretched taut, supporting all his weight, the pressure on his chest preventing him from taking more than shallow breaths. The pain in his leg had subsided to a pounding throb, and he'd managed not to bleed to death while unconscious, so he considered himself ahead of the game.

A glance at the sun told him he'd been out for a while. It had been off to his right when he'd regained consciousness the first time and now it was almost directly overhead, which meant he'd lost a couple of hours at least. He cursed himself for blacking out. Both sides routinely sent out patrols to check the wreckage in the aftermath of a dogfight. When they could, they'd scratch the pilot's name into the propeller and send it across the lines, so there wouldn't be any doubt as to the disposition of the men involved.

He had no doubt that his plane had been recognized by the opposition; the Jack of Spades painted onto the fuselage and the underside of the wings made sure of that. Like Richthofen in his bright red Fokker, Freeman wanted the enemy to know just who it was they were facing when deciding to take him on. A little psychological manipulation never hurt.

That very notoriety, though, would have started to work against him the minute his plane hit the ground. Shooting down the Allies' top ace was a coup no flier would want stolen from him by the lack of a "credible" witness, so they'd be sure to send someone to the crash site no matter how remote it might be, just to be certain of the kill. Enemy infantry could appear at any moment, and he had no doubt about what would happen to him when they did. If he hoped to live through this, he had to be long gone before they arrived.

So stop hanging around and get the hell out of here!

His subconscious had a point. The belt was a problem, however. To release it, he was going to have to get his weight off it long enough for him to unhook the shoulder strap. Most days that wouldn't have been an issue, for he was strong enough to support himself one-armed if need be, even in his current position.

But this wasn't most days.

He was light-headed and felt nauseated, both from blood loss and from hanging upside down all this time, and he kept slipping back down every time he tried to boost himself up high enough to slip the belt off the shoulder hook that held it in place.

After half a dozen tries, he was too exhausted to lift himself.

Fighting back tears of frustration, his gaze fell on the handle of the knife that he routinely carried in his boot, and it suddenly occurred to him that he could just cut himself loose. He cursed himself for not thinking of it in the first place, rather than wasting all that energy. The fact that it took him this long just showed how fuzzy his thinking was getting. The longer he hung here, the worse it was going to get.

Thankfully, the knife was worn on his uninjured leg and it only took him a few tries before he had it in hand. He gave himself a moment to catch his breath, then put the blade against the edge of the belt close to where it disappeared beneath the seat and started sawing back and forth.

The knife was sharp, the belt was tight, and it didn't take long for him to cut halfway through it. At that point the weight of his body proved to be too much for the worn old leather to bear, and he dropped free of the wreckage as the belt tore the rest of the way through.

He hit the ground with a heavy thud and a muffled scream as he landed on his injured leg. Darkness threatened again, but he fought it off, knowing that if he passed out again, he wouldn't have any chance at all of escape. Rolling onto his back, he sat up and then scooted himself backward a few feet so that he could lean against the trunk of the tree.

Freeman was surprised but thankful to find that he still held on to the knife. He used it now to slice through the scarf he'd wrapped around his leg earlier and to cut away the remains of his flight suit from midthigh down. He took a couple of deep breaths, steadied himself, and then looked down at the wound in his leg.

In the light of day, it looked particularly ugly, an open mouth gaping in the fleshy part of his calf that oozed blood out of the wound. He could see several wood splinters and a few small scraps of cloth embedded in his wounded flesh, no doubt shoved there by the passage of the broken spar as it forced its way through his leg. He used the tip of his knife to gently remove them one at a time.

His breath was coming in harsh gasps and his hands were shaking by the time he was finished, but the wound was free of any foreign matter. *That was good,* he thought, *for infection could kill him as quickly as anything else.*

He opened up the breast pocket of his flight suit and pulled out the first aid kit he kept there. It wasn't much—a couple of packets of sulfa, a vial of morphine, a few rolls of bandage stored in a small metal tin—but it would handle the chore ahead of him and that was all that mattered.

He put the bandages in his lap and picked up the packet of sulfa. The powdered antibiotic was designed to help keep the wound from getting infected, but he knew from prior experience that using it was no walk in the park.

This is going to hurt.

A lot.

To keep himself from crying out, he picked up a piece of the material he'd cut away from the leg of his flight suit and stuffed it into his mouth. Then he tore open the packet and upended the sulfa into the wound.

Agony.

Blazing liquid agony that ripped through his body like a bolt of lightning. He couldn't see, he couldn't think, was, in fact, completely unaware of the way his body arched against the pain, the cords in his neck standing out and his heels drumming involuntarily against the ground. All he could do was scream against the gag in his mouth until at last the pain's grip began to loosen.

When it did, he spat the gag from his mouth, gasped for air, and looked down to see a bloodstained yellow froth bubbling up from the wound. For all its ghastliness the sight was a welcome one, for it meant that the chemical was doing its job of washing the wound free of any contaminants. It hissed and bubbled for several minutes and then settled to a weak trickle. Once it had, Freeman used the bandage to wrap the wound tight enough to keep it clean but loose enough so as not to cut off circulation.

He knew that the sulfa packet contained a soporific agent that was designed to help numb the pain, and he could already feel it starting to work. While he waited for the pain to subside enough for him to move around, he took an inventory of what he had by way of supplies, which, disappointingly, didn't take very long. For weapons he had a Browning M1911 pistol in the holster on his belt and the knife. He had an extra magazine for the pistol, giving him a total of fourteen shots. The pockets of his flight suit held his first aid kit, now half used, a compass, a box of matches, a map, and a stick of chewing gum.

No food and no water, unfortunately.

He unfolded the map and studied it for a moment. He guessed he was about ten, maybe twelve miles behind the lines at Nogent. He could have crossed that distance in less than a day uninjured, but given his leg wound, he knew it was going to take him much longer than that. He figured that he could travel two miles a day in his current condition. Three, if he was lucky.

He was going to have to forage for food and water along the way or he'd die of dehydration long before he reached the area where the enemy had dug in along the front. Hopefully, there would be something left to find between here and there; the German army was not known for its restraint.

Ten minutes passed and he could no longer feel the wound in his leg, which he took to be sign enough that it was time to get under way. Using the tree behind him for support, he got one leg under him and pushed himself upright until he could stand on both feet without too much difficulty. The leg throbbed, but that was the worst of it. A few tentative steps gave him a bit more confidence and soon he was limping around fairly decently. He knew he was going to be in a world of hurt when the soporific wore off, but he'd worry about that when the time came.

For now, he had to get away from the wreckage.

A glance at the sky and he set off in an easterly direction, moving as quickly and quietly through the underbrush as he could.

CHAPTER SEVEN

★

BEHIND THE LINES

AT FIRST, THINGS weren't too bad. The soporific kept him from feeling any of the pain from his leg injury so he was able to travel at a reasonable pace for a few hours and managed to cover four, maybe four and a half miles in the process.

After that, however, things went downhill.

The woods abruptly fell away behind him, leaving him looking out across a vast expanse of rocky scrubland, broken only by old shell craters, rusting barbed wire, and overgrown trenches. It was just one of the many stretches of land that had once served as the front lines in a war that seemed to go on forever. Too wide to go around, it left him little choice but to make his way through it.

The rugged terrain didn't help his injured leg, and he was forced to stop frequently to rest and to retie the bandage around the wound. The first two times he took care to clean it out, but after it began bleeding for the third time, he just let it go, figuring he'd deal with the dried blood and sweat when he got to whatever place he found to hole up for the night.

After two more hours, the old trench lines gave way to overgrown fields, the farmers who used to work them long since having fled the coming of the kaiser and his undead army. Freeman kept going, crossing the occasional road. More than a few times he saw the ruins of a town or even an occasional intact farmhouse rising in the distance, but he avoided all of them, not wanting to stumble upon anyone who might be able to turn him over to those he was certain would be coming for him before long.

Eventually, though, the effort of stumbling along over rough ground became too much and when he wandered across a road in the late afternoon that was going in the right direction, he decided to follow it. The paved surface would be much easier to walk on, he decided, and if he had to get undercover quickly, he could always head for the hedges that seemed to line every damned road in France.

So it was that by late afternoon, tired, hungry, and in desperate need of some rest yet unwilling to stop for fear he might not get going again, Freeman found himself plodding along an old country track, his head pounding and his thoughts a thousand miles away. The combination of his condition and the monotony of walking hour after hour kept him from registering the sound when he first heard it. It just sat there, in the back of his consciousness, growing louder with each passing minute.

By the time it broke into his awareness and he recognized it for what it was—the hiss and grumble of an approaching engine—Freeman had nearly run out of time to do anything about it. He hobbled toward a line of hedgerows that grew a few feet back from the side of the road, fought his way between them, and threw himself into the shallow irrigation ditch on the other side. He'd barely settled into place when the truck rumbled into view.

With his heart pounding and his pulse in his ears, Freeman drew his pistol and positioned himself with his stomach against the side of the ditch so that he could peer out through the small gap between the ground and the bottom of the hedge, ready to go down shooting if his frantic rush for cover had been seen.

The vehicle he'd been hearing was a NAG four-ton lorry, the kind with the rounded hood and the open front cab; he'd strafed enough of them over the last few years to recognize one on sight. A guard stood up in the front next to the driver, watching the sides of the road with his Mauser rifle in hand. Both men wore the gray uniform common to the frontline German infantry divisions and Freeman guessed that's where they were headed.

The cargo area behind the guard was open to the sky, the usual canvas cover missing, and Freeman could see that they were carrying a full load of wooden crates, each one marked with the word *Minenwerfer*. He didn't know much German, but that was one term with which he was familiar. *Mortar shells*. And from the sizes of the crates, he'd bet they were the shells for the big boys, 25 cm mortars that routinely pounded the hell out of the men in the trenches. Seeing them made him wish he had an armful of hand grenades and a pair of uninjured legs; he would have lobbed a few explosives right into the midst of that cargo hold and gotten the hell out of there while the Boche were still trying to figure out what hit them.

Might as well ask for a Spad to fly home in while I'm at it . . .

A squad of soldiers marched two by two behind the truck, their rifles slung over their shoulders and their gaze on the ground in front of their feet. Most of them had that bored look that came with too many days of inactivity and for that Freeman was grateful. If they'd been paying attention, he'd probably be fighting for his life right now.

He was just getting ready to congratulate himself on escaping their notice when the third and final element of the German convoy came into view, and the sight of them made his blood run cold.

At first he thought they were just another group of shamblers. They had the same gray-green cast to their skin and wore the same threadbare uniforms. Even the stench of rot and decay drifting off them was the same.

But they didn't move like any shamblers he'd ever seen. They scurried along in a crouch, their hands touching the surface of the road in front of them almost as often as their feet did; Freeman was reminded of a wolf spider he'd once seen racing across the floor, all liquid motion and alien menace. Unlike the soldiers before them, who could have cared less about their surroundings, these strange new shamblers were constantly peering this way and that, their heads bobbing from side to side and then dipping back down toward the surface of the road, like dogs on the hunt, tracking a scent.

Tracking a scent . . .

Good God! he thought. *Was that it? Had these things picked up his trail somehow?*

As if in answer, one of the creatures paused at the exact spot where he'd left the road just moments before. It slowly raised its head and let its gaze roam along the hedge running parallel with the road, the same hedge that he was hiding behind.

Freeman froze, not daring to move, not even to blink.

Could it see him? Smell him?

Fear churned in his guts, and for a moment he considered attacking from ambush while he still had the chance. Going out under a hail of bullets from the soldiers' rifles would be preferable to being torn apart at the claws of that creature in front of him.

The rotting thing stopped moving, cocked its head to one side; its gaze locked solidly with his own, as if it could see him right through the protective cover of the hedge.

Maybe it could.

A drop of sweat rolled down the side of his face as his finger tightened on the trigger.

He was a half second away from firing when a web of electrical current giving off green and purple sparks danced along the outside of the creature's control collar, indicating it was receiving a command. With one last glance at the hedge, it turned about and scurried off toward its companions.

Freeman waited until it had moved out of sight with the rest of the convoy and then breathed a sigh of relief. He lowered his gun and rolled over onto his back, staring at the sky above as he tried to get his heartbeat under control.

After a few minutes, Freeman holstered his gun and then got unsteadily to his feet. His leg was shouting at him to give it a rest, but he wanted to put some distance between himself and that convoy of soldiers. If he cut across country, he might be able to avoid them. He took a moment to brush off the dirt and leaves from his uniform, then bent over and checked to be sure the bandage was still wrapped securely around his injured leg. The wound had started bleeding again, and the bandage would need to be changed whenever he stopped for the night.

He pushed his way back through the hedge only to find himself face-to-face with the strange new shambler that had been searching for him moments before.

Time seemed to stop as they stared at each other. The shambler was only about ten feet away and Freeman had plenty of time to draw his gun and fire, but he didn't dare do so as a gunshot was sure to bring the rest of the patrol running. He might be able to handle a single shambler, but a pack of them? Not a chance. Never mind the human troops that accompanied them.

As Freeman stood rooted to the spot, trying to figure out what to do, the shambler took the decision out of his hands. It sprang at him with an eager dexterity that belied anything he'd previously seen, taking a few short, powerful steps before launching itself toward him, arms extended.

Freeman reacted without thought, letting the creature's momentum work against it as he grabbed the front of its tattered uniform and went over backward beneath its weight, heaving it over his head in a well-timed throw.

Rolling over as he hit the ground, Freeman ended up poised in a crouch over his opponent. He snatched his knife out of his boot and plunged it deep into the shambler's throat.

He knew the strike wouldn't kill it, but right now killing it wasn't his primary concern. All he wanted to do was ensure that it couldn't communicate, couldn't shriek or howl or do whatever it was that shamblers of this sort did to summon others of their kind or its German handlers. Just to be safe he dragged the knife to the side as he pulled it back out, trying to cause as much damage as possible. As soon as his weapon was free, he scuttled out of reach.

As quickly as it went down, the shambler was back up on its

feet, spinning round to face Freeman where he crouched in a fighting stance a few yards away. It opened its mouth, perhaps to scream its defiance, but nothing but a weak hiss came out.

Unfortunately, the injury did nothing to slow the creature's attack.

It came at him again, slashing with a clawed hand in an attempt to disembowel, and Freeman was forced to backpedal furiously, each step eliciting a stab of pain from his injured leg, as he fought to stay upright and out of the creature's reach.

He managed to land a few blows with his knife in the process, but they had little effect. The blade simply sank into the shambler's rotting flesh and came back out again, with no harm done, as far as he could tell.

You're in trouble, Jack.

Damn right he was. This thing was not only faster and stronger, but it had the added advantage of being impervious to pain. He, on the other hand, was hobbling around on an injured leg while exhausted from all the miles he had covered since crawling out of the wreckage of his aircraft.

The shambler seemed to know it, too. Rather than rush him, as it had done before, it circled about him, darting in to deliver a blow here and there, testing Jack's defenses. It was all Freeman could do to stay on his feet and fend off each attack, and before long he was bleeding from half a dozen minor wounds on his arms and chest.

The damn thing seemed to be toying with him, forcing him to expend what little energy he had left, and he had no choice but to follow along. He couldn't turn and run; he wouldn't get three steps before it would catch him and bring him down. Getting in close enough to deliver the kind of blow that would put the thing down for good meant he'd have to expose himself to the creature's attack at the same time.

They'd been at it for several long minutes when the tide turned against him.

Scrambling backward to avoid the creature's latest attack, Freeman's heel struck a rock jutting out of the earth, tripping him. He pinwheeled his arms in an effort to keep his balance, knowing all the while that falling down would not be good for his life expectancy.

It was just the kind of opening the shambler had been waiting for.

It leaped atop him, its weight forcing him to the ground as it thrust its face forward, trying to sink its jaws into his neck.

Freeman responded by grabbing it by the hair with one hand and pulling backward, dragging its lips away from his flesh and holding it off him, but just barely. It twisted and turned, trying to break free of Freeman's grip, and he felt its scalp starting to give way, the pressure on its hair causing the rotting flesh to peel away from the skull. One good yank and it would break free in his hands, leaving Freeman at the thing's mercy.

Reversing his grip on the knife, Freeman jabbed the blade right into the shambler's eye, digging for that vital spot deep in the creature's brain that kept it animated long after the man it once was had died.

The shambler reared back, its hands going to its face but unable or unwilling to pull the blade free. Freeman took advantage of its distraction to buck his body upward, throwing the shambler off him. He scrambled away from it, watching in horrified fascination as it began to twitch and jerk like someone caught in the grip of an epileptic fit, thrashing about on the ground for a good minute before it finally went still.

"Sonofabitch!" he swore, panting in exertion, his hand unconsciously going to his neck as if checking to be sure he hadn't lost a chunk of it to the shambler's teeth.

The fight had just about done him in. His leg felt like it was on fire, and he could see that the bandage was now dark with blood. He needed to get off his feet and let the wound seal itself over, but he couldn't afford to do that quite yet. He had no idea if the soldiers would come looking for the missing shambler; if they did, he needed to be long gone.

A glance at the shambler's body showed his knife still stuck deep in the creature's eye socket. He hobbled over, pulled out the knife, and wiped the blade off on the shambler's uniform, and then returned it to his boot.

The convoy had been moving in the same direction he had, southeast, and so he decided to leave the road behind and strike out cross-country in a more easterly direction. He'd still be headed toward the front; he'd just have to angle southward once he drew closer.

Satisfied with his decision, he was about to head out when he felt a hand clamp tightly about his ankle. Glancing down, he found to his horror that the shambler had returned to life, the removal of the knife having restored whatever unholy force it was that animated the creature!

Before he could figure out what to do, he was yanked off his feet to fall directly onto his injured leg.

Freeman howled in agony, the pain sweeping over him like the tide and nearly rendering him unconscious. That surely would have been the end of him, for it would have given the newly reanimated shambler all the time it needed to finish him off.

Right now it seemed to be having trouble getting its lower limbs to work, but that didn't stop it from trying to find an unprotected piece of Freeman's flesh to feast on. It reached out and began pulling itself up his body, hand over hand, its teeth clacking together like some kind of deranged castanet, its one good eye rolling around in the socket as if no longer under control.

The shambler's spastic movements jostled Freeman's injured leg and sent waves of pain crashing through his system, forcing him to fight to stay conscious as he flailed at the creature, pushing against it with both hands in an attempt to get it off him.

It clung tightly despite his every effort to dislodge it. Its face was even with his stomach, and he suddenly had a horrible vision of it rooting around in his guts, its teeth sawing through his intestines as it burrowed deeper . . .

Better do something, Jack, before it's too late!

With his head spinning, Freeman did the one thing he'd been trying to avoid since first laying eyes on the hideous creature.

He drew his pistol, shoved it against the rotting flesh of the shambler's forehead, and pulled the trigger. Blood, brains, and bone splashed across his face as the shambler's skull exploded beneath the force of the bullet.

Heaving the now unmoving body off him for the second time that day, Freeman dragged himself several feet away and sat with his pistol aimed at the corpse, afraid that it might still find some way of coming after him despite all the damage.

That was how the German soldiers who had been summoned back by his gunshot found him some time later. So unnerved was he by the shambler's ability to continue fighting long after it should have stopped, he didn't even look away from the corpse as the soldiers snatched his gun out of his hands and dragged him to his feet.

CHAPTER EIGHT

THE LABORATORY

BURKE HAD BEEN awake for over an hour by the time Sergeant Moore showed up to escort him to his appointment with Professor Graves. Burke probably could have gone on his own, as it wasn't that far, but since he was still under the doctors' care they wouldn't let him out of the facility without an escort.

So with Charlie there to steady him if the distance proved too much for his recovering body to handle, Burke headed off down the hall and out into the early morning. He could smell the corpse fires the minute he stepped outside; they had been burning overtime to deal with the aftermath of the latest attack. The air had a greasy, sooty feel to it, and the taste of ash clogged the back of his throat.

Another beautiful day in the war effort, Burke thought sourly.

It was only a few minutes' walk from the entrance of the hospital to the bunker complex that Professor Graves had commandeered for use as his laboratory. The complex had started life as a deep dugout that served as protection for artillery and mortar attacks, and over the last several months had been expanded into a literal warren of passageways and rough-hewn chambers in which to test Graves's various projects. Burke had never been beyond the main chamber; he had no desire to venture into the dark depths of that underground kingdom. Dealing with the professor himself was creepy enough sometimes; he didn't want to see what peculiarities the man had generated down there in the dark.

Apparently, the same held true for Charlie. As the two men approached the entrance to the "facility," sandwiched as it was between piles of sandbags, the sergeant slowed, then said, "You all right from here?"

Burke cast a glance in his direction. "Aren't you going in with me?"

"Not a chance."

"Coward."

Charlie laughed. "I like to think of it as the better part of valor. I'll be waiting right here for you when you come out," he said, settling back against a pile of sandbags and reaching for his cigarettes.

"Thanks a lot."

"Anytime, Captain, anytime."

Entrance to the bunker was gained through a cast-iron door several inches thick. It was currently propped open with a packing crate to allow some fresh air to make its way inside. Two guards stood outside it and they nodded at Burke as he passed by. Just beyond the doors was a long flight of stairs, nineteen steps in all, which led down into the complex itself. Burke took his time on the stairs, not wanting to slip and fall with only one hand to brace himself.

As far as Burke had been able to ascertain, the professor had only two interests in life: mechanical devices and shamblers. While one was certainly better than the other, as far as Burke was concerned neither of them was all that natural.

Or healthy.

Graves was one of Nikola Tesla's prize students, so it made sense that he spent a good part of his time with his hands in the guts of a mechanical apparatus of one kind or another, be it the steam-driven lorries that they used around the base or the partially assembled automatons that the army was forever hoping might one day replace men on the battlefield. Success in the latter case would mean lessening the horrible cost of this war in terms of human lives and would have the added benefit of preventing the other side from resurrecting the Allied dead with their damned corpse gas.

Graves was obsessed with the shamblers.

It wasn't that he was just doing his best for the war effort. It went beyond that, into what Burke suspected was downright admiration for the foul things. All you had to do was see how excited Graves got when he was able to obtain another specimen to recognize that it was more than just simple duty.

He could often be found walking the trenches after an attack, studying the carcasses where they lay and collecting specimens to take back to his laboratory for later study.

Sometimes, Burke found himself wondering what Graves would do if all the specimens he hoarded down here in the dark suddenly decided to get up again and start walking around . . .

He shook his head vigorously, banishing the thought. He didn't need to focus on that stuff; he was here for his new hand.

The room at the bottom of the staircase was as long as it was wide, lit by several bare lightbulbs that hung down from the low ceiling above and cast shadows throughout the space.

The bitter smell of formaldehyde drifted through the air, most likely the reason for the open door above, and Burke followed it to where he saw a man's body stretched out on a table set all by itself in the center of the room.

As he drew closer, he could see that the body was in fact the decaying remains of a shambler, and it looked like someone had been operating on it. The chest was cut open, and the sides were peeled back and now held in place by a set of brass clamps that were stained with the creature's black blood. The rib cage had been removed and rested on one side of the table. An unintentional glimpse inside the body cavity showed that what was left of the creature's internal organs gleamed wetly in the stark light of the overhead bulb. Even the head seemed oddly shaped to Burke, and it wasn't until he'd walked partially around the table and gotten a good look that he realized the top of the skull had been cut off and the brain removed for God-knows-what purpose.

Burke glanced at the shambler's face and was surprised to discover that he recognized it. It was the creature that had attacked him in the trench the day before, the one that had seemed to think for itself and that Charlie had ultimately been forced to shoot with the suitcase gun.

What was Graves doing with it?

Burke wasn't sure he wanted to know.

The hair on the back of his neck suddenly stood up as he realized that he was no longer alone.

Burked whirled about.

A tall thin man with a hawklike face stood almost directly behind him. He was dressed in a butcher's apron, stained black with shambler blood, and wore a pair of thick rubber gloves on his hands. In his hands was a shallow metal dish full of some gray gooey mass that looked oddly familiar to Burke, though he couldn't place exactly what it was until he glanced back at the creature's empty brain pan and made the necessary connection.

"Be with you in a moment, Captain," the professor said as he stepped past the other man and set the bowl he was carrying down on the table in front of them. As Burke looked on, the professor picked up an empty jar from a stack nearby and then carefully poured the jellied mass of brain tissue from the bowl into the jar.

Burke had to look away.

When he heard Graves strip off his rubber gloves, he chanced a quick look. The table and the corpse it contained were now covered with a large black sheet. The professor untied and removed the butcher's apron he was wearing, then wiped his hands on a rag he picked up from somewhere nearby.

Then, and only then, did he turn back to address Burke.

"What can I do for you, Captain?"

Burke held up his left arm stump and wiggled it in the professor's direction.

"Ah, yes! Time to fit that new hand of yours. How could I have forgotten?"

I refuse to answer that, Burke thought.

"All right, follow me, please."

Graves stepped around the dissection table and led him across the room to where an open door awaited. Inside was a small operating theater, complete with banks of overhead lights, a rack full of surgical instruments, a good supply of bandages, and even a small sink. A reclining leather chair, like you might see in a barber's shop or dentist's office, sat in the middle.

Graves stepped over to the sink and scrubbed the shambler blood off his hands. "Climb up in the chair, Captain," he said, as he dried them on a towel, "while I retrieve your new prosthesis from storage."

Burke slid into the chair and settled back, letting his neck and head relax against the cushion. There was a quiet whirring sound followed by a rustle of movement, and something cinched itself around his stomach.

Burke looked down and found a thick leather strap with a metal buckle had just fastened itself around his midsection.

"Hey!" he said, surprised, and was answered when four more straps emerged from the sides of the chair and fastened themselves around his thighs and ankles respectively.

This time Burke was much more emphatic in his response.

"Professor Graves!" he shouted. "Professor!"

Footsteps sounded and Graves emerged from around the corner carrying a long and narrow wooden crate.

"Yes, yes, what is it, Captain?"

"These straps . . ."

Graves chuckled. "I'm sorry, I forgot to warn you about those. The arm we're giving you this time around is a considerable improvement over the earlier model," he said, as he unfolded a side table the same height as the chair and rested Burke's arm on it so that the stump extended off one end. Taking a couple of thin leather straps out of his pocket, Graves secured what remained of Blake's arm to the table.

"In order for it to work at the level for which we designed it for you, we're going to have to implant a kind of platform at the end of your arm in order to power and maintain the prosthesis long term."

Burke only caught one word, really.

"Implant?" he asked.

"Yes, yes. No worries, Captain, I've done this procedure hundreds of times now."

Something about the way he said it made Burke pause. He hesitated and then asked, "How many of those were on a living person?"

Graves laughed but didn't answer.

Burke began to have second thoughts.

"Maybe we should wait until Doctor Tesla returns . . . ?"

"Nonsense! You don't want to go two months without a hand, do you?"

Two months?

Finally satisfied with the arrangements, Graves opened up the box that he'd carried in with him. Inside, on a bed of satin, was Burke's new hand.

It came in two pieces; a small baselike attachment that would be attached to his stump and the fully articulated wrist/hand piece that fitted into it. Both pieces had been fashioned out of highly polished wood, brass, and steel. The fingers had three knuckles and only bent in one direction, just like real ones did, and judging by the cables and clockwork components running throughout, it certainly looked much stronger than his previous model had been.

Satisfied that Burke had seen enough, Graves put down the box and removed the base mount. "The first step is to mount this device onto your arm where it can intersect with the existing musculature.

"When the rest of the hand is slotted into place," he continued, picking up the hand and doing just that by pushing one into the other until Burke heard a sharp click, "the electrical impulses produced by your muscle will activate the miniature clockwork gears inside each finger, telling them what to do."

Graves smiled. "Nothing to it, really."

Before Burke could say anything more, Graves picked up a

bottle of ether, poured some on a cloth, and held the cloth tightly over Burke's nose and mouth.

For a second his eyes grew wide as he saw Graves looming over him, and then he was out like a light.

As Burke stumbled into wakefulness two hours later, he instinctively felt for his hand and encountered the smooth, metal surface of the new implant. It was heavier than he was used to, but he knew he'd adapt to that soon enough. Right now he just wanted to be sure it worked.

He held it up in front of him and then tried to bend his fingers. To his amazement, all five of them slowly bent inward toward his palm and then opened back up again when he tried to move them the other way. He could feel the muscles in his upper forearm moving as they powered the motion of his mechanical fingers, and he knew he was going to have to do some work in the days ahead to build up some strength in that area.

"How are you doing, Captain?"

Burke jerked in surprise, which caused his hand to snap shut with an audible click, and it was only then that he realized how much power he could generate with his new prosthesis. *Who knew? One day he might even need all that strength.*

Graves waited patiently for Burke to get his hand to unclench and then began to unstrap him from the chair. "Any dizziness? Nausea? Pain in the extremity?"

There wasn't. Nor were there any lingering effects from the ether. Graves gave him a quick check and then suggested he head back to his hospital room for some more rest, a suggestion Burke was more than happy to take him up on. He was anxious to show Charlie his new hand.

CHAPTER NINE

★

WHEN BURKE RETURNED from having his hand repaired in Graves's chamber of horrors, he found he had a visitor. An officer was waiting for him by the side of his bed, cap and clipboard in hand. His uniform was crisp and clean, with creases ironed so sharp as to be dangerous. The shoes on his feet were buffed to a glistening shine, which let Burke know that time at the front was not part of the man's regular duty. The silver eagle on either shoulder board told Burke he was outranked.

Despite his weariness, Burke snapped up a salute. It wasn't something they usually did on the front lines, for calling attention to an officer was as good as painting a sniper's target across the man's forehead, but they were a bit more "spit-and-polish" back in the rear; given the colonel's personal appearance, Burke figured the man would be a stickler for protocol.

"What can I do for you, Colonel?" he asked politely, after the other man had waved the salute away.

His visitor stuck out his hand. "Colonel Nichols, MID."

Burke's eyebrows went up in surprise. The Military Intelligence Division was a newly formed group within the aegis of the War Department in Washington. It was run by Brigadier General Morrissey, a man who was not afraid to get out and see what life in the trenches was actually like, as evidenced by the Distinguished Service Cross he'd won at Apremont for personally leading a charge against a German machine-gun nest while visiting there. MID's job was to learn as much as they could about the enemy's plans and then disrupt them as quickly and efficiently as possible. They'd been operating primarily on the Western and Italian Fronts to date, but even if only half of what Burke had heard about them was true, they were a formidable unit indeed.

Suddenly he was having a hard time reconciling this perfectly uniformed officer with his previously conceived notions of what a visitor from MID should look like.

Nichols didn't seem to notice Burke's confusion. "If you're feeling up to it, I'd like to speak to you about the action you were involved in the other morning."

Burke glanced longingly at his nearby bed, wondering what kind of hell he'd catch if he sat down in the colonel's presence without permission, and then decided he really didn't care and did it anyway. He was a patient, after all. *What were they going to do? Send him back to the front? They'd already ordered him to return there as soon as he was fit to do so.*

"What do you want to know?" Burke asked.

The colonel raised an eyebrow at his departure from protocol, but didn't pursue the issue. "Your report mentioned an encounter with a shambler that was acting strangely . . ." he said, letting the question hang in the air.

Burke nodded. "That's right."

"How so? What made it different?"

"It was aware, for one."

"Aware?"

Burke laughed, but there wasn't anything even remotely amused in his tone when he said, "The bloody thing changed direction when the block was deployed to protect the communications trench, Colonel. Instead of continuing forward, *it made the decision to turn around.*"

Nichols frowned, which let Burke know the colonel understood the implications of his statement, but the conclusion was one the colonel apparently wasn't yet ready to accept and he tried to explain it away. "Perhaps it was turned about accidentally when it came in contact with the trench block?" he suggested, an almost hopeful tone to his voice.

Burke would have loved to believe that too, but he'd seen the thing with his own eyes. "It stopped and turned around long before that, Colonel. And if that wasn't bad enough, I could practically see the wheels turning in its head as it worked to figure a way out of the mess it found itself in. It wasn't just instinct; it knew it was trapped and it wanted out!"

Nichols's expression grew more alarmed as he considered what Burke was saying. Burke had stood his ground in the face of more shambler attacks than he could count, and not once had he seen them act with anything resembling intelligent action. Once pointed at the Allied lines, they would simply shuffle forward. There might be a clear path through the barbed wire five feet to a shambler's left and the stupid thing would walk straight ahead, getting tangled in the wire.

Not only had this rotting sonofabitch sprinted out of the tunneling machine and headed straight for the rear, but it had recognized the trench block as a threat to its mission and had headed for the opposite side when the passage to the left was no longer an option.

Shamblers just don't do that, he thought, his own statement from moments before echoing in his head. But that wasn't all.

"It didn't move like any shambler I've ever seen, either. Shamblers can't move at anything faster than an unsteady shuffle. That's how they got their name, right? This thing was different. It came out of that tunneling machine like an Olympic runner right out of the blocks."

Despite the fact that the creature had once been a living, breathing soldier, Burke couldn't bring himself to call it "he." As far as Burke was concerned, it had ceased being human, and therefore deserving of human appellations, the minute it had gotten up after dying the first time around.

The colonel didn't seem to notice the pronoun issue. He was still trying to find a reasonable solution to what Burke had witnessed, for anything else might change the face of the war as they knew it. "Perhaps it wasn't moving as fast as you thought it was," he suggested. "I understand it was pretty touch-and-go there for a while. Are you sure your senses weren't simply confused by the strain of combat?"

Burke stared at him. He'd been fighting in the frontline trenches for more than three years. He'd lived through gas attacks, mortar bombardments, and wave after wave of shambler attacks. Sometimes all three at once. The idea that he'd be "confused by the strain of combat" was ludicrous and, frankly, a bit insulting.

He let the suggestion hang in the air unanswered.

To his credit, Nichols didn't turn away from Burke's aggressive silence, but calmly gazed back at him. When he was certain Burke wasn't going to reply, he said, "Right. I'll note that it moved faster than normal."

He's just not getting it, Burke thought.

"Look," he said. "This thing didn't just move faster than normal. If that's all it had done, I'd have written it off as an anomaly then and there and never mentioned it in my report. It was fast, yes, but it was also aware and that's not something we've ever seen in a shambler before. It knew where it was going, waited for the best opportunity to get there, and then actively sought a different solution when prevented from carrying out its orders."

"So what are you saying?"

Burke hesitated for a moment, then threw caution to the wind and plowed ahead. "I think we're looking at a new breed of soldier," he told the colonel.

Nichols nodded, but he didn't say anything to support or deny Burke's conclusion. Instead, he asked, "Do you remember anything else that might be significant about this particular encounter?"

"Like what?"

The colonel shrugged. "Did it look different? Smell different? Did it, God forbid, say anything?"

"No, nothing like that," Burke replied, as a chill ran up his spine. It was bad enough that the thing had acted intelligently. The idea that it might retain the mental faculties necessary to speak made him feel vaguely nauseated as he considered what that would mean for the man the creature had once been. Could it remember who it had been? Be aware of what it had become? He shuddered. "No reason to trust my observations, though. Professor Graves is carving the thing up like a Christmas turkey in his lab as we speak. He can give you more information than I."

The colonel opened his mouth to ask another question but was cut off when an orderly pulled the curtain aside and stepped into the "room." He went straight to Nichols, cupped a hand around his ear, and whispered something excitedly. Burke caught the words *Freeman* and *wreckage*, but that was about all.

Whatever was said galvanized Nichols into action. He turned to Burke, thanked him for his time, and hustled out of the room on the orderly's heels.

What have you done now, Jack? Burke wondered and then pushed the thought aside, irritated at himself for even being curious. That vainglorious SOB could get himself thrown out of the Air Corps for all he cared. Burke's years of giving a damn were long since over. Mae's death had seen to that.

Exhausted from all the day's activity, Burke settled back against his pillow and let his eyes slip closed. Several minutes later he drifted off into an uneasy sleep in which intelligent shamblers chased him through the trenches of his dreams.

CHAPTER TEN

★

"Verschieben!"

The command to move was punctuated with a rifle butt between the shoulder blades, causing Freeman to stumble forward and fall to his knees in the mud beside the truck from which he'd just emerged. It wasn't the first time he'd been struck violently since being taken captive, and he knew better than to protest. He'd done that the first few times, and the bruises on his face and body were testimony to the fact that they didn't care what he thought of their methods.

As he climbed painfully to his feet, he braved a quick glance around. They had clearly arrived at some kind of POW camp. A double chain-link fence surrounded the area, and guard towers with visible searchlights were strategically placed to give good sight lines of the perimeter. A cluster of wooden buildings stood to his left, and a German staff car was parked in front of the largest of them, a two-story affair that would have still looked like the French manor house it had once been if it weren't for the flag of the Imperial German Empire hanging in front of it. Freeman guessed that this was the commandant's headquarters and personal residence. A set of six low-slung rectangular buildings that reminded him of the makeshift hangars at the airfield stood off to the right.

They were in the corner of the camp and ramshackle enough to make it clear that these were the prisoners' barracks. In between were the usual assortment of buildings you'd expect to see as part of any military encampment—a motor pool, mess hall, workroom, laundry, and workshop.

Directly in front of him was a dirt field, and Freeman could see men working in it, using handheld hoes and shovels to move the soil around. The men were dressed in gray coveralls with the letter K stamped on the back. He knew the K was short for *kriegsgefan-gener*, which meant "prisoner of war" in German.

Beyond the field, in their own double-fenced section of the camp, stood another set of wooden buildings too far away to get a good look at. Freeman did notice that armed guards were stationed in the no-man's-land between the two fences, but they were facing outward toward the second set of buildings, rather than inward toward the rest of the camp.

Curious, thought Freeman.

An elbow struck his shoulder, rocking him forward a step, and he realized the time for sightseeing was over.

"Verschieben!" his guard snarled, and this time Freeman stepped forward quickly to avoid the rifle strike he knew the other man was preparing. Three other guards walked along with the one who was so free with the butt of his gun, making it a quintet.

The guards marched him over to the commandant's headquarters, where they went up the steps, across the porch, and inside to the office just beyond. A clerk sat waiting behind the wooden desk, a bored expression on his face and a lit cigarette in his mouth. Over the clerk's shoulder Freeman caught a glimpse of another office. That one was much larger and more comfortably furnished than the one he stood in. It was also currently unoccupied.

"Name?" asked the clerk.

Freeman hesitated. The articles of war required that the kaiser's forces properly record the arrival of all prisoners of war and pass their names and current conditions on to the International Red Cross. That information would, in turn, be relayed to the Allied authorities. On the other hand, he wasn't just another soldier. His record of eighty-two kills made him not only one of America's top aces, but a public figure as well. There was a fair amount of propaganda value they could gain simply by announcing he was a prisoner.

Then again, he thought darkly, *they might just decide to keep quiet.* It was much easier torturing information out of a man everyone thought was dead.

Aware that the clerk was getting impatient, and wanting to avoid another rifle butt to the back, Freeman decided that his notoriety might be more of a protection than a hindrance and took a chance. "Julius Freeman, major, American Expeditionary Force" and rattled off his serial number.

The clerk scratched something on the paper in front of him, consulted a notebook, and then said to his guard, "Put him in C Barracks and assign him to first shift. He can take the place of whoever is selected to meet the commandant tonight."

His guards led him across the camp to the six low-slung buildings that he'd correctly identified as barracks for the prisoners. There were several men lounging around outside the entrance to one of them, but the minute they saw the guards approaching they disappeared inside.

Freeman's escort marched him through the same doorway and into the building. While Freeman was still waiting for his eyes to adjust to the dim interior light, the guard behind him slammed the stock of his rifle into Freeman's kidney and the American flier went down like a rock.

For a moment, all he could see were stars, so great was the pain, but when his vision cleared, he discovered that he was lying on the dirt floor of a large, warehouse-like room. Bunk beds had been erected in orderly rows throughout most of the space, but there must not have been enough for all the prisoners who were housed, for men were lying on the floor in the spaces between the beds, wrapped in thin blankets.

As he struggled to pick himself up off the floor, the other prisoners watched dispassionately. No one volunteered to help him. In fact, there was a definite sense of hostility aimed in his direction.

He was a prisoner, just like they were. What had he done to them?

He found out a few seconds later. The lead guard called out something in his native tongue and pointed at one of the other prisoners. Before the man had a chance to protest, two of the guards stepped forward and grabbed his arms, dragging him toward the doorway.

A collective grumble of protest arose from the other prisoners, and several of them stepped forward, reaching toward either their companion or the guards, perhaps both, an act that proved too much for the guard in charge of the detail.

The sound of the shot was deafening in the confined space. The prisoner closest to the guards dropped to the ground, dead from the bullet that had struck him below the right eye and exited the back of his skull in a showery spray of blood and brain matter.

As his body hit the floor, the rest of the prisoners froze in place.

Lying a few feet away, Freeman realized that the guards were at a supreme disadvantage. All the prisoners had to do was rush them and they'd be overpowered in seconds. Sure, a few of the POWs were likely to die in the process, but the group would then be armed and they could use those firearms to gain more in the next attack.

But rather than seize the opportunity, the prisoners backed away from the confrontation, doing nothing more than muttering darkly and casting hate-filled glances at their captors.

The prisoner the guards had seized began to wail in French, screaming for the others to help and begging the guards to choose someone else, anyone else, just not him. Or, at least, that's what Freeman, with his rudimentary French, thought he was saying.

As expected, the guards ignored the prisoner's pleas and marched back out the door, taking the prisoner with them as they went.

In the aftermath of their departure, you could have heard a pin drop. Several of the men started toward Freeman, and from the expressions on their faces it was clear that they weren't coming to help him to his feet, but they were intercepted by a short, dark-haired man with a trim mustache.

He didn't say anything, just stepped out into the open space between Freeman and the oncoming prisoners, glaring in their direction. That was enough to bring the men up short.

The ringleader, a tall solidly built Irishman, said something to the short man that was too low for Freeman to catch. The other man answered in similar fashion, and whatever was said was enough to defuse the situation. The Irishman looked at Freeman, spat on the floor in his direction, but turned away, content for the moment to let the matter rest. His companions followed in his wake.

"Thanks," Freeman said from his position on the floor.

The mustached man turned to him and Freeman could see a blaze of anger in his eyes as he said, "Do not think for even a moment that I did that for you. Fighting is a punishable offense, and in this camp there are things far worse than death."

Mustache and the rest of the prisoners turned away, leaving Freeman lying on the floor wondering just how he was going to survive.

CHAPTER ELEVEN

★

AFTER THE SHOOTING and his subsequent shunning by the rest of the prisoners, Freeman found space against one of the walls to curl up in and quickly fell into a restless sleep. It had been too long since he'd had anything to eat or drink and he was feeling weak and light-headed. His condition was worsened, no doubt, by the pain of his injury from the crash and the physical exertion he'd undergone while trying to escape. If the other prisoners had decided they wanted to take revenge for the loss of one of their own, it would have been easy to slit his throat in his sleep, but Freeman was beyond the point of caring.

The guards came for him just before sundown.

A hush fell over the barracks, and the stomp of booted feet dragged Freeman back to wakefulness. He was just rousing himself when the guards grabbed him by the arms and literally dragged him across the floor to where an officer in the uniform of an oberleutnant stood waiting.

The man looked down at him and said something in German, but Freeman didn't understand and simply shrugged his shoulders in response. The oberleutnant sneered at him in disgust and then gave a rapid-fire round of orders to the guards before turning on his heels and marching out of the barracks.

The guards followed suit, dragging Freeman with them. They took him behind the workshop and pantomimed that he should strip off his dirty clothes, gesturing with their weapons when he hesitated. When he had complied with their order, they made him stand up against the rear wall of the workshop on a cement slab set into the ground and then retreated a dozen feet away.

So this is how it ends, Freeman thought to himself. He'd survived both an aerial dogfight with the famed Richthofen and the crash that followed only to face summary execution in a dirty POW camp by a couple of German thugs.

Freeman ignored the pain in his leg and did his best to stand tall, wanting to go out with some dignity.

To his surprise, one of the guards disappeared around the side of the workshop and came back a moment later carrying a fireman's hose. The guard threw the lever attached to the side of the nozzle, and a jet of icy cold water struck Freeman like a freight train, slamming him against the wall behind him and holding him there with the strength of ten men. The guard directed the spray up and down Freeman's body, using the water like an industrial-sized scrubbing pad, leaving the American gasping for breath as the force of the flow hammered him without mercy.

Just when he thought he couldn't take it anymore, the guard switched the hose off and Freeman collapsed to the ground, gasping for air. Now he understood the purpose of the slab he was lying on; it wouldn't do to have freshly scrubbed prisoners fall into the mud that was the dominant feature of the camp. While the first guard returned the hose, another approached and threw a gray coverall to Freeman, indicating he should get dressed.

When Freeman didn't move quickly enough for the guards' liking, they moved in and helped him get dressed, not caring how often they yanked or bumped his injured leg. By the time they were finished, he was gasping from the pain, but at least he was no longer naked. The prisoner's uniform he now wore also gave him the sense that he might be here awhile.

They gave him a moment to get himself together and then

marched him across the camp to the commandant's residence. Rather than going into the clerk's office, as he had earlier in the day, the guards led him in through a different door on the side of the house facing away from the camp and Freeman found himself standing in a well-appointed foyer. A butler was waiting for them, and after exchanging a few words with the guards, he turned to Freeman and said, "This way, Major."

Their destination turned out to be the dining room, where several German officers were seated around the table. Conversation ceased when he entered the room.

"Ah, Major Freeman, how good of you to join us!"

The speaker was a blond-haired, jowl-cheeked man in the uniform of an oberst, which made him the equivalent of an American colonel, one rank above Freeman. He wore a pair of pince-nez spectacles perched on the bridge of his nose and black leather gloves on his hands, though whether the latter was to hide an injury or as a personal affectation, Freeman didn't know.

"I am Oberst Schulheim, commandant of Stalag 113," his host said with a smile, revealing teeth that had been sharpened to points, "and I would be pleased if you would join us for dinner."

The thought of having real food made his stomach growl. He had no desire to eat with these men, but the chance to learn something more about the camp and his current situation was too valuable an intelligence asset to pass up. There was a chair at the end of the table directly opposite Schulheim, the only empty seat available, and Freeman made his way over to it. One of the other officers snickered at his limp, but Freeman ignored him.

Let them laugh, he thought. *Laughter never killed anyone. As long as they're laughing, they're unlikely to drag me out back to be executed.*

Though, with men like these, that might not be true.

"Gentlemen," said Schulheim, "this is Major Freeman, of the American Expeditionary Force. Major Freeman, my general staff."

No one introduced themselves, which was just fine. He didn't care who any of these officers were, and he'd happily shoot them in the head without hesitation if given the chance. All he cared about was getting something worthwhile out of Schulheim that he could use to bust out of this place.

He carefully lowered himself into his seat, wincing as his leg flared with pain. The wet stickiness he felt inside the leg of his coverall let him know his leg was bleeding again. The "shower" he'd received had no doubt opened the wound.

"Are you injured, Major?"

Freeman looked down the length of the table to find Schulheim watching him closely. For just a moment he thought he saw the man's nostrils flare, as if he could smell the blood from half the room away.

"A minor wound," he said. "It's nothing, really."

Schulheim seemed unconvinced. "If it pains you, please let me know; I'm sure something can be arranged to take care of it for you."

Freeman nodded, but didn't reply.

Schulheim watched him for a moment, then said, "You know, Major, there really is no need for a man of your rank and stature to spend the rest of the war huddled in a freezing shack like Barracks C. A little cooperation would go a long way to making life much easier for you here."

Freeman had no intention of cooperating, even in the slightest bit, but he thought it might prove interesting to see what the oberst had in mind. At the very least, it might tell him something about what he could expect from his captors.

"What did you have in mind?" he asked, a carefully neutral expression on his face.

Schulheim smiled. "What did I have in mind? Well, I'm sure that isn't too difficult for an intelligent man like you to determine. We could start with the disposition of your troops along the front near Provins and move on from there."

Freeman nodded. "Of course. And in return?"

"In return," Schulheim said, "I'm sure we can arrange private quarters, hot water, and even regular meals. You would be treated more like an honored guest than a common POW. Come now, you must admit that's a tempting proposition, is it not?"

Only for scum like you, Freeman thought.

Carefully controlling his feelings, Freeman said, "You've given me a lot to think about. May I sleep on it?"

"Of course," the oberst said, echoing Freeman's own comment from moments before, his voice practically dripping with false generosity. "Perhaps it might help your decision making to understand the alternatives as well."

He clapped his hands and turned expectantly toward the door. A moment passed and then the butler came into the room, pushing a serving cart ahead of him. On it was the largest covered platters Burke had ever seen. The aroma of meat basted in its juices filled the room, and Freeman found his mouth watering.

With the help of an assistant, the butler managed to lift the platter off the cart and to place it on the table in front of the oberst. Several of the officers leaned forward in eager expectation.

The butler lifted the lid from the serving platter, and Freeman stared in horror at what was sitting on the table in front of him.

The platter held a man's torso and head, roasted long enough that the skin had split and the liquefied fatty tissues were spilling out. An apple had been forced into the man's open mouth and was held there with the edges of his teeth.

That was bad enough, but what made the bile in Freeman's stomach surge upward toward his mouth was the fact that he recognized the face of the man on the platter.

It was the soldier who'd been removed from the barracks when Freeman had arrived earlier that day.

He made it a few feet away from the table before he was violently sick on the polished wood floor. As he fled the dining room, he could hear Schulheim's laughter chasing him down the hall as he went.

CHAPTER TWELVE

ROLL CALL WAS at six the next morning. The prisoners were roused by the shrill blast of a guard's whistle and had only a few minutes to assemble on the parade ground outside the barracks. One of Schulheim's officers showed up and supervised the prisoner count and then, when it was determined that all of them were present, led them over to the mess hall for their morning meal.

Given what he'd seen in the commandant's residence the night before, Freeman was leery of eating anything put in front of them, but as he watched the other prisoners settle down at the tables with their cup of gruel and hunk of black bread, he decided it was safe enough. The food didn't do much more than remind him of how hungry he was, and he knew that was part of their captor's strategy: keep them weak enough that they wouldn't have the energy to attempt a breakout. The poor food combined with the hard labor he knew would come would be enough to exhaust any man, never mind one who was wounded as he was.

When breakfast was over, they were divided into four groups for the morning work detail. Freeman ended up in the same group as the short, dark-haired man who'd saved him from being beaten by his fellow prisoners when he'd first arrived at the barracks, and

Freeman resolved to have a word with him if at all possible.

A pair of guards led them across the camp and over to the muddy field that Freeman had seen the day before. Men were paired up to work together, and Freeman ended up being paired with Mustache from the night before. He did not say anything to Freeman until they had been given their tools, a trowel and a hoe, and were led by the guard to their assigned stretch of ground.

After the guard had left them, the dark-haired man began to hoe the ground with short, sharp motions. Prisoners were not allowed to speak while working so he kept his voice to little more than a whisper and did not look at Freeman when he spoke.

"I believe we got off on the wrong leg, you and I, no?"

"Foot," Freeman replied automatically.

"I'm sorry?"

"*Foot*. We got off on the wrong *foot*. And yes, we did."

"Ah, foot. Yes, I shall remember that. I am Claude Demonet, capitaine, 29e Regiment d'Infanterie."

"Jack Freeman, major, Ninety-Fourth Squadron, American Expeditionary Force."

Claude was quiet a moment, then said, "You understand now? The anger of the men?"

Freeman flashed on the sight of a man's roasted head and torso artfully arranged on a silver serving platter and quickly shook his head to clear it. He wanted to say something to heal the breach, but what do you say to a man whose companion had been, quite literally, served for dinner the night before?

Finally, he settled and said, "I'm sorry. Was he a good man?"

Claude laughed. "No. But that matters not. No man should suffer such a fate."

Ain't that the truth.

"Does that . . . happen often?" Freeman asked, trying to imagine the guards showing up each evening to decide who would be on the menu that night. It was a horrifying thought, all the more so because he could almost believe it.

His fellow prisoner shrugged. "Once every week or so."

"You can't be serious!"

Another Gallic shrug. "Perhaps they take their cue from the walking dead. Meat is scarce, and if it's good enough for them . . ."

Freeman was horrified, as much by the Frenchman's calm acceptance of the situation as he was by the act of cannibalism itself.

"Good God!" he exclaimed. "How can you let this go on?"

Claude kept his head down, but his words carried clearly to Freeman. "Every attempt we've made to escape has ended in failure. No one has made it even fifty feet past the fence. The last attempt resulted in the execution of ten men. Five others were thrown in the pit. We could hear them screaming for hours."

"Surely that is better than sitting around and waiting to be chosen to grace the oberst's dinner table!"

This time the Frenchman did look up.

"The men who were executed had not even participated in the escape attempt!" he snapped, then spat upon the ground in disgust at the memory. "Schulheim's way of teaching us a lesson about obedience. All we did was provide more meat for his larder. Better to be alive, and await our chance for revenge, than die outright with nothing to show for it!"

A guard glanced in their direction, and Freeman immediately put his head down and tried to look busy. It must have worked, for the guard did not head in their direction.

After a few minutes, he dared to asked another question.

"The pit? What's that?"

But Claude would only shake his head and say, "Trust me, monsieur, you do not want to go to the pit."

Movement from the other side of the fence caught Freeman's eye, interrupting the follow-up question that was on his lips. He watched as several figures emerged from a barracks-like building in the distance, on the other side of another double set of chain-link fences. They were too far away from them to make out any details, but there was something definitely odd about the way they moved and carried themselves, like injured men who were just learning how to use their limbs again.

Claude caught him watching.

"*Geheime Volks*," he said in German and then, at Freeman's blank look, "the secret people."

Claude waited a moment for a guard to pass by and then went on.

"I know you are familiar with the walking dead."

Freeman nodded. At this point he couldn't imagine a single man, woman, or child in all of Europe being unfamiliar with the shamblers, the kaiser's death troops.

"What would you say is their biggest weakness?"

That was easy. "They're stupid," Freeman said. "Barely controllable, even with those collars they wear. They're effective as a weapon only in large numbers and with a simple objective before them."

Claude nodded. "And if they were no longer, how do you say, dumb?"

If the shamblers could be molded into cohesive, interworking units, the stalemate at the front would likely fall apart within weeks, if not days. Right now the control collars allowed them to be sent in specific directions and kept them from attacking the German troops that worked in conjunction with them, but that was all. If the devices could be improved to allow for independent action . . . that would not be a good thing for the Allies.

He said as much to Claude.

The Frenchman nodded his head toward the figures in the distance. "Someone is not satisfied with the status quo and has begun trying to improve the process. Already they are growing more intelligent, more capable of thinking for themselves."

As Freeman watched, the group of undead soldiers began to follow their leader through a series of simple tasks. March forward ten paces. Stop. Turn left. March forward ten paces. Stop. And so on. If any of them got out of line or seemed to lose focus, a switch would be thrown on the control box and a bright arc of electricity would dance for a moment across the surface of the shambler's collar, visible even from this distance.

He was about to ask Claude how they were instigating the change when he noticed the Frenchman had frozen in place, stiff with tension. Following the man's gaze, he saw Oberst Schulheim's black staff car parked by the edge of the field. The officer in charge of the work detail stood by the rear door, speaking to someone inside the vehicle through the partially opened window. It wasn't hard to guess who, either. As if to confirm his suspicions, Freeman saw a hand encased in a black leather glove emerge from the window and point directly at them. A moment later the officer signaled to several of the guards standing nearby, and the group headed in their direction.

"*Merde!*" Claude swore beneath his breath.

"What are you doing?" Freeman hissed, trying to keep his head down and appear like he was working while at the same time keep an eye on the approaching Germans.

"Whatever happens," Claude told him, "don't interfere. They don't like troublemakers, and they have their own way of dealing with them, as you discovered last night."

The officer, a hauptmann, or captain, and his entourage marched right over to where Claude was standing, waiting for them. The hauptmann didn't hesitate, just drew back his hand and backhanded the Frenchman for having the audacity to stand in his presence.

"The oberst would like you to join him for supper this evening," the hauptmann said in passable French, eliciting laughter from the men under his command.

Claude didn't respond, nor did he resist as the guards seized him by the arms and began dragging him toward the edge of the field.

Freeman, however, was not going to stand for another man being dragged away like a side of beef for the commandant's table. He rushed forward as fast as his injured leg would let him, carrying the hoe Claude had discarded in one hand and slamming his shoulder into the guard on Claude's right, knocking him to the ground. Before anyone could react, he'd whipped the hoe around like a baseball bat, getting his hips and shoulders into it, striking the guard on Claude's left right in the face with a solid *thwock*. Down he went, too.

"Run!" Freeman cried, as he spun to face the rest of the opposition, not giving any thought to where his new companion might actually run to but determined to provide cover long enough for him to make a break for it.

Out of the corner of his eye, he saw Claude just standing there watching him.

It was so beyond Freeman's expectation of what should happen that it literally brought him to a grinding halt. He stood there, staring at the other man in shocked disbelief.

"Why didn't you run?" he asked.

"Run where?" Claude replied.

That was all the explanation he was ever going to get. At that point the hauptmann stepped forward and smacked the wooden baton he carried across the back of Freeman's head, causing him to drop the hoe and sending him to the ground. The other guards moved in, kicking him with their heavy-soled boots and beating him with their batons.

CHAPTER THIRTEEN

★

The Pit

WHEN FREEMAN CAME to, he found that a guard had a hold of each arm and they were pulling him along, his feet dragging in the dirt. His head was spinning and he felt like throwing up, which was making it difficult to concentrate.

He must have blacked out momentarily, for when he was next aware of what was going on, he found that he was lying facedown in the dirt next to a large piece of iron. A sharp, discordant sound filled the air as the iron was dragged away, revealing a round hole several feet in diameter.

The pit, he thought dimly.

Even in his dazed state he recognized the pungent odor of death and decay that was rising up out of the ground. He didn't have long to think about it, though, because at that point the guards bent down, rolled him over a few times to get him closer to the hole, and then pushed him over the edge with a few kicks of their booted feet.

There was a brief moment of free fall and then Freeman struck the floor with bone-jarring force. The guards' laughter filtered down to him from above, followed by the sound of the lid being dragged back into place.

A bit of light was coming in around the edges of the metal slab and through a handful of holes bored in its surface, so he wasn't in complete darkness. He pushed himself up on his hands to take a look around and saw that he was sitting in a rough-hewn chamber about ten feet wide with a ceiling about the same distance above his head. Amid the shadows to his left he could just make out what looked to be the entrance to another chamber or possibly a tunnel mouth.

The terrible smell was so strong that it burned his nostrils and cleared his head of the lingering sense of dizziness he'd been feeling. As his eyes adjusted to the dim light, he was able to see that the ground around him was littered with human corpses in various stages of decay.

Here, what was left of a man's face was sliding slowly off his skull, the empty eye sockets staring back at him as if in accusation. There a woman's arm thrust up through a pile of rotting flesh in defiance, the fingers of her hand hooked into a claw. Dozens of corpses littered the floor of the chamber alone, never mind the hundred or more that had been haphazardly stacked against the walls and were now rotting together into a giant mound of decaying flesh.

He'd seen his fair share of horror during the war, but nothing that compared with this! He had to close his eyes and swallow hard several times to keep from vomiting.

Many of the corpses were still wearing the remains of uniforms. He could see several different colors; the horizon blue of the French, the tan or khaki of the British and American forces, even the dull gray worn by the Germans. There were a fair number of darker gray jumpsuits present as well, similar in style and cut to his own, identifying those who wore them as former prisoners. It was clear, though, that the dead prisoners were in the minority.

So where had all the dead soldiers come from?

It had been months since there had been a major battle in this area; the kaiser's troops had pushed the line west to its current location in midwinter of last year. Any remains collected after that battle would long since have rotted away. Yet he could see the corpse of a French infantryman who didn't look like he'd been dead for more than a week.

He didn't have time to investigate, however. As he stepped forward, intending to examine the corpse for any answers it might yield, movement off to his left caught his attention. He turned in that direction, only to see the largest shambler he'd ever seen step out of the shadows at the back of the chamber.

It was a good two and a half to three feet taller than he was, half again as wide at the shoulders, and was covered with knots of muscles that seemed to have grown haphazardly out of control like malignant cancers. It was dressed in the shredded remains of what might have once been a jumpsuit, reminding him of the Frankenstein monster he'd seen in one of those new silent pictures a year or two before the war started.

Freeman suddenly understood why the prisoners had feared the pit.

As it stepped into the weak light, he realized his initial impression was wrong. It wasn't a shambler at all, for shamblers have no need to breathe, and even from across the chamber he could see its massive chest heaving up and down as it struggled to take a breath against the weight of its own flesh. He could also see the pale white cataracts that covered much of its eyes and suspected that it would have a hard time seeing as a result. The sniffing sound that reached his ears seconds later added weight to his hunch.

The creature turned its head slowly from side to side, hunting for whatever disturbed its rest, and Freeman went still, hoping to escape notice, but it was not to be. The creature's oversized head swung in his direction and seemed to lock in on him like a stream of machine-gun fire. With a roar that shook the confines of the small space, the creature rushed at him.

For something so big it moved surprisingly fast, and Freeman had no choice but to throw himself to the side to escape its grasping hands. He landed amid a pile of decomposing corpses with a fleshy smack and tried to scramble away, but he was unable to get any traction as the flesh of the corpse on which he'd landed simply sloughed off against the weight of his hands and feet.

That was all the time the creature needed. It whirled around and snatched his ankle in one of its oversized hands. Without pause it lifted him off the ground and hurled him across the room.

Freeman flew through the air and slammed into the opposite wall, taking the brunt of the blow on his right shoulder and narrowly missing cracking his head open against the stone. He slid to the floor, dazed and disoriented.

The creature was on him in seconds. It bent over him and let out a thunderous roar, like a gorilla claiming its territory, then snatched him up and threw him again.

Freeman bounced off a pile of corpses and crashed to the floor, his head pounding and his thoughts scrambling. He was in trouble and knew it. There was no way he was going to beat this thing on strength alone; he was going to have to find a way to outsmart it.

The creature began to stalk toward him, its feet crushing the remains of what Freeman now assumed were its previous victims beneath each step, its breath wheezing in and out.

His hands scrambled through the muck, searching for something he could use to defend himself as the mutant creature moved toward him. His heart was pounding and his mind was screaming at him to run, but he knew there was nowhere to go. *There had to be something he could use . . .*

Just as the creature reached down to take hold of him once more, Freeman's fingers came in contact with a long piece of narrow bone. He snatched it up as the mutant grabbed him about the waist and lifted him up, pulling him closer to allow it to get a good look at its prey.

Freeman didn't think, just acted, slamming the jagged piece of bone he held into the creature's eye.

It screamed, a long howling cry of pain that echoed in his ears, and then dropped him like a hot rock. Blood was spurting from its face in a bright arc as it stumbled backward, its hands raised as if to pull out the offending material but afraid to touch it, and Freeman cast about, looking for his next move.

His gaze fell upon a long strip of treated leather lying nearby, the kind that might have once served as the strap on an ammo bag or haversack, and he snatched it up, gripping it with both hands and testing its strength between them. It was strong, the leather snapping sharply as he pulled against it, and a plan sprang fully formed in his mind as the creature shook its head and turned to face him. It roared in challenge and rushed toward him for the fourth time, no doubt ready to crush the puny figure that had dared to hurt it.

This time he was ready.

As the creature thundered toward him, he timed its approach, forcing himself to stay still despite every instinct screaming for him to get out of the way, waiting, waiting, and then, at the very last second, he made his move. Ducking under its grasping arms, Freeman grabbed hold of one of the many fibrous growths that covered the creature and swung up on its back, just like a child climbing aboard for a horsey ride. As the enraged creature reared upward, Freeman looped the belt over its head and reared back, one end of the belt in each hand, pulling it against the creature's neck. He locked his knees into the well between the thing's shoulder blades, steadying his position and giving him the leverage necessary for what was to come.

The creature might have been big, but it wasn't stupid. It recognized the threat right away and began trying to reach around behind its back to rip Freeman away from his perch, but its overgrown musculature and warped joints wouldn't allow it to reach that far back. Realizing that he was out of reach, Freeman reared back even farther and pulled with all his might.

When it couldn't reach him with its hands, the creature threw itself down on its back in a pile of corpses, trying to crush Freeman with its weight while simultaneously drowning him in a sliding pile of decaying flesh.

The position of the corpses worked in Freeman's favor, however, dispersing some of the shambler's weight and protecting him from the worst of the impact. When he realized he wasn't going to be squashed like a bug, Freeman redoubled his efforts, twisting the ends of the belt and hauling backward against the creature's thickly muscled neck. He could feel its breathing getting more irregular, as it fought both the weight of its own body and the terrible pressure that he was exerting against its trachea. Freeman refused to let go, determined that only one of them was going to live through this encounter and he had every intention of being the one.

It reared up, trying to get to its feet, but then let out a long rattle and toppled over, lying still.

Freeman kept the pressure on for another five minutes, just to be sure.

When he was convinced it was dead, he let go of the strap and crawled away from the oversized corpse.

Time passed, he didn't know how long, as he sought to recover his breath and calm the beating of his heart. Eventually, when he thought he was ready, he rose to his feet and staggered back over to the creature's corpse. He stared at it for a long time, trying to understand just what it was he was looking at, and finally came to the conclusion that it was the result of some kind of experiment gone wrong. It lived and breathed like a man, but had the gray skin and black veins of a shambler. The massive size and odd muscle growths supported the notion that whatever it had been, it hadn't been natural.

That line of reasoning made Freeman remember his initial thoughts about all the bodies surrounding him, and as he turned to examine the closest of those, the body of a man dressed in the uniform of a French soldier, he received another surprise. The thick black veins pressing out against the man's skin were unmistakably the sign of corpse gas exposure and infection.

He wasn't looking at the corpse of a man at all, but that of a shambler.

He turned to another body and discovered that it, too, had been one of the Secret People. So were the bodies that he checked on either side of that. Just to be certain, he got up, slogged his way across the room, and checked several bodies over there.

Shamblers.

All of them, shamblers.

Where had they all come from?

Freeman had been making flyovers of the German lines for years, and as a result he knew that the enemy had their own disposal units for the remains of the undead: men whose job it was to gather whatever was left of the shamblers after each battle and dispose of them in giant bonfires constructed just for that purpose. He'd never heard of shambler carcasses being collected and shipped anywhere else. *What would be the point?* he wondered.

If they weren't being shipped in from elsewhere, then it was logical to conclude that these carcasses had all come from somewhere right here at the camp.

That's an awful lot of dead shamblers.

That didn't make a lot of sense. As far as Freeman knew, shamblers weren't useful for much beyond pointing them toward the enemy and ringing the dinner bell. They were too stupid to use as servants and couldn't be trained to carry out even the most menial tasks because of their all-consuming desire to feed.

Yet clearly they were being used for something, given how many of them there were.

He was missing something.

Something important.

Since he was already covered in filth, Freeman grabbed the nearest body without hesitation. He dragged it over to the spot where he'd first fallen into the pit and used the light coming down from above to look the body over carefully.

It had been a young man, somewhere in his midtwenties. He was dressed in a green jumpsuit that looked remarkably like those Freeman had seen the *Geheime Volks* wearing. He stripped it away and then examined the body as best he could for any sign of injury, any evidence that might point to what had killed the man.

He came up empty-handed.

Could be a lot of things, he told himself. A heart attack. An aneurysm. The wrong kind of chemical exposure. Maybe even poison.

It couldn't mean what he was thinking it meant.

That the shambler had only died once and that its death had occurred *after* it had been raised!

How was that possible?

The question nagged at him, poking and prodding at his subconscious, the way his tongue would push at a loose tooth when he was younger, and he spent much of the night pondering the issue until he fell into an exhausted, fitful sleep.

CHAPTER FOURTEEN

✪

FIELD HOSPITAL

BURKE SPENT THE two days following his meeting with Colonel Nichols regaining strength and working with his new arm. While similar to the previous model, this version allowed for a greater range of motion and was supposed to operate in a smoother fashion. Or, at least, that's what he'd been told. He hadn't yet mastered the fine muscle control needed to pull that off and so he spent several hours each day learning how to control the clockwork mechanisms inside the iron and brass framework.

He was standing by the window waiting for his discharge papers to arrive so he could get back to his command when there was a knock at the door. He turned to find a young corporal standing there. The newcomer snapped a salute and then crossed the room to hand Burke a message slip.

"Colonel Nichols's compliments, sir."

Burke took the note, glanced at it, and then read it again more carefully. It said:

You've been temporarily reassigned to MID, per General Morrissey. Paperwork to follow. Briefing at 1500 hours. Corporal Davis to provide transport.
—Nichols

Reassigned? What the hell?

Burke looked up.

"Are you Davis?"

"Yes, sir."

"Says you're supposed to escort me to a briefing."

"Yes, sir. Colonel Nichols asked me to bring you there straight-away."

Burke hesitated. "Any idea what it's about?"

"No, sir. Above my pay grade, sir."

"Yours and mine both, Corporal," Burke muttered beneath his breath.

He didn't like the idea of being reassigned, not at all. He'd been with the 316th Infantry Regiment, 81st Division for longer than he could remember, and he considered many of those boys his personal responsibility. Leaving them behind was not something he'd planned on doing. At least not this side of a pine box, anyway. But there really wasn't much he could do about it. According to Nichols's message, the order had been approved by General Mor-rissey himself, which meant there wasn't anyone over Nichols's head with whom he could lodge a complaint.

Still, it didn't mean he had to disappear without saying good-bye. He turned the message sheet over and wrote a quick note to Charlie, letting him know what had happened. When he was finished, he ordered Corporal Davis to see that it was delivered immediately after he'd taken Burke wherever it was that he needed to go.

His task completed, there wasn't anything else to do but get on with it.

"All right, Corporal," he said. "I'm in your hands."

Davis led him outside and then asked him to wait a moment while he fetched their transportation. Burke didn't mind; the sunshine felt warm on his face, and it was good to be out in the open air, away from the reek of antiseptic and the stench of wounded flesh that he'd been dealing with for the last few days.

He opened up a fresh pack of Sweet Caporal cigarettes and

shook one out. He didn't care much for the mild tobacco they used, being a Chesterfield man himself, but he'd won the pack in a card game the night before and they were all he had. He lit the cigarette with his pocket lighter and took a deep drag.

"What I wouldn't give for one of those," a voice said.

Startled, Burke glanced to the side where he saw a man tied upright to the wheel of a parked artillery wagon a few yards away. Known to the British as Field Punishment #1, this common disciplinary action had been adopted by the AEF and used for lower-level crimes like public drunkenness.

In the early years of Burke's enlistment, when Mae's death and his own guilt surrounding the event were both fresh in his mind, he'd had a tendency for getting a bit hot under the collar. Any slight, real or imagined, had been enough to throw him into a fit of temper. More than once he'd ended up both drunk and disorderly, caught fighting while in uniform or verbally insulting an officer. As a result, he knew just what it was like to stand without chance of relief for hours at a stretch, your muscles burning with pain. It was that very knowledge that caused him to impulsively honor the man's request.

He walked over, held the cigarette up to the prisoner's lips, and let him take a drag.

"Damn, that's good," the prisoner, a corporal by the single chevron on his shoulders, said. "Thanks."

Burke nodded. "How much longer you got?" he asked.

The corporal glanced up at the sun, checking its position. "Coupla hours, I think. Depends how long that bast . . . um, the lieutenant thinks it will take for his point to sink into my thick skull."

"And his point was?"

"Anything the lieutenant says is the Gospel truth," the corporal said quite clearly, and then, under his breath, added, "Even if he doesn't know his ass from his elbow."

Burke laughed. He'd met his fair share of officers just like that and knew how infuriating they could be. The man's good humor in the face of what was sure to be a painful punishment showed a strength and hardheaded stubbornness that reminded Burke of himself.

Replacing the cigarette in the man's mouth, he said, "Perhaps you'd best keep that, then. You might be here for a while yet."

Corporal Davis pulled up behind them in a Dodge staff car. Burke said good-bye to the lance corporal and climbed into the front passenger seat.

"What'd he do?" Burke asked, nodding back over his shoulder at the prisoner as they made their way through the camp.

"You mean Jones?" Davis asked. "Shot a German officer."

Burke stared at him. "They're punishing him for shooting the *enemy*?"

The corporal shrugged. "His lieutenant said the shot was too far. Told him not to take it."

Now Burke understood. It hadn't been the fact that Jones had shot an enemy officer or even that he'd disobeyed an order not to do so. No, Burke would have bet the rest of his cigarettes that the lance corporal was being punished solely because his lieutenant, whoever he was, hadn't liked being proved wrong.

"How far?" he asked.

Misunderstanding, the corporal replied, "We're going to the other side of the camp."

"No," Burke said. "How far was the shot?"

Davis grinned. "Nearly a thousand yards. Wouldn't have believed it if I hadn't seen it for myself. It was almost as if that Hun had been smitten by the hand of God himself."

Burke glanced back, but the corporal was out of sight. *A thousand yards with a Lee Enfield? That was some damned fine shooting.*

Davis drove to an old farmhouse on the southeast side of camp that had been converted to a makeshift headquarters building. A pair of guards stood out front, but they did little more than nod at Davis as he led Burke inside the building. They then walked past the communications officers working on the first floor and up a flight of stairs. They went down a short hallway and stopped in front of a door at the end. In other, more peaceful times, it would likely have been a bedroom.

"Wait here a moment," Davis said, then turned, knocked, and disappeared inside. He was only gone for a moment; when he returned, he ushered Burke inside, closing the door behind him.

The bedroom furniture, if that was indeed what the room had originally been used for, was long gone. A table and chairs were set up in the middle of the room, and maps of the front were tacked to most of the available wall space. The smell of freshly brewed coffee hung in the air and Burke eyed the cart standing in the corner with envy. The scent of fresh coffee had him salivating where he stood.

Colonel Nichols was already there, along with three other men. Burke recognized two of them; Lieutenant Colonel Bishop was the division commander and in charge of the six units stationed along this stretch of the front, while Brigadier General Morrissey held overall command authority for the entire sector. Both men were heavy hitters, with more command authority than Burke ever even dreamed of aspiring to, and he reacted the way officers have been reacting since time began when in the presence of the hallowed brass. He snapped to a textbook perfect salute.

"At ease, Captain," the general said, waving the salute aside.

Duty taken care of, Burke turned his attention to the stranger.

He was dressed considerably better than the others in expensive trousers, a long-sleeved linen shirt, and a waistcoat. A gold watch chain ran from the button of his waistcoat into the left pocket. Burk noted a topcoat and hat hanging on a rack at the back of the room, and it didn't take a genius to figure out who they belonged to.

Who was this joker and what was he doing at the front? Burke wondered.

Colonel Nichols handled the introductions, answering Burke's unspoken question.

"You already known General Morrissey and Lieutenant Colonel Bishop, I assume."

"Of course," Burke replied, nodding a hello to each of them. "Good morning, General. Lieutenant Colonel."

"And this," Nichols continued, waving his hand in the stranger's direction, "is Clayton Manning. He'll be sitting in on our discussion today."

That was it. No explanation of who Manning was or what his purpose might be. Nor did Nichols's matter-of-fact tone give Burke any sense of how he should feel about the civilian's presence. Manning looked familiar to Burke, but he couldn't place where or when he might have seen him.

He shook hands and was surprised by the strength in the other man's grip. He might be dressed a bit like a dandy, particularly for a visit to the front lines, but there was no doubting the fact that Manning was a man who wasn't afraid of a little hard work.

Right now, Burke needed to figure out what he was doing in a room with the division's top brass and the gung ho colonel from Military Intelligence Division.

"Help yourself to some coffee, Captain," Nichols said, and Burke didn't need to be told twice. Cup in hand, he returned to the table and took the seat that Nichols indicated.

No sooner had Burke settled down than a flustered young lieutenant burst into the room, a disorderly stack of papers in hand. He went pale at the sight of senior officers, and for a moment Burke was certain he was going to rabbit out of there, but he just gulped and moved to his place at the front of the room.

"Whenever you're ready, Stephens," Nichols said, a touch impatiently, as the lieutenant fussed with his paperwork.

"Yes, sir. Sorry, sir."

The young man took a deep breath and then got under way, referring to the large map on the wall behind him throughout the briefing.

"Three days ago, four biplanes from the Ninety-Fourth Squadron took off from the airfield at Toul in response to the sighting of several enemy aircraft near the front."

The lieutenant's voice had an odd nasal quality that made Burke hope the briefing wouldn't last long.

"The squadron engaged an observation balloon and a pair of Pfalz fighters just over the line at Nogent. They were successful in downing all three."

Good for them, Burke thought.

"The flight leader opted to continue patrol and took his squadron across the line into occupied territory. When they did not return several hours later, they were declared missing in action.

"Word came through official channels two days later that the squadron had been shot down by pilots from Jasta 11, with Rittmeister Richthofen personally claiming credit for the death of the squadron leader."

Burke wasn't a flier, but he bristled at the mention of Richthofen just the same. They'd killed the damned sonofabitch twice already; the first time at the end of Bloody April in '18 and the second during the closing days of the Champagne Offensive in '20. How many times was it going to take to keep the bastard from getting up again?

Stephens paused. Emboldened by three days of rest and a hot cup of coffee, Burke took advantage of the opportunity to speak up.

"With all due respect, gentlemen, I don't see what any of this has to do with me or the reason for my transfer. I'm a grunt, at home in the mud and muck of the trenches, and wouldn't know an aileron from a propeller. What's this got to do with me?"

"Patience, Captain. You'll understand why you're here in a moment," Nichols told him, then nodded his permission to the lieutenant to continue.

Stephens opened a file on the table in front of him. He picked up a photograph and then passed it to Burke.

"This was taken earlier this morning from the back of a Bristol two-seater that was returning from a sortie outside of Arcis," Stephens said.

The photo showed what looked like an Allied soldier standing in the middle of a road somewhere, waving at the oncoming aircraft with his left hand as if he didn't have a care in the world, while around him men in German uniforms were diving for cover.

"The Bristol's pilot intended to strafe the enemy column, but the sight of the prisoner stayed his hand. The observer in the rear seat actually managed to take several photographs, but the rest were insufficient for our purposes."

Nichols waited for Stephens to finish and then addressed Burke directly. "Do you recognize the man in the photo, Captain?"

Burke frowned, then pulled the photo closer for a better look. The image was fuzzy, and it was hard to see the prisoner's face clearly. He did seem to be wearing the long flight suit and thick boots that had become the uniform de rigueur of the average American flier, but that was about all that seemed familiar.

Burke said as much.

Nichols stared at Burke for a long moment, then said, "The patrol was led by Major Jack Freeman."

Burke's frown deepened. There was a monocular viewing glass sitting on the table nearby and he snatched it up, using it to take a closer look at the photo.

Was it really him?

He couldn't tell. Yet he wouldn't be surprised if it was. Jack had a way of fucking things up even when he was trying not to. Managing to survive after getting his entire squadron killed would only be the latest in a long string of disasters that followed him around like a shadow.

Burke put a neutral expression on his face, set the viewing glass back down on the table, and sat back.

"Might be him. Might not. Hard to tell. Not much you can do about it either way, though. He's clearly in the hands of the enemy and likely to remain that way for a long time to come."

If he isn't eaten first, Burke thought.

Rather than answering, Nichols turned to Stephens. "Thank you, Lieutenant," he said. "That will be all."

"Yes, sir." The younger man saluted the brass and then made himself scarce.

Nichols waited until the door had closed behind the lieutenant before he turned to Burke.

"What I'm about to tell you is considered highly classified, with all the attendant penalties that go along with such material."

In other words, we'll shoot you if you tell anyone, Burke thought sourly. He had the sudden urge to put his hands over his ears so he wouldn't have to hear whatever it was Nichols wanted to tell him.

The colonel paused, as if debating how to say what he needed to say, then shrugged his shoulders in a *What the hell?* kind of gesture and just threw it out there.

"For several years now a branch of the German scientific community known as the *Geheimnisvollen Bruderschaft*, or Arcane Brotherhood, has dedicated itself to combining scientific experimentation with the occult and mystical arts. They believe that the pairing of these two disciplines will ultimately result in the creation of a superweapon that could be used against Allied forces in Europe and even on the North American continent."

The colonel's statement was so far removed from what Burke had been expecting that he could only sit and stare at the man for a moment. "You can't be serious?" he finally said with a laugh and then glanced at the other men in the room, waiting for the explosion of laughter that was sure to follow his acceptance of such a wild statement.

It never came.

The other men stared at him without expression, certainly without even the hint of a smile on any of their faces. In fact, Burke got the distinct impression that he was being pitied, the way a parent will pity the loss of a child's innocence the moment they learn there really is no Santa Claus.

Nichols didn't mince his words. "I assure you that I am. Quite serious, in fact. Where do you think the corpse gas came from, Captain?"

He'd always assumed the creation of the gas had been accidental, that some error in the production process had created that first batch and then, having seen its value, the enemy had simply continued replicating the error. He'd never even considered the notion that the gas had been developed for a very specific and deliberate purpose.

What kind of twisted mind did it take to come up with such a notion in the first place?

Nichols went on. "We've been monitoring the activity of the Brotherhood as best we can, but I'll be the first to admit that things haven't been easy. Most operatives only manage to get out one or two messages before going silent."

Burke didn't need to be told what that meant, and he found himself wondering just how many men had been sacrificed since the organization had been discovered.

"Unfortunately, this means we have a hard time separating fact from fiction. That leaves us in the rather unenviable position of having to act as if all the information we receive is valid in order to protect our country and our people."

Nichols got up, crossed the room to the coffee cart, and refilled his cup. Burke knew he was just buying time while he figured out what to say next, which was fine by Burke, as he was still trying to come to grips with what had already been said.

Occult practices and arcane arts? You've got to be shitting me.

But it all made sense, in a weird kind of way. He could even imagine the project getting ramped up considerably as a result of the success they'd seen in the corpse gas experiment.

Nichols hadn't told him the worst of it yet.

"About a week ago we received a report from our most recent operative, a low-level occult practitioner, a dabbler really, who we managed to turn with an offer to get his family out of Germany. This report outlined a project our man called the Long Touch, or *Lange Berühren,* in German. It is supposed to be a way for one of the Brotherhood to deliver some kind of psychic strike to a target across a great distance."

Burke wanted to laugh; the entire conversation was getting more bizarre by the moment.

The colonel went on. "With a sample of a man's blood or the blood of a close relative, the Brotherhood can home in on their target regardless of the distance between them. He could be in the next village or half a world away. It makes no difference. They can reach out with their power and kill him, just like that."

"And you think they've actually managed to perfect this?"

Nichols shrugged. "Three years ago I never would have believed the dead would get up and walk again. Now I do not have the luxury of disbelief. I must act as if the danger is real and the threat exists."

Burke turned that one over a few times in his head. "Damn!" he said at last.

Nichols smiled tightly. "My sentiments exactly. Which is why we're sending in a team to rescue Freeman."

Burke choked on his coffee.

"You're what?" he asked, when he'd finished sputtering.

"We're sending a team behind the lines to rescue Freeman," he said patiently, like a schoolmaster trying to explain arithmetic to a slow-witted schoolboy. Then he dropped the bombshell.

"And you're going to lead it."

CHAPTER FIFTEEN

BURKE STARED AT the four men before him, very conscious of the fact that he would have been laughing aloud at the absurdity of it all if he hadn't been so uncomfortably aware of just how serious they were.

He opened his mouth several times, attempting to offer a reply, but he couldn't seem to get his mouth to form the words, mainly because telling the brigadier general and his chosen representatives that they were, to borrow a phrase from his British friends, absolutely barking mad, wasn't the kind of thing one should say in a situation like this, no matter how hard you might be thinking it.

"Why me?" he asked, instead. "Jack and I aren't the closest of brothers. Your files must tell you that."

Nichols nodded. "We're well aware of the level of hostility you have toward him, but frankly, your feelings are immaterial at this point. You're the best man for the job."

Burke practically sneered at him. "Why's that?" he asked, expecting some bullshit about his time on the battlefield or the high level of leadership that he could bring to the mission.

To his surprise, Nichols didn't try to make it into something it was not. "You're one of only a handful of people who know that Major Freeman is the president's son," he began. "Of those who do know, you're the only one with enough direct combat experience to have a prayer of getting the job done."

The irony of the situation wasn't lost on Burke. The president's continued well-being depended on the son he'd spent years ignoring, who in turn had to be rescued by a brother who didn't care whether he lived or breathed. *The president must be quaking in his boots,* he thought. *Let's see how far they are willing to take this.*

"Why break him out? Wouldn't it be easier to just gun him down?"

Nichols was already shaking his head before Burke had even finished. "That was our first inclination. Doing so, however, would leave his body in the hands of the Germans. As long as they have access to a sample of his blood, they will be able to make an attempt on the president's life."

Burke stared at him, then glanced over at the other two officers. No one seemed shocked that Nichols had considered assassinating the president's son.

They're entirely serious about this.

General Morrissey opened up the folder sitting on the table in front of him and withdrew the first piece of paper from the stack inside. He handed it to Burke.

"I suspect you'll recognize this."

A quick glance was all Burke needed, for he recognized it immediately. It was the handwritten after-action report he'd filed a few days ago from his hospital bed. As he handed it back, he said, "Yes, sir, I do. Recognize it, that is."

The general laid the paper down on top of the folder, talking all the while. "Fritz hit us up and down the line that day. Fifteen different points of engagement, with one in three supported by those damned burrowing machines and carrying one of those new types of the undead.

"Hundreds of men up and down the line witnessed the actions of these damned things. They saw the explosives strapped around their waists. They watched as the creatures charged out of the tunneling machines and rushed the access points to the communications trenches. In more than one location they observed the things blowing themselves to bits when it became obvious that they were not going to succeed in carrying out their missions."

Morrissey's voice was filled with disgust as he looked up at Burke and asked, "Do you know how many reports I received telling me that these rotting bastards were different from the ones we've been fighting for the last four years?"

He didn't wait for Burke's answer.

"One!" Morrissey said, brandishing the now crumpled piece of paper in his fist. "One fucking report!"

Morrissey visibly took a moment to gather the fraying ends of his temper. "Care to take a guess who wrote that report, Captain Burke?"

A complete idiot, Burke thought, even as he said, "I did, sir," with more than a hint of resignation in his tone.

"You are correct, Captain," Morrissey said. "Which is why we need you to lead this mission. The partisans we're in contact with behind the lines feed us information on a regular basis, but they're a far cry from trained soldiers who know what is important and what's not.

"You've already demonstrated your ability to think on your feet and, if I may be so bold, your willingness to do what it takes to make it back alive," he said, inclining his head toward Burke's clockwork arm. "You also have considerable familiarity with the enemy. You've been on the front for how long now?"

"Five years, sir."

One thousand, eight hundred, twenty-five days and eleven hours, give or take a few minutes, to be exact, but who was counting?

Morrissey was nodding. "You have the experience to see this through. You understand the need for discretion. And perhaps most important of all, you know the man we're after and he knows you. He'll trust you."

Burke must have looked doubtful, so at that point Clayton Manning spoke up for the first time. "If I may, General?" he asked, and then turned to Burke when the general waved his acquiescence.

"Have you ever been hunting, Captain Burke?" he asked. "I don't mean for deer or pheasant but for the kind of game that can often turn the tables and hunt you in return?"

Burke shook his head.

"Hunting lions, tigers, even the bull elephants of the world takes a particular mind-set. You have to understand your enemy to a certain degree; know what they're capable of, yes, but also know how they typically react when facing a given situation. A tiger will disengage when faced with fire, for instance, but a lion will not. Fire simply enrages the king of beasts, and using it will cause him to attack with more determination."

Burke realized where he'd seen Manning before. He was the big game hunter the British government had hired to track and kill a man-eating tiger that had been terrorizing British settlements in the Hindu Kush back in the spring. Four other men had tried and failed before Parliament had hired the American to handle the job. He'd gone into the jungle with only his rifle and a few supplies and had come back out five days later carrying what was left of the tiger in a burlap sack. The photo of him holding up the beast's head, three times the size of his own, had made the front page of the London *Times*. A little piece of good news to distract the loyal Brits from the ongoing hell of the war, Burke supposed.

"What I think the general is trying to say is that you are a man who has been tested in the heat of the crucible and has emerged refined by the process. You know the enemy because you have spent the last five years thinking like the enemy, doing everything you can to anticipate his next move so that you can counter it. You have lived through everything he has thrown in your direction through a combination of knowledge, skill, and a ruthless determination to survive. Your actions at Cambrai are a perfect example."

Burke winced. *They were never going to let him forget that, were they?*

What he'd done that day had been born of desperation, not good leadership. With his platoon pinned down by machine-gun fire and a group of enemy tanks about to roll over their position, his only option had been to order an attack. He'd gone over the top and charged the nearest tank with a grenade in each hand, praying like hell that his men would follow. He'd come out of that day's events with a silver star for bravery and the nickname "Madman" Burke.

He wasn't particularly proud of either of them.

Exasperated with the turn the conversation had taken, Burke turned to Nichols. "Do you even know where they took Freeman?"

"We think so. Reports have filtered back to us that a man fitting his description recently arrived at the POW camp outside of Vitry-le-François."

Burke frowned; he'd never heard of the place. He got up and examined the map on the wall for several minutes. When he finally located it, he couldn't believe what he was seeing.

"That's sixty miles behind enemy lines!"

"Sixty-four, to be precise," Nichols replied.

Burke's exasperation with the whole idea finally burst free. "How in heaven's name do you expect me to lead a team that far behind enemy lines without being discovered?" he asked. "We'll be lucky to make it through no-man's-land, or did you forget that the entire German army is camped out on our doorstep?"

Manning laughed good-naturedly. "I'm sure Colonel Nichols will have it all figured out ahead of time, Captain."

"Easy for you to say," Burke replied, growing annoyed with the man's need to speak for everyone else. "Your ass won't be left hanging out in the wind if things don't go as planned."

The big game hunter smiled wryly. "On the contrary, I'll be right there with you."

For a moment Burke thought he hadn't heard correctly. Manning's smug expression didn't fade, however, and so Burke turned a confused look in Nichols's direction.

"MID has retained Mr. Manning's services for the duration of the mission," Nichols told him.

"For what?" Burke wanted to know. "It's not like we're going to be running into any tigers."

"I'm afraid that's classified."

Of course it is.

Nichols went back to his explanation.

"We'll get you to within ten miles of the POW camp. I can't tell you how at the moment—that's classified until just before the mission to keep leaks to a minimum—but we will get you there. From that point it will be up to you to ascertain where they are keeping Freeman, infiltrate the compound, and get out with him in tow."

For the first time since Burke entered the room, Nichols looked slightly uneasy as he said, "We're still working on the exfiltration plan, but I assure you that it will be firmly in place before the mission gets under way.

"We're assembling a team with a wide variety of skills in order to cover as many potential scenarios as possible, including an individual who speaks German like a native and one trained as a medic. You'll be able to round out the team with a few men of your own choosing, if you so desire, though I'll have final approval. You'll report to me for the duration and will be transferred back to your original division at the conclusion of the mission, if you so desire.

"Those selected for the team will receive a $1,000 hazardous duty bonus, payable upon departure to their account or next of kin, and a month's leave stateside upon their return, with transportation to and from the destination of their choice. Field-grade promotions to the next rank will also be automatic upon return."

Burke was surprised; it was a generous bonus, not something he was used to seeing from the army. Those who made it back alive would enjoy considerable liberty away from the hell of the front, something a lot of men would give their left arm for. The automatic promotions, never mind the bonus pay, would mean they'd have the cash to actually enjoy themselves, if they lived long enough.

"Questions?" Nichols asked.

Only a few hundred, Burke thought, but he knew the details would be hammered out in the planning process. With a mission like this, he figured they'd have a few weeks to get the men and materials in place and he'd have plenty of time to corner Nichols and pick the planning apart with a fine-tooth comb.

He was wrong.

"The rest of your team has been ordered to report to the motor pool at 1300 hours tomorrow. You'll have an hour to speak with them before shipping out."

Burke stared at him in shock.

"That gives us less than twenty-four hours to plan and prepare!"

Nichols smiled grimly. "Then you'd better get started."

CHAPTER SIXTEEN

AFTER LEAVING THE briefing, Burke found Charlie waiting for him outside the headquarters building with all his personal gear.

"Hear you're taking a little trip," the other man said.

Burke nodded, struggling to find the words to say what needed to be said. The two of them had been together for literally years, and the thought of not having Charlie there at his back when he needed him was disconcerting, to say the least. He was kicking himself for not having asked Nichols to assign Charlie to the squad, for doing so would have assured him of at least one man he knew he could trust with his life.

"Listen, Charlie, I just want you to know that . . ."

The big sergeant rolled his eyes and handed him a piece of paper. "You might want to read this before you get all weepy."

The paper contained a set of orders very similar to the ones Burke received earlier that morning. They indicated that Staff Sergeant Charles Eugene Moore was being transferred to the Military Intelligence Division under Colonel D. Nichols for temporary assignment and was hereby ordered to report for duty outside the company motor pool at 1300 hours the next afternoon.

Apparently Burke had underestimated Nichols.

He looked up at his friend with an expression of horror on his face. "Are you serious?" he asked, his voice quivering with melo-drama. "I mean, really. *Eugene?*"

The use of his middle name made Charlie glare ominously for a moment in response to the old joke between them, and then the two men were laughing with relief at the fact that the war had missed another chance to break them apart. Burke, in fact, was thrilled, for he'd have the benefit of Charlie's steadfast support and years of experience in what was sure to prove a very difficult operation. From his perspective, their chances of getting through the mission alive had just gone up considerably.

"So where are we headed, boss?"

Burke winced. "They haven't told you yet?"

"Nope." Seeing his reaction, Charlie asked, "It's not Passchen-daele, is it? Tell me it's not Passchendaele."

Memories of the weeks they'd spent thigh-deep in the muck and mire of that small village in Belgium sprang to mind and Burke shuddered. Men and horses had literally been swallowed alive in the giant fields of mud that composed the battlefield.

"No, it's not Passchendaele," he said thankfully.

The staff sergeant sighed. "Good. Anywhere is better than that hellhole."

I wouldn't bet on it, Burke thought, as he began to fill his companion in on the mission that lay before them.

THE TWO OF them spent the next several hours looking at the personnel files of the men that Nichols had selected for the mission, as well as everything available on the POW camp outside of Vitry-le-François. Which, as it turned out, wasn't much—just a few rough sketches of the compound and a handful of notes that had been smuggled out in the last forty-eight hours from a partisan group operating on the ground in the local vicinity of the camp.

The information on the mission logistics was less complete, which Burke hadn't thought was even possible and reminded him never to underestimate the army's ability to royally fuck things up. From what Nichols told them, the team would be transported across the front and to within ten miles of the POW camp. The exact method intended to accomplish that little miracle was classified, and no amount of begging on Burke's part could get the colonel to bend on the confidentiality issue. From there they would rendezvous with a group of partisans in an abandoned farmhouse close to the target site, who would then transport them to a spot just outside of the camp itself. It would be up to Burke's team to determine the best way of infiltrating the camp and rescuing Freeman. Once they had, the team would be transported by truck back to the front, where they would have to cross no-man's-land under the cover of darkness in order to reach friendly lines.

It wasn't what Burke would call a good plan. More like a list of hopeful possibilities than anything else, but it was all they had, and if they hoped to live long enough to spend that bonus cash, they were going to have to somehow make it work.

At least they'd be well equipped to give it a try. Around the time they were finishing up, Nichols sent over a stack of supply chits that could be used to draw whatever they needed from the company stores, and the two men decided to head over to the quartermaster's to deal with that task right away. They quickly discovered that the lack of information they were operating under made resupply a challenge, however, and they wound up with far more than they'd originally intended—food, ammunition, topographical maps, medical supplies, demolition materials—anything and everything that they could think of that might make the difference between success and failure once they were behind enemy lines. The last thing they wanted was to discover that they were missing something important when it was too late to do anything about it.

They commandeered a small, steam-driven "supply truck," which was really nothing more than a flat platform on wheels with an engine in the back to help push the weight of the load, and loaded it up with the gear they had selected. Leather straps were then looped over the boxes, slipped through metal rings set on the floor of the truck, and cinched tight.

The truck clanked and shook and hissed like a dragon when Sergeant Moore opened the pepcock that released the already heated water into the boiler, but it built up a head of steam quickly, and they were able to make the short drive to the motor pool without incident.

When they arrived, they found Colonel Nichols waiting for them outside the mechanic's shed. He took one look at the amount of equipment they were carrying and frowned.

"You're going to have to leave at least half of that behind," he said, waving at the gear piled in the back of the truck. "You're allotted three hundred pounds per man, no more, so essentials only, please."

How in hell did they figure what was essential and what was not, Burke wanted to know, *when they didn't know how they were getting there or just what they would encounter when they arrived?*

It was a valid question, but Nichols was unbending on the issue of operational security, and no further information was forthcoming. "You'll just have to improvise as best you're able, Captain."

Improvise, my ass, Burke thought, but kept the grumbling to himself. Antagonizing the new commander in the first twenty-four hours of a unit's formation probably wasn't the best strategy for long-term success.

"The team is gathered inside," the colonel said, using his thumb to indicate the mechanic's shed behind him. "You'll have a few hours to get your equipment squared away before the transport vehicle arrives, so use that time wisely. I'll be back to see you off."

With that, Nichols left them to get to know their unit.

The men were gathered around a table in a small room at the back of the shed. Burke could see them through the open door as he approached, and he did his best to hide his reaction when he saw Graves sitting at the table with the other men. He stepped inside and waited for Sergeant Moore to call the team to order.

When the necessities were handled, Burke waved them back into their seats and took a place at the head of the table. From there, he could see each of them in turn.

Clayton Manning sat to Burke's left. The big game hunter was dressed for a day in the bush, wearing khaki-colored canvas breeches and a dark-colored shirt, over which he'd pulled a worn leather vest festooned with pockets. A slouch hat rested on the table in front of him.

Next to Manning was Graves. He'd exchanged his lab coat for a standard doughboy's uniform, but the way he tugged at the sleeves and pulled on the collar showed how uncomfortable he was in it. Burke hadn't been expecting him and wondered about his presence, but he didn't want to call him out in front of the other men, so he simply nodded a welcome and moved on.

The rest of the men were unfamiliar to him, but he'd read their personnel files and mentally reviewed what he had learned about them as he glanced from one to the next.

Corporal Richard Compton was the squad's medic. Tall and fair haired, he came from a well-to-do New England family that valued career respectability over patriotism. Richard had entered Harvard Medical School later in life, and while he was studying to be a surgeon, his younger brother, James, had enlisted and gone off to war against the family's wishes. It was only after James's death at Cantigny that Richard gave up his studies and followed suit. At age thirty-nine, he was the oldest man in the squad. Compton's file indicated that he was a "quiet, resourceful type" but also noted that he harbored a deep-seated hatred for all things German following the death of his brother.

Next to Compton and directly opposite Burke at the other end of the table sat a heavyset farm boy from Missouri named Steven Strauss. His file had been extremely slim, perhaps a result of the fact that he was the only one in the room who had been assigned to MID prior to this mission. About the only thing useful in the entire file, aside from his marksmanship qualifications and a clean bill of health from the camp doctor, was a notation that he was to be the team's language expert.

On the opposite side of the table from Manning and Graves sat Corporal Harrison Jones, of the fabled thousand-yard shot. Burke had decided to include him when he'd realized that having another sharpshooter along might mean the difference between success and failure. Manning certainly qualified, but Manning was a civilian and Burke had no idea how he'd react under fire of a different sort than he was used to. Jones, on the other hand, had been tested on the battlefield, and Burke was confident he could keep the man's rebellious nature in check if it came to that.

Last, but not least, came Private Benjamin Williams. A dark, curly-headed kid from rural Virginia, he had never left his hometown before shipping overseas less than six months before. He was the perfect stereotype of a small-town boy suddenly thrust into the bright lights of the big city, and Burke was amazed that the war hadn't eaten him alive. For all his inexperience, Williams was on the team for his demolitions know-how. He'd been working in the coal mines since he was eleven and could do things with dynamite that Burke didn't even know were possible. Williams had been part of the team that had tunneled beneath the German lines that ran along the Messines Ridge at the Battle of Passchendaele and blew up their company headquarters in an overwhelming display of military pyrotechnics. According to his file, the kid was an explosives virtuoso; if they needed to blast their way into or out of a structure, he was the one to do it.

Including himself and Sergeant Moore, that gave them an eight-man squad. It was a strong enough team to handle a fair-sized confrontation with the enemy and yet still small enough to move around behind the lines without calling undue attention to themselves.

Or so Burke hoped.

As was his style, he got right down to business.

"You've all had the chance to talk with Colonel Nichols, so I won't waste your time reiterating the basics. We've got a job to do and we're going to do it, as quickly and efficiently as possible.

"Make no mistake—we're bearding the lion in his den. He's bigger, stronger, and faster than we are, and he'll tear us to pieces in a heartbeat if given the chance. It's going to take nerve and discipline to pull this off. If either I or Sergeant Moore gives an order, we'll expect it to be obeyed without hesitation. Your life and the lives of the men around you may very well depend on it. I don't care what you did before this, once we leave this room you're under my command. If you have a problem with that, it's best you say so now. I'll see to it that Colonel Nichols transfers you back to your unit without issue."

He paused, giving them all a chance to decide for themselves if they were going to go through with it or not. When no one moved, he continued.

"Good. Sergeant Moore will handle resupply. We're under specific orders to remain within certain weight limits per man, so check with him to be sure you don't go over that. Otherwise, we'll try to be as liberal as possible with regard to equipment.

"If you've got any last-minute business to take care of or letters to write, now's the time to do it. We ship out in two hours. Dismissed."

As the men got up from the table, Burke put his hand on Strauss's elbow, stopping him. "Stay for a minute, Private, would you?"

He waited for the rest of the men, with the exception of Sergeant Moore, to clear the room and then turned to the young man sitting nearby. He gave him the once-over, taking in the neatly pressed—and clean—uniform, the shoes that were well shined but seemed little worn.

"File here says you know languages?" Burke asked.

"Yes, sir," the kid replied earnestly, his Missouri accent thick as weeds, and Burke almost winced at Strauss's eagerness to look good in front of his new commander. "I can speak English, German, and French, real well, sir."

"You don't say," he replied. "Where did you learn all those?"

"My parents taught me, sir. My mamma, she was from Paris, and my daddy was born and raised in Berlin. They met shortly after arriving in the United States. I learned to speak French and German at the same time I learned English."

"Say something to me in German," Burke told him, and Strauss didn't hesitate, just rattled off a long phrase in German.

Burke glanced at Charlie, who just shrugged. Neither of them spoke a lick of German, though it sounded good to Burke.

"Where were you stationed before this?" he asked Strauss.

The private looked uncomfortable as he said, "Sorry, sir, that's classified. I've been asked to refer all such requests to Colonel Nichols, sir."

Burke frowned, pretending to be annoyed at the response but actually just wanting to see how Strauss dealt with the situation.

"I'm your new commanding officer, Strauss. Surely you can tell me where you were stationed?"

Strauss shook his head. "No disrespect, sir, but I've been told to refer . . ."

" . . . all such requests to Colonel Nichols," Burke finished for him. "All right, that's enough. Get out of here and get your gear assembled."

"Yes, sir." Strauss jumped to his feet, moved to salute, then thought better of it and just hustled out the door in the wake of his new squad mates.

CHAPTER SEVENTEEN

★

GIVEN THE THREE-HUNDRED-POUND restriction that Colonel Nichols imposed on each member of the team, the issue of resupply became more complex, and it took them considerably longer to get all their gear sorted and packed away.

In addition to their bedroll and a change of clothing, each man's field kit contained a mess kit with utensils and a condiment can, a personal kit with razor, comb, toothbrush, shaving brush and soap, and a first aid pouch with a couple of ready-to-use dressings and bandages. Inside the mess kit were four tins of corned beef, a supply of hardtack, and a little sugar and salt. The various pieces of the field kit were carried in a haversack.

The term haversack was a bit of a misnomer; the pack wasn't a sack at all, but rather two large pieces of leather strapped to a frame on which all the soldier's gear was laid. The two flaps were then folded up and secured around the gear.

The enlisted men, with the exception of Sergeant Moore, were armed with Lee Enfield rifles, the standard bolt-action magazine-fed repeating rifle that had first been adopted by the British back in 1888 and then later, along with the 1903 Springfield, became the standard weapon of the American doughboy. The Enfield fired a .303-caliber cartridge, and a well-trained marksman could get off anywhere between twenty and thirty rounds in sixty seconds, making it an extremely efficient weapon.

A cartridge belt at the waist carried twelve clips of five rounds each for the rifles. From a hook on either hip hung a canteen full of water, the canteen itself wrapped in cloth to quiet the sloshing of the liquid inside as the men moved. Each soldier also had a box respirator and gas mask, a trenching tool, and a sixteen-inch bayonet strapped to the outside of his pack.

Captain Burke and Staff Sergeant Moore were given the option of carrying one of the newly released Thompson submachine guns, and both of them jumped at the opportunity. The Tommy gun, or trench sweeper as it was also known, had, for the first time, provided the Allies with a portable machine gun that was as deadly as it was useful. The stocky weapon was fitted with a drum magazine that delivered its fifty-round capacity at a rate of six hundred rounds per minute and could be switched out in seconds by a trained operator.

In addition to the Tommy gun, they also carried a Colt .45-caliber 1911 firearm in a holster on their hips. A double-pocket magazine pouch containing two full magazines for the pistol were attached to their cartridge belts. They also carried two British Mills bombs, or hand grenades, that could be set to a timed delay of four to seven seconds before throwing.

Additional equipment—tents and pegs, coils of rope, candles, maps, compasses, matches, additional clips of ammunition—had to be divvied up so that they could meet Nichols's weight restriction.

The process raised the issue of what was behind the restriction and several of the men asked Burke about it, but he didn't know any more than they did. All he'd been told was that they were going to be taken by truck to Châteauroux. Once there, someone would see to it that they were informed about the next leg of the journey.

Burke didn't like it, didn't like it one bit, but there was very little he could do about it. Nichols had already made it clear that security was paramount and Burke wasn't getting anywhere pushing for more information.

That didn't mean he couldn't use the brain he'd been blessed with, however, and try to work it out for himself. Châteauroux was nearly 150 miles to the east of their current position, in the exact opposite direction they needed to travel in order to reach the POW camp where they believed Freeman was being held. If they were going that far out of their way, there had to be a good reason for it.

Perhaps they'd developed some new sort of transportation system, he thought, *something to carry them beyond the front and deep into occupied territory, like the burrowing machines that Fritz had used to infiltrate the trenches a few days before. Or perhaps the rumors he'd been hearing for the last few months about a platoon of armored walkers being developed for frontline combat were actually true and they'd been drafted to test the twenty-five-foot behemoths through their raid on the POW camp.*

While he was still pondering the issue, he heard a truck pull up outside and moments later Nichols's aide-de-camp, Corporal Davis, entered the shed and indicated that they were to begin loading their gear.

As the men were getting themselves and their gear settled into the back of the truck, Davis indicated that Burke was expected in the tent next door.

Leaving Sergeant Moore to handle the details, Burke slipped through the opening in the drab-colored canvas and found Colonel Nichols and Professor Graves waiting for him, a long table covered with odd-looking gear between them.

"Quickly, Captain," Nichols said, gesturing for him to come forward. "Professor Graves has some special gear for you, and we still need to get it packed up and loaded in time for departure."

As Burke hustled over, Graves turned to the table, picked up the first gadget, and handed it to Burke. It was a revolver, much like the Colt 1917, except the barrel was slightly longer, a lot wider, and was accompanied by an oversized cylinder that made it look slightly comical. He noted that there were eight openings in the cylinder, rather than the usual six.

"This is the Colt Firestarter," Graves said, "and it fires these . . ."

He handed Burke a two-inch-long cartridge that was as wide around as his thumb. "The bullet inside the cartridge has been coated with a special enzyme that has been designed to interact with a shambler's blood. One shot should be all it takes to put one of the things down for good."

There was a holster and an ammo belt with eight full cartridge loops to go with it, giving him a total of sixteen shots with the new weapon. "This all the ammo you got?" he asked, as he buckled the belt around his waist.

"Unfortunately, yes. The components that make up the enzyme are extremely rare, and we haven't yet found a practical way of making them in large quantities."

Which was too damn bad, Burke thought. *Putting a gun like this into the hands of every Tom, Dick, and Harry on the front lines could change the course of the war.*

Provided it worked.

Graves moved to a pile of half a dozen objects that looked like German stick grenades; each had a long handle with a fat tube on the far end. He handed one to Burke, who discovered it was a bit heavier than usual, which would make it harder to throw.

Graves caught his grimace. "I know; we've done everything we can to shave off some of that weight, but that's the best we're going to be able to do at this point. What you're holding is a magnetism grenade. Six-second countdown; you arm it by twisting the top." He mimed turning the fat end of the grenade, where Burke would normally expect the explosives to go.

"Magnetism grenade?" Burke wasn't sure he understood the point. He wanted his explosives to explode, and it sounded like this one might not do that.

He was right. "The device sends out concentric waves of magnetism that impart a positive charge to anything within an eight-foot radius from the blast point. Metal objects, especially anything with high levels of iron in it, will be seized and held in place for the duration of the effect," Graves told him.

"How long does it last?"

"About ten minutes."

Not bad. Not bad at all.

Graves wasn't finished yet. He moved over to where a wide-mouthed metal tube rested next to a plate about a foot square. The plate was made from something that looked like a combination of steel and ceramics, and Burke found it to be lighter than expected.

"Looks like a mortar tube," Burke said, and Graves nodded eagerly.

"It is. I'm calling it a pulse mortar," he said with a smile. "It is based on the same principles that created the suitcase device you used previously, but it is much more useful than the earlier device. Dropping the round into the tube triggers the firing pin, which charges the shell and sends it on its way. When the shell strikes the ground, it releases the energy contained in the warhead, sending tendrils of electricity arcing outward from it with enough power to knock a man unconscious. We can give you as many mortar rounds as you can carry."

Burke's gaze was drawn to the last piece of equipment on the table, a leather cuirass covered with narrow metal tubes that ran over the shoulders to a boxy collection of gears and wires that came together in a juncture box at the small of the back. Two wire-covered sleeves made from rubber and steel rested on the table beside the remainder of the "suit."

He looked at Graves with a raised brow. "Dare I even ask?" he said.

"Hercules vest" was the prompt reply. "Runs on a combination of steam and electrical power. Will effectively double a man's physical strength for a short period of time."

"How short?" Burke wanted to know.

Now it was Graves's turn to wince. "We're still having some

issues with the cooling mechanism. As a result, the feeding tubes have a tendency to overheat. Any usage longer than ten minutes runs the risk of bursting the tubes and scalding the wearer with superheated steam."

Burk took a step back, as if the device had a mind of its own and might suddenly turn itself on, but he was smiling when he turned to Graves and said, "We'll take them. Give the mortar tube to Jones, the rockets to Compton, and the Hercules vest to Sergeant Moore. We can distribute the grenades among the team."

As Graves disappeared outside to round up some help with packing up the gear, Nichols appeared at Burke's elbow.

"A final word, if you please, Captain?"

"Of course, sir."

Nichols led him into the shadow of a four-ton lorry a few yards away, then wasted a few minutes fussing with a cigar, getting it lit properly. Burke recognized Nichols's actions for what they were, a delay tactic, perhaps even some distaste over whatever was to come, and so Burke waited him out, having learned plenty of patience while dealing with his so-called superior officers over the years. At last, Nichols got around to the reason for pulling him aside.

"I wanted to stress again the importance of your mission, Captain. The president has been very clear; in no way can Major Freeman remain in the hands of the Boche."

"I understand, sir," Burke replied. "We'll get him out and bring him home."

Nichols shook his head. "You're good, Burke, I'll give you that. A damn sight better than some of the yahoos I've dealt with over the last year, to be sure, and the men under your command are all solid, reliable soldiers, but both you and I know the chances of actually getting Freeman back across the front are slim at best."

Burke stared at him in confusion. *What the fuck kind of pep talk was this?*

"I'm not sure I follow you, Colonel."

The colonel sighed. "No, no, I don't expect you do."

He looked away into the darkness, and for a moment Burke saw a fleeting expression cross the man's face. Frustration? Pain, maybe? He didn't know; it was there and gone again so quickly that Burke wasn't even sure he'd seen it at all. When Nichols turned back toward him, his face was set back into the same stone canvas it had been moments before.

He withdrew a piece of paper from his pocket, unfolded it, and read it aloud to Burke.

"If, after arriving at the prisoner of war camp and making contact with Major Freeman," Nichols began, his voice as flat as the Kansas prairie, "you determine at any time that it is unfeasible to escort him to the safety of the Allied lines, you are ordered to use any and all means necessary to see to it that his physical form does not remain in the hands of the enemy."

He handed the paper to Burke, who looked down at it in confusion, his mind still trying to process what he'd just heard. It was a telegram, addressed directly to him, and it was signed by none other than Nathaniel Harper, President of the United States.

You've just been ordered to kill your own brother and destroy his corpse!

By none other than the president!

It pissed him off. Years ago it would have been inconceivable that such an order would have even been considered, never mind given, but this crazy war had been going on so long that all the old rules had fallen by the wayside. Burke knew that the conflict was no longer about political ideologies or territorial expansion, no longer a question of "might makes right," but rather had become a fight for survival with the fate of the human race hanging in the balance.

Anything that weakened the ability of the Allied powers to stand in the face of the threat had to be eliminated. He knew that, but the order still stuck in his craw, and for a moment he considered telling them to go fuck themselves. It was an illegal order. He knew that, knew it as well as he knew his own name, but the coldly logical side of his personality also recognized it as a necessary order, one that was ultimately designed to protect the hard-won gains bought with the lives of thousands over the last several months. What was one man's life against the continued existence of an entire country, an entire way of life?

Besides, spending the rest of the war sitting in a six-by-nine cell somewhere after being court-martialed for disobeying a direct order wouldn't help anyone, least of all himself. They'd just order some other fool to head up the mission. If his men were going to be put in harm's way, and that's how he thought of them now, as *his* men, he'd be the one to give the order.

No, refusing was out of the question. Which meant that he'd just have to be sure that they succeeded in getting Jack out alive. It was as simple as that. Anything else was unacceptable.

Nichols took the telegram back and made a show of tearing the evidence into tiny pieces. "Are we clear, Captain?" Nichols asked when he finished, and for the first time Burke heard the edge of steel in the man's voice.

"Crystal clear, sir."

Nichols stared at him for a long moment, as if trying to see inside the depths of his heart, and then nodded. "Very well. Dismissed."

Burke saluted and then turned away. He hadn't gone more than a few steps before Nichols's voice called out to him.

"I trust this conversation will remain between us, Captain."

Burke hesitated, considered saying something, then just raised his hand in acknowledgment without turning around, because, really, what was there to say?

CHAPTER EIGHTEEN

✪

BURKE AWOKE TO a hand on his arm.

"We're here," Charlie said softly, leaning between the front seats to reach Burke from his position in the back of the truck.

The ride to Châteauroux had taken close to four hours and Burke had used the time to catch up on the one commodity you could never have enough of as a soldier—rest. Now, as the truck turned down the dirt track that served as the entrance to the airfield, Burke wiped the sleep from his eyes and looked out into the predawn light.

Even at this hour the airfield was a flurry of activity. Planes had been wheeled out of their hangars and were lined up on the grassy field that served as the takeoff and landing area. Men swarmed over them like worker ants on a mission, checking struts, tuning engines, and loading ammunition into the machine guns that were mounted in front of the cockpits. A group of pilots stood around a map pinned to a piece of plywood, more than likely discussing the morning's dawn patrol. A group of infantrymen emerged from the mess hall as they drove past, and Burke lifted his hand in greeting.

Corporal Davis drove the truck through the center of camp and out the other side. When Burke shot him a questioning look,

Davis said, "Almost there, sir," inclining his head in the direction they were going. Burke let it go, figuring the corporal knew where they were headed, and settled back in his seat.

They drove through what had once, in the days before the coming of the kaiser, been a farmer's field and followed the dirt track they were on into the woods just beyond. They continued for a few more minutes until the trees suddenly gave way and a clearing opened before them. Burke sat up, staring in astonishment out the windshield at the massive airship that came into view.

The gleaming cigar-shaped silver vessel hung fifteen feet off the ground, anchored there by more than a dozen guide ropes, its silver hide illuminated in the spotlights directed up at it from the ground below. Burke guessed it to be somewhere close to seven hundred feet in length, with a diameter in the neighborhood of eighty or ninety feet. The insignia of the British Air Corps, three concentric circles of blue, white, and red, was painted brightly on the airship's nose and tail fins. When one of the lights played across the bow, Burke was able to make out the name of the craft written in letters six feet tall.

HMS *Victorious*.

Two gondolas hung from its underside, one forward and one aft, connected to the bottom of the dirigible by thick brass columns. Large wooden propellers on gimbaled platforms jutted from the back of each of the gondolas, which Burke surmised were meant to assist the tail rudder in maneuvering the craft through the sky. A pair of smaller propeller platforms hung down from the middle of the vessel, perhaps to provide a little extra lift in case of an emergency.

From beneath the tail fin at the rear of the ship jutted several exhaust ports, most likely leading to several steam engines designed to provide the thrust necessary to move the big craft through the atmosphere. A large cargo door hung open, partially obscuring the view of the ports, and Burke could see men standing in its doorway and using a system of ropes and pulleys to bring up crates of supplies that were loaded by a group on the ground below.

Davis pulled to a stop in the shadow of the airship and the men of the squad climbed out of the truck, their eyes going wide as they caught sight, one by one, of the enormous airship looming over them.

Burke understood how they felt.

If was, by far, the largest airship he'd ever seen. The sheer size of the craft was impressive, but it was when you remembered that a ship like that could carry a man all the way across the Atlantic that the wonder of it all really hit home. He'd never ridden in an airship before, and the idea that this behemoth might be their transport made him as giddy as a schoolgirl.

Until he realized with a sinking feeling in his gut just what a bright, big target HMS *Victorious* would be.

While he was still pondering the implications of that realization, a slim young man in a dark blue uniform approached and asked in a heavy British accent which one of them was Captain Burke.

"That would be me," Burke said, stepping forward.

"Lieutenant Silverton, sir, His Majesty's Air Corps."

"Good to meet you, Lieutenant." The two men shook hands.

"If you'll follow me, I'll get you and your men squared away, sir."

Silverton led them toward the group loading the cargo. As they approached, Burke watched several crates being pushed into a wire-framed basket, which was then hauled upward to the men waiting above. Half a dozen other lines hung down from above and men were using them to climb up and down from the deck as their duties required.

"We've got your team bunking together in one of the forward wardrooms," the lieutenant told Burke. "When you get topside, ask for Chief Wilson and he'll help you get your gear stowed away and show you to the bridge."

Silverton glanced at Burke's clockwork arm, hesitated, and said, "If you'll give them a moment to unload, I'll have them send the basket down for you."

"Don't be ridiculous," Burke replied, irked that the lieutenant would assume his former injury left him less capable than the men he commanded.

He reached out, grabbed hold of one of the hanging lines, and began to pull himself upward, hand over hand. His mechanical arm actually worked to his advantage, for he was able to "lock" the hand in the closed position, fingers clamped tightly around the rope, and then hang from it without putting unnecessary strain on his muscles while he reached upward with his other hand. It took him a moment to get the rhythm, but once he had it, he went up the rope as if he'd been doing it for years.

He was met at the top by another British airman, this time a short, burly fellow with a shock of flaming red hair, who grabbed hold of the rope and pulled it over to the side so that Burke could step onto the deck.

"Welcome aboard," the airman said, by way of introduction.

"Thanks. I'm looking for Chief Wilson . . . ?"

"You found him," the man said with a smile. "Chief Machinist Wilson, at your service. I'm guessing you're the mysterious Yank we've been waiting on."

"I don't know about mysterious, but definitely a Yank. Captain Michael Burke, American Expeditionary Force."

The two men shook hands.

"My orders are to get you and your men squared away and then take you to see our captain before we launch. Okay with you?"

"Sounds just fine, Chief."

Burke spent the next few minutes helping the rest of his men aboard and making sure the crates Nichols had sent along made it on as well. After that, they collected their personal gear and told Wilson they were ready.

To Burke's surprise, the first thing the machinist did was lead them to the far side of the room where a large door stood open.

A glance through its open frame showed Burke the looming bulk of what looked to be a bank of engines or generators.

Wilson pointed toward them.

"That's the main engine room, which is where you'll find me when I'm not dragging you Yanks around by the nose," he said, smiling to show he meant no offense. "Unless you're a grease monkey like me, you probably won't have any need to set foot in there during the voyage, but it's always good to know where things are, in case you're assigned to damage control or something like that.

"This way, please," he said and led them back across the cargo bay to the end of a long catwalk that extended forward toward the bow of the ship far ahead.

Wilson explained that all the crew spaces were grouped in two areas, one forward and one aft, along the central axis of the ship and accessible by the main catwalk. The aft section included the engine room, the mechanics' quarters, several storage bays, and the loading dock, which was where they had entered the ship. A stern weapons platform was mounted beneath the bulk of the engines and accessible through the engine room, though Burke hadn't noticed it while on the ground.

The stern gondola, which housed one of the maneuvering engines and also served as the auxiliary bridge in the event something happened to the bow gondola, was located about a third of the way along the ship's length. It was accessed by a ladder that ran down the inside of a vertical shaft that pierced the floor of the catwalk and extended down through the roof of the gondola. Wilson pointed it out as they went past, piquing Burke's curiosity, but they didn't have time to drop down inside and take a look around.

Maybe later, he told himself, as he hurried to catch up.

Above them hung the *Victorious*'s three gas bags, strung horizontally in a line one after another and surrounded by a framework of steel and corded mesh to keep them confined to that particular area. Ladders and catwalks hemmed in the entire structure, providing access, Burke assumed, for the crew in the event repairs needed to be made while in flight.

Curious about what kind of gas could provide lift for a ship of this size and weight, he asked Wilson how it all worked. The chief machinist was more than happy to explain it to him as they walked along.

"Etherium," he said, with more than a touch of pride. "Only the best for His Majesty's Air Service." He pointed forward as he said, "Look there; that gas sack contains refined ether in as pure a concentration as we can get it. In the aft gas sack"—pointing again, but this time behind them—"is a mixture of hydrogen and helium in a 2:1 ratio."

The combination surprised Burke. "Wouldn't pure hydrogen give you more lift?" he asked.

"Yes, but it's also more prone to instability and therefore more flammable," Wilson told him. "The combination makes them all safer. It also burns easier, allowing us to get another ten percent efficiency out of the engines."

The forward crew area, set near the nose of the airship, was twice the size of the one in the rear and contained most of the major crew spaces within the vessel; officers' quarters and wardroom, the crew quarters, mess hall, the captain's cabin, the galley and pantry, the dry goods storage, and the ship's infirmary.

The wardroom that Burke and his men had been assigned to for the duration of the voyage was sandwiched between the galley and the sick bay. It wasn't all that big, especially for eight men and their assorted gear, but since Wilson didn't apologize for the lack of space, Burke didn't bring it up. For all he knew the British airmen were crammed into a space half the size. Four sets of wooden bunk beds had been bolted to the floor and the men quickly claimed their respective territory, with Burke automatically awarded the lower bunk closest to the door, as was custom.

Burke left the men in Sergeant Moore's hands and followed Wilson out the door. The vertical shaft that provided access to the forward gondola was located half a dozen yards back along the central catwalk and Wilson didn't waste any time in leading Burke over to it and then down the ladder into the gondola.

Burke's gaze was immediately drawn to the windows. They rose from waist height to just below the ceiling and provided a complete 360-degree view of the surrounding terrain. Right now all he could see were the trunks of the trees that encircled them, but once they were airborne he knew the view would be magnificent.

Tearing his attention away from the windows, he looked upon a finely appointed cabin done up like a gentlemen's club of old, with dark wood paneling, a deep maroon rug, and high-backed leather seats at each of the crew stations. The instrument panels were covered with a dizzying array of gauges, dials, and switches, all coated in brass that was sparkling from a recent round of polishing. Crew members were dressed in the bright blue jumpsuits the British Air Service had adopted as its official uniform and were hard at work at their various stations, calling information back and forth as they ran through the departure checklists. A ship's wheel was mounted near the front of the gondola, allowing the helmsman manning it to see where they were headed and to adjust course as necessary. Behind him, in the center of the command area, a gray-haired figure wearing the uniform of a senior officer sat in a raised chair watching over it all with an authoritative air while at the same time dealing with several issues brought to his attention by the aides clustering around him.

"Captain Connolly?"

Without looking up from the clipboard in his hand, the other man said, "What can I do for you, Chief?"

"Our 'package' is aboard, sir. The American, Captain Burke, and his team."

The captain turned, spotted Burke standing a few feet away, and, dismissing the aides for the moment, crossed over to him with a smile. "Good to meet you, Captain," he said. "Nigel Connolly, captain of Her Majesty's vessel *Victorious*. My people taking care of you all right?"

"They are, Captain. Thank you," Burke said politely, trying not to be rude as he continued to gaze in fascination at the control stations nearby.

"Good. If you need anything, you just let Chief Wilson know and he'll take care of it. I'll speak to you again after launch."

"Sounds good, sir. Thanks."

Captain Connolly nodded and then excused himself to continue dealing with the many items that demanded his attention. Wilson nodded his head in the direction of the access shaft, and Burke reluctantly turned away. They hadn't gone more than a few steps, however, before Connolly's voice cut through all the chatter.

"Captain Burke?" he called, and Burke turned to see him looking in their direction.

"Ever flown in an airship before?" the British commander wanted to know.

Burke shook his head. "Not had the pleasure, sir."

"Consider this an invitation then." Connolly pointed to an unused control station near the rear of the gondola. "Buckle yourself in over there and enjoy the ride. I'll see to it that word gets back to your men that you'll be occupied during the launch."

It was the opportunity of a lifetime! Burke hustled over to the appointed position and settled himself into it, buckling the lap belt in place and keeping his hands off the controls, lest he screw something up.

Fifteen minutes passed as the crew made their final preparations, and then they were ready to get under way. The executive officer, Lieutenant Jamison, signaled someone on the ground, and a moment later it grew brighter inside the cabin of the gondola as the massive canvas tarps that had hidden the clearing from the prying eyes of enemy aircraft were cut away and fell to the ground on all sides of the airship.

Connolly stabbed a button on the control panel in front of him with a thick finger and said, "Bridge to Engineering, this is the captain. Fire the engines."

A moment later there was a gentle rumble from the rear of the craft, and Burke could feel the airship strain slightly against the ropes that held it secure to the ground.

A voice came out of the grid on the control panel in front of Connolly. "Engineering to Bridge, Chief Machinist Wilson. All engines fired and operational. You have maneuvering power at your service."

Connolly nodded to himself, then turned to his exec. "Aft guide ropes away, Lieutenant," he ordered. Jamison delivered a hand signal to the men on the ground, and Burke felt the rear of the airship begin to slowly lift.

When he felt the ship begin to rise, Captain Connolly said, "Forward guide ropes away," and the same process was repeated, but this time it was the nose of the vessel coming up to meet the already rising stern. A few minor adjustments and the helmsmen had the ship rising smoothly toward the open sky above.

With his gaze glued to the window beside him, Burke watched the ground slowly slip away until they were out in open air and climbing into the gray light of the morning.

Captain Connolly let his ship rise unhindered for several more minutes and then pressed a button on the panel before him.

"Bridge to Engineering. Main engines all ahead full."

There was a moment's hesitation, and then the twin engines that Wilson had shown him during training kicked into gear, sending the *Victorious* moving forward at a steady pace.

"Lieutenant?"

"Yes, sir?"

"Signal the ground and let them know that Operation Orpheus is officially under way."

"Very good, sir!"

As the *Victorious* rose into the light, Burke was left wondering just who on earth thought it was a good idea to name the mission after a tragic Greek hero who descended into the Underworld to rescue his wife, only to fail at the last minute and lose her forever.

It wasn't the most auspicious of omens.

CHAPTER NINETEEN

★

AFTER THE EXCITEMENT of getting under way had passed, Burke returned to the wardroom. He stood in the doorway for a moment, watching his men move about their tasks, then slipped inside the room. He passed Private Strauss sitting near the entrance, cleaning the Lee Enfield he'd been assigned under Sergeant Moore's watchful eye, and the two of them nodded as Burke went by. Private Williams and Professor Graves sat on the next bunk over, the younger man seemingly spellbound by the older one's description of the infectious rot that sometimes spread like wildfire in the wake of a shambler bite, and neither man seemed to notice Burke's presence.

The next bunk held Corporal Compton, and as Burke moved closer he could hear him reading aloud to himself from the small, leather-bound book he held in his lap.

"You prepare a table before me in the presence of my enemies. You anoint my head with oil; my cup overflows. Surely your goodness and love will follow me . . ."

Manning was sitting on the floor, his back against the bulkhead and his legs stretched out before him. Burke couldn't be certain, thanks to the fedora pulled down low over the hunter's brow, but he was pretty sure the man was asleep.

Jones sat to Manning's left, and he nodded when the captain looked in his direction. Unlike the others, Jones had barely glanced at the *Victorious* when they'd arrived at the field, and Burke had the sense that the corporal viewed the airship as just another means to an end. The joy and wonder of flight held no interest for him; he was just marking time until they reached their destination and he could get back to doing what he was good at, which, in Jones's case, was shooting things. His eyes were bright, like a predator on the hunt, and something in his expression made Burke feel like he was being sized up, judged even. Having worked with men like Jones in the past, Burke kept his gaze firm and stared back at him without flinching, establishing who was in charge right from the get-go, until the other man looked away.

Jones's brashness was a good thing, provided it remained firmly focused on the enemy. But if he began to get the idea that he was better than the officers in charge, he'd start to push back, and Burke had to be ready to respond decisively if he did. A quick display of force would probably do more to keep Jones in line than anything else.

Burke settled down on his bunk and dug the map out of the inside pocket of his uniform. He took his time unfolding it, knowing he hadn't yet mastered the gentle movements needed to use his mechanical hand for such delicate tasks, and mentally clapped himself on the back when he managed to open the map up all the way without tearing it.

His satisfaction was short-lived. Charlie sat down on the edge of the bunk next to him, causing Burke's weight to shift to one side and his hand to jerk in the opposite direction, tearing a quarter of the map off in the process.

"Sonofabitch!"

Charlie took one look at the expression on Burke's face and burst into laughter. His laughter turned out to be contagious; Burke found himself busting up, right along with him. When the two men finally stopped cackling, they found the rest of the squad staring at them in puzzled concern.

Which just broke them up all over again.

It was a much needed relief to the stress of the last twenty-four hours, and both men felt better for it. To Burke's relief, the piece of the map that he'd torn free had been of the French coastline and not an area they were going to need for the mission.

Or, at least, not unless something went radically wrong, Burke thought.

Pushing that idea out of his head before it could sink its claws into his confidence, he turned his attention to the map and began discussing options with Charlie. They were still at it, over an hour later, when a voice suddenly intruded on their conversation.

"Captain Burke?" the voice asked.

The speaker had a British accent, which wasn't all that surprising on a British vessel, but what was surprising was that they couldn't tell where the voice was coming from. No one else had entered the room with them.

It came again.

"Captain Burke? Are you there, sir?"

This time they pinpointed the voice as coming from a small mesh-covered box mounted on the wall in one corner of the room.

It was a talk box, though a smaller version than the one Burke had seen Captain Connolly use on the bridge. The devices operated much like a telephone, he knew, with two-way communication between two stations that were dialed into the same channel, but they used radio waves to carry the transmission rather than wires. Now that he knew what to look for, Burke could see the control panel and microphone peeking out from behind some of the gear they'd stored on a nearby shelf.

"Just a moment!" Burke called out, then felt foolish for doing so because he knew the other man couldn't hear him unless he used the microphone. He got up and quickly crossed the room toward the equipment, the rest of the men on his heels.

The speaker must have recognized their lack of experience with such devices, for rather than continuing to call out the captain's name, he began to issue instructions on how to use the equipment—the dial to move to zero the channel in better, the button to push in order to talk at the base of the microphone, and so on. With his help, Burke was ready in just a few moments.

"Yes," he replied into the microphone. "Yes, this is Captain Burke."

"Ah, there you are. Good, good. Lieutenant Jamison here, from the bridge."

Burke waited a second to be sure the other man was finished speaking and then mashed the talk button down with his hand.

"What news, Jamison?"

"Captain's compliments, sir. He asked me to let you know that we've just crossed the line and are now in occupied territory."

That's it. No turning back.

"Thanks, Lieutenant. I appreciate your letting us know. My thanks to the captain as well."

"Very good, sir."

After signing off, Burke returned to his bunk and dug the envelope Nichols had given him out of his breast pocket. He knew the envelope contained additional information about their mission, but he'd been ordered not to open it until they had crossed the front line and Burke took those commands seriously.

Now, though, there was no longer any reason to wait.

He tore open the envelope and pulled out the folded sheets of paper that it contained. The first two were written agreements spelling out the terms under which Burke's team had undertaken the mission, which he barely glanced at, turning his attention instead to the third and final sheet in the set.

It was a communiqué directed specifically to him and marked TOP SECRET in bold letters right across the top of the page. It detailed the mission's parameters and requirements, including the specific roles each man was intended to play, and the key milestones that formed the backbone of the plan as it had been developed for them by Nichols's staff.

Burke skimmed through the dense typewritten lines, stopping to read certain parts more closely, such as the description of Graves's role as the team's "expert in regard to the sciences, both common and esoteric" and how he had been charged with the task of "collecting any and all information" relevant to those topics. Burke noted that the professor was also somewhat fluent in German, which, even though they had Strauss's expertise, might come in handy.

Graves's assignment made sense and Burke didn't think twice about it. What was surprising to him, however, were the orders regarding the big game hunter, Clayton Manning. According to the communiqué, Burke was instructed to give Manning a free hand if the opportunity arose for him to "expedite the removal of certain key members of the opposition." A list of half a dozen names followed. Burke recognized only one of them, that of Baron Manfred von Richthofen, commander of Jagdgeschwader 1 and the enemy's ace of aces.

But he didn't need to recognize the names in order to understand the role that Manning had been asked to play. Apparently it wasn't all that wide a leap from big game hunter to government assassin. No wonder neither Manning nor Nichols had wanted to talk about it at the briefing the day before. Killing a man in the heat of combat was one thing, but gunning him down like a rabid dog was something else, in Burke's view, and he would have protested the necessity of such tactics if he'd known about them.

Too late now.

As Burke expected, the remainder of the communiqué outlined the operational details for getting his team in place to make the assault on Stalag 113, the POW camp where they believed Freeman was being held. He turned to it eagerly.

The plan was simple and direct, which, as far as he was concerned, was the best kind. The *Victorious* was to carry them across the line and into occupied territory before depositing them ten miles from the camp. The *Victorious* would then retreat to the safety of a higher altitude, there to await the signal that the mission was complete. In the meantime, the squad would hike cross-country to a farmhouse where they would rendezvous with a group of French partisans.

Burke's contact among the freedom fighters was a man named Pierre Armant. According to the documents, Armant's group was responsible for several recent guerrilla raids against truck convoys and distribution centers. They were well positioned to help them with their strike on the POW camp. They had been watching the camp for the last few days and would relay their observations to Burke. Using that information, he would then decide the best means of infiltrating the camp, rescuing Freeman, and getting them all back out again, preferably in one piece. The partisans would provide backup during the assault and, once the squad busted Freeman out of the camp, would take the group deeper into occupied territory on the assumption that it would be the last place the enemy would look. Upon reaching the departure site, the team would signal the *Victorious* and journey aboard her back to friendly lines.

Burke wasn't thrilled with having to depend on strangers to provide them with an escape route, but really, what choice did he have? Familiarity with the local terrain might make the difference when it came to a successful exfiltration, and that certainly wasn't something he or anyone else on his team could provide.

In the end, the details of the plan were still a bit sketchy, but the general outline was there and that was good enough for Burke. It gave him something to work with, and that was more than he'd had when they'd left the ground.

He filled Charlie in on the details, both to get his input and to be certain that someone else in the squad knew what was supposed to happen. That way the mission wouldn't be in jeopardy if Burke suffered an injury or, God forbid, ended up killed in action.

The two men were deep in discussion of the particulars when Burke felt the ship rock beneath them.

Charlie must have felt it too, for he looked up at the same time that Burke did, glancing at the whitewashed walls around them as if they might provide some answer.

When, after a moment, the strange impact wasn't repeated, they shrugged and went back to examining the map that they had spread out before them on the bunk. Both men were trying to memorize as much of it as possible so that they wouldn't waste precious time having to consult it in the midst of the operation.

A few seconds later, the airship rocked again. This time it lurched downward, the angle of attack so steep that anything that wasn't held down—knapsacks, ammo belts, helmets, and the like—flew through the air. The men swatted frantically at the loose objects as they flew past, fighting to keep their balance and avoid getting struck at the same time.

The ship righted itself quickly enough, but that didn't stop the men from wanting to know what was going on and looking to Burke for answers. He just didn't have any to give them.

Or at least, not yet.

But he intended to find some.

The tramp of boots on the catwalk outside reached his ears. Burke moved to the door and hauled it open, startling the group of men who were passing by. Wilson, the chief machinist who had shown him around the *Victorious* earlier that afternoon, was one of them and Burke snatched at his arm as he tried to get past.

"What's going on?"

"We're under attack," he answered gruffly, his attention clearly on the task ahead of him. "Get back inside and secure yourself as best . . . Wait! Are you afraid of heights?"

Surprised by the question, Burke answered before he thought about why the other man might be asking. "No."

That was all Wilson needed to hear. He grabbed Burke's arm and dragged him along in his wake, his burly strength overcoming what little resistance Burke mounted before willingly deciding to comply. *Anything to get out of that cramped compartment and get a sense of what was going on.*

"We can use your help," Wilson told him, as they rushed down the catwalk in the direction he'd originally been going. "How comfortable are you with a Vickers gun?"

The Vickers was a heavy machine gun that used a 7.7 mm cartridge. Water-cooled, it had a tendency to jam too often for Burke's comfort, but the British had adopted it as their heavy machine gun of choice, and he'd trained with it earlier in his career. It was bulkier than the American Lewis gun, with which he was more familiar, but the basic operation was the same and Burke didn't think he'd have any trouble with it.

He said as much to Wilson.

"Good," the chief machinist said. "In that case, I'll load and you fire. I can't aim worth hell."

Burke was still trying to figure out where on earth they'd set up a machine-gun emplacement on a ship like this when Wilson dragged him through an unmarked door and into the room that lay beyond.

Much of the space was filled with a metal contraption that looked like a lion's cage with a reclining barber's chair in the middle of it. Mounted on a tripod in front of the chair was the Vickers, a belt of shells already loaded, with the bulk of an ammunition case sitting close by. A thick lever, like that seen at a railroad crossing, jutted up from the flooring next to the ammunition case.

Behind the strange-looking contraption against the far wall Burke could see what looked to be two bicycle frames, sans wheels, mounted about ten feet apart from each other. Large chains ran from the frames into the walls on either side of the room. They reminded Burke of the anchor chains on the merchant vessel he'd sailed aboard when being deployed to Europe, all thick links and solid iron. Two midshipmen sat on the seats, their feet on the pedals, and from the sweat staining their shirts it looked as if they'd been pedaling hard for a while.

A groan of pain from one side caught his attention, and he turned to find a medical orderly frantically trying to bandage the chest of a wounded man lying on the floor, the deck around them awash in blood. Another man lay slumped against the nearby bulkhead, a small red hole on the front of his uniform that at first glance didn't look too bad, but from the way he stared off into space, Burke knew he was already beyond help.

The airship rocked again, shuddering beneath their feet, and the time for sightseeing was over. Wilson pushed him forward, toward the contraption, and guided him into the seat in the center of it, right behind the Vickers. Burke had already sat down before he noticed the blood smeared on the seat beneath him and splashed across the inside surface of the cage nearby. His gut clenched at the sight, but it was too late to back out now; Wilson was already strapping him into place with thick, leather belts.

"What do I need those for?" Burke asked, as he shifted against the tightness of the straps and tried to get comfortable.

"You'll see," was all the chief machinist said.

When Burke was properly strapped in, he watched for a moment as Wilson thrust his feet into leather straps next to the chair and set about buckling them down tight over his boots, with extra straps wrapping around his ankles as well, then turned his attention to the gun before him.

It was mounted on a gimbaled tripod that supported its heavy weight while still allowing him to swing it up, down, and to either side with minimal difficulty, even with the lessened dexterity of his clockwork arm.

Now all he needed was something to shoot at.

"Better put these on," Wilson said and handed him a pair of goggles with thick lenses protruding for the eyepieces. Burke pulled them over his head and was still trying to get them adjusted when Wilson turned to face the far wall where the other men had gathered and shouted, "Ready!"

The men stationed on the bicycles began pedaling at a furious rate. A loud grinding noise filled the room as the exterior wall split in two across the center of its horizontal axis, revealing that the wall was in fact two massive doors. Burke watched in astonishment as the doors moved outward from the hull for a few feet before sliding in opposite directions, one up and one down. The gap beneath them widened as the crew continued pedaling, and Burke got his first glimpse at the gray sky just beyond. As the gap widened, a cold breeze rushed in from outside, filling the room with its hoary caress.

Burke immediately realized why Wilson had asked if he was afraid of heights.

"We're not going out there, are . . ."

That was as far as he got.

Wilson shouted, "Hang on!" and then hauled back on the lever beside his station.

The locks holding the gun emplacement sprang open and the entire platform shot out through the open door along a rapidly unfolding track to hang suspended thousands of feet above the ground.

CHAPTER TWENTY

Two Miles High

THE WIND WHIPPED and shrieked at them, trying to tear them from their perch with freezing fingers, and Burke was glad for the straps that held him in place even as he gazed about in amazement. The bulk of the *Victorious* rose behind them, filling the view in that direction with its steely gray hide, but the action was out ahead of them where the sky was filled with aircraft whirling and diving about one another and the massive airship in an intricate dance that made Burke dizzy from trying to watch it all. He was unable to pick out friend from foe; they all looked the same as they dove and spun about one another with seeming abandon. For the first time since he'd entered the war, Burke was thankful that he'd joined the infantry.

He tore his gaze away from the dogfight in front of him and glanced to the side. A bank of deep black thunderclouds loomed a few miles to the east and, despite the flashes of lightning he could see dancing deep within, the *Victorious* seemed to be headed directly toward them, climbing as she went.

The storm was the least of his concern though, as Wilson tapped his shoulder and frantically pointed out ahead of them into the distance.

At first, Burke didn't understand what the other man was pointing at; there was just too much going on. He reached up with his good hand, trying to clear the light mist that seemed to be gathering on the surface of his goggles, and discovered that the right-hand lens rotated through different settings, each one making the distant objects much clearer. By chance he landed on the proper one and the German biplane that was speeding toward them sprang sharply into view, its machine guns already spitting a hail of lead in their direction!

With his heart in his throat and his pulse beating a mile a minute, Burke grabbed the handles of the Vickers and swung it around at the oncoming aircraft, depressing the firing trigger even before he'd gotten it lined up properly.

A stream of tracers arced out across the sky toward the Albatros even as the German machine-gun fire bounced off the steel cage around the two men, the sound of the bullets lost in the howl of the wind and the hammering cry of the Vickers. The plane grew larger with every passing second, and Burke found himself screaming wordlessly in defiance as it filled his view, bullets flying back and forth between them.

At the last minute the pilot pushed the stick forward and the biplane dove beneath the firing cage to disappear somewhere beneath and behind them.

Burke didn't have a lot of time to worry about him, however, for another plane rushed into view, this one moving laterally across his field of vision, and he recognized the brilliant red paint job even in the midst of all the sensory overload. He swung the guns to follow it, sending a stream of bullets across the space between them, but the aircraft zigged when he thought it would zag and he never even touched it.

There wasn't time for regret however, for Wilson was already pointing out another German plane as it came into range and Burke spun the gun mount, trying to line up a shot. That's how it went for what felt like hours, Burke firing until the gun went dry and then waiting impatiently for Wilson to feed another belt into the firing mechanism before beginning the process all over again. The enemy, of course, was doing their best to kill them in turn, for Burke and his companion stood between them and their prize, the *Victorious* herself. Bullets constantly rattled against the outside of the firing cage, and there were more than a few close calls, including one in which a bullet came close enough to burn a crease down the side of Burke's cheek with the heat of its passage.

Burke's first kill was a Fokker D.III that came too close while trying to shake the Sopwith Camel on its tail. He chopped its tail assembly to pieces with a burst from the Vickers, sending the plane spinning earthward with a long spiral of black smoke pouring from the engine. Not long after that, while working in conjunction with one of the escort squadron's Bristols, he helped send an Albatros with silver-tipped wings to the same fate.

Each time they caused damage to an enemy aircraft, Burke screamed in primal triumph and pumped his clenched fist, high on bloodlust and the need to kill those who had come to deliver the same fate to him. The urgency of the squad's mission, the danger of the enemy guns, even the precariousness of his position in a simple cage of wire mesh and steel thousands of feet above the ground all brought his senses alive like only the heat of battle could. This was why he joined the war: to feel the pulse of life pour through his veins. He felt ready to take on the world and everything in it, and he found himself wishing it would go on and on, reveling in the excitement and the glory.

The Albatros appeared out of nowhere, its blue-and-gold-striped frame hurtling toward them from out of the morning sun, and Burke spun the Vickers in its direction, trying to line up the shot. The German pilot kept a steady stream of tracers headed in their direction while avoiding Burke's return fire, turning away only at the last second. As he did so he lobbed something toward them with his free hand.

The world slowed down as Burke watched the object tumble through the air, turning end over end in a manner that he was all too familiar with, for he'd seen it hundreds of times over the years as enemy soldiers rushed toward him across no-man's-land. Fear rose like a spectre in the night, threatening to overwhelm him, as his brain finally cataloged what his eyes had already recognized.

Grenade!

There was nothing he could do; he was strapped in tighter than a lunatic in a straitjacket. The potato masher would explode long before he managed to even get the first buckle undone, never mind free himself from the harness. Even if he did get free, there was nowhere for him to go. He'd never be able to crawl back along the rails supporting the gun platform to the safety of the airship's interior without slipping, not with the wind and the movement of the ship.

All this and more passed through his mind in the three seconds it took for the grenade to arc through the air, bounce off the top of the cage, once, twice, and then slip through an opening to disappear amid the wire mesh beneath their feet.

Burke closed his eyes and waited for the end.

A minute passed.

Then two.

Burke began to think he might just live.

"Why are we still here?" Wilson asked, his voice shaking, though whether from fear or relief Burke didn't know.

Burke's voice betrayed his own confusion when he answered, "Don't have a clue. Just be thankful we are."

The universe apparently didn't believe him, however, for the faulty grenade chose that moment to live up to the purpose for which it had been designed and exploded in a fury of sound and pressure.

For Burke there was a thunderous boom followed by a brilliant flash of light, and then the explosion enveloped him in its velvet fist.

CHAPTER TWENTY-ONE

GUN PLATFORM #3

TIME PASSED, THOUGH in his vaguely conscious state Burke didn't know how long. He didn't care, he just wanted to drift in the peace and silence, to let the world pass him by unhindered and unnoticed.

A voice began shouting at him, dragging him from his rest, but he couldn't make out what it was saying. He wanted to tell the voice to go away, to leave him alone and to let him go back to sleep, but for some reason he couldn't get his thoughts together well enough to form the words. That worried him, and the concern he felt was like a kick in the teeth, jarring him toward conscious awareness of where he was and what he was doing.

Which, as it turned out, was hanging by his harness from the remains of the gun platform.

It took everything he had not to scream when he opened his eyes and found himself bobbing there in midair with the earth lain out like a giant patchwork quilt thousands of feet below.

"Burke! Buuurrrkkkke!"

Apparently someone was doing enough screaming for both of them. The voice in his dreams was real, as it turned out. It was Chief Wilson.

Afraid to make any sudden moves, Burke kept his body as still as possible and just moved his head to one side, but he saw nothing in that direction but open sky. Turning back the other way, he found his partner.

Like Burke, the chief machinist was also hanging on by a thread, but in this case that thread happened to be his right foot. Somehow it had gotten caught inside a mess of wire and twisted steel and that was all that was keeping him from falling to his death.

One dip in the wrong direction and it was all over. There was no way Burke would be able to reach him.

Stop worrying about him and save your own ass, said a voice in the back of his mind, but Burke ignored it. Abandoning an injured man just wasn't in his nature. He told the dark side of his mind to shut the hell up and focused on figuring a way out of their predicament.

"Don't move!" Burke shouted, before realizing how stupid the order sounded. *Of course he's not going to move, you idiot. He's trapped, hanging upside down.*

Burke closed his eyes tightly as he fought to clear his thoughts. He, too, was trapped. His harness held him strapped into the firing chair, but the explosion had tipped the entire gun platform on its side, leaving the chair pointed downward. If he was going to be of any help to Wilson, he was going to have to get out of the chair and get himself onto the remains of the platform, all the while not making any moves that might change the balance of the wreckage.

At the moment he had no idea how he was going to do it.

Come on, Burke. Think!

He glanced around, looking for anything that might support his weight long enough to let him clamber into a more secure position. Half the cage had been torn away by the explosion, revealing wires, cooling conduits, and the guts of the gimbal system that had supported the firing platform. In particular, his attention was drawn to a long piece of rail on which the cage had traveled in and out of the airship's hull.

If he could reach that . . .

"Help me, Burke!" Wilson screamed, as his foot slipped slightly inside the twisted nest of metal.

I'm trying, you fool! he wanted to scream in return, but he said nothing, focusing instead on the idea that had just reared its head for a moment in the back of his mind. It was a crazy-ass plan, as plans go, but it was better than staying where they were.

As if to prove his point, a flurry of bullets from a passing German aircraft ricocheted off the wreckage around him. The aircraft swept past, headed for the bulk of the *Victorious* behind them. The gunfire failed to strike either Wilson or himself, but Burke knew they would only be lucky so long.

The wind was causing the cables to swing this way and that, and he waited until one drifted close enough for him to lunge forward and grab hold of it. His motion caused the ruins of the firing platform to creak loudly and dip lower as the metal rail that held it bent with the pressure.

"What are you doing?" Wilson screamed at him, while trying to remain still. "Stop!"

Sorry, man, no can do, Burke thought. *We're getting our asses out of here.*

With his right hand he pulled on the cable as hard as he could, wanting to be sure it could hold his weight. It seemed fairly solid, but he wouldn't really know until he put his full weight on it.

"I'm coming to get you!" he shouted and then prepared himself for what he had to do.

"What?" Wilson cried, trying to lift his head high enough that he could see what Burke was doing. "Stay where you are! You're going to get us killed!"

But Burke was already committed to his plan. If he stopped, they'd hang there until they were either cut down by a bullet from an enemy aircraft or dropped into oblivion when the remains of the gun platform finally broke free. He had no intention of waiting around for either eventuality.

Burke pulled the cable tight and then wrapped the end of it around the outside of his forearm, making sure that it wouldn't slip through his fingers. When he was ready, he took up the slack on the rope and smashed his mechanical hand into the hook that secured his body harness to the remains of the platform.

For a second he hung there, and then the hook surrendered to the application of a more powerful force and he was suddenly swinging through the air.

The cable held the few feet it took for him to reach his target, a thick metal pipe jutting out of the opposite side of the gun cage. At the apex of his swing, he reached out his mechanical hand and clamped it tight around the pipe, securing him in place. From there it was an easy matter to find footholds for his feet and to transfer his weight to what was left of the cage rather than the cable.

For the moment, he was safe.

Wilson was staring at him, his eyes wide in horror, terrified that Burke's motions were going to shake his foot free.

From where he now clung to the side of the firing cage, Burke could look down and see Wilson about six feet below him. To rescue him, Burke was going to have to clamber down the side of the cage until he was close enough to grab the other man's leg and pull him up onto the platform.

There was only one problem. He had no idea if that section of the wreckage would hold both of their weights.

He carefully began to clamber down what was left of the metal shell toward his companion. The frame creaked and groaned beneath his weight, but otherwise seemed to hold.

Burke had managed to get to within a few feet of the other man when he noticed something ominous. The rat's nest of tangled steel and wire that Wilson's foot had caught itself upon was tearing away from the main structure. Even as Burke watched he could see it bend, the metal turning white from the strain.

Burke lunged forward, his hand outstretched and hoping for the best.

"Gotcha!" he crowed, as his fingers locked around Wilson's ankle.

Just as he did, the piece of wreckage that had held Wilson's foot suddenly broke off and fell away from the rest of the gun cage, disappearing into the abyss, leaving the chief machinist hanging by his heel from Burke's outstretched arm.

"Pull me up! Pull me up!" Wilson was screaming.

When Burke tried to do just that, he discovered a new problem. He simply didn't have the strength to pull Wilson up. It was all he could to do keep his fingers locked around the other man's ankle.

"I can't!" he yelled back. "You're going to have to do it yourself! Reach up and grab my arm and then climb up over me. Can you do that?"

The *Victorious* was still moving under her own power as the dogfight raged in the sky around her, planes wheeling about, tracers cutting the sky with sudden bright flashes of color, and Burke suspected that most of what he'd said got lost in the wind and the roar of battle. Wilson must have understood because he began to rock his upper body back and forth like a trapeze artist.

What the hell is he doing? Burke wondered and found out a moment later when Wilson suddenly arched upward, using his stomach muscles to pull himself forward.

Wilson's fear worked as a powerful motivator, for he reached all the way up and grabbed Burke's arm in the first try. Once he had a secure grip, Burke let go of his foot and Wilson was able to climb up over Burke's body until he too was clinging desperately to the metal shell of the gun cage.

That's when the platform lurched beneath them.

Both men tried to sink themselves deeper into the metal against which they clung, praying the whole thing didn't break free, and they were surprised a few moments later when they realized that the platform was moving horizontally back toward the airship's hull. It could mean only one thing; someone inside the weapon's bay must have realized they were still alive and had begun to haul them in!

The damaged platform took twice as long to go in as it had to go out. The corpse of the British gunner, one side of his head nothing but a bloody, gaping mess, that greeted them when they stumbled out of the weapons platform and onto the deck of the *Victorious* served as a stark reminder of how perilously close they had come to dying.

Wouldn't be the first time, Burke thought as he fought to control the trembling of his adrenaline-fueled limbs while pulling the goggles off his face.

A hand gripped his good arm.

"You all right?" Wilson asked.

Burke nodded, not yet trusting himself to speak.

"Good. Sit tight." Wilson got up and stumbled over to the talk box on the far wall. He spoke for a few minutes, then returned to Burke's side.

"The captain's had no choice but to make a run for the storm, hoping the weather will give us some cover and allow us to leave the enemy fighters behind."

It sounded like a reasonable plan. "Will it work?"

"See for yourself," Wilson told him, pointing back out the open bay door behind them.

They watched the firefight continue for several long moments. Just when Burke was convinced there was no way of escaping, airplanes from both sides, friend and foe alike, began turning back as the *Victorious* reached the edge of the storm and slipped inside the clouds. The British escort craft kept their focus on the German fighters, who, in turn, were more than happy to oblige them with the same level of attention. Following the *Victorious* must have looked like a losing proposition.

Burke wasn't ready to breathe a sigh of relief, however. "So what happens now?" he asked.

Wilson shrugged. "I don't know. We've never flown into a thunderstorm before."

As the crew began closing the bay doors to keep out the wind and rain, Burke turned and looked hard at Wilson. "And why's that?"

For a moment, Wilson appeared surprised at the question, and then he burst into laughter. "Bloody hell, mate!" he said. "Did you forget where you are? A lightning storm's just about the last place we'd want to be!"

That's when it hit him. They were two miles up, trapped in what was, for all practical purposes, a six-hundred-foot cigar-shaped metal cylinder that was about to double as the world's largest lightning rod!

We are so fucked.

Seeing the expression on his face, Wilson clapped him heartily on the back. "Don't worry about it, mate!" he said, with the same maddening enthusiasm he'd shown throughout the rest of the day. "We're in a giant flammable balloon. If we get hit by lightning, it will all be over so fast you won't even know it!"

For a man who'd just avoided falling thousands of feet to his death, Wilson was awfully cheery about the fact they might suddenly blow up like a giant bonfire. Unable to foster the same kind of enthusiasm for going out that way himself, Burke suggested that it might be best if he returned to the wardroom to check on his men. Once there, he brought them up to speed on what was happening, though he carefully avoided any mention of giant flammable balloons.

They had enough to worry about as it was.

CHAPTER TWENTY-TWO

✪

MOST ORDINARY GERMAN pilots wouldn't have dared to follow HMS *Victorious* as she climbed into the bank of angry storm clouds to escape the German pursuit craft, but Manfred von Richthofen was anything but ordinary.

For the last few years, he hadn't even been human.

As the rest of his squadron turned the noses of their planes away from the storm, Richthofen grinned into the face of it and sped after the British airship.

At first it wasn't bad. The Fokker D.VII he was flying was a highly maneuverable aircraft, and it handled the increased winds without difficulty, chasing after the *Victorious* like a hound on the hunt. The sheer size of the vessel made it easy at first for him to keep it in sight, and he pushed his smaller craft for all it was worth, trying to close the gap between them.

But as the airship continued its steady drive deeper into the clouds, the impact of the storm grew worse. The winds buffeted Richthofen's craft like the breath of an angry god, tossing the Fokker triplane across the sky with seeming abandon, and it took all his not inconsiderable strength to recover from the wind shear.

The winds weren't the only problem. The rain gradually changed from a light sprinkle to a steady downpour, until it was heavy enough that water began to accumulate inside the cockpit and interfere with the action of his feet on the pedals. He was forced to periodically roll the aircraft to dump the water out. His clothes were soaked through, but his resurrected body no longer felt such human frailties and he was able to ignore both the wet and the cold.

What he couldn't ignore was the growing difficulty he was having following the airship. As the storm worked to push them farther apart, the clouds began to obscure his view, hiding the larger craft in their embrace for longer periods of time. Soon he lost sight of the enemy altogether, the black thunderclouds swallowing the ship whole, like Jonah in the whale. Unable to see more than a few feet in front of him, Richthofen was reduced to flying by compass alone. He kept the nose of his plane pointed due east, the direction the airship had been going when he'd first encountered it, and he hoped the pilot of the larger craft did the same.

Lightning flashed, lighting up the clouds, and for a moment he thought he caught a glimpse of the airship ahead of him in the distance, like a behemoth rising from dark seas, there for a flash and then gone again beneath the waves. There wasn't anything he could do about it though, for he had his hands full just trying to keep his plane under control.

Just when he thought it couldn't get any worse, the rain turned to sleet and hail, pelting his aircraft with fist-sized chunks of ice, threatening its integrity by tearing through the cloth-covered wings in several places. Ice began to build up on the leading edges of his wings and at that point Richthofen knew he'd pushed things far enough. With his quarry lost from sight and the storm threatening to knock him out of the sky, he chose prudence over pursuit and concentrated on breaking free of the storm.

But the storm had other ideas.

Once it had his tiny aircraft in its grasp, it didn't want to let go. It pushed and pulled him across the sky, preventing him from making any discernible headway toward finding the edge of the storm. Thinking the winds might be reduced at a lower altitude, he pointed the nose of the plane earthward and tried to find some gentler air below, but after descending several thousand feet, it only seemed as if things had gotten worse. Frustrated, Richthofen turned the nose of his craft skyward again. If he couldn't get out from under the storm, he decided, he'd just have to climb above it.

By now even his controls were covered with a thin sheet of ice, and it took a sharp rap with his knuckles to break the coating on the face of the altimeter. He watched as the red needle spun around the dial in conjunction with his rapid climb.

Ten thousand feet.

Eleven thousand feet.

Twelve . . .

The Fokker D.VII he was flying had a maximum ceiling of just over nineteen thousand feet and he could feel the thinner air starting to have an impact on the thrust of his engines and the lift beneath the wings, but he kept going, refusing to let the storm beat him.

Thirteen.

Fourteen.

At just over fourteen thousand feet the clouds suddenly fell away beneath him and he found himself in clear blue skies. To his surprise the vast bulk of the British airship loomed only several hundred yards away, its silver skin gleaming in the light of the sun and the blue, white, and red insignia on the tail fin looking like a giant bull's-eye.

If he'd been a religious man, he would have thought the gods were smiling on him.

He emerged from the cloud bank behind and below the airship, which meant for the next few moments he would effectively be hidden in their blind spot. From his position he had a good view of the engines that jutted from beneath the tail fin of the craft. While he'd never encountered this particular model before, he knew they all operated on the same general principles. Knocking out the main engines would effectively cripple the craft, leaving it unable to do anything more than maneuver against the wind. He'd then have all the time in the world to finish it off at his leisure.

Ever the careful combatant, Richthofen held back for a few minutes, observing the airship's course and making sure that none of its escort craft had followed it into the storm. When he was certain it was on its own, he opened up the throttle and started his attack run.

The airship was moving at a leisurely pace, the captain obviously believing that the fox had outrun the hounds, and it was literally child's play for Richthofen to line up the engines in the crosshairs of his guns and pull the trigger.

Tracers arced out across the sky as the twin Spandau guns spit bullets in the direction of the *Victorious* at a rate of four thousand rounds per minute, tearing into the engines and shredding their interior components into useless scrap. The airship visibly lurched as the thrust from the engines was cut off in midstream and great billowing clouds of black smoke began to spill forth.

Richthofen let up on the guns and shot past the twin gondolas hanging from the bottom of the airship, getting a good look inside each one as he did. The stern gondola was empty, but he was able to see the crew in the bow gondola quite clearly and smiled in response to the collective expression of fear he saw on their faces as he swept past. He knew they recognized his aircraft; after all, there was only one Fokker D.VII painted bloodred at a time in Jagdgeschwader I, never mind in the entire Imperial German Army Air Service. The psychological impact of that recognition was why he had ordered all the planes in the Flying Circus painted in such brilliant colors. He wanted the enemy to know that the ace of aces, the Red Baron himself, had them in his sights and it was only a matter of time before they would fall beneath his guns. Their fear would cause them to make mistakes, and he would use those mistakes to his advantage, hastening their demise.

Grinning wickedly in anticipation of what was to come, Richthofen arced away from the British airship, swinging around for another pass.

CHAPTER TWENTY-THREE

HMS *Victorious*

WITHOUT WARNING, THE airship rocked beneath their feet as if struck by a great blow. A couple of the men were thrown to the deck, and Burke would have followed suit if Charlie hadn't shot out a hand to steady him.

The men were quiet as they climbed to their feet, their expressions strained. It was one thing to face the enemy in the mud and muck of the trenches, where you could see who was shooting at you and even fire back when the opportunity presented itself. Being trapped here, inside the belly of the beast, unable to see or hear what was going on outside the airship, brought its own kind of anxiety.

Unable to say anything to reassure his men, Burke simply gave orders for them to secure themselves. For the next several minutes they all held on tightly as the airship careened this way and that, clearly trying to evade some external enemy that they, locked in the heart of the vessel, couldn't see. Their inability to know what was happening was maddening to Burke, so much so that he was beginning to wish he was back out on the firing platform as he'd been during the first assault. At least then he'd been able to see Death coming for him and not have to stare at the blank wardroom walls and wonder if he had only minutes left to live.

The ship was struck by another hammer blow, stronger this time, and the thunder of an accompanying explosion reached them from somewhere to the rear of their tiny compartment. Only Burke's earlier command to secure themselves kept the men from being tossed about like confetti. Rather than righting itself, this time the *Victorious* stayed skewed off center keel and pointed at a downward angle.

Charlie looked over at Burke.

"That can't be good!" he said.

Burke just nodded his agreement.

Seconds later a siren began to wail, filling the room with its banshee voice, letting anyone who hadn't already guessed know that they were under attack.

Having been through this once before, the men in the squad knew there wasn't anything they could do but lie there and hope for the best. As untrained and unfamiliar with the workings of the ship as they were, they knew they would just be in the way if they tried to help, and they accepted the fact that they should remain in the room out of the way.

But for Burke, who had been involved in the last dogfight and hadn't had to get used to lying on a bunk and praying for the best, the inactivity was intolerable.

"I can't take this anymore!" he exclaimed. He headed across the room to the control panel beneath the talk box. He was sitting in the operator's chair, fiddling with the dials and switches.

"What are you doing?" Charlie asked, joining him.

Burke didn't look up from the control board. "Trying to contact the bridge to find out what the hell is going on out there." His voice was full of confidence, but the truth was he didn't have a clue what he was doing. He was just throwing switches with his good hand and hoping to get lucky.

Charlie wasn't fooled. "Not like that," he said. "You're doing it all wrong. Here, get out of the way."

Burke got up out of the chair and Charlie slipped in behind him, running deft hands over the control panel. Within seconds they could hear everything that was going on inside the forward gondola thanks to the open channel.

It was like listening to a radio show, but one Burke hoped never to hear again.

Men were shouting, some issuing orders, others screaming in pain. Cries of "Doctor! Doctor!" were mixed up with warnings that "He's coming about again!" whoever "he" might be, and these were interspersed with the blaring of the siren that signaled they were under attack.

For a moment Burke could hear the captain shouting orders to take evasive action, and then everything was drowned beneath a cacophony of machine-gun fire and breaking glass.

In the aftermath of the gunfire, the only sounds that could be heard were the moaning of the wind and the hiss of static over the open line.

Charlie called out over the open mike several times, trying to reach anyone who might still be alive, to no avail.

"Now what?" Williams asked into the silence.

As if in reply, the door to the wardroom flew open, revealing Chief Wilson's compact form standing in the entrance. He didn't waste any time with pleasantries.

"We're going down," he told them. "I've been ordered to get you off this ship before we crash. Grab whatever equipment you can and come with me. Quickly!"

The squad didn't need to be told twice. Fighting against the tilt of the ship and the downward slope of the floor, they scrambled to grab their gear and follow Burke out the door.

Having expected Wilson to lead them forward toward the main gondola, Burke was surprised when the chief turned aft instead, requiring them to fight against gravity as they headed toward the engine room. Because of the incline they were forced to grab on to the guide ropes and literally pull themselves hand over hand up the treacherously canted walkway. One slip was all it would take to send a man tumbling into the steel structure of the airship's frame, and getting him out again would be an absolute bitch, so Burke kept a watchful eye on the men as they climbed ahead of him.

Chief Wilson led them up the central catwalk, past the various storage rooms they'd noted on their arrival, and into the cargo bay through which they'd entered the ship earlier that morning. Inside they found several of the ship's mechanics using crowbars to lever open a group of wooden crates, each one marked with the Military Intelligence Division's seal.

Burke had no idea what was in the crates, but Graves apparently did. When he saw what they were doing, the professor began to protest furiously.

"No! No! No!" he cried, rushing forward and waving his hands in front of him to emphasize his point. "Those shouldn't be here! I demand you stop what you are doing right this instant!"

The professor's energetic appearance caused the workers to pause, but when they caught Wilson's stern look over the other man's shoulder, they went right back to unpacking whatever it was that the crates contained.

"What are you doing?" Graves cried, rounding on the chief machinist. "Those are experimental devices that require extensive training to operate. I can't allow them to be used in a situation like this!"

Wilson didn't budge. "You don't have a choice," he said bluntly. "We're going down, and we're going down *quickly*. If you don't use those gizmos to get off this ship, you might not get off it at all. Is that clear enough for you?"

As his words sank in, the professor's expression went from outrage to abject horror.

The chief machinist steamrollered on as if he hadn't noticed. "My orders are to get you off this ship, and that's what I plan to do. We can do it the easy way or we can do it the hard way. I don't bloody care which. But you will be going, one way or another."

It was clear from the professor's expression that he wasn't used to taking orders, never mind taking them from someone outside his chain of command, but he clearly wasn't about to argue with the burly chief either. The man outweighed him by a good fifty pounds, and Wilson's manner said he wasn't about to take any crap from a scarecrow like Graves.

But Burke couldn't let it go that easily.

Get off the ship? How the hell were they supposed to do that? And what was in those crates?

"Now hold on a minute, Chief," he said, stepping between the two men in an effort to get things to calm down a bit. "I appreciate that you have your orders, but I have mine as well and I haven't heard anything about where or when we're supposed to land."

"That's because we're not. Landing, that is."

Burke took a step back in confusion. "Then how do you expect us to get off the ship?"

"With those," Wilson said grimly, pointing at the device two of his men were just now lifting out of one of the crates.

From what Burke could see, it had started life as a regulation greatcoat but it had evolved into something else entirely from there. For one thing, the metal frame of what he took to be a haversack had been sewn into the lining of the coat, with a variety of straps and buckles hanging from both lapels and a complicated structure of pipes and wires rising over each shoulder. Squares of what looked to be darkened glass, each one about three inches across, now covered the outside of the coat's sleeves. The squares caught the light of the cargo bay and reflected it back in scintillating colors.

As if that wasn't strange enough, there were the long rectangular planks of some reddish-black colored metal that were connected to the pipes jutting out of the back of the jacket. Each plank overlapped the one beside it, fanning out from the center in ever-increasing lengths like the feathers on the tail of a hawk.

"What the hell is *that*?" Burke asked.

Wilson opened his mouth, but Graves beat him to it.

"It's a man-portable person gliding device, or MPPGD for short."

"Uh-huh," Burke replied. "And that means what, exactly?"

"Think of it as your own personal flying device," Graves answered, with no small amount of pride, as he walked over and slipped his arms through the sleeves of the coat. He braced himself against its weight as the two men holding the device settled it on his shoulders. Graves began buckling the straps across his chest with the ease of long practice. "It is designed to use air currents in order to carry a man from a higher altitude to a lower one."

"Sounds like falling to me," one of the airmen quipped.

Burke thought so, too.

"It's not falling," Graves said, scowling in the airman's direction, "so much as a controlled descent. When fully extended, the wings will catch the air beneath them and provide lift, allowing the user to glide for an extended period, much like a flying squirrel does when jumping from tree to tree."

A flying squirrel? Burke thought. *Are you kidding me?*

He grabbed Graves by the arm and pulled him to one side, out of hearing of the rest of the men in the squad.

"Cut the crap, Professor. Do these things work—yes or no?"

"Yes. But . . ."

"But what?"

"But I've only tested them at an altitude of a few hundred feet. The air is much colder up here and that could significantly affect flight characteristics and overall lift."

"So you're saying they won't work?"

"No," the professor replied, clearly growing more anxious as the conversation continued. "I'm saying I have no data one way or the other on which to make an intelligent decision. They might work just fine, perhaps even better than anticipated. Then again, they could fail miserably and end up splattering us all over the landscape as a result. I just don't know."

Another shudder ran through the vessel around them, and Burke knew he was running out of time. He needed an answer and he needed it quickly.

"You built these things, right?" he asked.

At Graves's answering nod he said, "Then you know their capabilities better than anyone else. What's your best guess? Will they work? Yes or no?"

"If I had more time to test them . . ."

"You don't. We're falling out of the sky as we speak, Professor. Yes or no? *Will they work?*"

Burke didn't know if it was his insistence on an answer or the way the *Victorious* suddenly heeled over another ten degrees before rolling back up a little, but either way, Graves finally made his decision.

"Yes," he said. Then with a bit more confidence, "Yes. They'll work."

"Good man," Burke told him, praying as he did so that the other man was right.

At least we won't feel it for very long if he's not.

CHAPTER TWENTY-FOUR

★

In the Wild Blue Yonder

GRAVES GAVE THEM all a thirty-second crash course on how to operate the funny-looking devices. While they appeared rather complex at first glance, their use actually turned out to be quite simple.

The MPPGD was essentially just a big coat with metal wings. At this height the air was too thin to provide enough lift, so they would free-fall for several seconds before deploying the wings. To do so against the force of the air through which they were falling, they needed a sudden sharp burst of energy. That's where the second part of the device came into play. The glasslike tiles sewn into the sleeves of the coats were designed to pull electrical current out of the air as it rushed over them. When a strong enough charge had been built up, the globe attached to the belt running across the center of the chest would glow an electric blue, indicating it was safe to activate the wings. At that point the operator was supposed to slap the globe with the flat of his hand, releasing the charge into the electrical conduits running through the frame to the control box in the center of the backpack. This in turn would open the wings with a snap, and the resulting lift caused by the air rushing over the flat surface of the wings would allow the operator to glide for great distances.

When the wings extended, two control arms would drop down in front of the pilot. To maneuver, all the pilot had to do was pull down on one control arm or the other, depending on which direction he wanted to go. Landing was achieved by pushing forward on both arms at the same time; this would raise the nose of the glider and spill the air out from beneath the wing, stalling it.

There was just one critical command to remember.

"Don't hit the charge release too early," Graves cautioned. "If you do, you'll waste the energy buildup and the capacitors will need to charge themselves all over again. Depending on how close you are to the ground, you might have time to complete the recharging process before you strike the ground at terminal velocity and become part of the local terrain. Then again, you might not."

Burke stepped in at that point and addressed the men. "I'll be going first, so keep your eyes on me and make sure you don't trigger your wings before the man in front of you. If something goes wrong, don't panic, just wait for the charge to build up and try again."

And pray, he thought to himself.

"I want you all to watch the wings of the man in front of you and try to head in the same direction he's going. Once on the ground, we'll regroup and get ourselves organized before heading out. If you get separated from the group, don't waste time searching for us, just head to the rendezvous point and we'll meet there. Questions?"

Thankfully, there weren't any. Burke didn't know if he could have answered them if there were. Jumping out of the airship while wearing an experimental flying device wasn't high on his list of things to do in this lifetime, and he had to work hard to keep that from showing on his face. The doubt he saw on some of the other men's faces told him they were thinking the same thing.

They were soldiers, though, and he expected them to do exactly what soldiers had been doing since the invention of warfare—follow orders.

Wilson's crew worked diligently to get them all strapped into their rigs, double-checking the harness buckles and safety belts. The airmen also spent some time rigging the extra crates of equipment and supplies into something called a parachute. Burke had never heard of such a thing, but when they were explained to him, he wondered why they weren't using those instead of the MP-PGD. There would be less of a chance for a mechanical malfunction to occur if they were using equipment with no moving parts. Or at least it seemed that way to Burke.

Apparently, he wasn't thinking of the bigger picture.

"Your rate of descent will be several times faster by using the MPPGD," the professor explained. "That will take you through the lightning storm quicker and make you less of a target for any enemy aircraft that might still be lingering about."

Graves seemed insulted that Burke would even consider a different method after having the MPPGD explained to him. "If you prefer the parachute, I'm sure the chief can get you one," he said, and a bit snidely at that.

Burke shook his head. He didn't care about offending Graves, but it was the thought of hanging there, unable to do anything but wait to get struck by lightning, that turned the tide in favor of the glider gizmos. The faster he was able to get his feet on solid ground, the happier he would be.

When they were ready, the squad assembled near the cargo hatch they'd used to enter the ship.

Burke's on-the-spot decision to go first had been motivated by his desire to lead by example. He didn't believe in asking his men to do anything that he wasn't willing and ready to do himself, a principle that became particularly important in situations like this. He knew from past experience that leading in this way would make it easier for the men to step up later if the need arose. Once that decision had been made, it also made sense to leave Sergeant Moore and the professor to bring up the rear; the professor could answer any equipment-related questions that might arise from the rest of the team and Charlie could make sure the others listened when the professor spoke.

When Burke was ready, Chief Wilson ordered the cargo bay doors to be opened and then escorted Burke over to the drop position. Behind them, the rest of the team was lining up, getting ready for their respective turn in the shoot.

"We're going to be leaving a ten-second window between jumpers," Wilson told him. "That will keep anyone from accidentally jumping too close to the man ahead while also limiting the size of the area your team will be spread across when you reach the ground."

Burke nodded to show he understood as he fought to calm his pounding heart. Just a few hours before, he'd done everything he could to keep from taking a swan dive off the ship and now here he was getting ready to voluntarily do the very thing he'd fought so hard to prevent. The irony of his situation was not lost on him.

With a clank that startled him, the bay doors in the floor in front of him began to slowly draw apart, revealing the thick thunderclouds through which the airship was rapidly descending. The wind howled, buffeting Burke where he stood just a foot away from the opening and making it difficult to hear. Lightning flashed, lighting up the clouds, and Burke began having second thoughts.

"Steady on, mate," Wilson shouted while clamping a reassuring hand onto his shoulder. "Once you get through the cloud cover, everything will be much better. Just keep your head on your shoulders and you should be fine."

Right.

A thought suddenly occurred to him.

"What about you?" Burke shouted. "How are you going to get off the ship before she goes down?"

Wilson eyeballed the MPPGD one last time and then leaned in close so he wouldn't have to shout over the sound of the wind.

"We're not," he told him. "Captain's decided we'll ride it out and hope for the best, see if anything's salvageable once we're on the ground."

At Burke's look of disbelief, Wilson said, "Don't worry. She's a hardy gal. We should make it down all right. If you ever make it to Liverpool after the war, look me up. I owe you a beer after that cock-up earlier today."

If the *Victorious* was in so much danger that Burke and his men were being forced to abandon ship, it didn't seem likely the captain would be able to get her on the ground intact. Still, Burke agreed he'd do so and shook the man's hand. There really wasn't anything else to say.

Good-byes over, he faced forward, took a deep breath, and then calmly stepped off into space.

CHAPTER TWENTY-FIVE

FREE FALL

Burke fell.

He dropped away from the *Victorious* with his heart in his throat, suddenly terrified that Graves's device wouldn't work and he would end up crashing down to earth, a modern-day Icarus with wings of brass and iron replacing those of feathers and wax.

The wind howled in his ears and it was hard to breathe, both because of the thinness of the air and the fact that it seemed like a living thing, cramming itself up his nostrils and down his throat, filling the space whether he wanted it to or not.

After a few seconds, the sensation of falling diminished, replaced instead by the sensation of being buoyed up by the very air through which he sped. It was an oddly curious sensation, one that was heightened by the thick cloud cover that he was descending through.

Unable to see much of anything but the air a few feet in front of him, he focused instead on the small squares of glasslike material sewn into the arms of his jacket. Nothing was happening. They looked the same as they had the moment he'd jumped out of the airship.

Then, little by little, the squares began to glow deep down in their centers, as they sucked the electrical charge out of the air as it whistled over his body. Burke stretched his arms out ahead of him, trying to expose as many of the squares to the passage of the wind as possible, praying that all Graves's calculations had been correct.

If they were not, and the charging device failed as a result, it was going to be a long way down.

As the squares collected power, brilliant blue sparks of electrical current began to jump between them. The glow grew brighter, the sparks moved faster, and just when he began to worry about having all that electrical current dancing around so close to his skin, the activation light in the center of his harness sprang to life. He didn't hesitate, just smashed the button with his right hand and braced himself for the wings to open.

Nothing happened.

You have got to be shitting me.

Telling himself not to panic, a decidedly uneasy task when he felt like he was falling through the air with all the artfulness of a brick, he looked down at the round switch and saw that it was still glowing bright blue. Apparently, he hadn't dissipated the charge with his failed attempt to activate the wings, so he tried again. This time he held the button down, praying it just needed more time to send the necessary signal.

With a snap loud enough to be heard over the wind rushing in his face, the layers of metal jutting out from the pack on his back extended, spreading open like an oriental fan. It caught the air currents with nary an effort, and Burke went from falling through the sky like a dropped stone to swooping over the countryside with grace, riding the wind the way a surfer rides the crest of a wave.

He did as Graves instructed, pulling down on one side of the harness. That caused the wing to dip slightly, which in turn put him into a long, gentle spiral that was designed to carry him the rest of the way to the ground without mishap. He made a couple of turns, and then suddenly the earth spread out before him like a giant patchwork quilt as the cloud cover broke for a moment, letting him catch a glimpse of his destination far below.

That view was all it took. In that moment all of Burke's fear evaporated and in its place rose such a feeling of wonder and amazement the likes of which he hadn't experienced since he was a young boy. Aircraft hadn't even been invented when he was a boy and now here he was, gliding through the air with the greatest of ease, a mechanical angel adrift in the heavens.

He was flying! Really flying!

He laughed aloud at the wonder of it all.

Unfortunately, his joy didn't last long.

The *Victorious* hove into view several hundred yards away, her bow pointed earthward as she plunged past on what could only be her final flight. Burke could see that the airship's tail section was ablaze, the fire eating away at her glistening skin and revealing the blackened steel of her frame, and he was amazed that she hadn't already exploded. Even in her current condition she was fighting to stay aloft, but that one look was all it took for Burke to know that this was a battle she would not, could not, win. The pride of the British air fleet was going down and there was nothing anyone could do about it.

While the sight of the dying airship was certainly enough to dampen one's spirits, it was the glimpse of the enemy aircraft following in the *Victorious*'s wake, the black crosses standing out sharply against the red paint of its wings, that was even more sobering. Unarmed as they were, Burke and his men would be sitting ducks if the pilot chose to come after them. He had no idea if the enemy had witnessed their evacuation of the airship, but he couldn't afford not to take the possibility into account and was therefore forced to act as if they *had* been spotted.

They had to get down while they still had the chance!

Burke pointed the nose of the glider earthward and increased the angle of attack between the edge of the glider's wing and the air passing over it, tightening the circumference of the circle he was following while increasing his rate of descent. He kept his eyes peeled for the enemy aircraft, expecting it to come charging out of the clouds at any minute, machine guns firing, and he didn't take his eyes off the horizon around him until he drew so close to the earth that he had no choice but to pay attention to the landing ahead of him.

As he drew closer, he began to make out the details of the terrain below and was not encouraged by what he saw. The rolling green grassland he'd been hoping for was nowhere in sight; in its place was the war-torn, crater-filled wasteland. He could see old trench lines and fortifications strewn willy-nilly across the area, and in more than one place the seemingly endless spring rains had flooded a section until it looked like a small lake. He steered for the flattest section he could see and hoped for the best.

He couldn't do anything else.

The ground was coming up quickly now, and he mentally reviewed the landing sequence Graves had taught them, knowing he had only one chance to get it right. So far they'd been lucky but that could all change in an instant, and a broken ankle would be just the kind of thing that would send their carefully made plans into the shitter and compromise the mission overall.

Closer . . . closer . . .

He shifted his weight and brought his legs up in front of him, flaring the nose of the glider upward and using the wing on his back as a primitive braking device, praying he wouldn't overdo it and end up flipping over.

Closer . . .

He hit the ground with both feet churning and kept running forward, not wanting the weight of the glider to come down on top of him, especially at the speed he was moving. For a second the glider stayed horizontal to the ground, then gravity took over and began to pull it the final few feet earthward. By that point Burke was ready for it, however, and he tipped the wings on their side and let it slide across the earth until it hit a rock and brought him up short, panting from the exertion.

He stood there with his hands on his knees and his body leaning toward the wing of the glider, pulled by the harness he still wore, and took a moment to catch his breath.

Once he had, he unbuckled the straps, slipped out of the jacket, and stepped away from the MPPGD. He looked skyward and was relieved to see the other gliders on their way down; he hadn't realized how concerned he'd been about being trapped behind enemy lines alone until he saw them descending toward him. He could also see, higher above the gliders, the twin parachutes that held his supply cache.

So far, so good.

Burke watched the first two men in his squad come in for a landing—neither of them would have won any points for style but they ended up on the ground uninjured—and then he turned his attention back to the MPPGD.

They couldn't afford to leave the devices where they might be discovered by the enemy, so the decision had been made to bury them at the landing site. Burke pressed a trigger on the rear of the device and watched in satisfaction as the wing folded back in on itself, reducing its size by at least half. After that it was simply a matter of pulling out his entrenching tool and getting to work.

When he was finished with his efforts, he moved on to help the next nearest member of his team. In this fashion they quickly completed the work, until they were all gathered together around the professor's glider.

That's when Jones asked the question of the day.

"Where the hell is Strauss?"

CHAPTER TWENTY-SIX

Behind the Lines

ACCORDING TO SERGEANT Moore, Strauss had exited the airship as planned and had correctly deployed his MPPGD. He entered a cloud bank shortly after that, however, at which point Charlie lost sight of him. In the effort to get the gliders under cover before they could be spotted from the air by enemy aircraft, no one had noticed he wasn't with them.

Burke suspected that Strauss had come down too quickly, perhaps even crashing into a bomb crater or an old trench line, and been knocked unconscious, so he sent the men out looking for him. It was in the midst of the search that they discovered another piece of bad news.

Burke was walking along the edge of a series of bomb craters when he heard his name being called. Hopeful that some sign of Strauss had been found, he jogged ahead to where he found Private Williams and Corporal Jones standing atop a small ridgeline. They were looking at something on the other side, and from the expressions on their faces it wasn't good news.

"Did you find him? Did you find Strauss?" Burke asked as he climbed to meet them.

"Nope," Jones answered in his usual laconic style, "found our supplies. You're not going to like it, though."

When Burke got his first glance at what lay on the other side of the ridge, he knew Jones was right.

He stared down into an enormous crater and estimated it to be at least a hundred feet across and a good twenty feet deep, though it was hard to pinpoint the latter because it was three-quarters of the way filled with brackish water the color of rust. To make matters worse, there was a thick, oily-looking film covering much of the water's surface, the detritus of too many gas attacks in too short a period. The stuff was clearly toxic, for the edges of the makeshift "lake" were littered with the carcasses of rats, birds, and other small animals.

Their supply crates had come down smack-dab in the middle of it all. Or, at least, he thought they had. Right now all he could see were the two parachutes, bobbing gently in the contaminated water.

"Shit!" Burke swore, once he'd taken a good look.

He couldn't think of any way to recover the crates. Not with the materials they had on hand, at least. Even if they were able to figure something out, the supplies they needed would no doubt be ruined by the time they managed to get the crates to shore. The crates weren't waterproof, and from the look of things, the water they'd fallen into was toxic in more ways than one.

It was a setback, and a big one, too. Losing Strauss, their linguist, was bad, yes, but losing those crates was damn near catastrophic, for they held almost all the food and water, never mind the vast majority of ammunition.

He sent Williams to round up the rest of the men and figure out just how much food and water each man was carrying. In the meantime, Burke sat down with the map and tried to figure out exactly where they were. Based on the relative speed and position of the *Victorious* when they had abandoned ship, he estimated that they were about ten miles from where they were supposed to be after disembarking from the airship. That meant that the farmhouse where they were meeting the French partisans was at least twelve, maybe as many as fourteen miles from their current position.

Originally, the plan was for them to land, make their way cross-country to the farmhouse, and lay low until the partisans arrived sometime that evening. Burke would have preferred arriving under the cover of darkness, but he understood why they hadn't; even the bravest of men would have quaked at the idea of paragliding down from the *Victorious* in complete darkness.

The plan had clearly gone to hell in a handbasket. There was no way they were going to make it to the farmhouse by nightfall, not with a hump of that distance in front of them. Best they could do was get there as quickly as possible and hope the French were still there waiting when they arrived. If they were, the team could resupply and not worry about the gear they had lost.

If they weren't . . . well, he'd worry about that when the time came.

By the time he'd finished planning their route, the rest of the men had assembled around him at the bottom of the ridge. He explained the situation, and they did a quick inventory of supplies. The corned beef and hardtack the men carried in their personal kits would get them through the next two days, as would the water they carried in their two canteens.

Weapons and ammunition were a mixed bag. Each man had several full clips for his rifle, with Burke and Moore carrying three drums apiece for the Tommy guns. Burke also had the Firestarter and its sixteen rounds of ammo. Jones had been carrying the mortar tube strapped to his pack, but Compton had only been carrying four of its projectiles. The rest were no doubt at the bottom of the lake. Burke wasn't happy. If they ran into trouble, something that was all but guaranteed given how far behind enemy lines they were, they had enough ammunition to fight back for only a few minutes, at best.

Hopefully, they would be able to resupply once they hooked up with the partisans.

With no sign of Strauss and no way of recovering their supplies from the middle of the lake, Burke made the decision to get the team under way. Staying in one place for too long wasn't a tactically intelligent move, especially if that fighter pilot witnessed them bailing out of the *Victorious*.

He took one final glance at the map and got the squad moving.

THE TERRAIN PROVED difficult to negotiate. The landscape was littered with old trenches and bomb craters, both big and small. The misshapen contours of the ground made travel slow and difficult; Burke half expected one of them to tumble into an unseen ditch and wind up with a broken ankle or leg. They'd been hiking cross-country for almost an hour when Manning gave a short exclamation of surprise and hustled over to the edge of a shallow crater. Jutting out of it were the remains of Strauss's glider.

Manning was carefully examining the ground at the edge of the crater when Burke and the rest of the squad approached. The big game hunter held up his hand, signaling that they should hold back, and they stopped a few feet away.

From where he stood Burke could see that the glider looked more or less intact. It had a long tear in one of the wings, but that was all. It wasn't enough to cause the glider to crash, even if it happened in midflight, which Burke didn't believe it had. It was much more likely to have resulted from a poorly executed landing than anything else.

Manning seemed to think so, too. "The area right around the wreckage is a bit of a mess, but we've got one clear set of tracks leading off in this direction. Standard army-issue boot print, so it must be Strauss."

Burke put Manning on point, and the squad headed off in the same direction as the tracks. They hadn't gone more than a hundred yards before they found Strauss's backpack.

Or, what was left of it, rather.

The pack had been shredded, its contents strewn over the space of a half-dozen feet. While the rest of the men were passing it back and forth among them, examining the long narrow tears through the tough material, Manning called Burke a few yards farther down the trail and pointed out several sets of new tracks that had converged on Strauss's.

"Looks like at least four, maybe as many as six," Manning said quietly.

"Human?" Burke asked.

The other man shook his head. "I don't think so. At least not after seeing the condition of that pack."

It wasn't what Burke wanted to hear, and it certainly wasn't good news for their missing private. Strauss had a chance against a squad of human soldiers, maybe even a lone shambler or two, but a pack of shamblers was more than a man of his experience could be expected to handle.

Burke got the squad under way once more, moving faster this time, hoping they might catch up to their errant squad mate before it was too late.

Only a few minutes up the trail, however, the late morning quiet was split by a scream of pain. It hung in the air for a moment and then died, too quick for any of them to get a fix on its location.

"Did you hear that?" Williams asked, his voice trembling with tension as he glanced around, trying to pinpoint where the scream had come from.

Burke had, but he'd been no more successful than any of the others in pinpointing the location. He turned in a slow circle, listening carefully, waiting to see if it would come again.

When it did, it was followed by a shouted plea for help.

Strauss!

Manning gestured for his attention, and Burke hurried over to him.

"It's coming from over there," Manning said, and Burke took him at his word. The man had been hunting big game for years and was the most experienced in the squad for this kind of thing.

"Lead on," Burke told him.

Moving as quickly and as quietly as they could, the squad followed Manning as he made his way closer to the source. They hadn't gone more than another dozen feet before the scream came again, louder, and this time it continued, a long ululating wail that made the hair on the back of Burke's neck stand up straight.

Manning led them around a series of bomb craters to where some low hills rose ahead of them. The screaming seemed to be coming from the far side, so Manning led them up the low-grade slope toward the top. Near the top he frantically motioned them down to the ground and waited for Burke to crawl forward to meet him.

"It's definitely Strauss," Manning told him quietly.

With the man's screams ringing in his ears, Burke lifted his head up over the edge of the ridge and looked down into the hollow on the other side.

That one glance was enough to sear the horror of what he was seeing into his memory forever.

Corporal Strauss was stretched out on the dirt in the center of the hollow, surrounded by shamblers and screaming in pain as they feasted on his body. Even as Burke looked on, one of the creatures reached inside a large hole in Strauss's abdomen and pulled out a stretch of intestine before sinking its teeth into the ropelike organ to more of Strauss's screams.

Burke had to turn away lest he lose what little was in his stomach. Jones came up beside, took a look for himself, and then whispered a horrified "Sweet Mother Mary!" as he, too, saw what was going on.

It was a bitch of a situation, and Burke didn't immediately know what to do about it. On one hand Strauss was as good as dead already. Even if he survived the feeding, which at this point didn't look likely, he'd be dead from the infection that often followed a shambler bite in less than a day. It was not a pleasant way to go.

Neither is being eaten alive, his subconscious reminded him.

Which was precisely the reason that they couldn't let Strauss continue to suffer.

The problem was the shamblers.

There were at least six of them, maybe more; it was hard to tell with them bunched up around Strauss the way they were. The minute Burke and his men took action to deliver Strauss from his painful misery, they would be alerting the shamblers to their presence. Despite the horror of what he'd been looking at, Burke hadn't missed a vital fact.

These were no ordinary shamblers.

Their motions while feeding were too controlled, their balance and coordination too fine for them to be average run-of-the-mill shamblers. If they had been, they'd have ripped Strauss's throat out the moment they'd dragged him to the ground. The way these creatures were intentionally feeding on the nonvital parts of his body, thereby keeping him alive in the process, was evidence in Burke's eyes that they possessed a rudimentary level of intelligence at the very least, and perhaps one considerably more advanced than that.

Taking action would put the men in danger from the shamblers in the hollow ahead of them, but walking away would earn him the enmity and disrespect of his men, which would probably do more to derail the success of their mission than anything short of getting killed.

Never mind that the shamblers would probably hunt them down if they didn't deal with them here and now.

When he opened his eyes, he found the men watching him closely. He quickly explained what was happening.

"We can't just leave him like that," Compton said, voicing what the others must have been thinking as they watched Burke wrestle with the decision.

"I don't intend to," Burke replied, and he felt rather than saw the collective sigh of relief that went up from the men in the group. They knew the potential consequences and still they were willing to take the risk to help one of their own, even if it was just to put him out of his misery.

It was a good sign.

Burke beckoned them all in closer, so he could keep his voice down while he explained what they were going to do. He had no idea how good the creatures' hearing might be, so he wasn't taking any chances.

"I'm going to take care of Strauss," he told them. "But when I do so, we're going to attract the attention of those shamblers. It can't be helped; we can't leave one of our own out there like that."

There were grunts of agreement from around the circle.

"So here's what I want you all to do . . ."

It took a few moments for them all to get into position. Burke remained where he was, with Jones on one side and Manning on the other. The other four split into pairs of two—Compton and Williams, Moore and Graves—and circled around the outer edges of the hollow, one set to the left and one to the right. They settled down along the rim, slightly downslope so they couldn't be seen, and took aim, waiting for the signal to fire.

Burke had swapped his Thompson submachine gun for Compton's Lee Enfield, as he needed a precision weapon for what he was about to do and the trench sweeper was anything but. Resting the butt of the weapon against his shoulder, Burke eased the muzzle over the lip of the hill and carefully lined up the sight at the end of the barrel with a spot in the center of Strauss's forehead.

He felt Jones and Manning adjust their positions on either side of him.

Strauss was thrashing around, screaming and wailing in pain as the creatures continued to tear into his flesh, and Burke was amazed that he hadn't passed out from the pain. What Burke had to do would have been much easier if Strauss had been immobile, and for a second Burke thought about asking one of the other two men beside him to take the shot. Their marksmanship, particularly with the Lee Enfield, was far more accurate than his own and they'd have a better chance of succeeding with just the single shot he wanted to take, but he couldn't bring himself to do it. As commanding officer, Strauss was his responsibility.

"Steady," he said softly.

One of the shamblers feeding on Strauss must have struck a nerve bundle, for Strauss suddenly raised his head, shrieking at the top of his lungs, and Burke saw his chance. For just a moment, he had an unobstructed view of his target.

"Now!"

Burke squeezed the Lee Enfield's trigger, sending a .303-inch cartridge whistling toward its target at a muzzle velocity of 2,441 meters per second. In the blink of an eye, a round red hole appeared in the center of Strauss's forehead and he abruptly stopped screaming.

The crack of Burke's rifle was still expanding into the open air when Jones and Manning joined the fray. A well-trained soldier could fire up to thirty rounds per minute, a practice commonly known as the "mad minute," with a Lee Enfield rifle, and consummate marksmen that they were, Burke's two companions were no exception. They poured shot after well-placed shot down onto the creatures in that hollow, targeting the creatures' skulls to be certain they didn't get back up at a later time. Bone exploded and blood flew in the wake of their accuracy. When the rest of the squad joined in, it became a veritable free-for-all.

The shamblers reacted just as Burke suspected they would, scattering in every direction quicker than he thought possible and charging the men's positions at the rim of the crater. Thankfully none of the shamblers made it past the first ten feet.

In seconds it was over.

The stink of blood and cordite filled the air as they cautiously made their way down toward the bodies. The corpses of the shamblers were cautiously checked to be certain that they were well and truly dead. Two quick shots finished off the ones that were discovered to be still moving.

Burke advanced on Strauss's body and took care of the business of removing one of the young man's identification tags, small metal disks worn around the neck that contained the surname and serial number of the soldier in question, leaving the other to be buried with the body. He had no idea if anyone would ever come to recover the man's remains, but if they did, Burke wanted them to know exactly whose remains they were looking at. He looked for Strauss's gun but didn't see it. *Probably lost it when he was first attacked*, he thought. He went through Strauss's pockets, removing a pocket watch, a rosary, and a half-written letter on a piece of folded stationery, all of which would be sent back to his family. He took the ammo from Strauss's ammo belt and distributed it among the men.

With the necessary tasks handled, the men picked up Strauss's body and carried it out of the crater and away from the sight of the attack. They found a nice spot a hundred yards away in the shade of a tree where they laid him down on the grass. In unspoken agreement, the men pulled out their entrenching tools and began to dig a grave deep enough to keep his remains out of the hands of roving animals, including shamblers. When they were finished, they laid him in the depths of the hole and gently covered him up, stacking a pile of loose rocks over the earth to provide a further layer of protection.

Corporal Compton pulled his Bible out of his uniform pocket and read from it in a clear, calm voice.

"There is a time for everything, and a season for every activity under heaven," he began, his voice growing strong with every passing word. "A time to be born and a time to die; a time to plant and a time to uproot; a time to kill and a time to heal; a time to tear down and a time to build; a time to weep and a time to laugh; a time to mourn and a time to dance; a time to scatter stones and a time to gather them; a time to embrace and a time to refrain; a time to search and a time to give up; a time to keep and a time to throw away; a time to tear and a time to mend; a time to be silent and a time to speak; a time to love and a time to hate," he said, then paused just slightly before stating the last line, "a time for war and a time for peace."

Ain't that the truth, Burke thought as he turned away from the grave and got the team marching forward once more. They still had a long way to go to make the rendezvous with the partisans, and time wasn't about to wait for them.

CHAPTER TWENTY-SEVEN

⭐

RICHTHOFEN STALKED DOWN the hallway, the heels of his flight boots knocking against the marble floor. The scowl on his face had the servants scurrying out of his way the moment they laid eyes on him, leaving him to find his way to the grand hall on his own. He barely noticed, his thoughts elsewhere.

He'd had been plagued with an odd sense of restlessness since his duel with the American ace, Freeman, three days before. He'd tried to drown the feeling in activity, going out on patrol at all hours of the day and night, a routine made easier by the fact that he no longer had need of sleep since arising as a revenant, but even that was unsatisfying. Where before he'd met each new combat patrol with an air of expectation, hoping each time that he would meet a pilot worthy of his opposition, now he simply went through the motions, racking up an impressive number of kills, eleven in two days, but without the satisfaction that usually came along with them. Even the massive British airship he'd taken down that morning had not buoyed his spirits the way it normally would have.

Part of the problem, he knew, was the lack of closure with regard to Freeman's death.

Adler's search teams had located the wreckage of the American's airplane, but they had been unable to locate the body. Richthofen knew this wasn't all that unusual; the twists and turns that a dying aircraft went through as it plummeted toward the ground had a tendency to separate the pilot from his aircraft, particularly if the pilot chose not to use his safety belt.

Still, it nagged at him.

He'd visited the crash site just yesterday. He'd recovered what was left of the propeller, had an aide carve Freeman's name onto the blade, and then arranged to have it sent to the commanding officer over at the 94th Squadron by way of the Red Cross. Letting them know that their favorite ace had fallen at the hands of the Baron was simply good psychological warfare and needed to be done, despite his own personal unease with the lack of a corpse.

He'd even gone so far as to check wind levels and scheduled gas attacks. He'd felt foolish when the idea first occurred to him, but he had reminded himself that stranger things had happened in this war and done it anyway. As it turned out, there simply was no way for an effective dose of T-Leiche to have drifted that far behind the lines and thus no way for Freeman to have risen anew as a result.

There was, of course, the possibility that Freeman had somehow survived the crash and abandoned the scene under his own power. It was that possibility, however small, that was the source of Richthofen's unrest. It would not do to proclaim to the world that he'd killed the American ace, only to have him show up alive and well at some point in the future.

He ordered more search teams into the field, but the size of the territory they had to cover prevented them from completing the task with any real speed and as of that moment, they were still looking.

To get his mind off the problem, he'd decided to attend a strategy session being held at the kaiser's summer estate outside of Berlin. He'd received word that both Field Marshal Hindenburg and General Erich Ludendorff were going to be in attendance, and he made a point of trying to limit their influence on the kaiser whenever he could. Wilhelm had been taking too much of a hands-off approach lately, content to hide in his palaces and make the social rounds while letting his generals manage the war, and that was a recipe for disaster if he ever saw one.

A pair of double doors loomed ahead, two of the kaiser's personal guards standing outside them. They snapped to attention as Richthofen approached, saluting the Blue Max he wore at his throat as much as the man who wore it. The Baron knew he was well liked among the Imperial staff and now, as always, he took a moment to speak to the guards, man to man, to ensure that he maintained that relationship. There would come a time, in the not too distant future, when he was going to need friends among those surrounding the kaiser . . .

He slipped through the door to find the meeting already under way. A large table had been set up in the middle of the room, a map of both the Eastern and Western Fronts tacked down on its surface. Wooden models representing the forces currently in theater were arranged there and could be moved around to illustrate the results of various battles or proposed strategies. For months now there had been little change in the positions of the various armies, and Richthofen barely glanced at the map as he approached.

The kaiser sat on a wooden throne on a raised dais next to the table, his legs crossed in front of him and his left arm resting on the hilt of his sword, as if he might draw it at any moment. Richthofen knew it for the sham it was; the kaiser's withered limb didn't have enough strength to draw the sword, never mind wield it. The fact that Wilhelm did all he could to hide the infirmity was a constant source of annoyance for the German ace. Hiding the injury was a clear sign that the kaiser cared how others saw him and that, in Richthofen's eyes, was a weakness that no leader should exhibit. It was why he never covered the wound along his jaw except to keep food or drink from falling out. The opinions of other, lesser men meant nothing to Richthofen, and he despised the kaiser for showing his personal vanity and weakness to the world in such a fashion.

No matter, he thought, calming himself before his temper could flare up. If his plan went well, there would soon be another on the Iron Throne anyway. He could be patient.

His resolve to do so, however, was severely tested when he saw Field Marshal Hindenburg and General Ludendorff standing at the foot of the throne, wide beaming smiles on both their faces. A servant was in the act of pouring a glass of champagne for the kaiser and his guests, which was another bad sign.

Wilhelm looked up as Richthofen moved across the room to join them.

"Ah, Manfred! So good of you to come! You're just in time to celebrate with us."

"Celebrate?" he asked, as he accepted a glass of champagne of his own.

"Yes, yes!" Wilhelm said, beaming with nervous energy. "I've just appointed Field Marshal Hindenburg to the position of chief of the general staff and General Ludendorff to the role of first quartermaster-general. The future of the war, and of the German Empire, is now assured!"

Richthofen's grip tightened on his glass, and it took considerable effort not to crush it in his fist.

Easy, Manfred, easy . . .

He turned and nodded politely to the other two men, holding up his glass in salute.

"Congratulations. Is it too early to ask what your plans might be to break the stalemate at the front?"

Von Hindenburg looked at him with an expression of superiority and disdain, there being no love lost between the two men, but at the kaiser's urging he moved over to the map to illustrate the plans he and Ludendorff had developed for the next offensive.

As he followed the newly appointed chief of staff over to the map, Richthofen had to restrain himself from ripping the pompous fool's head clear off his shoulders. He could picture himself putting his hands on either side of the man's head and twisting sharply, could almost feel the fountain of blood as it sprayed upward, and he had to shake his head to clear the red haze that was starting to creep over his vision as his control began to slip away.

Von Hindenburg picked up a pointer and began indicating several units arranged a short distance from the front. "The Seventh, Eighth and Ninth Armies are here, near Mons. As soon as we have resupplied, we will swing north past Lens and break the back of the British's positions along the river Somme with our new tank divisions. Having done so, we should quickly roll over what is left of the French Army and take Paris from Allied hands with minimal difficulty."

He stepped back, nodding to himself as if the effort had already been made and the objective accomplished.

"And how long do you expect this offensive to take?" Richthofen asked in a carefully controlled voice.

This time it was Ludendorff who answered. "With twelve new battalions of Tottensoldat being brought to Mons by rail as we speak, we expect to launch the offensive in the next week. Once begun, I anticipate that it will take no more than four weeks to seize the French capital."

The kaiser was nodding his head with enthusiasm. "With France in our control, it should be an easy matter to get the British to sue for peace. At that point we can turn our attention back to the east and deal with Russia once and for all!"

Richthofen looked away, lest his expression reveal how he was truly feeling. The notion that they could seize Paris inside of four months was absurd, given what they were working with. The tank regiments were a disaster; they kept getting bogged down in the mud of the front, becoming another set of targets for the Allied artillery men to practice upon. Never mind that another twenty-five battalions of Tottensoldat wouldn't be able to smash through the defenses along the Somme. They had been dug in there for more than five years now, and it would take more than barely controlled zombie troops to break that line.

His trip here had been a waste, he realized. The kaiser's action in turning over control of the Imperial Army to these two buffoons, the same two buffoons who had been unable to conquer Russia in the early phase of the war, was just another example of how badly the empire needed new hands on the tiller. Now, more than ever, it was clear that he needed to act, and act soon, in order to save the empire from a slow death.

Outwardly he congratulated the other three on their foresight and forward thinking, pledging the support of his air corps to make the offensive a resounding success, but inwardly he seethed, impatient with the need to act before it was too late. It was that impatience that finally forced him to bid good-bye to the others and slip back out of the room before he said or did something he would later have cause to regret.

To get his mind off the imbeciles now running the war, Richthofen decided to make the short flight over to Verdun and drop in on Eisenberg. The good doctor was due to deliver his latest report on the *Geheime Volks* project in another week, and Richthofen decided that keeping him from getting too comfortable was worth the extra trouble. It was imperative that Eisenberg remember just who was in charge of the whole endeavor, and an unexpected visit from his patron would go a long way in establishing the pecking order. That, in turn, would add to Richthofen's satisfaction with the situation.

The winds were fair and the flight uneventful. Richthofen didn't bother circling the airfield, as was his usual style, but came in directly for a landing to limit the amount of warning Eisenberg would have regarding his arrival.

It did little good. Apparently Eisenberg's people were more on the ball than expected. By the time Richthofen had taxied to the side of the field that served as the compound's takeoff and landing zone, the doctor himself was waiting patiently in front of his staff car, ready to ferry his patron back to the comfort of his personal residence. Eisenberg was a chubby little man was a fat face and a tendency to sweat, but he was a literal genius when it came to these kinds of programs.

"Herr Richthofen! A pleasure to see you!"

Richthofen ignored him, walking right past to climb into the backseat of the staff car.

Always good to keep him on the defensive, he thought.

Eisenberg slid in beside him. The driver must have been briefed previously, for he started the vehicle and headed for their destination without having to be told. A few minutes after landing, the two men were ensconced in Eisenberg's private study.

"How can I help you today, Herr Richthofen?"

"Let's start with an update on the T-Leiche enhancements."

Eisenberg took a moment to gather his thoughts. "A new round of testing utilizing batch 3472 was initiated at Stalag 108 last night. I suspect that this will be the most successful variant yet, but it will be a few days before we will know for sure."

"And the others?"

"Testing on batch 3419 continues at Stalag 113. The initial success rate was startling, as you know, and we nicknamed the breed the *Geheime Volks,* the secret people, in order to differentiate them from the *Totenarbeitskraft* and *Tottensoldat* breeding programs."

Richthofen nodded to show he was following along, but Eisenberg wasn't telling him anything he didn't already know. He'd been the one to suggest the names for those first breeds, after all. The death workers and the death soldiers had been named for precisely the tasks they'd been developed to perform.

"Surprisingly," the doctor said, "we're noticing an increase in the overall intelligence of the G.V. who survive the transformation process. They are able to carry out simple commands and make basic decisions when obstacles are placed in their path, which is similar to the results we've been getting with the Tottensoldat breed for the last few months now."

"That's encouraging," Richthofen said, and it was. The Tottensoldat program was designed to make the soldiers' battlefield resurrections more useful, the idea being that if a stronger sense of identity and independent function could be maintained in the undead following their revival, they would be easier to control and therefore more adaptable to different situations on the front line.

If the same could be done in the Geheime Volks program, which used living subjects, the doctor and his assistants would be one step closer to ending this war, with the empire fully in control of all of Europe.

And one step closer to having the right man sitting on the Iron Throne as well, Richthofen thought.

But Eisenberg wasn't finished.

"It *is* encouraging, yes, but it is offset by the recent discovery that this particular breed has a tendency to grow more aggressive as time passes. We're not sure what's causing it at the moment, but we're looking into it. Our first line of thought was that . . ."

Richthofen let the doctor prattle on for several minutes about chemical structures, the characteristics of gaseous bodies, and the rate at which gases were absorbed into the human form through the pores of the skin before he decided he'd heard enough and prompted the doctor to move to the next topic of discussion.

"Where are we on the new breed of hounds?" Richthofen asked.

The *Tod Hunde,* or Death Hounds, were another result of the experiments that Dr. Eisenberg was attempting. Recognizing that the composition of the gas could be used to highlight certain features and capabilities while downplaying others, the doctor had worked hard to heighten the creatures' olfactory powers while limiting their free will and intelligence quotient. The result, a strange batch of creatures with limited humanity but incredibly efficient tracking abilities, had shown a good degree of promise, so much so that Richthofen recently authorized their use outside the camp on a limited basis. Two "packs" had been assigned to the teams searching for Freeman's remains.

"The latest enhancements have also increased the creatures' aggressive nature, making them more difficult to control, but I think we can filter that back out again in the next experiment."

"Excellent," Richthofen replied, honestly pleased with the development. A little aggressiveness might even make the creatures usable on the front line, so he didn't necessarily see that as a bad thing.

He changed focus again, moving to a new subject, one the good doctor might find less comfortable, just to keep him on his toes.

"What is this I hear about a group of test subjects escaping from Stalag 113?"

Eisenberg's eyes widened and Richthofen knew the doctor had not been aware that the information about the escapees had leaked, never mind that it had made its way back to Richthofen himself.

"Uh . . . um . . . yes, the escape," the doctor replied. "I was going to fill you in on the details of that in my report to you next week."

Richthofen remained silent.

"A transport vehicle broke down shortly after leaving the compound. The newly altered soldiers it was carrying were not secured properly and they managed to overpower the guards and escape. The search teams are trying to locate them as we speak."

Richthofen nodded. "Good. I want it made clear to the rest of the staff that such poor attention to detail will not be tolerated. When the escapees are rounded up, feed the guards to them in front of the other staff, so they understand the consequences of failure."

The doctor paled but nodded in agreement.

One of Eisenberg's young pages burst into the room at that point, a piece of paper held tightly in his hand.

"Please excuse me, Major," Eisenberg said, as he motioned the page over to him. The doctor took the note, glanced at it, and then passed it across to Richthofen.

"My apologies. It seems the message is for you, Herr Richthofen."

It was a telegram from his adjutant, Corporal Adler, and it contained a surprising revelation.

Freeman alive. Stop. Being held at Stalag 113. Stop. Request instructions. Stop. Adler.

If Richthofen's heart hadn't already been a shriveled lump of dead tissue, it would have skipped a beat in his chest. He finally understood what it was that his instincts had been trying to tell him the last several days; Freeman had survived the crash!

Possibilities flooded through his mind in rapid-fire sequence. Richthofen knew that Freeman was more than just the Americans' top ace. He'd discovered the truth while reading an intelligence dispatch that he'd intercepted, a dispatch intended for the kaiser. In the right hands, Freeman's unique relationship to the head of the American political system could be used to gain incredible leverage, which was one reason Richthofen had chosen to keep the information to himself. He fiercely believed that the good of the empire would best be served by having someone other than Kaiser Wilhelm sitting on the Iron Throne, someone who was no longer hampered by the emotions and faulty reasoning that plagued mankind as a species.

And if that individual had Freeman in his actual control . . .

Richthofen turned the message slip over and quickly wrote on the back. Handing it to Eisenberg's aide, he said, "Send this to Corporal Adler at once."

As the aide scurried off, Richthofen turned to Eisenberg and said, "I have a special task for you, Docktor . . ."

CHAPTER TWENTY-EIGHT

STALAG 113

THEY LEFT HIM in the pit overnight, with only the dead for company. Freeman slept with his back against the wall and his hand on a sharpened piece of bone, reassured by the simple knowledge that he had something with which to defend himself.

As the morning light filtered down from above he expected the guards to come check on him, but as the hours passed and no one came, he began to suspect that they wouldn't do so until the next troublemaker needed punishing. Which could be ten minutes or ten days from now.

Not good.

After several days without adequate medical care, his leg was inflamed and aching horribly. If it hadn't been infected before he'd been dropped into the pit and forced to roll around in the remains of previous victims while fighting off a starving shambler, he had little doubt that it was now. At this rate he wouldn't live out the week.

First things first, he reminded himself. *You've got to get out of this pit.*

He found a section of the wall where there weren't any corpses stacked and moved in, hoping to pick out a route he could use to climb to the top. The wall glistened, and when he touched it, he discovered that it had been covered with some kind of a slick substance—*animal or human fat perhaps?*—higher than he could reach. The grease made it impossible to find a handhold.

When that didn't work, he moved over to where a stack of bodies reached halfway up the wall and began to clamber up them, hoping that by doing so he could get himself high enough that he was above the grease line. The bodies slipped and rolled beneath his feet, making his position more precarious the higher he climbed. His injured leg wasn't helping matters either.

He had just about reached the top of the stack when his foot burst through the rib cage of the corpse beneath him, causing him to tip forward unexpectedly. The sudden movement caused the corpse to slide in the opposite direction, sending the entire stack of bodies tumbling downward to the floor and burying Freeman beneath them.

It took him nearly a half hour to dig himself free, leaving him covered from head to foot in bits of rotting flesh and bodily fluids. Exhausted from his ordeal and weak from hunger and thirst, Freeman dragged himself over to a clear space against the side of the pit and slumped down against the wall, determined to husband what was left of his strength.

He must have dozed, for he awoke to the sound of the metal plate being dragged to the side above his head. Sunlight flooded into the pit as he climbed to his feet and moved into the center of the space so he could see. Squinting up against the glare, Freeman saw four guards stationed around the hole, looking down at him in surprise.

Didn't think I'd still be here, did you, you bastards?

His satisfaction was short-lived, however. One of the guards pointed his Mauser down into the pit and barked something at him in German. Although Freeman didn't speak the language, the motions that went along with the command made it clear that they wanted him to back up. When he did, one of the guards lowered a ladder into the hole and then sent two of the others in after him.

Freeman braced himself for another beating and was therefore surprised when he realized the guards were unarmed. He watched them warily approach and nearly fell over in shock when they offered, with hand gestures, to help him over to the ladder.

What the hell?

He shrugged off their assistance and hobbled his way over to the ladder. Trap or not, he wasn't going to pass on the possibility of getting out of this hellhole, and he'd do it under his own power, thank you very much. But the task proved too much for his energy-sapped body, and he had to resort to letting them guide him along. It was either that or fall off the ladder back into the muck of the pit.

There was a lorry waiting near the hole, and the guards helped him over to it when he reached the surface. From there it was a short drive over to the infirmary, where a short, elderly gentleman and two male nurses were waiting for him. The man introduced himself as Dr. Taschner. Even better, he spoke passable English.

"Sit, please, Major," he said, pointing at the wheeled chair he had waiting.

"Someone want to tell me what this is all about first?" he asked. He had visions of being strapped to an operating table and carved into little pieces for the glory of the empire.

"I couldn't honestly tell you, Major. All I know is that I've been ordered to clean you up, and that includes treating your leg. Which, from the smell of it, is probably not a moment too soon. Another day or two and we'd most likely have had to amputate."

Having had it pointed out to him, Freeman was suddenly aware of the rotting meat smell that was wafting off his injured leg and clothing.

They wheeled him into a communal shower, cut the clothes from his body, and then thoroughly washed him down. The nurses were well trained and extremely efficient; Freeman eventually stopped trying to help and just let them take over. He screamed several times when they were forced to clean the exterior of his wound, but they left the job of routing out the infection and the pus it had generated to Dr. Taschner.

When they were finished, they sat him naked in the chair and wheeled him into the examination room where the doctor was waiting.

"Better, Major?"

Freeman nodded, still wary but feeling better about the situation as the minutes ticked past.

Taschner indicated the exam table beside him with an extended hand. "I need to look at that wound on your leg," he said.

Freeman let them help him up onto the exam table. He lay down flat on his back at Dr. Taschner's suggestion.

That's when they threw the leather straps over his arms, legs, and chest, six in all, cinching them tight before he even knew what was happening.

"Hey!" he yelled, fear in his voice for the first time since arriving at the camp. There was something about being strapped down, helpless, at your enemies' mercy . . .

"Relax, Major," Taschner said. "I assure you again, I mean no harm. Cleaning a wound in that condition is going to hurt, a lot, and I'm afraid I haven't been authorized to use any of our limited supply of morphine or ether to numb your pain. The straps are there for your protection, nothing else."

Freeman was only slightly mollified by the explanation, but at this point there was nothing he could do. Struggling against his bonds got him exactly nowhere; he was trussed up tighter than a Christmas goose.

The doctor stepped out of view for a moment and returned carrying a cloth-covered tray. He set the tray down, picked a scalpel up off it, and said to Freeman, "As I said, this is going to hurt."

Then, without hesitating, the doctor used the scalpel to slice open the partially healed wound on Freeman's leg.

Freeman screamed, a long wailing cry that matched the white-hot explosion of pain that went off in his mind. Amazingly, he didn't pass out.

A few seconds later he wished he had, however, as he caught sight of the gallon-sized glass jar one of the nurses carried into the room and the wormlike creatures it contained. At nearly an inch in diameter, their pale blue-gray bodies twisted and churned about one another like a nest of maggots gone wild with abandon.

"Are you familiar with the African rotworm, Major?" Taschner asked. "Marvelous creatures. They'll clean the wound and allow it to heal properly, something you've been unable to get it to do on your own, I'm sorry to say."

"Keep those things away from me, Doc," he said, but of course the doctor ignored him.

The nurse held the jar and waited patiently as the doctor unscrewed the lid and then reached inside with a pair of long-nosed forceps. He caught one of the wriggling things with the forceps and lifted it out of the jar.

"I'm warning you! Keep that fucking thing away from me!" Freeman screamed.

Dr. Taschner gave him a sympathetic glance and then placed the worm on Freeman's calf about two inches away from the open wound.

Freeman was strapped down so tightly that he couldn't even shake the worm off his leg. He stared at it in sick fascination.

For a moment nothing happened.

Then the worm lifted the front of its body, questing this way and that like a dog searching for a scent. When it caught the smell of decay rising out of the wound in Freeman's leg, it first stiffened and then slowly wiggled its way forward.

Freeman watched in horror as the rotworm slid closer to the gaping wound in his leg. His eyes opened wider as the creature drew closer. His breathing took on a harsh, panting rhythm.

When the worm reached the thick line of blood, pus, and fluid that was draining from inside of the wound it paused for a half moment.

Then, quicker than he thought possible given its slow rate of motion up until that point, the worm shot forward and disappeared directly inside the wound.

"Excellent!" Dr. Taschner cried. Using the forceps, he removed a second rotworm from the jar. "Shall we try another?" he asked.

CHAPTER TWENTY-NINE

THE MEN WERE quiet after Strauss's death and subsequent burial. They marched on, but if the mood of the group had been subdued before discovering their missing comrade, it was downright anemic afterward.

Like any good commander, Burke felt responsible for the loss of one of his men, but he knew he couldn't have prevented it. The attack on the *Victorious* had forced them to improvise, and it was the very nature of that improvisation that had led to Strauss's death. His best guess was that Strauss had lost sight of the man in front of him when he'd entered the cloud bank and had become disoriented in the midst of it all, unwittingly changing his flight path.

Unfortunately for him, he'd apparently survived the landing only to run into a pack of shamblers when he'd gone looking for the rest of the unit.

In the end, Private Strauss had fallen victim to the bane of soldiers everywhere—simple bad luck.

Thirty minutes later the muck and mire of the old battlefield gave way to grassy fields and short stretches of uncultivated forest between. This allowed them to increase their pace significantly, and they covered another three miles before Burke called a short halt. Packs were shed, rations divvied up, and they sat down for a quick meal.

At the rate they were going, they wouldn't reach the farmhouse until well past sundown, but Burke wanted to push through anyway. Doing so would give them a relatively safe location to bed down for the night and might also provide some much needed supplies.

Who knew? Maybe their contact would wait for them.

After a short break, Burke signaled Sergeant Moore to get the men back on their feet. There was the usual grumbling about sore feet and endless marching, which Burke took as a good sign. Having the energy to complain meant that the morale was still pretty high; he'd been worried that the loss of Private Strauss would send the men in a downward spiral. With Sergeant Moore in the lead, they headed out.

Tensions were high, as every step took them deeper into enemy territory. The few farmhouses they encountered were given a wide berth, as they had no way of knowing if the inhabitants would be amenable to their cause or more interested in bringing the Germans down on their heads. They were forced to cross several major roads and even ford a fast-moving river, but they managed to do so without incident.

They had just left the shelter of the trees behind and were in the midst of crossing a wide meadow when their luck ran out.

Manning heard it first, his hunter's instincts picking up the sound seconds before anyone else. He stopped short, catching the next man in line, Williams, by surprise and causing the eager young private to walk right into him.

Williams immediately apologized. "Sorry, Mr. Manning," he said, in his usual overly loud voice. "Didn't mean to walk into ya like that, but ya stopped suddenly and I didn't . . ."

"Quiet!" Manning hissed. He turned his face skyward and began to move in a slow circle, searching for something.

Burke was bringing up the rear of the column several yards behind the two men and he had a second to wonder just what Manning was looking for before he heard it himself.

The rumble of an approaching engine.

They'd all heard it by that point, and many of them were looking around, trying to pinpoint where it was coming from. The tall trees surrounding the meadow weren't much help, for they dispersed the sound, bouncing it to and fro, making it hard to get a fix on the location.

Burke turned to look behind them and that's when a biplane burst over the treetops, the sound they'd all been hearing finally resolving into the growl of a Mercedes engine. This far behind enemy lines the chances it was an Allied fighter were slim, but seeing the equal length of the upper and lower wings, a common design on the French Nieuport, Burke was momentarily hopeful. Then he got a good look at the rounded cowl and smooth unbroken curve of the rudder rising up over the fuselage in back, two traits that immediately identified the aircraft as a German Albatros, and he knew that they were in trouble. The thick black crosses that adorned the underside of the aircraft's wings were nothing more than an afterthought for him at that point.

There was no doubt that the pilot had seen them, for he pointed the plane in their direction, clearing his guns as he started his dive.

Fear caused Burke's heart to lurch in his chest.

He knew what the pair of Spandau machine guns the Albatros sported could do to a man's unprotected body, and he didn't want to be anywhere near them when the pilot pulled the trigger.

"Move, move, move!" he yelled, grabbing the nearest man, Graves it turned out, and shoving him toward the trees even as the sound of the dreaded machine guns filled the clearing.

Rat-tat-tat-tat-tat!

Bullets stitched their way through the air and pounded the dirt track the squad had been following, the guns thundering in that rhythm that had become so familiar to him over the years. The squad scattered like rabbits at the sight of a fox, charging off in different directions to avoid providing a single, large target for the pilot to focus on.

Burke was turning toward the trees to his right, intent on getting under cover as soon as possible, when he saw Manning throw up his hands as if in surprise and crumble to the ground. Without a second thought he changed direction, scooped up the man's limp form, and ran hell-bent for the protective boughs of the trees some twenty yards away.

The long grass dragged at his legs and seemed to be actively trying to hold his feet to the ground as he forced his way forward with Manning flung across his shoulder in a fireman's carry. He had no idea how badly hurt the other man was, but he couldn't take the time to stop and look. That Albatros would be back for another go at them, and he had to get under cover before that happened.

The twenty yards felt like twenty miles. All he could hear was the pounding of his heart and the hiss of his breath through his labored lungs. He could see one of his men in the trees ahead of him, waving him on, and so he put his head down and ordered his feet to move faster.

As Burke reached the trees, Charlie stepped out and helped him lower Manning's still, unconscious form to the ground. As the big sergeant began examining their injured squad member, Burke looked back out over the clearing, praying that no one else had been hit, and was shocked to see Jones still standing there, watching the aircraft as it began to loop round for another run.

"Get under cover, you fool!" Burke yelled. "That's an order!"

He was certain he'd been heard, for Jones looked briefly in his direction and then turned his face to the sky once more.

Jones had just ignored a direct order.

Burke was tempted to shoot Jones himself.

Seeing the look of anger on Burke's face, Charlie said, "I'll get him," and started forward, but Burke grabbed his arm and held him back.

"No time," he told his friend and then pointed to where the Albatros had completed its turn and was diving back down toward the lone man standing in the middle of the clearing as if daring the German to try to kill him.

As the two men looked on, Jones unslung his Enfield rifle from over his shoulder and knelt down in the middle of the game trail they'd been following as if he were on a duck hunt and didn't have a care in the world. The roar of the German fighter's engine grew louder, and the crack of the machine guns added their sound to the chorus as Jones raised his rifle and aimed it at the diving aircraft.

"That stupid sonofabitch is going to get himself killed," Charlie muttered, and Burke could only nod his head in agreement. There wasn't anything they could do about it, except watch it all play out.

The German pilot began firing his guns the moment he had them lined up on his target. Jones was a sitting duck. The game trail acted like an arrow pointing to the target, and all the pilot had to do was follow it with his shots.

Burke's stomach churned at the thought of what was about to happen, but he couldn't turn away.

To his amazement, Jones calmly ignored the line of bullets walking their way toward him, churning up the earth less than one hundred feet away.

Burke watched as Jones opened and then closed his forward hand on the stock of the rifle, adjusting his grip for better comfort.

Fifty feet.

Lowered the muzzle of the rifle slightly.

Twenty-five feet.

The pilot couldn't miss; the bullets would cut Jones in half if he didn't get out of the way.

Jones opened his mouth, closed it . . .

. . . and pulled the trigger.

As soon as he'd taken the shot he threw himself to the side, rolling over and over again through the grass, desperately trying to get out of the path of the bullets, his rifle tucked up tight against his body so that it wouldn't snag on something and slow him down.

Burke watched in silence as the Albatros roared over the spot where Jones had been just seconds before, the machine guns still hammering out their deadly song. The plane banked slightly, as if preparing to come around a third time, and then it continued its arc and nosed over, its guns still firing even as it slammed into the earth with a splintering crash at the far end of the clearing some forty yards away.

Silence settled over them for a long moment as everyone tried to come to grips with what had just happened, then Williams let out a whoop from the safety of the brush on the other side of the clearing and rushed out toward where Jones was just now getting to his feet and dusting himself off. The younger man met the sharpshooter with enthusiasm, a wide smile on his face.

Without taking his eyes off the two men before him, Burke asked, "How's Manning?"

"Damned lucky is what he is," Charlie replied. "The bullet only grazed the side of his helmet. He'll have a headache to end all headaches when he comes to, but other than that he'll be okay."

Burke nodded. Wouldn't be the first time luck had saved a man's life and certainly wouldn't be the last. Hell, every single one of them was just a hairsbreadth away from death at any moment in this crazy war, but he tried not to think about that now. He had a bigger problem on his hands.

"What are you going to do about Jones?" Charlie asked him, but Burke only shook his head. He wasn't sure yet.

No doubt about it though. Something had to be done. He couldn't have men disobeying orders. This far behind enemy lines, the slightest hesitation at a crucial moment could get them all killed.

"Stay with Manning," Burke said and then set off across the clearing.

The rest of the squad had come out from undercover and were converging around the wreckage. As Burke approached, he could see them pulling the body of the pilot out of the cockpit and laying him on the grass. The lopsided shape to the dead man's skull told them everything they needed to know about the accuracy of Jones's shooting. He could hear the men congratulating him on the precision of the shot, and it was clear that they were, almost to a man, impressed with Jones's skill. Burke was equally impressed—hitting a melon-sized target moving at roughly fifty miles per hour while that target was trying to turn you into Swiss cheese was no easy feat—but he couldn't let his admiration show.

Disobedience could not be tolerated.

The other men saw him coming and one of them—he thought it was Compton but he wasn't sure—said, "Captain, did you see . . . ?"

Burke wasn't listening. He closed on Jones and got right up in the man's face, his expression and tone of voice as hard as stone.

"Corporal Jones. Did I or did I not give you a direct order?" he asked, in a low but steady tone.

Jones, flush from his success, either didn't notice or simply chose to ignore Burke's evident anger, perhaps hoping it might go away if he didn't deign to acknowledge it. Instead of answering the captain's question, Jones said, "Did you see that shot? Had to have been at least two hundred . . ."

"Shut up."

The words were spoken with the same volume that Burke had used a moment before, but this time they cut through the chatter like a knife and caused everyone in the group, including Jones, to snap their mouths closed and stand at attention.

"I asked you a question, Corporal," Burke said softly, but with all the menace of a rattlesnake.

Jones squirmed, but answered his question nonetheless.

"Yes, sir."

"Yes, sir, what?"

"You gave me a direct order. Sir."

Burke leaned in even closer, his gaze locked on Jones's own. "Do you know what they call it when a soldier disobeys a direct order in the midst of combat, Jones?"

The corporal shook his head.

"Treason," Burke replied.

He let that word sink into their heads for a minute. Burke wasn't just speaking to Jones; he wanted each and every one of the men to understand the gravity of what had just occurred. He couldn't keep them alive if they didn't follow his orders.

"How about the penalty for treason? Do you know what that is?"

Burke didn't wait for a reply, but barreled on ahead. "The penalty for treason, Mr. Jones, is death by firing squad."

Jones's bravado was gone now. His face turned pale, and Burke watched a single line of sweat roll down the side of it.

"I'll shoot you myself if you disobey another direct order, is that clear, *Private* Jones?"

The other man nodded.

Reducing the man one grade in rank was a trivial punishment, particularly as it had no real meaning out here behind enemy lines, but Burke needed to keep Jones's head in the game and avoid any smoldering resentment at the same time. The truth of the matter was that Burke needed every gun they had at their disposal. That was why he was so annoyed at the incident in the first place. Jones should have known better.

Satisfied that his point had been made, Burke stepped back and turned his attention to the body of the German pilot. A quick search through the man's pockets didn't turn up any information relative to who he was or the unit, or Jasta as the Germans called them, to which he belonged. Nor did Burke recognize the personal insignia, a knight's head with two lances crossed behind it, painted on his plane. Knowing someone somewhere would want to know what happened to him, Burke ordered the insignia cut from the aircraft and stuffed it into his back pocket for later delivery to the Red Cross.

They didn't have time to bury the pilot nor did they want to call attention to themselves by lighting a funeral pyre, so they arranged his body in a burial position and left it in the shade of his aircraft.

Manning was still unconscious, but Burke knew they couldn't stay put. *What if someone came looking for the missing aircraft and its pilot?* They needed to be long gone before that happened, so the decision was made to carry their wounded comrade. Each man would take turns, starting with Charlie, until either the big game hunter woke up or they reached their destination.

As they left the clearing behind, Burke took one last look back at the wreckage of the German aircraft.

One hell of an amazing shot.

CHAPTER THIRTY

An hour later, Burke crouched with the rest of his men at the edge of the tree line and stared out at the farmhouse ahead of them. The sun was just setting, casting long shadows across the yard and the stone walls and wooden shutters of the one-story structure. He stayed still for several long minutes, watching, wanting to be certain the coast was clear before he sent someone over to make contact.

Truth was, he didn't like what he saw. There was no smoke coming from the chimney, nor could he see any movement behind the window's partially opened curtains.

That wasn't right. They might be late but at least they were expected; someone should have been watching for their approach.

Even worse, the house felt empty. Not just empty, but deserted. As if it had been that way for a long time.

Something's wrong.

He glanced behind him, caught Charlie's eye, and waved him over.

"I don't like it," he said, when the other man slipped up beside him. "There should be somebody down there, waiting for us."

Charlie studied the rear of the building for another minute and then said, "Maybe they're just lying low. Trying not to call attention to themselves."

Burke turned the idea over in his head a few times. He had to admit that it was possible. Lord knew he wouldn't want to do anything to attract attention living this far behind enemy lines. There were simply too many things that liked the taste of human flesh these days to get careless.

The explanation made sense, but it didn't fit the situation.

Or at least, it didn't feel that way to him.

"I'm going to check it out. Once you see me go inside, start counting. If I'm not back out by the time you reach thirty, skip the rendezvous and head for the POW camp on your own."

It was clear that Charlie wanted to go with him, but they both knew that wasn't going to happen. Someone had to lead the team if Burke got into trouble, and the best man to do that was Charlie.

"Good luck," Charlie finally told him as he settled himself into position to provide cover fire in case Burke needed it.

The captain clapped him on the back and then turned to the others. "Williams, you're with me. The rest of you keep your eyes peeled and get ready to join us when I give the signal."

One last long look and then Burke took off running, Williams on his heels.

The twenty yards from the tree line to the farmhouse felt like half a mile. Burke's world narrowed down to just the back door and the windows to either side of it, his gaze never leaving them as he rushed forward, watching for any flicker of movement, some sign that they weren't alone. With his heart pounding in his chest and the sound of his own harsh breathing in his ears, he raced toward the door ahead of him, expecting at any moment to hear the crack of a shot and to be thrown to the ground as the bullet slammed into his body.

Thankfully, that didn't happen.

He reached the rear of the house and threw himself against it to the right of the door. A second later Williams did the same on the left.

From his current position Burke could see that the door was slightly ajar. Catching the younger man's eye, he held up the fingers of his mechanical hand and counted down from three, then shouldered the door open and rushed inside, his Tommy gun at the ready, his gaze flicking this way and that as he searched for a target.

They moved through each room—kitchen, living room, and bedroom—quickly and efficiently, covering each other as they went.

The house was empty.

Satisfied that they were alone and that no one was going to suddenly pop up from behind the couch and start shooting, Burke stuck his head out the back door and gave the signal for the rest of the squad to join them.

Once the men had assembled inside, with the unconscious Manning laid out on the farmhouse's only bed, Burke split the rest of the team into pairs for a more detailed search of the property. He didn't want any surprises in the middle of the night, and the best way to avoid that was to know exactly what they were getting themselves into.

Right away they discovered evidence that someone had been there before them, and recently, too. Williams found an empty bottle of wine, a few drops of liquid still clinging to the inside of the glass, under the bed where someone might have kicked it accidentally. According to Sergeant Moore, the coals in the fireplace were no more than two, maybe even only one day old. The big find of the day, though, was a sack that contained a slab of cured meat, several potatoes, and two bottles of wine; they were discovered when Corporal Compton noticed a loose board in the floor of the living room and pulled it up to see what was hidden underneath.

From a tactical standpoint the farmhouse had some pretty solid advantages. It was isolated, standing in a small clearing all by itself, with a clear line of approach on all sides. It would be nearly impossible for anyone to sneak up on them. A single forest road provided access, ending in a small clearing in front of the house. Tire tracks in the mud of the clearing showed that there had been at least one, possibly two large vehicles parked there recently. Charlie thought the tracks looked like those from a two- or three-ton lorry, but Burke wouldn't have known the difference even if he'd had the actual tires right there in front of his face. He took his sergeant's word for it and let it go.

There was a porch attached to the front of the house, and beyond that a small yard enclosed by a stone fence that stood about waist-high. There was an opening in the fence that lined up with the front door and served as a gate. When Burke paced off the distance between the fence and the house, he found it was about thirty feet, which gave them some room to defend themselves if the need arose.

Out behind the house was a chicken coop, currently empty, and a toolshed. Judging by the state of disrepair of both structures, they'd been that way for several months at least.

Given that it was already nightfall, any smoke coming from the chimney would be hard to see, so Burke gave Sergeant Moore permission to use the fireplace to whip up some dinner for the squad. Charlie immediately took control of the entire bundle of food that Compton had discovered and got to work making a stew, using one of the bottles of wine as a broth, leaving the other to be shared with the meal. While the meal was cooking, Clayton Manning finally regained consciousness, and, much to Burke's relief, he seemed to have avoided serious injury.

"What's your name?" Compton asked him, as Burke looked on from the doorway.

"Clayton Charles Xavier Manning the third," the former big game hunter answered and with that one reply managed to eliminate any concerns either Doc Compton or Captain Burke might have had about his mental faculties.

No way could he be suffering from brain damage if he can remember a name like that, Burke thought.

Compton ran through a few simple tests of dexterity and motor function—asking Manning to tell him how many fingers he was holding up, having him touch the forefinger on each hand to his nose, and walk across the room in a straight line—before pronouncing him fit enough to travel. Sergeant Moore's initial diagnosis had been correct; Manning had woken up with a terrible headache, but otherwise he was fine.

Dinner was eaten in shifts with those not gulping down their portions of the meal guarding the property. From Burke's view, all the evidence they'd uncovered so far in the house suggested that whoever had been here most likely intended to return. To make sure they weren't caught with their pants down when that happened, Burke set up a rotating watch schedule for the rest of the evening, with two men awake at all times, one watching the front of the house and the road while the other monitored the rear approach through the woods.

The night passed quietly. When it was his turn to sit watch, Burke settled into a chair in front of the window in the kitchen and watched the road, his thoughts on what was to come. They knew the location of the camp, so if the partisans didn't show by midmorning, Burke intended to set out on their own. Every day Jack spent in the company of the enemy was one more day that the enemy had to discover his connection to the president. Hell, for all Burke knew, Freeman's secret had already been discovered and everything Burke and his men had done to date had been for nothing!

Thinking that way's not going to help anyone, he scolded himself. *Stay positive until you have reason to be otherwise. These men are looking to you for their cues, and it won't do to be dragging down morale.*

He focused instead on trying to figure out a way to get Freeman back to friendly lines after they broke him out of the POW camp. With the downing of the *Victorious,* the original plan to have the airship return for them was no longer possible. Nor did it make sense for them to try to cover the distance on foot. After busting down the walls of the prison camp, they'd have half the Germany army after them. Eventually, they'd be tracked down and captured.

No, he thought, studying the map, *walking will never do.* What they needed was some kind of mechanical transport. If they could steal a truck or maybe even a plane, they could cover more distance in quicker fashion, increasing their odds overall. Of course, they'd have to find it before they could steal it.

He was still looking for a suitable solution when he sensed movement to his left.

"Rumor has it that you don't like him much."

Burke turned to see Manning standing there in the semidarkness. "Like who?" Burke asked.

"Your brother. Jack."

Burke scowled. "He's not my brother."

"Okay, fine," Manning said. "Your half brother then."

Burke looked back down at the map he'd been studying, then back at Manning. "What's it to you?"

"I've known Jack for several years. I'm risking my life to save him. It makes a difference to me that the man's own brother might not see the value in doing the same."

"Anyone who's known Jack for more than ten minutes would know he's an arrogant jackass who hasn't had an unselfish thought in decades, so no, I don't see the value in risking all our lives to save him," Burke replied.

Manning was silent for a moment, then asked, "So what happened?"

Burke scowled. "Jack happened, that's what. Now if you don't mind, I have work to do." He returned to staring at the map and when he looked up a few moments later, Manning was gone.

The comment lingered though. *"Rumor has it that you don't like him much."*

No, he didn't. Didn't like him at all, in fact. The man's reckless behavior and irresponsible nature had plagued him throughout childhood and had nearly destroyed him as an adult.

What Manning said was true. They *were* half brothers—they shared the same mother—but that's where the similarity between them ended. Jack came from a life of wealth and privilege in the Hamptons on Long Island. His father, a member of the country club set who'd met their mother when she'd been working as a chambermaid, had married her on a whim and had just as easily divorced her two years later. He'd taken his son with him when he left, letting the boy be raised by a succession of live-in nannies until he was old enough to go to boarding school. At that time an arrangement was made. Jack would be registered under his mother's maiden name to help keep his identity secret and in order to not have the divorce affect his father's growing political career. In return, the boy would spend two months every summer with his mother and his half brother, Michael, at their little house in New Jersey.

Eloise Freeman had remarried by then, taking the last name Burke. Her new husband, Sam, was a solid, dependable sort, a few years older and a good bit wiser than her previous husband, and a man who would have moved mountains for his wife and four-year-old son. Their happiness was short-lived, however, for an accident on the factory floor left her husbandless for the second time in her life and their young son, Michael, without a father.

Things might have been different had Sam lived, Burke knew. His father had a way of reaching people with his strong but gentle manner, and Jack might have taken other paths had he been influenced during those formative years the way Michael had. Instead, Jack's sense of entitlement and his constant need for approval from his mostly absent father made him an angry, spoiled child, one his mother had difficulty controlling. That attitude heavily influenced the boys' relationship, for Jack often took his frustration out on his younger brother. As they'd grown older, their differences gained a nasty, competitive flavor, the two men goading each other into behavior that even a blind man could see would never turn out well.

They might have continued that way indefinitely if it hadn't been for that fateful night in the summer of 1913. Burke had been dating Linda Mae Stevens, Mae to her friends, for two years by then, and they had plans to marry the following spring. They'd been out at a dance hall together when Jack had shown up looking for them. He told them that Eloise had fallen off a ladder, bumped her head, and had been admitted to the county hospital with a possible concussion. The three of them had piled into the car and driven to the hospital, but since visiting hours were over, only family was allowed in to see her. Having already lost one parent and worried sick about the other, Burke agreed to let his half brother drive his fiancée home.

It was a decision he would come to regret.

Along the way, Freeman convinced Mae to stop off and have a drink with him. One drink led to two, two to three, and before they knew it they were both a bit drunk. From what Burke would hear later, Freeman began to mouth off to a group of local factory workers, who in turn didn't care for the slick rich-boy attitude he was throwing in their faces. More than a little drunk themselves, the foursome decided to teach Freeman and his girlfriend a lesson. They waited until Jack and Mae left the bar and then intercepted them in the dark parking lot. While two of them beat Jack with their fists and stomped him with their work boots, the others put a scare into Mae, groping her with their hands and intimidating her with their size. By all indications they didn't intend her any real physical harm, but Mae didn't know that, and she reacted as if her life depended on it.

Breaking away from the two of them, she raced through the darkness between several parked cars and out onto the street, possibly hoping to wave down an oncoming car.

The driver of the truck that hit her claimed later not to have seen her until it was too late.

Mae's body had been tossed aside like so much discarded waste. In the wake of the accident, the assailants scattered, leaving Jack unconscious and Mae bleeding to death in the street.

Burke's eyes were dry as he remembered that night, the pain and misery he'd felt burned away by all the anger he'd harbored since. He'd spent the rest of that terrible evening at his mother's side, only learning of the death of his fiancée when Jack called from the county jail, having been picked up by the police in the wake of the accident.

How you feel about Jack, good or bad, doesn't matter, he reminded himself for what was probably the tenth time since taking the mission. His half brother's status as a POW put the country in danger, and the Intelligence Division's fears couldn't be allowed to come to fruition. It was as simple as that.

One way or another, he would see to it that Jack's presence in that camp was no longer a threat to the president or to the country itself.

One way or another . . .

CHAPTER THIRTY-ONE

THE FARMHOUSE

COMPTON WOKE HIM shortly after sunrise the next morning with a hand on his arm.

"Got a truck coming down the road, sir," the doc said when he saw that he had the captain's attention.

"Wake the others," Burke told him, as he grabbed his Tommy gun and headed for the kitchen.

Sergeant Moore was standing near one of the windows, looking out through a small gap in the curtains, when Burke slipped into the room.

"What have we got?" Burke whispered, as he took up position at the other window.

"Two-ton lorry. One man in the cab. Back of the truck is covered with a tarp."

As Burke looked out the window he was just in time to watch the driver in question bring the truck to a stop facing the front of the house. Burke couldn't see the driver's face clearly through the windshield, but something about the man's posture gave him the sense that he was looking at something above their heads.

It took Burke a moment to figure it out.

Smoke.

They'd let the fire die down earlier that morning, but there must still be a thin trail of smoke coming out of the chimney, and it had apparently caught the driver's eye.

After another moment's hesitation, the driver opened the door and climbed down from the lorry's cab.

He was dressed simply in a dark shirt, trousers, and black boots. He wore a thick workman's coat, the kind that fell below the waist, and had a plaid cap on his head over his curly hair.

He took a few steps forward and shouted something toward the house in French.

"*Bonjour! Quelq'un personne est ici?*"

"What's he saying?" Charlie whispered.

Burke shook his head. He'd picked up a fair bit of French over the years, but the man's accent was too thick for him to understand.

Outside, the newcomer paused, then yelled again.

"*Quelq'un personne est ici?*"

To Burke it sounded like the same phrase as before, but he couldn't be certain.

Moving a few steps away from the window allowed Burke to see the rest of the house as he checked the position of his men, nodding in approval at what he saw. Jones and Manning were watching the back, while Williams and Compton had each taken one of the side windows, checking to be certain that no one tried to flank them through the trees. That left only Professor Graves. Since he'd admitted that he wasn't all that great a shot, Burke decided to hold him back in case of emergency, which was why he was now crouched beside the bed, keeping his head down but watching the others to see if he was needed.

Satisfied, Burke stepped back over to the window. The Frenchman hadn't moved; he still stood facing the house, an uncertain expression on his face.

"Time to meet the locals," Burke said beneath his breath, then opened the door and stepped out onto the porch. He had the strap of the Tommy gun over his right shoulder and was holding on to the grip with his right hand. This allowed him to keep the weapon ready without having to hold it out in front of him, something that was sure to be seen as aggressive. He pulled the door shut behind him with his free hand.

No surprise showed on the Frenchman's face at Burke's appearance, though he did glance behind him at his truck.

Burke did the same, but didn't see anything, and so dismissed it as simple nervousness on the other man's part. *Perhaps he was making sure we aren't sneaking up behind him.*

After glancing around and double-checking they were still alone, Burke descended the steps and slowly made his way across the yard toward the Frenchman.

As he drew closer, the other man spoke up in halting English and asked, "Capitan Burke?"

The sound of his own name caused some of Burke's tension to dissipate. There was only one person this far behind enemy lines who would know who he was and that was their contact from the local partisan group. Apparently Pierre, if that was even his real name, hadn't given up on them, after all, despite their late arrival.

Let's hope he doesn't want his wine back.

"That's right, I'm Burke," he replied, pointing to himself with his mechanical hand as he said his name so there wouldn't be any mistake.

Pierre glanced behind him again. This time, when he turned back, his hand dipped suddenly into the pocket of the jacket he was wearing.

Alarm bells went off in Burke's head.

He threw himself to the side just as the gun secreted inside the pocket of the Frenchman's coat went off, the bullet whizzing past Burke's head with only inches to spare.

Burke's finger tightened on the trigger of his own weapon even as he was falling. The Tommy gun roared and a stream of bullets stitched their way across Pierre's chest, causing him to jerk and shake with their impact.

Glass broke somewhere behind him, and the sound of Charlie's Tommy gun reached his ears as Burke hit the ground. He landed on his shoulder and let his momentum carry him forward into a short roll, coming up on one knee with his weapon pointed ahead of him. Gunfire was flying in both directions, and all it took was one look to understand why.

The tarp on the back of the lorry had been thrown off, allowing half a dozen German soldiers, all of them human as far as Burke could tell, to clamber out, take cover behind the vehicle, and begin firing at the house. Burke's men were firing back at them, the sharp crack of their rifles punctuated by the roar of the Tommy gun in Charlie's hands. Burke added his own firepower to the mix, felt the machine gun jerk in his hands, and watched with satisfaction as the enemy soldier he'd been targeting fell off the truck with blood pouring from a wound in the center of his chest.

As several of the enemy soldiers shifted their attention toward his position, Burke decided it might be prudent to find some cover. There was no way he'd make it back to the house; there was too much distance to cover and he'd be exposed all the way to the front steps, even with the help of covering fire from his men.

If you can't go backward . . .

Surging to his feet, he kept a steady volume of fire directed at the truck as he rushed forward. Every step seemed to take forever and his feet felt like cement blocks as he fought his way across the half-dozen yards that separated him from the protection of the stone wall at the front of the yard. Bullets filled the air around him, whipping past like a swarm of angry bees, and he felt one clip the side of his ammo belt just as he threw himself down behind the fence.

Somewhere in those last few seconds the drum on his Tommy gun ran dry, so he hit the switch to drop the empty one on the ground, grabbed another one off his belt, and moved to slap it into place.

Movement caught his eye and he looked up to find a German soldier leering at him over the top of the wall, the barrel of his Mauser pointed right in Burke's face.

Time slowed.

Burke's left hand smacked into the bottom of the drum magazine, knocking it into place, even as he began to bring the barrel up toward his foe. His mind was screaming *Too late! Too late! Too late!* even as he tried to bring his weapon to bear, praying the other man had a misfire or some other failure . . . anything to let him live.

Someone was apparently listening to him.

A small red hole appeared in the center of the man's forehead and he toppled backward out of sight.

There wasn't time to thank whoever had taken the shot. Another enemy soldier suddenly ran through the gate, searching for a target, but he turned left instead of right and Burke was able to cut him down with a burst from his Tommy gun.

Even as that man fell, another took his place, firing point-blank at Burke as he did the same, and then there were two dead Germans in front of him and God knew how many more in the truck.

Letting go of his Tommy gun for a second, Burke snatched one of the two grenades he carried off his belt. He hooked the index finger of his mechanical hand through the ring hanging off the grenade and pulled out the arming pin. He counted to three and then lobbed the grenade over the stone wall in the direction of the truck. As soon as he let go, he shoved himself against the stone wall, trying to make himself as small a target as possible for when the shrapnel began to fly.

There was a shattering roar and a sudden blast of heat as the grenade found its target and exploded. Pieces of wood and metal and human flesh began to rain out of the sky, including an arm that struck Burke on the shoulder and nearly made him scream. Burke held his position, and when a German soldier rushed through the gate, his body on fire, Burke calmly put a bullet in him.

A few gunshots followed, and then silence fell over the battleground.

For a moment Burke stayed where he was, Tommy gun in hand and ready to fire. When he felt enough time had passed, he slowly stood up and looked around.

The lorry was a blazing ruin. Flames several feet high consumed it and what was left of the men who'd been trapped inside when the grenade had gone off. The bodies of several other German soldiers lay in the area around the truck, all of them dead.

Burke heard the door to the house open behind him and he turned to see Sergeant Moore and Private Jones standing there, guns at the ready, their heads turning to either side as they searched for targets.

"We're clear," he told them.

Burke stepped over to the Frenchman and was surprised to discover that he was still alive. He was about to call for the doctor when he noticed the blood bubbling up from two wounds in the middle of the man's chest, and Burke knew there wasn't anything they could do for him. He was literally drowning in his own blood and probably wouldn't last more than a few more minutes. The best they could do was to make him comfortable until he passed.

To that end Burke took the man's hand and held it, letting him know he wasn't alone. The Frenchman gripped his hand with surprising strength and pulled him closer as he tried to tell him something.

Burke didn't understand.

The Frenchman tried again.

"Pardonnez-moi," he said, as he coughed up a thick mass of blood.

Forgive me.

Burke glanced away, trying to order his thoughts, to find it in his heart to honestly forgive the man, and at that moment the Frenchman's grip suddenly when slack. When Burke looked back, the man was dead.

The man's attempt to beg for forgiveness didn't sit right with Burke until he ripped open the man's shirt and found the red welts that showed where they had burned him with a hot poker.

After that, it wasn't too hard to figure out what must have happened. The Boche must have stumbled on the partisan safe house, discovered that Pierre was waiting for someone, and had then tortured him to get information. Maybe they'd seized his family, threatened them as well. In any case, Pierre had cracked, and once he'd done so they'd used him as bait in an attempt to lure the Americans out into the open.

What was done was done. Nothing to do about it now.

"Your orders, sir?" Sergeant Moore asked, from where he was patiently standing off to one side. Burke hadn't even heard him approach.

He shook his head to clear it of the extraneous thoughts and focused on the task at hand. The truck fire was still burning, and great, greasy plumes of black smoke were wandering skyward. If the locals weren't wondering what was going on, they certainly would be soon. It was time to leave.

"Let's grab what we can from the bodies—maps, ammunition, even local currency if they have any—and then get out of here. I want to be back on the trail in fifteen minutes."

"Yes, sir!"

As Sergeant Moore hurried back toward the house, Burke took another look at the devastation around him.

Guess our days of running without discovery are over.

CHAPTER THIRTY-TWO

WHEN FREEMAN CAME to, he found himself being pushed down the hall in a wheelchair.

Or, at least, that's what he thought was happening.

He couldn't be sure if his senses were completely accurate; his vision was blurry and kept fading in and out, so all he was getting were quick snapshots of whatever was happening nearby. He could hear people speaking around him, but their voices sounded like they were talking underwater, all liquid tones and incoherent sounds.

He caught sight of a doorway coming up and tried to reach out, intent on stopping any forward movement until he regained some control over his faculties, but his arm refused to obey the commands his mind was giving it. That convinced him that maybe he'd been injured in a firefight, that the POW camp and the pit and the rotworms they'd put in the wound on his leg had all just been hallucinations, a result of the injury he had sustained. Fear shot through him like a three-alarm fire in a paper factory! The idea that he'd been injured made him think that he couldn't get his arm to move because his arm wasn't there anymore, blown off in a mortar attack or severed during a plane crash, and he was about to start screaming for a doctor when the wheelchair went over a small bump on the floor and his head tilted down, showing him his arms and hands resting comfortably in his lap. He focused his attention on them, willing them to move, but they just lay there, like lumps of discarded meat, and no matter how hard he willed them to move, he couldn't get them to budge.

Apparently things were much worse than he thought, for he hadn't lost his limbs at all, he'd lost the ability to move them. He must have been paralyzed, maybe even brain damaged!

Oh Lord, he thought, *please Lord, don't do this to me, don't, don't, don't do this . . .*

A hand reached down and patted him on the shoulder as his wheelchair was turned into a room.

"You need to relax, Major," said a familiar voice, though at the moment he couldn't figure out to whom it belonged. "The rotworms secrete a rather active psychotropic compound that affects people in different ways, so you might be feeling weird at the moment. I can assure you that you are not paralyzed; just relax, all right?"

Must have spoken aloud, Freeman thought to himself and then wondered if he'd done it again.

He didn't have the chance to find out. A siren began to sound, wailing in and out, an eerie cacophony that drowned out everything else for several long minutes. When Freeman could hear again, he realized someone else had entered the room with them and was having a conversation with his caretaker.

" . . . have escaped!" the newcomer said, rather urgently. "They've broken through the first fence line and are swarming over the prisoner barracks as we speak!"

"Why are you telling me? Inform Obertleutnant Brandt. His troops are the ones assigned to deal with outbreaks."

"I already have, sir," came the reply, and this time even Freeman, doped up as he was, recognized the fear in the man's voice. "Oberleutnant Brandt took a team into the compound when the trouble first began. No one has seen him since."

In the silence that followed Freeman finally remembered who

the voice belonged to. It was the doctor who had him removed from the pit and ordered him cleaned up and his wounded leg attended to, Dr. Taschner.

But what were they talking about? And why did they sound so afraid?

"Can you drive?" Taschner asked.

"Yes, Docktor!"

"Good. Get a staff car from the motor pool and bring it around to the rear of the building. You are to take this man to Dr. Eisenberg at the Verdun complex. Is that clear?"

"Right away, sir!"

Freeman must have gone off in his head for a few minutes, for when he came back to himself two soldiers were lifting him out of the wheelchair and into the back of a black staff car with the Imperial Hohenzollern eagle painted on the front doors.

Around them was chaos.

Gunfire and screams split the air, and squads of men in the blue-gray uniforms of the German army ran past, headed for some confrontation deeper in the camp. The guard who was helping him into the vehicle had a couple of long, ragged tears in his uniform tunic, as if he'd tangled with a wild animal, and he kept casting nervous looks over his shoulder as if to make sure that nothing was sneaking up behind him.

When they had Freeman settled into the rear seat and buckled into place, one soldier climbed in beside him while the other took his place behind the wheel.

As the driver pulled away from the infirmary, Freeman glanced out the window and what he saw shocked the fog from his senses.

A man wearing the light gray coverall that designated him as a prisoner of war was running toward them, seemingly intent on catching the car before it could leave the camp. Something about him looked familiar, and by the time the runner had closed half the distance, Freeman understood why. It was Demonet, the French captain the guards had hauled away the day before.

He looked stronger than Freeman remembered him being, as

if he'd been eating four-course meals for the last few months in captivity rather than the meager sustenance that their captors provided, and any trace of the limp he'd moved with yesterday was gone. As he drew closer Freeman could see black lines running beneath his skin, like routes on a map, but his head was too full of rotworm secretions to understand just why he should be alarmed by that fact.

It seemed to him that Demonet was moving extraordinarily fast as well, for he closed with their vehicle even as it was picking up speed, and Freeman's anxiety grew accordingly the closer the other man got. A normal human being shouldn't be able to do that, Freeman told himself, and he knew that it was more than just a visual illusion caused by the drug in his system.

Something was wrong.

Demonet was no longer Demonet.

Freeman tried to move, to alert the soldier beside him, but all he succeeded in doing was jerking his foot back and forth ineffectually beneath him.

As it turned out, he needn't have worried; Demonet managed to get their attention all on his own when he leaped ten feet through the air and landed with a loud crash on the rear of the vehicle, sinking his claws—*claws?*—into the surface of the trunk.

The soldier in the rear seat spun around to see what had caused the ruckus and found himself face-to-face with the thing that had once been Claude Demonet.

The man yelped in fear and snatched at the pistol in the holster on his belt, all the while shouting something at the driver in German.

Apparently the shouts had been a command for the man to take evasive action for the driver began swerving the vehicle back and forth in an effort to dislodge their unwanted passenger. The shambler just sank his claws deeper into the metal and wouldn't let go. When the driver was forced to straighten the car out for a moment to avoid running down a group of fellow soldiers, the shambler scurried up to the rear window and peered inside.

The creature's mouth split open in a wide, froglike grin, and Freeman could see row upon row of razor-sharp teeth lining it.

The shambler drew back one fist and prepared to smash the rear window, but the soldier finally had his gun out and fired through the glass.

The bullet struck the shambler in the chest and knocked it right off the rear of the vehicle, rolling several times in the street before coming to a rest.

It wasn't moving, but Freeman wasn't convinced it was dead, either.

Then the driver shot through the gates of Stalag 113 onto the open road beyond.

CHAPTER THIRTY-THREE

★

THE RIDE WAS long and uneventful. At first Freeman tried to speak to his guard, wanting to talk about what had happened back at Stalag 113, but neither of them spoke the other's language and gestures weren't adequate when discussing the transformation of men into monsters and attacks by rampaging shamblers. Unable to communicate, Freeman settled back against his seat and quickly fell asleep, exhausted both mentally and physically from all he'd been through over the last several days. The relative safety and the rocking motion of the car lulled him into a deep sleep.

The guard nudged him awake as they approached the main gates to the facility at Verdun. The driver had a brief conversation with the guards, the barriers were lifted, and they drove through. This camp was much bigger than the previous one and there was a great deal more activity, causing Freeman to wonder just why he was being brought here.

The driver took them through camp, giving Freeman a good view of the local garrison and the shambler pens, and then he stopped in front of a row of small cottagelike buildings. An officer stood in front of one of them, accompanied by several soldiers, all dressed in the blue-gray of the German infantry. They were waiting patiently, it seemed, for his arrival.

When the car stopped, the guard beside Freeman ordered him to get out. Expecting to have difficulty with his leg, the Allied pilot was surprised to discover that it felt as good as new. The flesh beneath the bandages no longer felt hot and swollen, and it supported his weight without difficulty when he went to stand on it.

The officer, a lieutenant from the insignia on his uniform, stepped forward, and Burke tried to suppress the instant reaction that overcame him at the sight of the man. It was clear that he was no longer human. His black veins stood out prominently against his gray skin, and his eyes had the yellow cast to them that was so common in the shamblers. But he walked and talked and moved like one of the living.

Freeman's first guess was that he was looking at a revenant, one of those extremely rare shamblers that came back with their physical and mental faculties intact, much like Richthofen himself. But from what he'd heard, such creatures didn't exhibit the physical characteristics of the shamblers, either, and Adler certainly did.

Perhaps he's a new breed of shambler, Freeman thought. He'd already encountered one variation, in the houndlike creatures that had hunted him after the crash. Could this be another?

The officer said, "Welcome to Verdun, Major Freeman. I am Leutnant Adler. Rittmeister Richthofen regrets that he could not be here to meet you personally. If you would follow me, please."

Richthofen! So the bastard had lived.

Freeman wasn't surprised; after all, he himself had managed to walk away from the crash. Doing the same when you were already dead must have been that much easier. Still, it was disappointing to hear. He'd hoped he'd downed the German ace once and for all.

Adler didn't appear to notice his scrutiny but turned and led him inside the building before them.

The little cottage turned out to be the visiting officer's quarters, with a bed and a desk and a small sink for washing up. A clean set of clothes was laid out on the bed, and there was a plate of fresh fruit on the desktop.

As Freeman stepped inside, Adler said, "Rittmeister Richthofen will be with you as soon as he can. If you need anything in the meantime, ask the guards and they will contact me."

It sounded good, but from the tone of his voice, Adler made it clear that he didn't expect to be bothered for any reason. Nor did the way he pulled the door shut without a backward glance leave any room for misunderstanding.

Freeman waited a moment, until he heard the car pull away out front, then he opened the door.

The two guards stationed outside turned to face him, their weapons at the ready and pointed in his direction.

Freeman smiled tightly at them, then shut the door before they could say anything.

He crossed the room and looked out the window on the wall opposite the door. Another guard stood a few feet away, watching the house from that direction, ostensibly preventing Freeman from climbing through the window and making a run for it, though where he would go in a camp surrounded by hundreds of enemy soldiers was up for grabs.

The sound of an approaching plane drew his attention away from the guard to the airfield he saw on the northern edge of the camp. A red triplane was just coming in for a landing and Freeman watched the pilot put the aircraft down, a sense of jealousy stirring in his heart. It had been days since Freeman had been in the air and his longing to be up among the clouds was like a physical weight, dragging him down. He'd flown nearly every day since arriving at the front; being stuck dirtside was its own special torture. Richthofen had to know what he was going through; otherwise, why situate him where he could hear and see the airfield all day and night?

He moved to close the curtains only to discover there weren't any.

Oh, Richthofen knew all right!

Bastard.

Wandering back over to the sink, Burke found a straight razor and a cup of shaving powder resting on the edge. He eyed the razor for a long moment, as thoughts of using it to kill the guards out front ran through his mind, but he dismissed them as quickly as they came. He was starting to understand that everything about his presence here was calculated, no doubt by Richthofen, and snatching up the weapon and trying to use it was exactly what they expected him to do.

He refused to be their patsy.

Instead, he decided to have a shave. He'd always kept himself clean-shaven, and his face itched terribly from the several days of beard growth that now covered it. A good shave would make him feel better mentally as well as physically. Once he was finished with that, he changed into the clean set of clothes and sat down on the bed to await whatever was next.

They came for him an hour later.

He heard the car pull up and was on his feet by the time there was a swift knock on his door. He opened it to find Adler waiting on the step outside.

"If you would come with me, please," Adler ordered.

Freeman had the sudden urge to tell him no, just to be a pain in the ass, but he conquered the feeling and did as he was told.

Adler let Freeman precede him into the rear of the vehicle and then leaned forward to give some instructions to the driver in German.

As the driver pulled away, Freeman was unable to keep himself from glancing out the window toward the airfield and was met with a startling sight. A massive airship was now moored alongside one of the hangars, the black crosses painted on its tail stark against its gleaming silver skin. It was at least three times the size of any he'd seen before, with an oversized gondola to match, and had several flat platforms hanging beneath its bulk. He caught a glimpse of long rows of narrow openings piercing the underside of each platform. He didn't know what they were for, but one thing was certain; if those were weapon bays, that ship would carry one helluva punch. The airship must have just arrived, for mooring lines were still being secured and a ground crew was working frantically to get it settled into a makeshift berth.

The driver pulled up before a two-story manor house and let them out. Adler led Freeman inside. The American glimpsed several richly furnished rooms as they passed by. He was led into a study at the far end of the hall.

"Please make yourself comfortable," Adler said. "Rittmeister Richthofen will join you shortly." He left Freeman alone in the room, pulling the door shut behind him as he left.

Freeman assumed this was Richthofen's personal residence. He wandered about the room, trying to get a sense of the man he was about to meet, the man who had been his personal nemesis for what felt like years. Richthofen clearly enjoyed reading, as the walls were covered with shelves full of well-worn books, mainly historical treatises or military examinations of particular battles and tactics. A copy of the Baron's own *Der Rote Kampfflieger,* or the *Red Battle Flyer,* the autobiography he had written just before being killed the first time, was stuck between a copy of Caesar's *Gallic Wars* and Bismarck's memoirs. Freeman found himself wondering how the Baron would deal with his subsequent "deaths" if he ever got around to writing a revised version.

He left the bookshelves, glanced idly at the papers on the man's desk; most was correspondence to his brother, Lothar, it seemed. He turned his attention to the chessboard set up on its own table in the corner. He was standing in front of it, studying the game already in progress, when a voice spoke from behind him.

"Knight to Queen's Rook 4. Checkmate in 16."

Freeman turned around and found himself looking at a man who, just days before, he'd done his best to kill and who had tried to kill him in turn.

Rittmeister Manfred Albrecht Freiherr von Richthofen.

The Red Baron himself.

He was dressed in a well-tailored uniform of dark gray that buttoned across the front in double-breasted fashion. A red ribbon around his throat held a medallion in the shape of a blue-enameled Maltese cross with eagles of gold between its arms, which was Germany's highest military honor, the *Pour le Mérite,* otherwise known as the Blue Max. Hung over the back of his shoulders was a fur-lined leather flight jacket that looked as if it had seen a fair bit of use.

Richthofen wore his hair slicked back and parted in the middle, which only served to exaggerate his long, narrow face and to highlight the spot along his left jawline where Freeman could see bone poking through a section of missing flesh the size of a half dollar, a remnant left over from when the Rittmeister's body had started to rot after being shot down and killed the first time.

"Do you play?" Richthofen asked, indicating the board and watching with blue hawklike eyes as he crossed the room.

"Occasionally," Freeman replied, glancing down to buy some time while he tried to get his thoughts in order.

He had no idea what he was doing here or what it was that Richthofen wanted from him. Make no doubt, Richthofen wanted something; you didn't think sixteen moves ahead in chess and not apply that kind of thinking to everything you did. There was a reason Richthofen had rescued him from that pit and brought him here, wherever the hell *here* was. Not that he was complaining; this was a damn sight better than being surrounded by the rotting corpses of dead shamblers, so he wasn't about to look a gift horse in the mouth. He needed to remember, though, that the German ace had a purpose for rescuing him, even if that purpose wasn't obvious.

Richthofen shook his head, as if he'd just remembered something. He marched across the room to stand before Freeman and extended his right hand.

"Please, forgive my rudeness. I am Freiherr von Richthofen."

Determined not to let the other man get the better of him, Freeman shook the offered hand.

"Major Jack Freeman," he said as he did so, pleased that his voice didn't betray any of the discomfort he felt at the cold, clammy feel of the other man's skin.

"Your reputation precedes you, Major."

"As does yours," he answered politely.

Richthofen moved over to the pair of leather chairs near the fireplace and settled into one of them. He waved his hand at the other. "Please, join me."

Not seeing any reason to not do as he was asked, Freeman sat down opposite the German ace.

Richthofen got right down to business. "I wanted to apologize for what you went through while under the supervision of Oberst Schulheim. I acted as soon as I learned that you had survived the crash, and I give you my word, both as an officer and a fellow flier, that he will be dealt with appropriately."

Freeman shrugged, not knowing what to say. Richthofen sounded sincere, but Freeman had no way of knowing if his captor truly meant what he said or not. The best strategy seemed to be to say nothing at all.

A few moments of silence passed as Richthofen seemed to evaluate what he wanted to say. At last, he asked, "Tell me, Major, why did you join the AEF?"

The question surprised Freeman. "To fly, of course," he replied.

That, apparently, was an answer Richthofen could understand. "It is glorious, is it not? To slip the bonds of earth and soar among the clouds? To pit your skills against those of another flier, like knights of the air fighting for the favor of the Queen?"

Freeman was surprised. It was almost as if Richthofen had reached down right into the center of his soul and read his secret heart. *Knights of the air, indeed!*

"Flying has certainly been one of the few pleasures of this war, yes," Freeman replied, not wanting to admit how the other man had struck the heart of his emotions.

Richthofen's next comment, however, showed he wasn't fooled by Freeman's casual reply.

"It must be hard, for a man like you, to deal with the realization that your flying days are over. At least, that is, for the duration of the war."

Was that a hint of mockery he heard in Richthofen's voice?

The German ace didn't seem to notice Freeman's sudden tension. He went on in the same matter-of-fact tone that he'd started with earlier. "It doesn't have to be that way, you know."

Freeman laughed. "Somehow I don't see you giving me an aircraft and sending me on my merry way."

Richthofen smiled, revealing the sudden flash of wet bone at his jawline. "On the contrary, Major, I'd be happy to do so." He paused, then concluded, "Provided you were to join me."

The American wasn't certain he'd heard him correctly. "Excuse me?"

Richthofen leaned forward, and Freeman could see what he could only term an unholy light shining deep in the German officer's eyes. "How many kills do you have now, Major? Seventy-four? Seventy-five?"

It was actually eighty-two, but he just shrugged and said, "Something like that, yes."

"Ha! You are lying; I can tell. But no matter. A little modesty can be an asset for gentlemen like you and me," Richthofen replied. "The truth of the matter is this. Whether it is seventy-five, eighty, or even one hundred kills, you are clearly the Allies' top ace."

Freeman didn't try to argue. A fierce competition had sprung up in the early days of the war between fliers on both sides of the conflict. At first it had been a race first to see who could make five kills and become an ace, but as the war ground on and the better pilots lived to fight another day, it became a race for the top, to become the ace of aces, the ruler of the sky.

Richthofen had been clearly in the lead with eighty-nine kills when he'd been shot down that first time. That had been an incredible achievement, but what he'd done since was absolutely astonishing. In the last two years he'd bested twice as many pilots as he had in the four years prior to that, bringing his current total to 267, last Freeman knew. It could have gone even higher in the days Freeman was in captivity.

One of those "kills" was me, Freeman thought.

Richthofen seemed to sense what he was thinking. "If you had not steered your plane into my own, there is a good possibility our encounter might have ended with you as the victor, rather than me."

Freeman didn't agree, but he politely inclined his head to acknowledge the implied compliment.

"We are the two best pilots on both sides of the conflict. Were you to join my Circus, there would be none who could oppose us! We would own the sky and could dictate whatever terms we wanted from the losers on the battlefield. Forget being a knight—you could be a duke, nay, a prince of the air!"

With you as king, of course, Freeman thought in a slightly dazed fashion. Being asked to betray his country and join Richthofen was quite possibly the last thing Freeman had expected to hear. He was literally shocked into silence.

Richthofen went on. "I assure you, the *Auferstehung* process is a painless one, and it has been considerably refined since I underwent it as one of its first subjects, accidental as that incident might have been."

The freiherr leaped to his feet, caught up in his own passionate rhetoric. "No longer will things like hunger or thirst plague you!" he said, pacing back and forth across the room. "No longer will your body be susceptible to the plights that can befall an ordinary man. You will be smarter, stronger, faster than you ever were before. None will be able to stand against us! The empire will be ours to command!"

Freeman knew at that moment that he was in the presence of a madman. The very notion that he would betray his country and join the man he had spent the last few years trying to send to his just reward was absolutely ludicrous, yet Richthofen obviously believed it might be possible or he wouldn't have made the offer. That worried Freeman more than he wanted to let on, for if he turned Richthofen down, who knew how he would react?

Trying to buy some time during which he could figure a way out of the situation without getting shot on the spot, Freeman asked, "The Auferstehung process? What is that?"

The question seemed to bring Richthofen back to his senses. He stopped, shook his head as if to clear it, and looked hard at Freeman, as if checking to see if Freeman had noticed his irrational behavior.

Freeman made sure his expression did nothing to convey what he really thought: *coming back from the dead twice had certainly messed with the German ace's mental stability and emotional health.*

Apparently satisfied with what he saw, Richthofen relaxed. "I will explain the Auferstehung process tomorrow, when you've had a chance to rest. I'm sure what you've been through has been particularly draining. I will have Leutnant Adler escort you back to your quarters and see to it you are fed properly. We'll talk again tomorrow."

Just as quickly as it started, his audience with Richthofen was over. The German ace strode from the room without another word, only to be replaced several seconds later by his aide, Adler.

Soon thereafter, Freeman was returned to his quarters, as Richthofen called them, and locked inside to await whatever craziness tomorrow might bring.

As he listened to airplanes coming and going in the field outside, Freeman did his best to forget what Richthofen had said, but the words kept echoing inside his head.

Your flying days are over.

Your flying days are over.

Your flying days are over.

CHAPTER THIRTY-FOUR

ONCE FREEMAN WAS led from the sitting room, Richthofen returned. Gone was the sense of manic behavior that surrounded him only moments before, and in its place a cold, reptilian-like logic remained.

The truth was, his instability had all been an act. He wanted Freeman to underestimate him, so that when the time came, he'd be able to break the American flier without effort.

Richthofen was pouring himself a scotch from the decanter in the corner when he heard the door behind him open and then close again.

"Care for a drink, Docktor?" he asked, glancing over his shoulder at Eisenberg who stood in the room's doorway.

"That would be excellent, Herr Richthofen."

Richthofen handed the other man a glass full of the deep amber-red liquid and then picked up his own. With the requisite toast to the kaiser out of the way, he took a long pull on his drink, holding a folded piece of white cloth over the hole in the side of his jaw with his other hand while he did so, not wanting to waste any of the hundred-year-old liquor. He could barely taste it anymore, but he was determined to continue enjoying some of the activities common to his earlier life, and a good glass of scotch was one of them.

"You heard?" Richthofen asked, knowing the other man had been listening in on his exchange with Freeman.

"Of course. I thought your performance was quite remarkable, actually."

Richthofen ignored the compliment; Eisenberg's constant need to curry favor could be highly annoying, but right now Richthofen was too pleased with how the meeting had gone to care.

"What do you think? Will he survive the transformation process?" Richthofen asked.

"I believe so. He appears determined to survive regardless of what happens to him, which is an excellent sign that he'll have the mental stamina necessary to come through with his mind intact. And thanks to Taschner, the infection in his leg is gone, giving him the physical toughness he'll need to withstand the change as well."

"Excellent," Richthofen replied. He had plans for Freeman, important plans, and he preferred that the American ace come through the resurrection process with his sanity intact.

"Where are we in regard to Operation Stormcloud? Can we launch as anticipated?"

Eisenberg nodded. "We started production of the gas several weeks ago, when Taschner first let us know about the success rates he was seeing with the new compound. We completed the first batch at 1500 hours this afternoon.

"We'll need thirty-six to forty-eight hours to properly load the canisters onto the *Megaera* and another five to six hours to prime the deployment system. After that, it will be entirely up to the pilot."

Richthofen was pleased. The airship was ready to be loaded, and reports from the other facilities were equally positive. It looked like there was very little that could stop his forward momentum at this point. If he could turn Freeman to his cause, all the better, but one way or another, the Allies were about to learn what it meant to face the German juggernaut when it was led by one worthy of the role.

Then, when he had finished eliminating the empire's enemy, he would turn his attention to the emperor himself. The Grand Council would be only too happy to replace that weak, insipid fool who currently occupied the palace with the man who had won this war quickly, decisively, and with a minimum of German casualties.

Feeling generous, Richthofen said, "I'm going to invite Taschner to join us for the launch. He deserves to understand the impact his contributions will have on the war effort. Besides, it will be good to finally meet the man."

"As you wish, Herr Richthofen."

Which, when you got right down to it, Richthofen thought, *was what this was all about anyway. What he, Manfred von Richthofen, wanted. Nothing else really mattered.*

CHAPTER THIRTY-FIVE

ON THE ROAD TO VERDUN

WITH THE HELP of a map found on the body of an oberleutnant at the scene of the ambush, Burke led the squad away from the farmhouse less than five minutes after the last shot had been fired. He was concerned that the truck fire would bring reinforcements, so he cut eastward through the forest rather than follow the contours of the road as he'd originally intended. He set an accelerated pace, worried as he was about what might happen to Freeman if word of the patrol's destruction should reach the wrong ears. The men, too, seemed to understand the necessity; if they did not, they at least kept their complaints to themselves.

The forest was full of well-cleared trails and they made good time, covering several miles in short order. When they stopped for a break, Burke gathered the men together for a quick strategy session.

"We're about two and a half miles from our objective. Without the intel from the partisan group, we don't know what kind of defenses to expect at the camp, so from this point on we make as little noise as possible. If you need to communicate on the trail, use hand signals only. I want everyone to keep their eyes peeled as well. The last thing we want to do is walk into an enemy observation post."

At the rate they'd been traveling, Burke anticipated that they would reach their objective, a thickly wooded area that overlooked the west side of camp, by late afternoon. They'd observe the target from that location and hopefully get an understanding of where Freeman was being kept. Once they knew that, they could decide on a specific plan to get him out.

The last section of their march proved uneventful. They made good time and reached the outer reaches of the camp right on time. But when they reached the tree line and looked out from cover at their objective, they received a major shock, leaving many of them staring openmouthed in surprise.

Stalag 113 was no more.

In its place was a battle-torn and fire-ravaged shell that had ceased functioning as a POW camp and was now nothing more than a silent witness to the catastrophe that had claimed it.

Several of the outlying buildings were nothing more than smoldering ruins from which smoke still drifted. Large holes had been torn in the fence line, and one of the guard towers looked like it had been smashed flat by a giant's foot. For a moment Burke wondered why they hadn't seen the smoke during their approach, then realized the thick tree cover had prevented them from doing so. Now they couldn't miss it, just as they couldn't miss the bodies littering the ground inside the compound.

Jack might be down there, dead or dying, Burke thought and was surprised by the anxiety it caused. He hadn't thought he had any feelings left for his half brother, especially not good ones.

With a wave of his hand, Burke led the squad forward.

They stopped just inside the broken front gates and surveyed the death and destruction before them. Bodies lay everywhere they looked. Some were dressed in the bluish-gray uniforms that were the hallmark of the kaiser's army while others wore lighter gray coveralls with the letter K on their backs, an abbreviation Burke knew was used to reflect their status as prisoners of war. Strangely, the positions of the bodies made it clear that the two groups had died side by side manning the barricades against what appeared to be a third group.

Just who, or rather what, they'd been defending against became clear a few yards deeper in the camp as Burke and his squad stumbled over the corpse of their first shambler.

This one had been cut almost in half at the point just below its ribs. The upper half of its body lay at an angle to the lower half, connected by only a few ragged strands of tissue near the spinal column. The creature's guts were spread out along the ground beside it. The shambler was dressed in a green jumpsuit, now stained dark with blood. Burke was about to step over it and move on when what he was seeing actually registered on the conscious side of his brain and brought him up short.

The shambler was dressed and not in the usual rags. No, this one was wearing a drab, olive-colored jumpsuit that clearly served as some kind of uniform and a new one at that.

Sonofabitch.

The realization forced him to look closer at the corpse, which caused several other differences to spring out at him.

Most shamblers he'd encountered were physically damaged from whatever violent act had taken their life before they were brought back as one of the walking dead. If they had been dead long enough, they might have even started to rot. This particular shambler looked physically intact. In fact, if you ignored the thick black veins visible beneath the creature's skin and the fact that its torso had been all but cut cleanly in half, it actually looked, well, healthy.

That's not right.

Burke squatted down next to it to get a closer look.

To his untrained eye, there seemed to be some evidence that the creature's face had undergone physical changes during the resurrection process, not the least of which was a bony ridge running from the nose, up over the top of the head and down the back of the skull. Its fingers were elongated, and there was an extra joint on several of them. The fingernails had thickened and grown out by several inches, creating a natural weapon that, judging by the dried blood and scraps of flesh caught beneath them, had been useful in the fight that had taken the creature's life.

"What is it, Captain?" Graves asked, noting his interest in the body.

As Burke glanced in the professor's direction, the shambler at his feet opened its eyes and lunged for him from the waist up.

It took a split second for Burke to realize he'd never move fast enough to get out of the way, to see the shambler's lips open revealing a mouth stuffed full of row after row of sharp-looking teeth, to hear Graves's shout of surprise as if from miles away . . .

The top of the shambler's head blew apart just before the sound of the rifle's report reached Burke's ears, and the creature flopped back down against the hard ground, dead once more.

His heart pounding, Burke looked up to find Jones lowering his rifle from his shoulder, a thin wisp of smoke drifting from the end of the barrel.

The two men eyed each other.

Then Graves broke the spell by passing between them as he threw himself down next to Burke in his eagerness to examine what was left of the shambler.

"Did you see that?!" he exclaimed, acting like a kid in a candy store. "It's got fully articulated . . ."

Burke tuned out the rest. He climbed to his feet and found Charlie standing next to him, ready to help. That made him realize how shaken he was by the shambler's attack; he hadn't heard his sergeant approach.

"You all right?" Charlie asked.

"Yeah, I'm good," he told him, then he raised his voice so the others in the squad could hear him. "Double-check any shambler carcass you come across. There's plenty of ammo lying around, so don't hesitate to put a bullet through every skull in order to be sure they are dead; we don't want these things getting back up again when we're not looking."

They had no idea how many of the undead might still be moving on the base, so they stuck together, wanting the increased firepower they could bring to bear. Splitting into pairs might have made the work go faster, but it was a risk Burke was unwilling to accept. If one of their isolated teams ran into a pack of live shamblers, they'd be overwhelmed in seconds, just like the base's original inhabitants. No, they'd stick together, even if it took all day to cover the base in its entirety.

They moved quickly but carefully, checking each corpse for signs of life by nudging it with the barrel of a rifle or the sole of a boot while a partner kept a bead on its skull with his own weapon. If it didn't move, and it was human, they checked to be sure it wasn't the corpse of Major Freeman and then searched it for anything useful—ammo, grenades, even cigarettes. Those they found were quickly confiscated and passed around.

Every building had to be searched to ensure that there weren't any shamblers hiding in the shadows, so they developed a system to reduce the risk. Two men would wait on either side of the door, weapons ready, while a third would kick it in. The minute he did so the others would spin around the doorjamb and take out anything waiting inside. When the first room was cleared, they moved on to the next. It was time consuming, and the sheer tension of expecting a group of shamblers to come charging out of every doorway had their nerves on edge. Several times they were forced to put down an injured but still struggling shambler, but thankfully they didn't encounter any uninjured ones roaming the grounds.

When they'd cleared all but the large, two-story building that appeared to be the base headquarters, Burke headed in that direction, hoping to find some answers. They still hadn't found any evidence that Jack had ever been here and the idea that they had come all this way for nothing was not sitting well with him.

CHAPTER THIRTY-SIX

A STAFF CAR was parked just in front of the building. The car's windshield was cracked and its tires shredded to ribbons. It was surrounded by the half-eaten bodies of several German soldiers. A handful more bodies, both human and shambler this time, led up the stairs and through the shattered front doors of the building. Burke surveyed the carnage, eventually deciding that the command staff had tried to make a run for it and had been forced to retreat back inside the house when the shamblers attacked.

A quick search of all but the commandant's office confirmed that the rest of the house was empty. They left the office for last, because of the barricade that guarded the entrance. The men assigned to hold the position had died where they stood, but the doors beyond were still intact and gave Burke some hope that there might be someone still alive in there who could give them some answers.

Those hopes were dashed, however, when they broke down the doors and discovered the commandant, one Oberst Schulheim, according to the plaque on his desk, sitting in his chair, dead from a self-inflicted gunshot wound to the head. On the floor nearby was a second man, this one lying in a puddle of his own blood. From the bullet holes in the back of his white lab coat it was clear that he had been shot from behind by the commandant. A briefcase lay near the man's outstretched hand, the files inside spilling out across the floor.

While Charlie checked the rest of the room, Burke walked over, scooped up the files, and began looking through them.

They were in German, but Burke was still able to recognize their contents as scientific notes of some kind. The long chemical formulas were a dead giveaway. He could pick out certain words here and there, mostly names, like that of Manfred von Richthofen. In fact, Richthofen's name appeared in various places in several of the files, which Burke found curious.

"Anything interesting?" Charlie asked, from where he was currently rifling through the papers on the commandant's desk while trying not to get the dead man's blood on himself.

"I'm not sure," Burke replied, still looking at the papers. "Ask Graves to come in here, will you?"

Charlie nodded and stepped outside to find the professor.

While he waited, Burke tried to quench the sense of unease growing in his chest. The intelligence they'd received claimed Jack was being held at this facility, but so far they had found neither hide nor hair of him. If he'd been here, he was gone now.

With no clue as to what might have happened to him or where he might have gone, their options were severely limited. Occupied France was an awfully big place. Jack, if he was still alive, could be anywhere within its boundaries. *Hell,* Burke thought, *at this point he could be anywhere within the German Empire.*

Equally disturbing were the events that had apparently unfolded prior to their arrival. How had a group of shamblers gotten loose among the general population of the camp and gone on a feeding frenzy, attacking guards and prisoners alike? It was clear that faced with a common enemy, the two groups had banded together in an attempt to stop the threat, but what wasn't clear was how it had all started. He could guess at the end, though; large gaping holes in the outer fence suggested the surviving shamblers had forced their way out of the camp only to disappear into the depths of the forest.

Where they were now was anyone's guess.

Charlie returned at that point with Graves in tow, stopping Burke's musings. Burke handed the professor the files he'd been looking at and asked him to translate as best he was able.

It didn't take him long. "Hmm," Graves said, as he looked them over. "These look to be records of experiments, some current, some going back several months. This one is from February, this one from the November before that, and this one . . . wait a minute. What's this . . . ?"

Graves began reading aloud, mumbling about chemical reactions and methodologies to get specific populations to react within certain guidelines and . . .

The professor abruptly stopped talking to himself, flipped forward several pages, read some more, and then collapsed into a nearby chair, a shell-shocked look of horror on his face.

"It can't be," he said, more to himself than the others.

Burke heard him clearly, though, and something in Graves's tone sent shivers up his spine. Whatever it was, it couldn't be good news, and that made him nervous.

"Talk to me, Graves," he said. "What do they say?"

The professor looked up, and in his eyes Burke saw that wild look that people get when they're on the verge of panicking. The man kept glancing down at the pages of the file in front of him and then around the room, like a caged animal searching for a way out.

"Take it easy, Professor," Burke said. "It can't be all that bad."

But apparently it was, for rather than answering, Graves began flipping through the file again, frantically rereading certain sections and muttering to himself. "No . . . no no no . . ."

That was as much as Burke could take. "What the hell's going on, Graves?!"

The professor started and then visibly pulled himself together. He turned to Burke and took a deep breath.

"They've found a way to modify the corpse gas so that it affects both viable and necrotic tissue."

Viable and necrotic.

Living and dead.

Burke couldn't believe what he was hearing. If Graves was right, the implications were staggering. The war would be over in a matter of days, the kaiser's army sweeping over the Allied defenses as the gas turned everyone it touched into flesh-eating monsters.

"Are you sure?" Burke said at last, when he'd found his voice.

"No," Graves replied, "but I think I know a way to test my theory."

He got to his feet, handed the files to Burke, and disappeared out the door. He was only gone a moment; when he came back, he was dragging the corpse of a shambler by its heels.

"Don't just stand there; give me a hand with this," he said, when he realized the other two men were staring at him in surprise.

Charlie jumped to help, and they managed to get the corpse up onto the commandant's desk. Like the shambler that had attacked Burke earlier, this one too was dressed in a green jumpsuit. Graves pulled a knife off his belt and began to cut the clothing off the body, explaining as he went.

"I've examined hundreds of shamblers over the last several months. Most were frontline soldiers killed in the line of duty and raised by a touch of the gas, only to be killed a second time by our troops."

He finished cutting the jumpsuit open and peeled it back, revealing the shambler's gray skin.

"Every shambler I've examined had had two sets of mortal wounds as a result, the one that most recently ended its unlife and another, earlier wound that served as the original cause of death. If the information in the files is accurate, if our enemy has, indeed, managed to alter the composition of the gas enough to impact living tissue . . ."

" . . . then we should only see one set of injuries," Charlie finished for him.

"Sergeant Moore is correct," Graves replied, bending over to examine the corpse more closely. "This should only take a few minutes."

Burke didn't want to watch. Excusing himself, he stepped outside for a bit of fresh air, pulling the pack of cigarettes he'd been carrying since this whole mess started out of the inside pocket of his uniform as he went. One final cigarette stared back at him. He hesitated for a moment, muttered a low "Fuck it," and then lit up.

A few minutes later, Graves came out the front door, wiping black shambler blood off his hands with a towel he'd picked up from somewhere inside. Charlie followed close behind. Seeing the troubled expressions on their faces, Burke asked, "Well?"

"One set of injuries. Definitely postmortem," Graves said.

"Which means what, exactly?" Burke didn't want there to be any room for misunderstanding.

"Either that . . . man in there died of some internal injury, a heart attack, maybe even a stroke, something that might not be obvious any longer due to physical changes incurred during the resurrection process, or else the files are correct and he was alive when he was exposed to the gas."

Shit.

CHAPTER THIRTY-SEVEN

BURKE OPENED HIS mouth, not yet knowing what he was going to say to Graves but knowing he had to say something, when a sharp whistle caught his attention.

Glancing toward the sound, Burke saw Private Jones standing in the watchtower by the gate, pointing frantically to something out on the road.

A moment's study revealed a vehicle of some kind making its way toward the camp. It was traveling quickly, kicking up a plume of dust behind it, which was what had caught Jones's attention. It would be here in a matter of minutes.

Burke turned and began shouting orders to the rest of the men. "Manning! Get up in that watchtower with Jones! Charlie, you're with me. The rest of you get out of sight back inside the commandant's office. Move! Move! Move!"

Burke hunkered down behind the nearby staff car with Charlie at his side. From their position they had a clear view of the vehicle as it approached the gates. It was a single-seat motorbike, the kind that couriers use to take messages between locations. The driver was dressed in a long coat and a leather cap with goggles. He must not have been paying attention, for he was through the gates before he seemed to notice the wreckage in front of him. When he did, he braked hard and brought the bike to a sliding stop.

Charlie tensed, as if about to step out from behind their cover, and Burke put a hand on his arm to stop him. "Wait," he said, "let him get off the bike . . ."

The driver straddled the bike for a long moment, looking around. When nothing came charging out at him, he cut the engine, put down the kickstand, and climbed off.

That was all Burke needed.

He stepped out from behind the car with his Tommy gun in hand and shouted, *"Einfrieren!"*

Freeze.

The driver, already spooked by what he saw around him, didn't listen. He started to turn, a pistol appearing in his hand from the depths of his coat. The crack of a rifle split the afternoon air before he'd completed even a quarter of that turn, and a bullet plowed into the ground directly in front of him in such a way that it was clear the shooter had missed only because he'd wanted to. Faced with an enemy he could not see, the German did the only reasonable thing, dropping his weapon and putting his hands in the air.

Within minutes the man was tied up with some rope they found in the wreckage of the headquarters building. While Sergeant Moore kept watch, and the rest of the team rejoined them outside now that the immediate danger had passed, Graves read and translated the dispatch cable the messenger had been carrying and then filled Burke in.

"It's addressed to a Doctor Taschner," he said.

> *Operation Stormcloud to launch as planned. Prisoner 459831 arrived and will be prepped for resurrection process. Bring sample of new formula and all relevant data to Testing Facility 89 Verdun soonest. Richthofen.*

The paper was marked with Richthofen's personal seal, a black eagle with its wings outstretched over a pair of grinning skulls, confirming its authenticity.

Burke wasn't interested in the insignia, however. His attention was on the contents. *Operation Stormcloud? Prisoner 459831?*

Burke pointed at the messenger and said to Graves, "Ask him about Stormcloud. What is it and when is it supposed to happen?"

Graves nodded, then spoke a few words in German to the sullen-faced messenger. The reply was both short and swift.

"He doesn't know," Graves translated. Burke wasn't surprised. He would never trust a courier with sensitive information like that, so expecting the other side to act differently was asking too much. Still, one never knew what men like this overheard, which was why he bothered to ask in the first place.

"What about prisoner 459831? Does he know anything about who that might be?"

Graves spoke to the other man again, and this time there was a bit more back and forth. Burke waited patiently for them to finish.

Finally, Graves turned back to Burke and said, "He says all he knows is that a new prisoner arrived at the camp yesterday and is being treated more like a guest than a POW. Rumor has it that the prisoner's an important American officer, but our man here doesn't know for sure."

Burke did though; it had to be Jack. There just wasn't any other prisoner who might be worthy of that kind of treatment. If they were going to use him as a propaganda piece, they would want to be sure he was being treated decently.

Knowing Jack's whereabouts presented a bit of a dilemma to Burke. He'd been ordered to rescue his brother, or, at the very least, keep him out of enemy hands. But that had been before they'd discovered the advances the enemy had made with regard to that damned corpse gas. Word of those advances had to get back to the Allies; if they were caught unprepared, the consequences would be apocalyptic. Entire cities could be gassed, their populations turned into hordes of the hungry dead.

The problem was that he didn't have enough proof yet to be certain those higher up the chain of command would listen. The files he had would be enough to show that the Germans were working on the process, but Graves said that there weren't any documents claiming it to be a complete success. Burke doubted that would be enough. There would be plenty of naysayers claiming it wasn't possible, that the enemy couldn't have made the requisite scientific advances quickly enough for the threat to be real, and the urgency of the problem would likely get lost in the bureaucratic tendency to talk everything to death before taking action.

It was clear this Operation Stormcloud had something to do with the new gas, otherwise, why would Richthofen have mentioned the two in the same message? But the brass wasn't likely to risk the kind of assault they would need to eliminate the threat completely, especially this far behind enemy lines, without concrete proof.

Thankfully, Burke knew just where he could get that and perhaps rescue his brother at the same time.

"Graves, see what you can do about getting him to draw us a map of that testing facility mentioned in the communiqué. Charlie, I want you to round us up some enemy uniforms, including a couple of lab coats if you can find them. Williams, you're with me. The rest of you round up as much food and water as you can find. Go!"

As the men split up to handle the various activities assigned them, Burke and Williams walked over to the motor pool they'd searched earlier.

The large garage contained several vehicles in various stages of repair. Burke selected a staff car and a two-ton lorry, then asked Williams how long it would take to get them up and running.

The younger man gave them a quick inspection.

"An hour, maybe two?"

Burke nodded. "All right, get to work. I'll send a couple of the other boys down to help you out."

WILLIAMS WAS AS good as his word. He had the staff car and the lorry back together and running smoothly inside of ninety minutes. At that point it was time for Burke to gather the men and let them know what he had planned.

"Our target has been moved to a scientific research station outside of Verdun," Burke began, "so that's where we are headed as well. I, for one, am sick of walking, however, so we're going to be taking some alternate transportation."

He jerked a thumb over his shoulder, where the two vehicles Williams had repaired were parked, and that earned him a cheer.

"We're going to need to blend in as much as possible in case we pass another convoy coming the other way, so we're going to look the part. Grab a uniform from Sergeant Moore and put it on. If you're out of ammunition for your Enfield, grab some ammunition for it or take one of the Mausers from the pile over there. We leave in twenty minutes."

As the men moved to obey, Burke pulled Graves aside and handed him one of the two officer's uniforms he'd scrounged up. "How do you feel about impersonating a German scientist?" he asked.

THE ROADS TO Verdun were well paved and, for the most part, intact. This far behind enemy lines the team didn't have to worry about nonsense like roadblocks or random checkpoints, and they were able to keep to a decent speed.

Burke, dressed in a leutnant's uniform, drove the staff car with Professor Graves posing as Dr. Taschner in the back. They passed several other motorized vehicles headed in the other direction, and each time one appeared Burke would stiffen, worried that their ruse would be discovered. Visions of being run off the road, dragged free of the wreckage, and executed flashed through his head, but each time the other vehicles simply drove past without bothering them, leaving Burke to breathe a sigh of relief.

In the end, it took them a little over two hours to make the fifty-mile trip between Vitry-le-François and Verdun. About half a mile short of their destination, Burke spotted the narrow dirt track the messenger had told them about and pulled onto it, leaving the main road behind. He drove far enough into the woods that they wouldn't be easily visible from the main road, then pulled to a stop. He shut off the engine and got out of the car.

Behind him, in the lorry, Charlie did the same.

A sharp whistle from the sergeant brought Graves out of the staff car and the rest of the men out of the back of the truck. The group gathered between the two vehicles, using the lorry's headlights to check their weapons and adjust the stolen German uniforms they wore. Graves actually looked right at home in the dead doctor's lab coat. When they were ready, Burke addressed them all.

"This is it," he said, pointing behind him into the copse of trees. "There's a small ridgeline on the other side and from that we'll be able to look down on the camp and get an idea of what we're facing. Manning and I will check it out while the rest of you stay here with Sergeant Moore. Keep your eyes open and be ready to fade into the trees if you need to."

With a final nod at Charlie, Burke slipped into the trees, Manning at his heels.

The courier had been correct; the hike up to the top of the ridge took less than ten minutes. From there they could look down a few hundred yards below.

This facility was laid out similar to the last, though it was about twice the size of the other. From up on the ridge they could see several clusters of buildings and even a small airfield on the far side of camp. Burke was digging in his pack for his viewing goggles when he felt Manning stiffen beside him.

"What is it?" he asked.

The other man hesitated, then inclined his head slightly. "Look. The airfield."

Burke glanced in that direction and was just in time to see several mechanics pushing a bright red triplane inside the field's solitary hangar.

He didn't need to be told whose plane it was, as there was only one bright red Fokker triplane in the entire German Air Corps.

Richthofen!

Burke watched the mechanics for a moment through the open doors as they went to work examining the aircraft, one climbing up a small stepladder to access the engine while the other walked around the craft itself, checking the fuselage for God knew what.

A flurry of activity from beside him drew his attention away and back to Manning. The other man had his pack off and was digging through it, pulling out cloth-wrapped items and laying them down on the ground in front of him. A palpable sense of excitement washed off him in waves.

"What are you doing?" Burke asked, more curious than worried at that point.

"What I came here to do," Manning replied.

His tone was all business, as were his actions—swift, sure, but decidedly unhurried as he unwrapped each cloth-covered piece and began to assemble the object before him.

A glance at the various pieces told Burke it was a gun, but as it came together he had to admit it was a gun unlike any he'd seen before. It looked as if it had started life as a Lee Enfield, but had morphed from there into something with cooling tubes, an extra barrel, and a snap-on sight. Manning sighted through the glass and then began dialing it in with the help of a small geared mechanism to the left of the optics.

No sooner had he done so than Manning let out a startled "Sonofabitch! That's him!" and scrambled to lower himself into a firing position.

Alarmed with the speed at which things were happening, Burke tried to get control of the events around him. A figure could now be seen standing on the front porch of a house not far from the airfield, watching a black staff car approach from up the road. Something about the man's stance screamed "officer" to Burke, and he slipped his goggles down over his eyes and dialed them in for a better look.

The indistinct figure on the porch resolved itself through the lens of his goggles and Burke noted with surprise that Manning was right.

It was Richthofen.

As Burke realized who he was looking at, the door behind Richthofen opened and another man stepped into view. The newcomer was dressed in the standard jumpsuit that served as a POW uniform, and although Burke hadn't seen him in several years, he still had no problem recognizing his own brother.

Jack stepped over to Richthofen and they exchanged a few words.

"Come on, get out of the way . . ." Manning said, beneath his breath.

Thinking Manning was speaking to him, Burke pulled off his goggles and glanced in that direction, only to find the other man lining up to take a shot at Richthofen!

"What are you doing?" Burke hissed at him.

"Killing that undead bastard," Manning answered quietly. "Exactly what I was sent here to do. Do you want me to solve your problem too while I'm at it?"

"What?"

The big game hunter pulled his eye off the scope and looked over at him, his impatience plain on his face.

"You know exactly what I'm talking about! Now hurry up and make up your mind before we lose our chance!"

For just a moment, Burke considered letting Manning do just what he'd suggested: gunning down both men right where they stood. As options went it wasn't such a bad one. The biggest threat to Allied air supremacy would be eliminated, they'd relieve the enemy of one of their best military minds, and they'd be protecting the president, and by extension the country, all in one fell swoop. For just a moment, it seemed the perfect way out. If he let Manning take that extra shot, he'd be saving his men from having to infiltrate the base and all the danger that went hand in hand with just such an operation. He expected several of them to be injured, possibly even killed, before the assault was over, and he could avoid all that with one simple shot. He wouldn't even have to pull the trigger.

But then the moment passed, and Burke came to his senses.

"Put the gun down, Manning. We're here to recon and that's all."

Manning ignored him and went on fumbling with the buttons and knobs on his strange-looking gun.

"I'm ordering you to put down that weapon, Manning."

The other man let out a short laugh. "Sorry, Captain, but I'm not really in your chain of command, now am I?" he said, as he pulled back the hammer on the rifle. He put his eye up against the optical sight, getting ready to fire.

Burke didn't hesitate. He snatched the Colt Firestarter from his belt and jammed the barrel into the side of Manning's head.

The big game hunter went absolutely still.

"I said put the gun down. Now either do what I ordered you to do or so help me God . . ."

Very carefully, Manning lifted his finger away from the trigger of the rifle.

"Push it away from you," Burke said, and then waited for the other man to do so before he took the Firestarter away from Manning's head.

Below them, the staff car reached the house where the two men were waiting. Richthofen climbed into the backseat. Freeman followed. The car pulled away and disappeared deeper into the camp.

Burke let out a breath he didn't know he'd been holding.

Manning waited another moment or two, then reached out and retrieved his rifle. Burke didn't stop him. They eyed each other warily for a moment.

Manning broke the silence.

"If you'd pulled that trigger, you would have given us away."

"True, but at least I wouldn't have the death of my brother on my conscience either."

"Might still come to that."

Burke nodded. "Yes, it might. But we'll deal with that if and when we come to it. For now, we stick to the plan."

Manning sketched a quick, sarcastic salute, before heading back down the ridgeline, rifle in hand.

Burke followed.

Back at the rendezvous point, Burke relayed what they had seen, making no mention of the altercation between him and Manning, and was grateful that the other man let it rest as well. Burke sketched out a quick map and laid it on the hood of the truck where everyone could see.

The plan was simple. Using their stolen uniforms, the team would infiltrate the base, passing themselves off as German soldiers. If they stuck to the plan and didn't engage anyone in conversation, they should be all right, as it was after dark and the uniforms would help them blend in.

"We're going to enter through the main gate," he said. "That will put us reasonably close to where we think Major Freeman is being held, either in this area over here," he said, pointing to a group of buildings surrounding a larger one labeled Commandant's Residence, "or with the rest of the prisoners here," pointing to a section on the west side of the map that was labeled POWs.

"He'll be guarded, but to what extent and by how many men is something we won't know until we get in there."

He looked around the circle, meeting their gazes, looking for any hesitation or doubt. They were about to try and scam their way in through the front gate of a major enemy base. Confidence was key; they needed to look and act like they belonged.

He needn't have worried. All he saw were the confident expressions of men ready to do the job they had come here to do. What had started as a misfit bunch had coalesced into a team who knew they could depend upon one another, and that was something that could only be forged in the crucible of combat.

If anyone had a chance of pulling this off, they did.

Burke was proud of them.

He caught Charlie watching him and knew the sergeant was thinking the same thing.

"Remember, once we're past the gates, you are to stay in the truck and avoid interaction with anyone unless ordered to do so. Our cover demands it."

That last was especially important, given how little most of them knew of the German language. Any attempt at conversation would quickly reveal that they weren't who they said they were, so their success or failure depended upon how long they could avoid calling attention to themselves.

"Once we secure Major Freeman, we'll turn around and get out of there the same way we came in. If all goes well, we should be in and out again in twenty, twenty-five minutes tops."

He was oversimplifying everything, as there were only about a million things that could go wrong, but at this point he was operating on nothing more than a wing and a prayer; the plan, however weak it might be, would have to do.

It worried him, though he made sure it didn't show. Everything they knew about the camp ahead of them had come by way of the dispatch messenger they'd taken captive back at Stalag 113. The messenger could have been lying, for all any of them knew. If he led them astray, they were going to be in for a boatload of trouble.

Stop worrying, Burke, he told himself. *You'll be lucky to get past the front gate.*

Forcing a smile to his face, he turned to the others and said, "Let's do this."

CHAPTER THIRTY-EIGHT

While Burke and his men were pulling their vehicles off the road not far from the gates of the Verdun testing facility, inside those same gates Major Freeman was being driven to another meeting with Baron Richthofen. His minders took him to the base headquarters and escorted him into the Baron's office.

Unlike the day before, when he'd been meticulously dressed in a carefully pressed uniform, complete with the Blue Max at his throat, today Richthofen was wearing a loose shirt, trousers, and a pair of leather flight boots. His attire suggested that he would be airborne soon, and Freeman felt a stab of jealousy. He did his best not to let it show on his face, however, as he knew that was precisely the reaction Richthofen was no doubt hoping for.

"Ah, Major," Richthofen exclaimed when Freeman was ushered into the room. "Thank you for coming."

Like I had a choice, Freeman thought.

"You are being treated properly? Better than with that pig Schulheim, yes?"

Just about anything would have been better than the treatment he had received at the hands of the oberst—after all, the man had been eating his prisoners—but Freeman didn't acknowledge that fact. It seemed clear that Richthofen was trying to establish himself as the good guy in the equation. So rather than telling him what he really thought, he said simply, "Yes. Thank you."

"Good," Richthofen replied, smiling. "We wouldn't want your illustrious father to hear that we have been treating you in anything less than the gentlemanly manner that you deserve."

Freeman had been expecting the truth of his heritage to come out ever since his capture, so he barely flinched at Richthofen's remark. Not that it mattered, for Richthofen went on before Freeman could formulate a reply.

"Have no fear, Major. Your secret is safe with me. I only bring it up to show that we are not so different, you and me. Our fathers are both great men who have little time for anyone but themselves, isn't that right?"

Freeman shrugged. He was not going to get into a conversation about his father with a man who should have been dead twice over. It was as simple as that.

Noting his reluctance, and no doubt satisfied that his point had been made, the German ace turned to another issue.

"Have you thought any further about the offer I made yesterday?"

Freeman cleared his throat. "With all due respect, Herr Richthofen, I cannot accept."

Richthofen watched Freeman for several long seconds, then broke the silence by saying, "You do realize, do you not, that you cannot win? That sooner, rather than later, the *Sturmbataillons* will drive the rest of your forces all the way to the Atlantic? That my Flying Circus will rule the air and therefore control all movement on the ground? The empire is *destined* to win this conflict."

Freeman shook his head. "Be that as it may, we will still fight you to the end."

"Of course you will," Richthofen replied with a sigh, "but that is precisely what I am talking about. You will fight and you will die, and in the end we will still be here. Where is the good in that?"

He paused, seemed about to say something further, but then

jumped to his feet. "Come," he said. "I see you need more than words to convince you."

With Freeman at his heels, Richthofen left the commandant's office, crossed to his staff car, and slid into the backseat. Freeman climbed in after him. The two men sat in silence while Richthofen's driver took them across the camp to a series of buildings on the east side of camp. The driver pulled up in front of a long, low building set off a bit from the others. It was only when he got out and saw the armored locomotive parked behind the building that Freeman understood he was looking at a train station.

A train must have arrived earlier, for prisoners in gray jumpsuits were hard at work unloading the cargo when Richthofen and Freeman appeared around the far side of the platform. The thick smell of putrefying flesh wafted to him along the breeze, and Freeman had to keep himself from gagging. As they got closer, Freeman wasn't surprised to see that the "freight" the train carried was the bodies of German soldiers, all human, killed in combat.

The corpses were still dressed in the uniforms they'd worn while alive, and Freeman could see from the unit patches on their blouses they had come from quite a few different units. Each corpse was taken off the train by prisoners wearing face masks and gloves, and then laid out next to each other, shoulder to shoulder, on the nearby platform. Even as Freeman watched, a trio of white lab-coated scientists moved among those that had already been unloaded, marking some of them with a quick slash of white chalk across the bottom of the corpses' boots.

Richthofen spoke from behind him. "I have seen your corpse fires burning, all day and night, as you try to keep your countrymen from responding to the call of the gas. Tell me, Major, what is the biggest problem you and your Allies now face?"

Freeman didn't respond. He didn't need to; Richthofen was already answering the question for himself.

"Come now, Major. It's no secret. Manpower. That's what the Allies need more than anything else. Manpower. Each one that falls rises to fight against you. Soon you will run out of men to throw into battle. What will you do then?"

Richthofen paused to watch as the scientists loaded several of the corpses that hadn't yet begun to rot onto a wheeled cart. When it was full, they pushed it along the platform toward the next closest building. Richthofen followed and Freeman had no choice but to do the same.

"We do not have that problem," Richthofen said, continuing his earlier train of thought. "The Western Front. The Italian Front. The Russian Front. It does not matter where our brave soldiers fall. If they are intact, they are brought home, to facilities like this one, where we return them to functional status."

Freeman couldn't resist. "You mean turn them into mindless zombies, don't you?"

Richthofen stopped and turned to face him. "Is that what you think? That all those who survive the resurrection process are mindless drones? No wonder you were not interested in my proposal yesterday!"

The scientists and their grisly cargo disappeared inside the doors of the building ahead of them. Richthofen glanced in their direction, looked back at Freeman, and apparently made up his mind.

"This way, Major. I think you will find this interesting."

They passed through the doors and found themselves in a narrow corridor that seemed to stretch the length of the building. A thick black line was painted down the center.

"It's probably best if you don't let your feet stray from the path," Richthofen said, then started walking forward.

For a moment Freeman considered turning around and heading out the door behind him as fast as he could go. *If he could make the fence line . . .*

The idea passed as quickly as it had formed. He couldn't outrun a bullet, and he had very little doubt that the sentries would fire on him the moment they thought he was escaping. If by some miracle he did make the fence without being shot down like a dog in the street, he wasn't convinced that he could get over it. Days of injury and infection had taken their toll; his leg was feeling a hundred percent better, but that didn't mean the rest of his body was in any kind of condition to make the attempt.

Forget running. It was best if he just held out and waited for the right chance to come along.

With a sigh, he followed Richthofen.

The corridor was only dimly lit, and his companion was already disappearing into the shadows ahead of him. Normally this wasn't something that would have bothered Freeman, but for some reason the whole building had him on edge and so he hurried to catch up.

In the process, he didn't notice that the walls on either side had given way to vertical iron bars, like those you find in a prison, nor that he had strayed from the centerline.

The only warning he had was the animalistic whine that came from his left as something moved in his peripheral vision. Years of reacting on instinct as enemy aircraft dove at his own from out of the clouds had him shifting away from whatever it was beside him even as he turned to look.

The shambler howled in dismay as its hands closed on empty air rather than around Freeman's neck as planned. The creature was close enough that Freeman could see that its nose had rotted away, leaving a gaping hole in the middle of its face between two eyes that focused on him in ravenous hunger.

Freeman stepped back to the centerline, out of reach.

With his heart pounding from the close call, Freeman looked around, noting for the first time the prisonlike cells that lined either side of the hallway and the dozen or more shamblers that occupied each one. They all reacted the same way when they saw him, lumbering over to the bars and reaching their hands through them just as the first one had, howling and moaning with unholy need, setting off a cacophony that filled the narrow hall until Freeman was forced to put his hands over his ears and run ahead.

Richthofen didn't say anything to him when he finally caught up, just led him a few feet farther down the hall until they came to a viewing window set into the wall.

The room on the other side of the glass contained a dozen or more tables, each complete with a set of leather straps attached to each side, and the cart full of corpses that had just come in from the train platform. Two men dressed in gray jumpsuits that identified them as prisoners of war were working inside the room, moving the recently selected bodies from the cart up onto the tables, taking care to strap each of them down securely before moving on to the next.

Given the previous conversation with Richthofen, it was obvious to Freeman that the men were getting the bodies ready for the resurrection process. Unlike the troops manning the trenches, he had never seen the dead actually rise, and he found himself leaning forward in anticipation of what was to come despite his abhorrence of the idea. He watched as the POWs finished strapping down the last body and then moved to leave through the door at the far end of the room.

He glanced at Richthofen. "What happens now?"

Richthofen didn't seem to hear; he was watching those in the room with a focus that could only be described as predatory, and it drew Freeman's attention back toward them. He immediately recognized the problem; the door had accidentally locked behind the POWs, and they were now pounding on it and yelling to be let out.

Their fear heightened his own anxiety. "Someone's going to come help them, right?"

Richthofen didn't respond.

The men turned, looking for another way out, and one of them saw that Freeman and Richthofen were watching through the glass. He ran over and put himself face-to-face with Freeman, his palms flat on the glass, as words in French began to tumble desperately from his lips. Freeman couldn't understand the words, but there was no mistaking the sense of what he was saying. "Help us," the man pleaded. "Get us out of here before it is too late!"

"Why isn't anyone helping them?" Freeman asked, alarmed

now. If the bodies inside that room came back as shamblers and managed to get loose, the two men would be torn apart by the newly resurrected dead within minutes of their awakening. "Let them out!"

But Richthofen shook his head. "It's too late; the gas has already been released." He pointed toward the ceiling.

Both he and the Frenchmen followed the Baron's pointing finger until they spotted the brass nozzles that had descended several inches from their seats in recessed niches. A pale green gas began to jet from each nozzle, and soon the room began to fill with a rapidly expanding and billowing cloud.

The men trapped inside reacted in earnest, pounding on the window glass, screaming for help as the gas descended toward them.

Richthofen stared at them, his eyes alight with excitement.

Freeman tried to turn away, but Richthofen's hand shot out and grabbed him around the back of the neck, squeezing with such tremendous strength that he was afraid the Baron might snap it in two.

"Watch!" Richthofen hissed in his ear. "It is not what you expect!"

The gas drifted down from the ceiling and enveloped the living and the dead alike. The two POWs fell to the floor, coughing and gagging as the gas sent its questing fingers down their throats and up their noses, worming its way inside their bodies to wreak its deadly changes. At the same time, the bodies on the tables began to twitch and shake, the gas sliding over flesh long since devoid of any signs of life and causing a chemical reaction like nothing nature had ever intended.

Perhaps most shocking, however, was the transformation that the POWs were undergoing. As the gas wrapped them in its cold embrace, the veins beneath their skin stood out in a twisting network of deep black lines that contrasted sharply with the greenish-gray cast that slowly took over their flesh. Freeman was watching them both closely and was certain he knew the exact moment that exposure to the gas killed them, just as he recognized when that mystic spark flashed back into their eyes as their new unlife took them into its unholy grip.

It was like watching two trains roaring down the tracks toward each other; you knew it would end terribly but you couldn't look away, you had to watch to the very end . . .

The formerly dead soldiers that had come in on the train had all revived and were thrashing against their bonds, their mouths opening and closing as the never-ending hunger every shambler feels stole over them. Freeman could see in their eyes that there was no one home; the passage from life to death and back again had robbed them of any recollection of who or what they had been.

He'd been right; they were nothing more than mindless drones at this point.

But the POWs . . .

The POWs were a different story. First one and then the other climbed to his feet, both shaking their heads as if trying to clear an unpleasant memory from the forefront of their minds. They looked down at their hands, turning them over to examine the thick black veins bulging against their flesh and then, as one, they lifted their gaze and looked in Freeman's direction.

The one who had pleaded so strongly with Freeman before his change took a few steps forward, until his face was only inches from Freeman's own. The only thing separating them at that point was the thin pane of glass in the viewing window.

The strange new type of shambler looked at him and smiled.

Then it spoke.

"Ouvrez la porte."

Open the door.

In that moment of shocked horror, as he grappled with the realization the gas had worked on the living as well as the dead, Freeman's thoughts flashed back to the pit at Stalag 113 and the piles of shambler bodies he'd shared that dark hole with all evening. He finally understood now what his mind had been trying to tell him then; the shamblers tossed into that pit had not passed through the gates of death before being exposed to the noxious gas. Instead, like the two men he'd just observed, they'd been exposed while alive and had either not managed to weather the transformation process or else had been dispatched after the fact for some unknown reason.

For the gas to have reached this level of effectiveness the kaiser must have been pursuing the program for some time. Freeman had no doubt there were dozens of other pits like the one he'd been thrown into on bases across occupied France, full of the bodies of those who'd played guinea pigs for the gas's development.

But that wasn't the worst of it, not by far.

The realization of what this would mean to the war effort hit him like a blow to the face.

On the other side of the glass, giant fans came on, sucking the remnants of the gas out of the room; when it was clear, the door on the far side opened, admitting several of the enhanced shamblers who quickly moved to subdue the new "recruits."

"I call them the Geheime Volks, the secret people," Richthofen said, watching as the groups struggled with each other on the other side of the glass. "As you can see, they are a step above the Tottensoldat, which can barely be controlled even with their collars in place. But these new soldiers retain their mental and physical functions even after returning from the dead. They do not need collars, for they can follow commands as well as you and I. They are the future, Major Freeman, and with each new batch we refine and improve the process further."

Richthofen turned to face him, a ghastly smile on his face.

"Do you understand now, Major? Today, tomorrow, next week, or next year, it does not matter to me—you *will* fall. My *Stosstruppen*, my shock troops, will push you out of the trenches and all the way to the coast, until they force you off the Continent. As you scurry back to your homeland, we will be there, too. But this is just the beginning. Come!"

There's more? Freeman thought. *Just how bad could this get?*

Richthofen led him to a door at the end of the hall, which

opened into a private office. The German flier walked across the room and opened a door set in the far wall, revealing a staircase that led down several steps into a large warehouse-like room. Several large machines were connected to tanks of some strangely viscous liquid. The machines seemed to be pumping the liquid out of the tanks, down a conveyor belt, and into large glass ampoules. These in turn were sent down a series of belts to workers standing at various stations. The workers took the ampoules, carefully fitted them into the noses of cannon and mortar shells that reached the workers along a movable track, and then passed them along to the next station to have the nose cones fitted into place.

Hundreds of shells were being produced at any given moment, with hundreds, maybe even thousands more moving along the conveyor belt behind them.

The sight of all that corpse gas made Freeman want to be physically ill.

"In less than forty-eight hours, the *Megaera* will launch, carrying with it more than three thousand canisters of the newly improved gas bound straight for the heart of the British Empire. Tell me, Major, how long do you think your Allies will continue to fight when they learn that their loved ones at home have become the very things they despise, wandering the streets of London, trying to slake that never-ending hunger that burns in their breasts?"

Richthofen laughed and it was a cold, brutal sound.

"While the kaiser fumbles with his generals at the front, lost in the insanity of doing the same thing over and over again while expecting different results, I will be securing the glory of the empire for the centuries to come!"

CHAPTER THIRTY-NINE

BURKE DROVE THE staff car at a steady pace toward the gates of Testing Facility 89. He did his best to ignore the yawning pit in the depths of his stomach. What they were about to do would either go down in the annals of history as the height of stupidity or as a masterful stroke of daring; he didn't know which.

He could see Charlie and Manning sitting in the cab of the truck behind him, their faces set into masks of boredom, their weapons held casually but at the ready in case they had to use them quickly to extricate themselves if things went wrong.

Burke hoped it wouldn't come to that.

The gates loomed before him, the guards in the watchtowers on either side casting long shadows ahead of them that seemed to leap and dance on their own when seen through the veil of Burke's nervousness. He did what he could to calm himself. Everything depended upon their getting inside those gates.

"Showtime, Professor," he said over his shoulder to Graves who was riding in the backseat.

Burke drove forward, hoping the guards would see the staff car and simply open the gates without any questions, but Lady Luck still had not deigned to honor them with her presence. The gates stayed firmly closed.

At the last minute, Burke braked, then leaned on the horn to get the full attention of the guards as he came to a stop. A moment passed, and then a guard wandered out of the nearby gatehouse to meet them.

The side windows of the staff car were made of a dark, smoky glass, so the guard was obliged to knock on Burke's window. Burke waited a moment, playing the "I'm-more-important-than-you" game, and then cranked his window. The guard said something in German, which was, of course, incomprehensible to him.

Fear snatched at his guts like a vise.

How did I think this would ever work . . . ?

Graves said something sharply from the backseat, and Burke was surprised at the commanding tone he heard in the other man's voice. The German soldier apparently heard it too, for he snapped to attention and gave a quick salute.

The professor reached forward and tapped Burke on the shoulder. That was their prearranged signal for Burke to hand over the personal cable from Richthofen, and the captain did so with practiced disdain.

The guard's swagger vanished the minute he saw the emblem at the bottom of the page. He handed the paper back to Burke, turned to face Graves, and, if his tone was any indication, began to immediately apologize.

Graves rattled off another long stream of German. When he was finished, the guard saluted once more, then turned and signaled for his partner to open the gates. As the twin chain-link gates swung inward, the guard waved Burke forward. A glance out the rearview mirror showed the guard doing the same for Charlie without bothering to check with him specifically.

They were in!

"Nicely done, Professor," Burke told him.

The other man met the compliment with a nervous laugh. "Nicely done? I thought he was going to see right through me at any minute. Thank God we had that cable with us!"

The guard had informed Graves that "the American pilot" was

being housed in one of the buildings for guests in the officers' section of the camp and provided directions, which Graves now relayed to Burke. In turn, the captain did his best to follow them, slowly making his way through the camp as groups of soldiers moved about on various tasks.

Burke had to stop once to let a company of shamblers move slowly past, their handlers keeping them in line with repeated shocks from the control devices held in their hands that were connected to the masklike collars that surrounded the shamblers' necks and rose up the left side of their faces. He marveled at seeing the technology in action up close. The Allies still knew entirely too little about the creatures, and now it seemed they might have a whole new breed to contend with.

After parking the car, Burke got out and, playing the role of chauffeur, opened the rear door for Graves. The guards took in the officers' uniforms the two newcomers were wearing and snapped to attention.

Walking over, Graves spoke to the guards for a moment, then turned on his heel and stalked back over to the car. He waited by the door, every inch the Prussian scientist he was pretending to be, and Burke had no choice but to play along, waiting until the other man was seated before shutting Graves's door and then taking his own seat behind the wheel.

"We've got a problem," Graves said the minute the door had closed behind Burke. "The sentry at the front gate must have called ahead; they knew why I was here before I had even opened my mouth."

"So where is he?"

"That's the problem. He was summoned to a meeting with Richthofen several hours ago and hasn't yet returned."

A problem was right.

Graves wasn't finished, however. "The guards here weren't the only people the gate sentry alerted either. He also rang Richthofen and informed him that his guest, 'Dr. Taschner,' had arrived. Richthofen left an order that we are to join him right away."

They had hoped to avoid Richthofen or any of his immediate staff in case they knew Dr. Taschner. It was too much to expect that anyone who worked with the man wouldn't immediately know that Graves wasn't Taschner.

And yet with some aggressive action it might be for the best.

The guard had said that Freeman and Richthofen were together. Depending upon who else was in the room with them, they might be able to overpower Richthofen and his companions, releasing Freeman in the process. That would serve the dual purpose of freeing their target while neutralizing their biggest threat.

He quickly explained his thinking to Graves, who agreed that they didn't have much choice. Ignoring Richthofen's summons wasn't an option; he'd find them the minute he realized he'd been duped. Their best bet was to stick with their chosen subterfuge for as far as it would take them and then be ready to act decisively.

Convinced that they were making the best choice possible under the circumstances, Burke started the car and drove deeper into the enemy camp, searching for the commandant's office in answer to the Baron's summons. Charlie, and the rest of the men in the stolen lorry, followed close behind.

CHAPTER FORTY

★

AFTER SEEING THE inhuman conversion of the prisoners and listening to Richthofen talk about what would happen to his countrymen and allies when Operation Stormcloud was launched, the stunned and dejected Freeman followed the Baron back from the conversion facility to the manor house in a daze. He knew that Richthofen was trying to break him, to tear down his mental and physical defenses until in a fit of despair he agreed to whatever the other man wanted, and he had to admit that it was working. Millions of people were about to die and there was nothing he could do to stop it.

The sight of the *Megaera*, its massive silver bulk filling the sky and seemingly looming malevolently on the horizon over them, made him want to scream in frustration, but he would not give Richthofen the satisfaction.

They returned to the same room where he and Richthofen had their discussion the day before and found an overweight, dark-haired man in a white lab coat waiting for them.

"Ah, Docktor Eisenberg," Richthofen said, as he caught sight of their visitor. "Allow me to introduce Major Jack Freeman of the AEF."

Freeman felt like a bug under a microscope as the other man

examined him thoroughly with just a glance and then dismissed him as entirely irrelevant. Freeman didn't care; he was still racking his brains for a way to keep Operation Stormcloud from going off as planned.

Eisenberg turned to Richthofen and said, "We've just received a message from the gate that our guest has arrived. I took the liberty of ordering him directly here in your name."

"Excellent! I look forward to it."

Richthofen was about to take a seat to await the arrival of his guest when he was interrupted by the arrival of an aide. The man handed over a message slip, saluted, and disappeared back out the door.

A frown crossed Richthofen's face as he read the note.

"Is there a problem?" Dr. Eisenberg asked.

"A minor issue with the flight controls on the *Megaera*, it seems," Richthofen replied. "I'd best speak to the chief engineer. Please, give my apologies to Docktor Taschner. I will join you both shortly."

Richthofen disappeared out the front, and a few moments later Freeman saw him through the window, striding toward the airfield. Never in his life had Freeman felt the need for a gun in his hands more than he did at that moment. He had no doubt that if Richthofen's plan succeeded, he would use the popularity the strike generated among the German High Command to push the kaiser from the throne. Nor was it hard to imagine why so many would choose Richthofen over the weak and crippled Kaiser Wilhelm, emperor in name but not action. With his strike at the heart of England, Richthofen would break that stalemate and take the war to a whole new level.

There had to be a way to stop him . . .

His thoughts were interrupted as the door opened a second time and two men entered.

The first was a tall, hawk-faced fellow with thinning hair who wore a white lab coat over his officer's uniform and carried a wide-mouthed satchel in one hand.

Freeman's attention was riveted almost immediately, however, by the second man. Or, rather, by the fact that everything from the man's left elbow on down had been replaced by a bronze and iron substitute that did a remarkable job of mimicking a human wrist and hand, right down to having knuckles on each artificial finger. He was dressed in a leutnant's uniform, but he held himself with a coiled tension that spoke of his familiarity with violence, giving the impression that he was a multiyear veteran of the conflict. This impression was supported by the casual yet familiar way he carried the Mauser in his right hand.

As his gaze rose to meet the other's, Freeman received the biggest shock of his life.

The man with the clockwork arm, the one who was looking at him with grim determination, was his younger brother!

Eisenberg looked up at the interruption and said something sharply to the newcomers in German. Freeman didn't understand what he said, but given the puzzled expression on the senior scientist's face, he imagined it was something along the lines of "Who the hell are you?"

The tall fellow replied in the same language, reaching into his bag as he did so.

Eisenberg apparently didn't like the reply, for he scowled and moved to get up out of the armchair he'd been sitting in.

"Not so fast," Burke said, swinging the Mauser up and pointing it in Eisenberg's direction. "Sit down before I put a bullet in your skull."

BURKE WAS PLEASED to see Freeman's captor do as he was told, though whether that was due to his ability to understand English or to the gun pointed at his head, he didn't know.

Nor did he care.

He saw that Graves now had his own pistol out of his satchel and was pointing it at the man, so Burke did a quick check of the other rooms, making certain they were empty, before he felt comfortable enough to turn his attention to his brother. He found Jack staring at him with a look of utter surprise on his face.

Bet I'm the last person he expected to walk through that door.

"Where's Richthofen?" Burke asked.

The fact that he was being rescued suddenly seemed to register and Freeman jumped up, rushing over to stand with his brother. "He was called away a few minutes ago. Something about a problem with the airship."

Burke gave his brother the once-over. He had a few cuts and bruises, but he looked to be in decent shape, considering what he'd been through over the last several days. Burke was pleased to see it; they had a long way to go before this was through.

"You all right?" he asked.

His brother nodded. "We should get out of here," he said nervously, glancing out the window in the direction he'd seen Richthofen take. "He could be back at any second."

"All right, all right, we're going. Here, take this." Burke passed him the Mauser and then drew his .45 from the holster on his belt. He would have preferred the Tommy gun, but it would have been an immediate giveaway and he'd left it back in the truck with the others. He pointed at their prisoner. "Help Graves tie this guy up while I check the desk."

Freeman shook his head. "No, you have to kill him."

Burke stared at his brother like he'd gone mad. "I'm not going to shoot an unarmed prisoner, Jack. I don't know what . . ."

Freeman didn't wait to hear the rest. "Fine, I will," he said. Even as Burke looked on, Jack brought the gun up and pointed it at Eisenberg.

Before he had a chance to fire, however, Burke snatched the weapon out of his hands.

"What the fuck are you doing, Jack? Pull that trigger and you'll have half the guards in the camp headed our way."

His brother was practically frantic, pointing at the smaller man with fear in his eyes. "You have to kill him, Mike! You have to! He's a monster."

Burke frowned. "A monster? This guy?" He certainly didn't look like much.

But Jack was adamant. "Yes. He's Richthofen's chief scientist. And they're getting ready to drop so much corpse gas on the city of London that there won't be anything but shamblers living there inside of a week!"

That didn't make sense. Corpse gas only worked on . . .

Burke heard Graves gasp half a second after he made the same connection for himself. The files they'd grabbed at Stalag 113 had talked about a new kind of gas, one that worked on the living as well as the dead. And if they had already produced it in quantity . . .

"The new formulation of the gas? It's here?" he asked.

His brother stared at him. "You know about the gas?"

"Yes," he told him, waving aside the questions he could see forming on Jack's lips. "Talk to me! Is the gas here?"

"Yes. That's what the zeppelin is for. They're going to use it to carry the gas across the channel and bomb London." Jack quickly sketched out what Richthofen had told him while touring the production facility, and the information changed everything for Burke. His orders were to rescue Jack and return him, alive if possible, to Allied hands. In order to have the best chance of doing that, he knew he should ignore everything else, get everybody back in the truck, and get the hell off the base as expeditiously as possible.

And yet he couldn't ignore the clear threat that this Operation Stormcloud posed, and not just to Allied troops on the Continent. From what Freeman had said, Richthofen had made it clear that he wouldn't hesitate to use the gas on civilian populations as well, which put not only London, but Paris and even any of the major American cities on the eastern seaboard at risk, including New York and Washington.

What good would it do to rescue the president's son, only to lose the president and the rest of the American government in the process?

He didn't have a choice.

"How heavily guarded is that production facility?" Burke asked.

CHAPTER FORTY-ONE

After determining that Freeman had only seen a handful of guards when he'd been inside the lab earlier, Burke decided they would strike at two different objectives, thereby increasing their chances of actually disrupting the operation before it could get off the ground. Burke, Freeman, Graves, and Williams would take out the laboratory, and its stockpile of corpse gas, while Moore, Jones, Compton, and Manning would deal with the *Megaera*. That way, even if only one team managed to succeed, they would delay Stormcloud long enough to get a warning back to friendly ears. Hopefully at that point someone with a higher pay grade than Burke's would figure out what to do next.

All thoughts of getting Freeman off the base were put aside. For one, Jack wouldn't go, and two, now that he'd found him, Burke didn't dare let him out of his sight. If worst came to worst, he could always make use of the final solution as suggested by Colonel Nichols, but to do that he needed Jack nearby.

Abandoning the staff car because of its high-profile nature and the fear that it would be easily remembered, the team piled into the lorry. Sergeant Moore took the wheel with Burke at his side. They drove calmly through the base, the two of them nodding to the soldiers they passed who were moving about the camp on foot, doing everything they could to give off the sense that they were just another unit going about their duties.

Several times they got a glimpse of the *Megaera* looming over the camp from its mooring on the north edge, and each time Burke marveled, just as he had with the *Victorious*, that something that big could move through the sky. Knowing what Richthofen had chosen to do with that vessel made its general appearance even worse than it really was.

Charlie pulled the truck to a stop in front of the production facility. Two guards watched them from either side of the door, and Burke half expected them to open fire the minute he climbed down from the cab. When they didn't, he could only assume it was because no one had discovered their trussed-up prisoner yet. He waited until Graves had slid out of the truck behind him and then headed for the door, looking for all the world like a senior officer's escort. Or so he hoped.

When the guards snapped to attention at the sight of Graves's uniform, he knew they had them. He headed right for the door, ignoring the guards on either side, but when he drew even with them, he didn't hesitate, lashing out at the one on the left with the stock of the Tommy gun, knowing that Williams would do the same on the opposite side. Freeman and Williams were close behind.

The guard didn't have time to do more than utter a surprised squawk before the impact knocked him into unconsciousness. Williams was equally successful on the right. They grabbed the guards about the ankles and dragged them inside where they wouldn't be stumbled upon by a casual passerby. Freeman used one of the guards' rifles to jam the door behind them and then led the team deeper into the facility, past the room where he'd seen the Frenchmen converted into the hideous undead creatures they'd become as a result of the gas, and finally to the office that overlooked the production facility where the gas was actually produced.

Burke knocked on the door and then entered the room without waiting for an answer, his pistol already in hand. A man wearing a captain's uniform looked up from where he was trying to enjoy his evening meal seated behind Eisenberg's desk. His eyes went wide at the sight of the gun in Burke's fist, and he made the mistake of going for his own weapon.

It was the last mistake he ever made.

Burke pulled the trigger and his bullet struck the captain in the center of the forehead, splattering the wall behind him with a thick shower of blood, brains, and bone. With the shot still ringing in their ears, the four men quickly moved to the door leading onto the production floor. Burke counted down to three with the fingers of his mechanical hand, then grabbed the knob and threw the door open. He went through it in a rush, with Williams on his heels.

AFTER DROPPING BURKE and the others off in front of the laboratory, Charlie turned the truck around and headed back toward the airfield. It wasn't hard to find, for the long gleaming body of the *Megaera* could be seen from halfway across the camp. A line of trucks similar to his own were moving in that direction, no doubt carrying supplies and other cargo to be loaded aboard the vessel for her forthcoming voyage.

Figuring that hiding in plain sight might be his best option, Charlie got into line behind a couple of other trucks and followed them up to a gate in the fence that separated the airfield from the rest of the base. A guard was on duty there, but once he'd waved the lead vehicle through he barely looked up at the rest of the trucks in the miniconvoy. Charlie tried to look as bored as he imagined the guard must feel as he drove past, and minutes later he was within range of his target.

There was a lot of activity close to the airship. Lights were set up close by, shining upward across the massive hull, allowing both those on the ground as well as those in the cargo bays above to see what they were doing. Men were working steadily, transferring crates from the backs of the trucks over to the cargo nets, which were then hauled skyward into the belly of the beast through the open maw of the cargo doors above.

Charlie drove through the edge of the turmoil, passing the other vehicles until he found a dark patch of ground a few hundred yards farther on, away from the lights and activity. He parked the truck so the tailgate was facing the airship and then slipped between the seats to join the others in the rear.

Compton was standing by the tailgate, peering out at all the activity through a small slit in the tarp that covered the rear of the truck. "There are German troops everywhere, Sergeant. How are we supposed to get to the airship and back out again without being caught?"

"We're not," Charlie said. He turned to Jones. "Are you still carrying that mortar tube?"

"Yes, Sergeant."

"Good. Here's what we're going to do."

Ten minutes later Charlie climbed out of the truck's cab and wandered back toward the tailgate, fishing in his pockets as if looking for a smoke. He glanced around, noted that no one was paying them the slightest attention, and then rapped twice on the tailgate.

At the signal, the men inside the truck jumped into action. Manning flipped the tarp up, revealing the squat frame of the mortar pointed in the direction of the airship. Jones bent over the sight reticle, made a final adjustment, then nodded at Charlie.

"Fire!" the sergeant said.

Compton dropped the mortar round into the tube.

Foomp!

The shell raced skyward with a sharp whistling sound, trailing a stream of dull-colored smoke. It had barely passed the top of its arc when it slammed into the airship's side, about a third of the way from the nose.

For a moment nothing happened, and in the stillness Charlie was sure he could have heard a pin drop, but then a sharp crack split the night air, like a hundred lightning bolts striking the same place all at once, and bright blue tendrils of electricity danced out across the *Megaera*'s hull.

Jones made a minor adjustment to the targeting.

"Again!" Moore ordered.

There was another dull thump followed by a shell arcing skyward to explode against the airship's hull.

Webs of electrical power were slowly spreading out from the impact points, dancing across the surface of the airship now, popping and buzzing with unsuppressed power. When they collided with each other, there was another flash of brilliance and then it was moving faster, sweeping down along the length of the airship until it reached the engines. There was a thunderous crash, a loud explosion, and then flames could be seen spreading out across the tail section of the zeppelin.

Foomp! Foomp!

Compton didn't wait for the order this time around, firing twice more in rapid succession, his eyes alight with glee as more explosions lit the night sky and the first of the screams of the injured reach their ears.

"Time to get out of here!"

The attack had only taken moments, but Charlie was worried about those last two shells. All eyes had been on the *Megaera* after that first, unexpected strike, and if someone had seen the second shell strike the airship, they probably wouldn't have been able to trace it back to its source. But by the time those last two shots had been fired, it would have been clear that the airship was under attack from outside forces and heads would have started turning in their direction.

It was time to leave before someone put two and two together.

Jones and Compton were working to dismantle the mortar. It was of no use to them now that they were out of ammunition for it, but they didn't want to leave it behind for fear the Germans might be able to turn it to their own ends. Manning pulled the tarp back into place over the rear of the vehicle and Charlie helped him tied it down, hiding the other men from sight. As soon as they were finished, he climbed into the driver's seat and got ready to leave.

Charlie was reaching for the ignition switch when he caught movement out of the corner of his eye. In the next instant his door was thrown violently open and he found himself flying through the air as if hurled from a cannon. He hit the ground hard, rolling over several times from the force of the throw before coming to rest on his back several yards away.

Get up! his mind screamed. *Get up now!*

He staggered to his feet.

A figure was stalking toward him out of the darkness, and there was no mistaking the stranger's intent, for a sense of murderous rage was coming off him in waves.

He not only means to kill me, Charlie thought, *but rend me limb from limb.*

Before he could give it too much rational thought, Charlie reached inside his shirt and flipped the switch on the leather vest he'd been wearing ever since the moments before they'd jumped out of what he considered to be a perfectly good airship.

The Hercules vest hummed and shook and came to life as the stored battery charge superheated the water running through the device's power system and fired up the servos. For a moment Charlie felt the rubber sleeves squeeze his arms, and then the sensation was swept away as a flood of energy passed through his system.

It was just in time.

No sooner had the vest come to life than his pursuer was upon him. Charlie recognized him immediately; the Baron's skeletal grin had graced the front pages of enough French and German newspapers over the years for him to know it on sight. There was a murderous look in the revenant's eyes as he reached out, intent on snatching Charlie up a second time.

Except this time Charlie was ready for him.

The suit was aptly named, for it more than doubled his strength. As Richthofen grabbed him about the shoulders, Charlie brought his arms up inside Richthofen's and broke free of his grip. He planted his feet, twisted at the waist, and sent a staggering right into the German pilot's face. He followed it up with a left to the body and felt something inside Richthofen's resurrected form crunch with the impact.

The damage didn't seem to do any harm to the other man but only served to enrage him further. He bellowed in defiance and backhanded Charlie across the chest, picking him up and dumping him to the ground several feet away.

If the blow had struck Charlie in the face, it likely would have taken his head off. As it was, it damaged the vest, sending a blast of superheated water across his left abdomen, burning his flesh and causing him to scream in pain. He could feel the strength ebbing out of him as the power generated through the servos was reduced by the damage, and as he watched Richthofen stalk toward him he knew he was in serious trouble.

He scrambled backward, trying to figure out what to do, as Richthofen rushed toward him.

The night was suddenly filled with lights and the sound of a body being struck at high speed, followed by the squeal of brakes, and the roar of a truck's engine being slammed into reverse. He looked up to see Jones leaning down out of the cab of their lorry, his hand extended and an anxious look on his face.

"Come on!" he shouted. "Before he gets up again!"

Charlie let him pull him up and then climbed into the cab behind the wheel as the other man scooted over to the passenger side. A glance out the windshield showed the Baron's body lying several yards away in the glare of the headlights.

Even as Charlie stared in fascinated horror, Richthofen began to stir.

"Drive!" Jones shouted.

Charlie thought that was a pretty good idea.

He stomped on the accelerator and sent the truck rocketing backward, then slammed on the brakes and swung it around in a 180-degree turn. The *Megaera* swept into view, fully ablaze now, and the scene was utter chaos as men rushed everywhere, either trying to save what they could or get themselves as far away as possible from the inferno before it exploded.

No one was paying them any attention.

He heard Manning firing out the back of the truck and decided that he was going to look to see what he was aiming at. The idea that Richthofen might have gotten back up after being run down by a two-ton lorry was a reality he just didn't want to face right now. Instead, he threw the truck into drive and went to look for Captain Burke.

THE GUARDS IN the next room had been warned by the previous gunshot, so they were already rushing toward the steps leading to the door even as Burke came through it. At the sight of him, they skidded to a halt on the wooden floor, raised their guns, and opened fire.

Bullets were whipping through the air and plinging off the metal steps around him, but none found their mark. Even as he fired back he knew he couldn't stay there; eventually one of those shots would find its target. Unable to move forward due to the enemy soldiers in front of him and unable to move back due to having Williams immediately behind, Burke did the only thing he could think of.

He vaulted over the railing and disappeared over the side.

It was a good fifteen-foot drop to the floor, but it felt like nothing after the experiences he'd endured lately, including leaping out of an airship that was plunging to the ground from twenty thousand feet.

He hit the ground, rolled, and came up shooting. With Williams using the door frame at the top of the steps for cover as he fired downward and Burke firing from the side where he was partially shielded by the staircase, the German soldiers didn't last long at all.

But it was the sight that met Burke's eyes when he looked up from the bodies of the men he'd just killed and over to the floor of the assembly line that made him swear aloud.

"Sonofabitch! What's wrong with these people?" he asked no one in particular.

The assembly-line workers hadn't left their posts, not when the bullets starting flying nor when two of their numbers were struck and knocked to the ground by errant shots. They were still standing there, carrying out their tasks, without even looking in the direction of the firefight.

Burke's companions joined him on the assembly-line floor and cautiously moved closer, weapons at the ready.

It was Graves who figured it out first.

"They're shamblers!" he whispered suddenly, bringing the whole group up short. He pointed at their faces. "Look at their eyes! And their mouths!"

A glance was all it took.

The eyes, like their mouths, had been sewn shut.

"Sweet Jesus!" Freeman said, and that about summed it up for Burke too.

Now that Graves had pointed it out, it was clear that the things working the machines in front of them were no longer human. Their bodies were in different stages of decomposition and they were chained to the tables at which they worked tirelessly to create the gas-filled shells that the German army used all along the front.

Burke felt only revulsion for the creatures before him. Things like that didn't deserve to walk the earth, and he intended to take as many of them with him as he could. He turned to Williams and said, "Let's set the charges and get the hell out of here."

Freeman stood guard while Williams and Burke moved through the room, carefully placing the twelve charges where they thought they would do the most good.

After placing the explosives, Burke moved back through the room twisting the dials on all the timers, setting them for five minutes. Freeman and Williams were already waiting at the stairs when Burke gave the setup one last glance and then hurried to join them.

Professor Graves, however, was nowhere to be found.

"You have got to be fuckin' kidding me!" Burke said and began to run back along the assembly line, looking for Graves. He found him examining one of the shamblers up close, way too close, and Burke kept waiting for the thing to spin around and attack. He grabbed Graves by the arm and started to pull him across the room.

"No! You don't understand," he cried. "We can learn so much this way!"

Burke was as unrelenting as the clock that was ticking its way down. "There are twelve explosives about to blow this place sky-high, and if it's all right with you, I'd rather not be here when that happens."

The word *explosives* was what did it. Graves suddenly snapped out of his dazed fascination with the creatures around him and rushed toward where the others were waiting.

"Let's get out of here!" he said, racing past Freeman and taking the steps two at a time.

The rest of them followed rapidly on his heels.

They burst through the door at the end of the hall and slammed to a halt.

The massive airship they'd seen on entering the building still loomed over the horizon, but now it was completely ablaze. Lurid red and yellow flames danced about its frame, casting back the darkness and lighting up the night sky like a beacon. Even as they watched, small explosions enveloped parts of the vessel where the flames had eaten their way through the skin and reached the gas bags inside.

They were so caught up in the horrid beauty of the sight that they didn't notice the oncoming truck until it squealed to a halt in front of them. Burke instinctively stepped in front of Freeman, though how he would have protected him if the truck turned out to be full of enemy soldiers he didn't know.

"Get in!" Charlie shouted from his place behind the wheel. "They're right behind us!"

The four men scrambled to comply. Freeman, Graves, and Williams rushed to the rear of the truck, where the rest of the men pulled them inside, while Burke scrambled up into the front passenger seat next to Charlie.

"Go! Go!" he cried, but Charlie needed no urging. He slammed the truck into gear and mashed his foot down on the accelerator. The tires spun for a second in the loose gravel that served as the base's roads and then they caught, sending them speeding away from the laboratory.

Burke stuck his head out the window, looking back, and was just in time to see part of the building's roof blow off as the explosives they'd set went off with a bang. The shock wave caught up with them a second later, pushing them along in a blast of super-heated air.

"No hiding from them now!" Charlie shouted, as several more explosions rocked the night.

The scene around them was chaos. Men were running in several directions, responding to the shouted commands of their officers. Many probably didn't even know what was going on but were simply reacting to the need to do something, anything, in the wake of what looked like an attack by Allied or partisan forces. Trucks raced by, headed in the opposite direction. Burke knew it wouldn't be long before someone noticed that they were racing away from the commotion.

Charlie smoothly maneuvered the lorry through the chaos, headed back toward the residence where they had left the staff car, hoping to pick it up again before heading on. Their plans were disrupted, however, when they turned the corner and saw a group of individuals gathered together outside the manor house.

"Don't stop!" Burke said urgently, and Charlie shifted up, accelerating them past the group as quickly as possible.

Burke glanced out the window, taking in the crowd and searching for any sign of Richthofen.

He didn't have to look far.

Richthofen's gaze locked with his own, and in the dead man's eyes Burke caught a glimpse of hell itself as the other man realized who they were.

"Shit!"

"What?" Charlie asked.

"Richthofen!"

Charlie made a couple of quick turns and suddenly the front gate flashed into view.

"Here we go!" he shouted over his shoulder to the rest of the team in the back. He pointed the truck at the center of the gate, intending to drive right through it, closed or not.

Recognizing his intentions, the sentries at the gate began firing at the lorry. Most of the shots missed, but a few slammed into the grille across the front of the truck and one tore away the mirror on Burke's side of the vehicle.

The gate loomed large in the windshield, and Burke steadied himself with a hand on the dash and his feet flat on the floor.

"Brace yourself!" Charlie cried.

They hit the gate doing a good fifty miles per hour and smashed through it with ease, the tires bouncing over its remains before biting into the surface of the road again.

Burke looked at Charlie and let out a whoop of excitement. "We're through!"

The open road stretched out before them, and Burke imagined that they might just make it out after all.

At least until the shooting started behind them.

CHAPTER FORTY-TWO

★

BULLETS SLAMMED INTO the tailgate of the truck as the thunder of a light machine gun split the night.

Charlie yanked the wheel to the right, taking them out of the line of fire, and giving Burke a chance to look behind them at the bad news waiting there.

They were being pursued by several smaller armored vehicles, both of which were faster and easier to maneuver than their own two-ton truck. The AVs were accompanied by a black staff car that looked similar to the one they'd used to bluff their way onto the base, except this one had Richthofen's personal crest, a two-headed eagle looming over a pair of skulls, on the front doors.

Both the armored vehicles sported light machine guns, and as Burke pulled his head back in the truck the guns opened up again, hammering the fleeing vehicle and causing those in the back to flatten themselves against the floorboard hoping like hell they wouldn't get hit.

A series of turns came into view ahead of them, forcing Charlie to slow down slightly to negotiate the narrow road and allowing the lead vehicle to catch up with them slightly. The machine gun went off again, stitching holes up and down the fabric that covered the cargo area where the rest of the team were hiding out.

The AV driver pulled up directly behind the lorry, the gunner aiming the machine gun across the cargo area at Sergeant Moore's unprotected back, waiting to get it lined up perfectly before he took the shot . . .

Manning popped up in the back of the truck and snapped off a shot from his pistol that took the gunner right in the face. The driver swerved away and fell back a few yards.

The driver of the second AV was apparently braver than the first, for he took the opportunity to close the distance with the lorry. The machine gunner lit up the night sky with a blast from his weapon, joined by two other soldiers who leaned out the side windows and fired at them whenever opportunity allowed.

Burke's men responded by laying down their own barrage of rifle fire from the back of the lorry, the barrels of their weapons pointed over the tailgate.

Sergeant Moore continued to do his part, swerving the lorry back and forth across the road at unexpected intervals, trying to keep the enemy from catching them in a concerted stream of fire.

"We're not going to make it," Charlie shouted. "Not like this anyway."

Burke knew he was right. Their pursuers knew the roads and local area. If they were in communication with any other units, which was highly likely, they could easily coordinate a joint effort to run the fugitives to ground. Burke and his squad would be intercepted long before they could reach the front.

They needed to throw their pursuers off their trail long enough to find an alternate means of escape.

"When I tell you, I want you to hold it steady for a sec," Burke shouted back.

Charlie nodded.

Burke turned, then yelled at Compton so he could be heard over the sound of the gunfire.

"We need to stop those AVs!" he shouted. "Do you still have those grenades Professor Graves created?"

Compton nodded.

"Here's what we're going to do . . ."

When Burke was finished, Compton flashed him a thumbs-up and disappeared back to the tailgate of the truck to pass the word to the others.

Burke waited a few seconds, wanting to gauge the timing just right. When Charlie hit a straightaway, he yelled, "Now!"

As one, Compton and the other men pulled the pins on the magnetic grenades in their hands, counted to three, and then dropped the devices out the back of the truck.

The explosives rolled down the street toward the pursuing vehicles as Charlie stomped on the gas pedal, trying to coax a little more speed from the already laboring engine.

Burke watched as the grenades rolled beneath the pursuing vehicles. He saw a brief flash from beneath their frames and in the next second their forward momentum was stolen completely as the now magnetically charged ground beneath them seemed to reach up and grab the iron frames of the trucks like a vise, bringing them to an immediate, shuddering halt. Frames crumpled and tires blew as the opposing forces fought against each other. He half expected bodies to come flying out the windshields from the sudden transference of g-forces, but then realized that they, too, would likely be struggling to lift themselves off the floor of the vehicle as the magnetic force acted on anything metallic that they were wearing.

For just a second, he felt a tug back in the direction of the wreckage as the magnetic charge tried to ensnare them as well, but the distance was too great and they broke free. Burke couldn't see what happened to the staff car behind the AVs, but was confident that they had gained a few minutes' advantage. The dense forest on either side of the road wouldn't let Richthofen's car pass, and the wreckage of the trucks would be immovable until the magnetic charge wore off.

It might only last for a few minutes, but even that would give them some time and distance to come up with a plan.

The solution must have occurred to him and Charlie at the same time. They looked at each other, the same thought running through their heads. *We need a decoy to lead pursuit away from the rest of the group . . .*

"I'll do it," they said simultaneously.

Charlie barely slowed as he whipped the truck around a hairpin turn and then stomped back down on the pedal as they hit the next straightaway. Without taking his eyes off the road he said, "Sorry, sir, but I can't let you do that. Somebody's going to have to lead the team all the way back to the front, and you've got a better chance of holding them together under pressure than I do."

Burke braced himself as they jolted over several bumps in the road.

"If you think I'm going to just leave you behind after all we've been through . . ."

Charlie cut him off. "With all due respect, you don't have a choice. You need to get Freeman and the information he has back to the other side or none of this will matter."

He was right; Burke knew it, too. But that didn't make it any easier.

The big sergeant glanced at Burke and smiled. "I'll meet you farther down the line. Just be ready to pick me up when the time comes."

They both knew it would take a miracle for him to do so once he drew the pursuit vehicles away from the rest of the squad. The enemy troops would run him down and shoot him on sight once they had.

Charlie didn't stand a chance.

No way was Burke going to admit that though. His friend deserved better, and if it helped him make the sacrifice he was about to make, Burke would happily plan their reunion if that's what Charlie wanted.

The grenades they'd dumped in the road gave them a bit of distance from their pursuers, but it wouldn't be long before they would catch up again. If they were going to do this, it was now or never.

"There's a big partisan group near Reims. Make your way to

them. They'll take you in and should be able to get word to us that you made it out all right."

"Will do." Charlie stuck out his hand. "Good luck."

Burke gripped his friend's hand tightly, then turned and spread the word to the others in the back of the truck. They held on as Charlie took them through series of turns and then brought the truck to a screeching halt.

"Go!" he shouted.

Burke didn't waste any time with further good-byes, just flung open his door and scrambled out of the truck. The rest of the men were piling out of the back at the same time and he counted heads as they joined him, only to come up one short. Glancing back toward the cab, he saw Manning climbing into the passenger seat beside Sergeant Moore.

"What the hell are you doing?" he shouted. "We've got to go!"

"Sorry, Captain," Manning replied. "I've still got a shot at bagging that bastard Richthofen and I'm going to take it. Give my regards to Colonel Nichols when you see him."

Before Burke could say another word, Charlie threw the truck into gear and slammed his foot down on the accelerator. No sooner had he sped off than lights appeared on the road behind them in the distance.

"Into the woods! Hurry!" Burke cried, waiting for all his men to head out before turning and running like hell for the safety of the trees.

Burke paused in the darkness around them and watched as the enemy sped past in a pair of lorries and Richthofen's staff car. At the speed that they were going, he estimated that Charlie had a two-, maybe three-minute lead on his pursuers.

That wasn't much. Charlie was going to need every trick in the book to get away.

Burke tried to get one last glimpse of the fleeing vehicle through the trees, but it was already out of sight.

"Godspeed, my friend," he whispered into the darkness.

It took Burke ten minutes to catch up with the others, at which point he called a quick break. He put two of them on guard and let the others grab a few minutes of rest while he tried to figure out their next course of action.

Time was of the essence. Sergeant Moore and Clayton Manning wouldn't be able to hold off their pursuers indefinitely. At some point, Richthofen would discover that he had been duped and the hunt would be on for Burke and the rest of his men. They needed to be miles away before that happened.

Their options were limited, however. Roads in this region were few, and all the previous traffic they'd seen had been military in nature. Burke had no objection to hijacking a truck if the opportunity arose, but the problem with that strategy was that they hadn't seen a single vehicle traveling on its own all the way from Stalag 113 to the testing facility in Verdun.

The more vehicles there were, the more soldiers they'd have to face. No, there had to be another way to . . .

"Why do I get the feeling that this wasn't part of the plan?"

Burke looked up from the map to find Jack watching him steadily and waiting for an answer. His half brother had pitched his voice low enough that the rest of the men wouldn't hear his comment, which Burke appreciated. Not that such subterfuge was necessary; Burke's men knew the plan had been screwed the minute the *Victorious* had been shot out from underneath them.

Seeing no reason not to tell the truth, Burke said, "Because it wasn't. We were supposed to rendezvous with the British airship that brought us behind the lines."

"And we're not doing that now because?"

"Because the Boche shot it down."

He turned back to the map, running his finger along a possible route that might get them a few miles farther from the camp without exposing them. *If they stuck to the woods, they might be able to get as far as . . .*

"I don't want to tell you your business, but have you thought about the train?"

Burke stopped and looked up.

"The train?"

Jack nodded. "The one that was parked behind the gas factory when you arrived at the camp."

Burke had no idea what Jack was talking about. "Show me," he said, handing him the map.

CHAPTER FORTY-THREE

Somewhere Behind the Lines

"You should have left when you had the chance!" Moore shouted, doing his best to make himself heard over the crack of the rifles and the thunder of the light machine gun hammering away at them from behind.

"And miss all this fun?" Manning replied. "Never!"

It hadn't taken long for more vehicles from the base to catch up with them, and they were now being subjected to a withering hail of gunfire from behind. Even as they traded bravado, a series of well-placed rifle shots whipped through the space between them, striking the windshield and shattering it into dozens of fragments that peppered them with cuts on their faces, necks, and hands.

The wind coming in through the space where the windshield used to be made it difficult to see, but Charlie didn't dare slow down.

They still had a job to do. Every minute they kept ahead of the enemy was another minute that Captain Burke and the rest of the squad could use to make their escape.

Sergeant Charlie Moore was many things, one of which was a realist. He had little hope that they'd get out of this mess and had long since stopped worrying about whether they would or not. How could he? He had no idea where he was or where he was headed; he'd lost track of everything just moments after smashing through the gates of the complex. All he was doing now was keeping the truck facing forward and pushing it as hard as he could, while Manning kept up a constant stream of fire directed behind them.

Moore knew how important it was that Burke get away, which was why even now, as the enemy closed in, he was praying for Burke rather than himself or Manning.

Manning had already emptied the sergeant's Tommy gun back at their pursuers and now had his pistol out, firing back over his seat—*Crack! Crack! Crack!*—at the enemy behind them.

He spun around, ejected the magazine, and slapped in a new one. "That's it. Last magazine and then I'm out."

Charlie opened his mouth to reply and almost bit his tongue in half when the driver behind them rammed the rear of their vehicle with his own.

"Get us the hell out of here, Sergeant!" Manning yelled, as he snapped off a couple of quick shots in the enemy's direction.

"I'm trying!"

Crash!

The other driver did it again, jamming his rear bumper up against the tailgate of their vehicle while trying to push them off the road.

Charlie jerked the wheel left, then right, but couldn't seem to get away.

"Shoot the sonofabitch!" he shouted at Manning and glanced back that way.

He was just in time to see the grenade arc through the air and skip—*tink, tink, tink*—across the floor of the cargo space behind them.

"Grenade!" he shouted, trying to warn his companion, but there was really no need. Manning had seen it too and he was already moving, hurling himself between the seats and scrambling to get his hands on the projectile as it rolled around behind them.

He's insane! Charlie thought. *No way he can grab that before being blown to bits!*

But to his surprise Manning did just that, snatching up the grenade in his right hand and side-arming it out the back of the truck.

Manning threw himself down to the deck of the cargo area, doing his best to make himself as small a target as possible as he huddled up against the thick metal tailgate, and was just in time to avoid being ripped to shreds by shrapnel as the grenade went off just after he released it. The explosion buckled the tailgate inward, but Manning survived unscathed.

Charlie couldn't believe it!

Neither could Manning. He popped up on his knees, shouting with relief to find himself all in one piece. "Damn, that was close!" he cried.

Crack!

The rifle shot took him square in the center of the back, blasting his spine into splinters as it tore through him from back to front and came out the other side with a wet splat. As Charlie watched in the mirror, Manning looked down at his chest, staring in stunned amazement at the blood pouring out of the fist-sized hole that had appeared as if by magic to the right of his sternum, and then toppled over on his face, dead.

"God damn it!" Charlie shouted at the sky above, not afraid to use a little blasphemy if that was going to catch the Lord's attention. "I need some help down here!"

But it was not to be.

As Charlie came speeding around the next curve, his headlights fell on the three German vehicles parked across the road. He realized in that instant that nothing he did would change the outcome of what was about to happen and so he didn't even bother to try. He just pointed the truck at the parked vehicles ahead of him, gripped the steering wheel tighter, and hoped for the best.

The lorry slammed into the roadblock nearly dead center, the momentum carrying the vehicle up and over the others, twisting over on its side as it went. It sailed through the air for a dozen feet before coming crashing back down and sliding along the roadside until it slammed nose first into a tree, stopping its forward momentum.

Inside the truck's cab, nothing moved.

RICHTHOFEN STOOD TO one side and watched as his men pulled the Americans from the wreckage.

The first man was already dead, the victim of an apparent gunshot wound. From the lack of blood around his neck and shoulders, the flier had to assume that the decapitation had happened postmortem.

The driver, on the other hand, was still breathing when they pulled him from the crumpled steel that had once been a two-ton lorry, protected by the thick vest he was wearing, a vest made from reinforced leather and steel. He was bleeding from his mouth, which suggested internal injuries, but at least he was alive.

Just two men.

Richthofen wanted to rip the bodies apart with his bare hands in frustration. Somewhere between here and the gates of the base, the rest of the infiltration team had disappeared, taking President Harper's son with them. Finding them now would be the equivalent of searching for a needle in a haystack.

Richthofen stood over the driver, pistol in hand, considering whether he was going to shoot the man outright and be done with it, or wait, see if he lived, and then get what he could from the heavyset American.

In the end, the lure of the unknown won out.

He beckoned several men over. "Do whatever you need to do to keep this man alive. If he dies, you'll be next."

CHAPTER FORTY-FOUR

AN HOUR LATER, Burke and what was left of his team were huddled in a ditch next to the station house, staring at a black steel behemoth. The train had started life as a standard steam-powered locomotive, but he could see that it had been through some extensive modifications, not the least of which was a thick set of armor that covered all but a small viewing slit in the front of the cab. A battering ram had been welded to the front of the engine, and two heavy machine-gun emplacements could be seen atop two of the cars. The armor told Burke that Freeman was right—the train most likely made regular visits to the front, which was just what they were looking for. If they could commandeer the train, they might be able to ride it all the way to the rail station on the enemy side of the lines at Nogent. Burke had no idea how he was going to get across the lines once they arrived there, but he'd worry about that later.

"What do you think, Professor? Can you handle a train that large?"

Graves seemed offended by the question. "It's powered by steam, isn't it?" he replied, as if that was answer enough.

And maybe it was.

Burke scooted up a little higher against the embankment and

took a long look down the tracks, letting the plan formulate in his head.

From his position opposite the train's engine, he could see a pair of guards, ostensibly guarding the locomotive and keeping unauthorized individuals from getting close enough to do it any harm.

He inched up even higher and chanced a quick look down the length of the train. He could see only one other guard, who stood about four cars from the front, near another boarding point. The guard had his gun slung over his shoulder and his hands in his pockets.

No threat there.

Burke slid back down into the cover of the ditch and motioned the others closer.

"That train is our ticket out of here. If we get lucky, we might even be able to ride it all the way to the front, but first we need to make sure it's fully under our control."

He pointed at Compton and Williams. "I want the two of you to make your way around the station house and into the ditch on the other side. When you hear us start the attack, you're to neutralize the guard and get aboard the closest car as quickly as possible. Understand?"

They nodded, excitement warring with fear on their faces.

"We're going to be waiting until the last possible second, so don't be late. Take out that guard and get onboard that train. Now get going."

The two men slipped out of the ditch and faded into the trees.

Burke watched them for a moment and then turned his attention to the others. "We have to get inside that cab before the engineers figure out what's going on. If they do, we're dead in the water, understand?"

Jones, Graves, and Freeman all nodded.

"When I give the signal, here's what we're going to do . . ."

Knowing Compton and Williams would give the station a wide berth, Burke gave the two of them ten minutes to get into position. That was, unfortunately, all he *could* give them, for right about that time the engineers boarded the locomotive and began their preparations for leaving.

"Let's get 'em!" Jones whispered and started to get to his feet, only to have Burke grab him and haul him back down.

"We go when I say we do!" he hissed, his face just inches from Jones's. "We want that engine up and running before we make our move, you idiot."

Burke knew that their best opportunity was to wait until the last moment and then seize control of the cab. Doing so would reduce the opportunity for anyone inside the train station to respond to the crisis.

The seconds ticked past.

Smoke began to drift out of the chimney atop the locomotive as the engine built up a head of steam powerful enough to move it along the track.

"Get ready," Burke whispered to the men beside him, his gaze on the guards outside the cab. In his peripheral vision he saw Jones settling the stock of his Enfield against his shoulder.

The shriek of a whistle split the night air as the motorman signaled their readiness for departure. The pair of guards that were standing near the door to the engineer's cab threw away their cigarettes and got ready to board the train.

"Now!" Burke cried and launched himself out of the ditch, hitting the ground running and heading straight for the cab and the engineers inside. The guards were slow to respond to his sudden appearance, unable to reconcile the conflict posed by the fact that he was wearing a German uniform and yet was running toward them with his gun at the ready and pointed in their direction. Their hesitation cost them their lives; Jones fired over Burke's shoulder, taking each of them down with a single shot to the head. Their bodies hadn't yet hit the ground as Burke rushed past them, his attention focused on the door of the train, knowing that if the engineers managed to close it before he got inside, there was no way to breach the cab.

A figure appeared in the doorway before him, a gun in hand, and Burke felt the passage of the bullet as it screamed past him only inches from his ear before he even realized that a shot had been fired. He responded with a quick squeeze of the trigger of his own weapon, the chatter of the Tommy gun filling the air with its *rat-a-tat-tat* sound as the bullets stitched their way across the man's chest, flinging him away from the door and into the depths of the compartment behind him. Off to Burke's right, farther down the length of the train, he heard more gunfire and knew that Compton and Williams had joined the fight.

Burke had no time to worry about them, however, for the door to the engineer's cab loomed before him and he bounded through it, taking it all in with a sweeping glance. The body of the man he'd shot lay crumpled on the floor in front of him. Motion to his left told him there was another man, possibly two, waiting there. He spun in that direction while still moving forward, unable to stop his momentum that quickly, and his foot landed squarely in the pool of blood spilling across the floor from the first man he'd shot.

Burke's foot went out from under him, sending him crashing to the floor.

The fall saved his life.

The coal shovel the fireman swung at Burke's head passed harmlessly overhead, missing him by inches.

Burke wasn't waiting around to give him another shot either. He was already pulling the trigger as he crashed to the floor; his first few bullets obliterated the man's face, the rest of them ricocheting around the small compartment as they bounced off the iron doors of the firebox.

Silence fell as the Tommy gun ran dry.

Burke scrambled to his feet, knowing that reinforcements could be only seconds away. They didn't have any time to waste. He stuck his head out the door and was relieved to see Jones running toward him with Graves and Freeman at his heels. A glance down the length of the train showed Williams and Compton climbing unhindered aboard, four cars back.

They'd taken the train!

Graves went straight to the control station as soon as he was aboard, with Freeman at his heels. Burke and Jones took up positions on either side of the door, their gaze on the station house.

No sooner had they settled into position than several gray-clad German soldiers rushed out of the building, weapons in hand.

"We need to leave, Graves!" Burke called out, risking a glance in his direction. "And I mean NOW!"

"Working on it, Captain," the professor shouted back, as he rushed from control panel to control panel, pushing buttons and pulling levers, while telling Freeman to shovel coal into the furnace.

The German soldiers sent a flurry of shots toward the train, forcing Burke to flatten himself against the side of the car to avoid getting hit. The small space was soon filled with the sounds of bullets striking metal and ricocheting away in different directions. Thankfully the armor on the train was more than up to the task of protecting them against small-arms fire. Burke grabbed the engineer's pistol and sent a few shots of his own winging toward the enemy. He wasn't really trying to hit anyone, just encourage them to keep their heads down. His philosophy was that they couldn't shoot if they couldn't see, and every minute that passed brought them one minute closer to departure.

The train lurched a few feet, nearly throwing Burke off balance. As he steadied himself, he realized they were picking up speed.

"Go! Go! Go!" he shouted toward the men in the cab, and Freeman shot him a weary but wide smile in return.

It was when he turned back again, not wanting to let the enemy out of sight for too long, that he saw the 18 mm mortar.

A team of three was hustling it into position on a clear spot just outside the doors of the station. While one man secured the legs, another stockpiled a dozen or more shells beside it. The mortar crew was going to stop the train one way or another, it seemed, and blowing it up didn't seem to be a problem.

Burke couldn't let that happen.

He caught Jones's attention, pointed toward the mortar crew, then showed him the grenade in his hand. The corporal stole a quick look and then pulled his head in before it could get shot off by one of the industrious soldiers providing cover for the mortar crew.

"On the count of three," he shouted, over the din of the gunfire. Burke nodded.

Jones counted it down and as he reached three, the two of them spun into the doorway. While Jones laid down some covering fire, Burke leaned out the door and heaved the German stick grenade toward the mortar crew. It flipped end over end and struck the ground a few feet in front of them. The resulting blast lifted the soldiers up and tossed them like rag dolls into the outer wall of the station.

As the train picked up speed, Burke whooped in satisfaction!

Several of the defenders scrambled to their feet and began to run toward the nearest car, hoping to jump onboard, but they were quickly cut down by shots from Williams and Compton.

The train gathered momentum, and within moments they had the station and its defenders behind. Soon they were rolling across occupied France at a rate many times what they would have been able to do on foot. Burke started to think they might have a prayer of surviving after all.

CHAPTER FORTY-FIVE

⭐

RICHTHOFEN MANAGED TO make it back to his office before the rage that had been building since leaving the crash site got the better of him. The next ten, maybe even fifteen minutes vanished as he lost himself in his fury, only coming back to himself when someone began pounding urgently on his office door.

He shook his head, clearing the red mist from his vision, and found that he was standing amid the wreckage of his office with the half-eaten corpse of a sentry in one hand. He turned in a slow circle, taking it all in.

His bookshelves had been pulled from the walls, the volumes they had contained now shredded and strewn about the floor. The chess set had been ground underfoot. The top of his desk had even been smashed in half.

Not one of his calmer rages.

Richthofen tossed the corpse aside and kicked his way through the wreckage and over to the door. He paused a moment to wipe some of the blood and uneaten tissue off his face with the back of his hand and then opened the door.

The messenger who stood on the other side managed to hand him the telegram before losing control of his nerve and falling to his knees, pleading for his life.

Ignoring him, Richthofen shut the door and read the hastily jotted message. It informed him that one of their troop transport trains was acting erratically, bypassing scheduled stops and ignoring attempts to flag it down.

He stalked back across the room to where a map of the region still hung on the wall and traced the route of the train forward from its last known position all the way to the end of the line, marking its path with the blood that stained his finger.

The route ended at Nogent, a small town very close to the front. *The missing fugitives were on that train!*

He hunted through the mess he'd made until he found the phone and put in a call to his headquarters at Jasta 11, one of the few locations that were currently set up to use the new communication device.

When Adler answered the phone, Richthofen said, "There is a train currently running on track 89, bound for the front. I want it stopped."

"Of course, Herr Richthofen. I will have the conductor contacted and . . ."

Richthofen cut him off. "The train is no longer under our control and may, in fact, be in the hands of the enemy. I want that train stopped, intact if possible, but do what you have to do to keep it from reaching the front lines. Do I make myself clear?"

"Yes, Herr Richthofen!"

"Good. I am returning to base and will join you in your efforts from the air as soon as I am able."

Richthofen left the phone hanging as he rushed out of the office, headed for the airfield and the aircraft waiting there.

CHAPTER FORTY-SIX

★

"How are we doing, Professor?" Burke asked as they labored to climb up another hill.

Graves shrugged. "As good as can be expected, I'd think. We'd move a bit faster if we could get rid of some of these extra cars though."

Burke wanted to hit himself for not thinking of that sooner. The train consisted of about a dozen cars, if you counted the locomotive and the tender car. By jettisoning the majority of them, they could save on fuel consumption while at the same time reducing the danger of derailment. The machine-gun emplacements were on cars three and eight, so he figured he would keep the first three and get rid of the rest.

He listened carefully as Graves told him how to release the clamp that held the cars together and then headed aft to do the job.

"Need help?" Compton asked.

"Nah, I should be all right. I want you and Williams to come with me and check out the machine-gun emplacement atop car number three, though, in case we need it."

"Right."

The three of them moved aft. The cars were connected by a

small wooden platform at either end with about two feet of space between them, which granted the engineers access to the coupler arms. Burke could see the thick pin that held the couplers together, which blocked the switch from being set to the release position accidentally. To release the coupler between cars three and four, he would have to climb down between the cars, balance on the couplers, and pull the pin with the help of an engineer's wrench before he could throw the switch. For now though, he just jumped lightly across the gap between the cars and hauled down on the handle that opened the door to the next.

Behind him, Compton and Williams followed suit.

About half the passenger seats in the third car had been torn out to make room for the machine-gun crew. A ladder had been welded into place in the center of the railcar, giving access to a small platform that hung down from the hole that had been cut in the ceiling. Above the platform on a swivel mounted to the top of the train was a Hotchkiss machine gun. To operate it the gunner stood on the platform with his head and shoulders outside the top of the train so that he could swivel the gun into whatever position was necessary to fire on the target.

Burke left his subordinates to check out the condition of the machine gun and continued aft, intent on uncoupling the cars. When he arrived at the junction of cars three and four, however, he happened to glance inside and discovered that he was looking at a private kitchen/dining car all rolled into one. The men hadn't had a decent meal in a while, so dumping the dining car before they had a chance to raid it for anything edible just didn't seem right. Having come to that conclusion, Burke decided to check out the other cars, just in case there was something usable there as well.

He made his way through the dining car, out onto the platform, and then stepped over the gap to the opposite platform and the door leading into car five. He pulled down on the handle and slid the door open.

A shambler stood on the other side, so close it must have been pressed right up against the door. Behind it, a horde of others filled the car, packed in so tightly that they had no room to move. At the sound of the door's opening they all turned and looked in Burke's direction.

"Oh, shit."

Burke went for his .45.

The lead shambler went for Burke.

It fell upon him, slamming him backward, its weight carrying them both off the platform as the door slid shut. They fell down into the space between the railroad cars, the .45 spinning out of Burke's hand and disappearing.

Burke let out a sharp yelp of pain as they landed hard on the coupler arms, the shambler atop him struggling to get close enough to take a bite out of his flesh while he worked to keep it from doing so. The wind whipped past, buffeting them on their precarious perch.

With his right arm between them like a brace, holding the shambler back, Burke began to beat at the shambler with his left. The heavy, mechanical arm smashed repeatedly into the creature's face and head with savage force, causing blood and flesh to fly. At the same time, Burke wrapped his legs around the coupler arm and squeezed them tight, not wanting the momentum of his own movements to accidentally knock him free of the train. He prayed there wasn't anything sticking up from the tracks ahead of them that might snag his foot and tear him free, then promptly forgot about the danger as he focused all his attention on the problem in front of him.

As expected, the shambler made no effort to avoid his blows, and it was starting to develop a considerable dent in the side of its head, but Burke was worried he wouldn't finish it off before the rest of the shamblers managed to get that door open. Now that they'd seen how it was done, it might not hold them as long as it had the first time. He needed to solve this and solve it fast.

As he levered another devastating blow to the shambler's face, it occurred to him that while he might have lost his .45, he was still carrying a firearm. The Colt Firestarter Graves had given him to test was still in its holster on the left side of his belt.

Without giving himself time to think about all the things that might go wrong with an untried weapon, Burke used his mechanical arm to push the shambler back a bit and snatched the gun out of its holster with the other, shoving the barrel against the creature's chest and pulling the trigger.

The shot tore right through the shambler, blowing a fist-sized chunk of flesh and bone out of its back before it embedded itself into the door behind them with a solid *thunk*.

Burke barely noticed, for he was too busy staring at the shambler. The enzyme that coated the round went to work on the creature's flesh, sending scorching trails of liquid lightning burning through its veins like fire following a trail of gasoline until open flames belched forth from the shambler's eyes, ears, and mouth. Burke jerked his metal hand up over his face to protect himself against the sudden eruption of fire, managing to keep himself from being scorched to a crisp and coming away with only a few patches of singed flesh, and then shoved the still-burning corpse to one side where it was swept away.

As the other shamblers lurched toward him, Burke opened up with the Firestarter again, causing those closest to him to erupt in blazing funeral pyres as flames tore them apart from the inside out. The sight of the walking dead dying so easily from just a single shot practically had him shouting with glee. When he'd cleared those closest to the door, he scrambled to his feet and climbed up onto the platform between the cars, knocking the burning creatures over the side with a quick thrust of his mechanical arm.

A glance through the still open door showed more of them moving forward, those behind pushing against the backs of those in front as they clambered over one another in their desire to reach him. Burke had no intention of giving them the chance.

He fired on the closest shambler, hitting it right in the face and sending the shot into the creature behind it as well. He then made use of the resulting confusion inside to leap for the door, intent on sealing the creatures back up again.

Except the door wouldn't move.

A hunk of burning shambler flesh was wedged in the track, jamming it open and preventing Burke from getting the door closed. As he struggled with it, the shamblers inside the car managed to get around their blazing comrades, lurching forward, almost within reach . . .

The rifle fire that sounded over his shoulder was uncomfortably close, but it did the job. The shamblers were knocked back into the crowd behind them, giving Burke the moment he needed to kick the unidentifiable piece of flesh out of the way and haul the door shut just as the shamblers inside reached the opening. Without hesitation, Burke used his mechanical hand to bend the handle until it broke off in place, sealing the door shut.

He turned to find Jones standing on the opposite platform, his Enfield in hand and a relieved grin on his face.

"Guess we should have searched the train, huh?"

Burke didn't bother to answer. It was a stupid oversight, one they were lucky to survive. If he'd come along a few minutes later, if the creatures had managed to get the door open, all their efforts would have been for nothing.

It didn't bear thinking about.

As Jones kept watch to make sure the shamblers didn't find a way to knock the door open with sheer numbers, Burke climbed down between the cars, making sure to keep his feet on the portion of the coupler that was attached to the dining car, and then grasped the pin in both hands. He heaved upward, expecting it to come right out.

Nothing happened.

The pin was stuck.

"Damn it!" he shouted. "You motherfuckin' stupid piece of . . ."

The rest of his statement was drowned out by the shrieking sound of the train's whistle as Graves tried to get his attention.

Hold your horses, Professor . . .

Burke raised one foot and hammered his boot against the pin, trying to free it from its seat. One kick. Two kicks. Three. Four. Five.

The fifth time was the charm. The pin rattled in its seat, and Burke wasted no time grabbing it by its ring with his mechanical fingers, hauling it upward, disengaging the locomotive from the rest of the train and causing it to surge forward now that it was free of all the weight behind it.

Congratulating himself on a job well done, Burke let Jones help him back up onto the platform, and the two of them rejoined the others in the locomotive. As they came through the door, Graves turned to Burke and said, "Station coming up," pointing through the front window at the building looming ahead.

Burke recognized the unspoken question.

"Don't stop," he told him. "Don't even slow down."

The professor did what he was told.

They rolled through the station without slowing, ignoring the surprised shouts of those on the platform who'd been expecting the train to stop. They did the same thing a half hour later, when they reached the station at Saint-Mihiel.

Word must have gotten out about the runaway train shortly after that, however, for when they began their approach to the station at Commercy they could see that the platform had been cleared, the potential passengers replaced with several riflemen and a three-man machine-gun crew. A flagman was also present, and he began waving his flags in a series of signals the minute they came into view.

Burke had no idea what message the flagman was trying to impart to him, nor did he care. Stopping was out of the question. When it became clear that the train wasn't going to heed their signals, another order was given and the machine gunner opened fire on the train.

Burke instinctively ducked, as did the rest of his men, but then straightened up and laughed aloud as the armor that covered the front of the train deflected the bullets with ease. Graves pushed the throttle forward, giving them more speed, and they shot through the Commercy station unharmed.

The element of surprise was lost now, though. Word would be going out to all the stations on the line that the train wasn't answering commands to stop, and resistance to their movement would only get worse. Burke's biggest fear was that the enemy would blow the tracks ahead of them, effectively ending their run for safety. That's what he would do if he were in their position. There wasn't a damn thing he could do about it if that was the option they chose.

He could, however, prepare for other possibilities. He ordered Compton to man the machine-gun turret on the roof of the train and put Williams and Jones at the windows in the dining car just behind him. He took up a position on the platform behind the tender car, where he could see what was coming but still communicate with Jack and the professor without trouble.

At both Saint-Dizier and Vitry-le-François, the enemy repeated what they'd done at Commercy, flooding the platform with troops who fired at them with an assortment of small arms and what few crew-operated weapons they had on hand. Compton opened fire as soon as the opportunity arose, cutting the enemy down with long bursts from the Hotchkiss on the roof above, and Burke was suddenly reminded of the corporal's prayer from days before, his desire to kill as many of the enemy as possible. *Seems someone upstairs was listening,* Burke thought, and then said a prayer of his own just in case they still had the big man's attention.

They rolled through a long stretch of open country without encountering any resistance, and Burke found himself staring out the window, wondering how Charlie was doing. He hoped like hell that the big sergeant had managed to lose his pursuers and slip away into the woods. If he could evade pursuit long enough to rendezvous with the freedom fighters outside of Reims, he'd have a chance of making it back to the other side of the lines.

His thoughts turned from his friend to his brother. The sheer bedlam of their escape from Verdun hadn't left Burke with any time to think, never mind sort through the conflicting feelings he had about the mission in general. He'd been surprised by the concern he'd felt when Jack had turned up missing back at Stalag 113 and even more surprised when the sight of him had failed to stir the old anger that he'd kept carefully banked and burning for so many years in his heart. Before today he would have scoffed at anyone who'd dared tell him that time heals all wounds, but perhaps he'd finally begun to see the truth of that statement.

Then again, maybe he was just tired.

He had just decided to return to the engine car and check up on the professor when a speck of motion out on the horizon caught his eye. He leaned farther out the door, staring at it, trying to make out just what it was.

The object grew larger as it came closer, but still he couldn't tell just what it was.

Something about it troubled him.

Something about the size.

Or the color . . .

"Sonofabitch!"

Burke hauled the door open to the car behind him and shouted, "Stay sharp, Compton! Aircraft at 10:00!"

"I'm on him, Captain!"

Burke returned to his previous position on the platform between the cars and watched as the speck on the horizon resolved itself into a Fokker triplane painted a brilliant red.

Richthofen!

The German ace came in with guns blazing, which were answered a moment later by the stutter of the Hotchkiss as Compton returned fire. As the Fokker swept overhead, Burke joined the fray, unloading what was left in the Firestarter's cylinder at the aircraft as well, hoping for a lucky shot that might send the undead bastard at the controls up in a blazing pyre of artificial fire.

The Fokker swept past, unharmed, and banked around, preparing for another pass.

That's when Jack began screaming for him from the front of the train.

"Mike! You better get up here, Mike!"

Burke abandoned his position and made his way between the two cars to the engine, where he found Graves bent over the controls and Jack standing in front of one of the forward viewing ports, an expression of real fear on his face.

"What now?"

"You better take a look for yourself," Jack said, stepping aside as Burke pressed his face to the viewing slit.

Squatting on the tracks ahead of them was a massive armored contraption the size of a small house. It rested on two large treads, each one nearly as tall as the troops standing next to it, and sprouted no less than six major armaments—a 57 mm cannon and five machine guns—all of them currently pointing in their direction.

Burke recognized the contraption as an A7V, the largest tank built to date and one the Allies were having trouble dealing with on the battlefield. If the damned things hadn't been so prone to mechanical issues, they might have pushed the Allies all the way back to Paris. Its appearance here meant that the Germans had finally decided stopping the train was more important than stopping it intact.

Things were about to get ugly.

Burke had previous experience with the A7V, having faced down a trio of the massive vehicles during the fourth Battle of Ypres several months before. He knew that it required a crew of twenty to operate it at full capacity, but trained crewmen were in high demand, and odds were this one didn't have the manpower needed to run it 100 percent effectively.

That might not help them much, though, because this one was parked with its treads straddling the train tracks, and even from this distance they could see a spotter standing up in the hatch, a small scope in one hand.

"I think he's going to . . ."

That was as far as Burke got.

The forward-facing 57 mm cannon hurled a shell in their direction.

It wasn't a difficult shot, as the train was headed right for the tank and all the gunner had to do was point the barrel of the cannon in the right direction.

"Everybody hold on!" Burke shouted behind him and then locked his mechanical hand around the nearest support, bracing himself for what was to come.

The shell screamed toward them, crossing the distance in mere seconds and impacting right against the sloping piece of armor that covered the front of the locomotive. Most of the explosion was forced aside thanks to the armor, but enough got through to really shake them up. Both Jack and Graves were thrown to the floor, though neither of them was hurt in the process.

"More speed!" Burke shouted. "We need more speed!"

Graves shook his head. "I can't! That's all she's got!"

Burke didn't think it was enough.

He sent Jack to fetch Williams and turned his attention to the furnace, feverishly shoveling wood into the feeder, hoping to raise the temperature of the fire and thereby produce a greater head of steam. When the others returned, they added their efforts to his, stuffing the hopper almost to overflowing.

He could hear the staccato shout of the Hotchkiss and the answering roar of the Spandau machine guns on Richthofen's aircraft as it swept by on another pass, but there was nothing he could do to help Compton now. If they didn't deal with the tank, it was all over anyway.

Another round screamed toward them, missing by inches and going past the train on the left side, so close that Burke imagined he could have reached out and touched it.

A glance at the gauge told him they were creeping up over sixty miles per hour now, which was faster than Burke had ever gone before.

"Five hundred yards," Graves called out, and Burke rushed over for a quick look, his mind racing, trying to come up with a plan but knowing that their only hope was to ram the tank and pray for the best.

His gaze fell on the stretch of land behind the tank, and he was surprised to see the rolls of concertina wire and abandoned trenches that marked the edge of no-man's-land, that boundary between the opposing armies that shifted back and forth as ground was lost, gained, and lost again.

If they could get past the tank and into no-man's-land . . .

"More fuel!" Burke ordered. He reached past Graves and pushed the throttle all the way forward, trying to squeeze another few miles per hour out of the engine.

The tank fired again, scoring another hit on their front end, and this time it tore away the armor, exposing the bare bones of the locomotive underneath.

One more shot and it was going to be all over . . .

The distance between the two vehicles seemed to close in a heartbeat, and Burke was suddenly screaming for everyone to brace themselves as the front of the tank loomed in their windshield.

There was a tremendous crash, and Burke felt himself flying through the air only to slam into something less yielding than he was.

CHAPTER FORTY-SEVEN

★

THE WHISTLE OF a mortar attack brought Burke awake with a start. The sound of the shells screaming through the air was one that any trench soldier learned to listen for, and hearing it now sent his heart hammering in his chest and his head swiveling from side to side, searching for a place to hunker down and wait out the attack.

That's when he realized he wasn't in a trench at all, but in some kind of metal bunker . . .

. . . the train!

It all came back to him in a rush. Freeman's rescue. Charlie's sacrifice. The seizure of the train and the long ride across occupied France to the front at Nogent. The battle with the tank and the collision that had ended it.

He pushed himself to his feet and shuffled his way over to the nearest window. Looking out, he could see the cratered earth and lines of barbed wire that were indicative of no-man's-land.

And there, a few hundred yards beyond that, the first of the trenches that marked the Allied lines.

They were so close!

The sound of the mortars came again, the shrill screaming whistle of a shell moving at subsonic speed. He found himself ducking down as multiple shells slammed into the ground and exploded less than a dozen yards away from the train.

Something about their placement bothered him, but he was still pretty fuzzy from the crash.

He tried to puzzle it out.

Something about where the shells were landing . . .

Shit! We have to get out of here!

He glanced around the dim interior and saw the rest of the team lying in the wreckage. Worried that they had only moments available to them, Burke rushed over to the nearest man, who turned out to be Graves, and shook him awake.

"The Germans are firing on the train," he said as soon as Graves could focus. "We need to move!"

The professor was still groggy, but he was able to function enough to drag himself over to Jones and begin to revive him while Burke moved to his brother's side. Jack was just starting to come to when Burke knelt down beside him and saw blood on his brother's shirt.

"How badly are you hurt?" Burke asked.

Freeman put a hand to the back of his head and when he took it away there was fresh blood on it. Still, he only grimaced slightly when he said, "Must have banged my head. It's a bleeder, but I don't think it's too bad."

"Can you walk?"

"Yeah."

"Okay, on your feet then!" Burke helped him up, then slid an arm under his own and helped lead him out of the train car behind Graves and Jones. They took shelter in a large shell hole about ten feet from the wreck as Burke went back for the others.

The whistling came again, and Burke flattened himself on the ground just as the mortar rounds slammed into the earth nearby. The earth shook savagely, but the explosives did little more than throw a lot of dirt into the air. The shells were starting to zero in.

Time was running out.

Burke clambered back inside the wrecked train and hunted

through the first couple of cars until he found Williams and Compton. He found Compton tending to his unconscious squad mate.

"Can you walk?" Burke asked him.

The other man nodded.

"The rest of the team are hunkered down in an old shell hole about fifteen feet to the right. Start walking and I'll be there in a minute to help you; I'm going to get Williams out of here first."

Compton struggled to his feet and began to shuffle in the right direction. One of his arms hung at an unusual angle and Burke realized that it was broken.

Still, a broken arm was better than being blown to bits in a mortar attack.

Burke slipped his arms underneath Williams's unconscious form and stood up, taking the young private with him. He adjusted Williams's weight, getting the grip right so he wouldn't drop him along the way, and moved to follow Compton.

He heard the engine before he realized what it was, and by then it was too late.

Compton had managed to get halfway to the shell hole when the sound of the aircraft's engine caught his attention. Burke was looking right at him when Compton looked up, caught sight of the aircraft, and then twisted and shook as a stream of bullets slammed into him, sending his body crashing to the ground.

"No!" Burke screamed, but he knew it was too late.

The plane roared overhead, the black Iron Crosses on the underside of its wings standing out sharply against the bright red paint that covered them.

The German ace wasn't ready to let them go.

CHAPTER FORTY-EIGHT

★

As Richthofen swept by overhead, Burke used the time to make a run for the shell hole where the others were waiting. He heard the scream of the incoming mortar rounds just seconds before he reached the hole. He threw himself and Williams over the side as the shells plunged to earth.

This time, the spotter got it right.

The shells slammed into what was left of the locomotive, sending shrapnel flying through the air in every direction. If they'd been out in the open, they would have been cut to pieces, but because they were hunkered down below ground level they managed to withstand the barrage without further injury.

Jack grabbed him by the arm as soon as the shelling stopped.

"Now what?" he shouted, trying to be heard over the ringing in all their ears.

Burke pointed toward the Allied lines a few hundred yards away. "We make a run for it."

His brother stared at him. "Are you crazy? We'll never make it."

"We don't have a choice."

If they stayed out here, the enemy would eventually get them, be it Richthofen, the mortar operators, or the German troops who couldn't be that far behind them on the other side of the wreckage.

Their only hope was to make it to Allied lines, and there was only one way to do that.

Run like hell.

RICHTHOFEN CIRCLED HIGH above the battlefield, watching and waiting for the right moment. He had no intention of letting Major Freeman and his rescuers escape his grasp.

He'd already killed one of their number with his last pass, watching with satisfaction as the shells of his Spandau machine guns tore him apart where he stood. When the rest of his companions emerged from that foxhole they were hiding in, he'd dive down and eliminate them as well.

"LOOK THERE!" FREEMAN said, pointing to a spot about halfway to Allied lines, between two large sections of barbed wire.

Burke looked in that direction, not getting what his brother was pointing at. There were a number of abandoned positions from when the British had retreated after an earlier strike, what looked like half-buried bodies of former soldiers, and . . . an empty machine-gun nest, complete with a Lewis gun still on its tripod!

"I see it, Jack," Burke said. "What do you have in mind?"

Freeman looked skyward, searching for Richthofen's plane but not seeing it. He knew the German ace wouldn't be gone for long.

"Richthofen is going to swoop down on us the minute we leave the cover of this shell hole. There's no way we can outrun his plane, not over rugged terrain and having to deal with barbed wire at the same time. We'll never make it.

"But we can make that gun," he said, eyeing it greedily. "And if it's in working order, we can use it to defend ourselves until reinforcements come or until there is a lull in the fighting long enough to make a run for it on our own. What do you say?"

Graves and Jones were listening in, and they all agreed it was the best option available to them. Burke was ready to rush out and make a run for it, when Jones pulled him back into the hole.

"Hang on a minute, Captain," the other man said. He fished around amid the debris near the edge of the shell hole and picked up a shiny piece of metal that must have come from some interior section of the locomotive. Jones settled on the edge of the shell hole, facing Allied lines, and began catching the sunlight with the metal and flashing it toward the infantry men in British uniforms that he could see manning the Allied line.

There was no response.

Jones tried again.

Still no response.

"I don't think it's going to work," Burke began and just then it did. One of the soldiers in the trench flashed a message back to Jones, who read it with a smile before flashing out a reply.

"What did he say?" Burke asked.

"I told him we are Americans with my first message and asked him not to shoot us when we make a run for it. He must not have believed me. He asked me who won the World Series last year."

Burke frowned. "But the Series was canceled last year."

"Exactly. And when I told him so, he knew we are who we say we are."

"So he's not going to shoot?"

Freeman laughed. "I sure as hell hope not. Getting shot by our Allies after surviving all this would really put a damper on the postmission celebration."

Burke definitely agreed.

They were getting ready to make a run for it when noise from behind them caught their attention.

Burke and Freeman turned around, only to be met by the sight of a pack of shambler hounds clambering up the side of the train's wreckage.

"What the hell are those?" Burke asked.

"Hounds," said Freeman, "now run!"

Without waiting to see if he followed, Freeman leaped to his feet and ran for it.

CHAPTER FORTY-NINE

TOWARD THE ALLIED LINES

FROM HIGH ABOVE, Richthofen's superior eyesight saw one of the Americans, he didn't know which, burst from the shell hole and make a run for the Allied lines.

That was the signal he'd been waiting for.

He banked his plane over to the left and headed for the ground in a steep dive.

BURKE SAW THE strange new shamblers charging toward him across the crater-strewn ground and didn't need to be told twice that it wasn't a good idea to stick around and see what happened. Nothing that moved that fast or had that many teeth was ever friendly.

He screamed at Graves and Jones to run for it, then scooped up Williams's unconscious form and charged out of the shell hole in their wake.

Burke kept his gaze locked firmly on Freeman's back, letting that be his guide. He concentrated on putting each foot down on solid ground and pumping his legs as fast as he could get them to go.

Out of the corner of his eye he saw the British men who were lining the trenches raise their guns to their shoulders, getting ready to unleash a volley. With his arms full, he couldn't even wave them off.

But when the shots were fired, neither he nor Graves nor Jones were targeted, but rather the pack of shamblers that was closing in behind them. Burke only realized they were that close when the skull of the nearest creature exploded from a well-placed shot, splattering him with gore.

He forced himself to run faster.

RICHTHOFEN BROUGHT HIS Fokker triplane racing along the battlefield at just a few dozen feet above the ground. He could see the Americans running for safety in the distance, and he had no intention of letting them reach their goal.

In his anger and excitement, he triggered his guns before he was fully in range.

FREEMAN REACHED THE barbed wire and spent a few precious seconds searching for a way through the barrier. At last he found it, a long vertical slit that some earlier sapper must have cut in the wire, and he pulled the sides apart and slipped through, doing his best not to look back, knowing that it would only slow him down.

He charged forward the last few yards and threw himself into the foxhole, scrambling for the machine gun.

Out of the corner of his eye he saw the approaching aircraft and heard the sound of its guns long before it was in range.

BURKE HEARD THE growl of the Spandau guns and knew Richthofen had returned, but he could only keep his legs churning forward and pray that he would be quick enough to save himself and Williams. The foxhole next to Freeman's was only a half a dozen yards away now. They were so close . . .

Something grabbed his ankle and yanked him off his feet. Williams's unconscious body went tumbling away from him.

RICHTHOFEN SAW THE hounds take down one of the Americans and smiled in satisfaction. His eyes gleamed and fury rose in his heart as he came swooping in like the avenging eagle on his personal crest, determined to punish those who dared stand in his way.

His finger tightened on the trigger . . .

FREEMAN JUMPED UP behind the Lewis gun, pulled the charging handle, and let loose with a stream of bullets directed at the Fokker triplane as it came across his field of vision.

The bullets slammed into the aircraft directly in front of the cockpit, sending bits of wood and canvas flying away through air, and riddling Richthofen with .303 mm rounds that tore through his flesh as if it were paper.

He watched as Richthofen reacted like any good pilot would do when faced with the same circumstances, pulling back on the stick and climbing nearly straight up in an effort to evade the guns. Freeman thought Richthofen had miraculously survived to fly another day until he watched the aircraft reach the apex of its arc and then just twist over and come speeding back down toward the earth in a completely uncontrolled fall.

The triplane sped downward, faster and faster, slamming into the earth nose first somewhere behind the German lines.

Freeman couldn't believe it.

He'd shot down the Red Baron!

FREEMAN'S TIMELY INTERVENTION kept Burke from being splattered all over the landscape by Richthofen's machine guns, but it also left Burke to deal with the shambler that had seized his ankle and yanked him off his feet.

For once Burke didn't mind. He was tired of running, tired of backing down from a fight for the greater good of the unit. Now all he wanted to do was avenge the death of his friends, and the shambler in front of him made the perfect target.

Like the shamblers they'd seen feasting on Strauss's body and the ones Freeman had seen at the testing facility, this shambler moved with far more dexterity and cunning than any Burke had ever encountered. No sooner had it pulled him off his feet than it was scrambling to overwhelm him on the ground, trying to pin him beneath it where it could rake at him with both its hands and feet.

Burke caught hold of the creature's limb and executed a well-timed judo throw, tossing the creature over him, giving him time to scramble back to his feet before it came charging again.

This time he was ready for it.

As it rushed forward, Burke drew back his fist and fired a solid right hook into the creature's chin, lifting it off its feet and sending it toppling over backward.

Before it had a chance to recover, Burke flung himself atop it, using his right hand to pin its neck to the ground. He raised his left hand, the mechanical one, and plunged it directly into the creature's chest, smashing through the rib cage and wrapping his fingers around its spine.

Grinning savagely at the creature pinned beneath him, he tore its backbone in two.

The shambler snapped at him as he climbed off it, still alive but unable to get up with its spine severed in two. As Burke staggered to his feet, he heard cheering and turned to see a squad of British soldiers headed his way, led by Jones.

Gathering Williams in his arms, Burke went to meet them.

EPILOGUE

BURKE STARED AT the piece of paper that Colonel Nichols was extending toward him as if it were a deadly snake filled with poison, with the promise of a long, slow death. Reluctantly he took it, doing what he could to summon the nerve to look at what it said.

Word had come in several hours before, but Burke was still numb from the news. Two massive airships, sister crafts to the one Burke had destroyed at the facility near Verdun, had taken off from undetermined locations. One had crossed the English Channel and bombed London while, less than an hour later, the other had moved down the American coastline to do the same thing to New York.

It was his worst nightmare, magnified a thousandfold.

Then Nichols had shown up, paper in hand.

"You've earned the right to see this," he said quietly, handing it to Burke.

It was a signals traffic report, the kind of thing that was routinely used to collect information being relayed from one location to another, usually by telegram. Burke recognized the three-digit code in the upper-right corner indicating that the traffic had originated from the embassy in London and that it had been sent with the proper encryption.

The first telegram was dated several hours earlier.

ENEMY AIRSHIP OVERHEAD. STOP. ANTI-AIRCRAFT BATTERIES INEFFECTUAL. STOP. BOMBS ARE FALLING. STOP.

Burke stared at the words, willing them away, as if by sheer force of thought he could wipe the words from the page and by doing so turn back the clock and keep the horror from engulfing them all. The universe, however, refused to hear his plea.

He knew what the next cable was going to say long before he shifted his gaze lower on the page to read it.

GAS AFFECTING LIVING AND DEAD ALIKE. STOP. WINDS CARRYING IT THROUGH THE CITY. STOP. ALL PERSONNEL ORDERED TO REMAIN INDOORS. STOP. THE DEAD HAVE TAKEN TO THE STREETS. STOP.

Like a horrendous train wreck that he just couldn't look away from, Burke lowered his gaze to the next cable on the page, the paper rustling in his shaking hands.

CONTACT WITH WHITEHALL LOST. STOP. MAIN GATE OVERRUN. STOP. THE DEAD ARE IN THE BUILDING. STOP.

And then, finally, one last communication. Just a single line with a notation that this one had been sent in the clear.

GOD HELP US ALL.

"We lost contact with the embassy shortly thereafter," Nichols said gently.

Burke nodded. He didn't need to be told what happened after that.

Thousands of pounds of gas had been dropped on each city during the attacks, turning untold scores of people into flesh-hungry ghouls. No one knew how many were dead, either in the initial bombardment or in the hours that followed as the creatures spread through the cities.

Plans were being made to destroy the bridges and tunnels leading to Manhattan in the hope that cutting the island off from the rest of civilization might be enough to contain the spread of the creatures. Five million people were being written off, just like that. Burke had to fight not to be sick at the very thought of it.

And England? No one knew what the hell they were going to do about England. London was not so easily segregated from the rest of the country . . .

"There was no way you could have known, Burke. You were there to pull Freeman out, that was all."

Burke didn't say anything. In his mind's eye he kept seeing the name on that massive airship.

Megaera.

One of the *three* Furies of Greek mythology.

He didn't have to ask to know that the other two ships had been named *Alecto* and *Tisiphone* and cursed himself for not seeing it earlier.

If only he'd made the connection in time . . .

After several moments of silence he looked up and asked the question he'd been waiting several hours to ask. "Any word on Sergeant Moore or Corporal Manning, sir?"

Nichols shook his head. "I'm sorry. Nothing. But you'll be the first to know, Captain."

Burke wondered if that were true.

Two hundred miles away, Dr. Eisenberg stared at the prisoner in front of him. He was a hulking fellow, with the grizzled look of a veteran, and had passed all the physical fitness tests he'd been given.

He was a perfect choice for testing the next phase of the process.

The fact that his injury kept him from remembering who or what he was made his selection even more interesting.

Eisenberg finished setting the dials on the control panel and stepped back out over to his companion.

"Are you ready, Sergeant?" he asked.

The former American nodded.

"Good," said Eisenberg. "I know this procedure will help you remember some of what you have lost. I'm going to strap you down so you don't injure yourself while you are in an unconscious state, all right?"

Again the nod.

Eisenberg wondered if the subject might regain his capacity for speech after the procedure as well.

The subject lay down on the table the doctor selected for him and then lay docilely while the straps were secured about his arms and legs.

Eisenberg pretended as if he'd forgotten an important document from his office and excused himself from the room, taking care to lock it behind him.

Returning to the control panel, he flipped a few switches.

In the room on the other side of the viewing screen, a pale green gas began to flow.

NIGHT FELL OVER the battlefield, and the usual flood of rats emerged from their warrens to see what might be available to feast upon that evening.

There were relatively slim pickings that night, for both sides in the conflict had policed their wounded and dead pretty well, removing them from the place of battle. Only those who had died somewhere between the two sides, in the region known as no-man's-land, still lay where they had fallen.

One particularly enterprising rat wandered deep into the heart of the conflict and was rewarded with the discovery of an entire corpse trapped within a cocoon of wood and canvas. The rat stared at the corpse for some time, debating, and then moved forward on its stubby little legs to sink its teeth into the decaying flesh and feast.

No sooner had the rat gotten close enough to take a bite than the corpse came alive with a jolt, its hand snapping out, seizing the rat in its unyielding grip and squeezing until it could no longer be counted among the living.

The hand retracted back into the shadows beneath the wreckage of the brightly painted aircraft, only to be replaced by the sounds of eating a few seconds later.